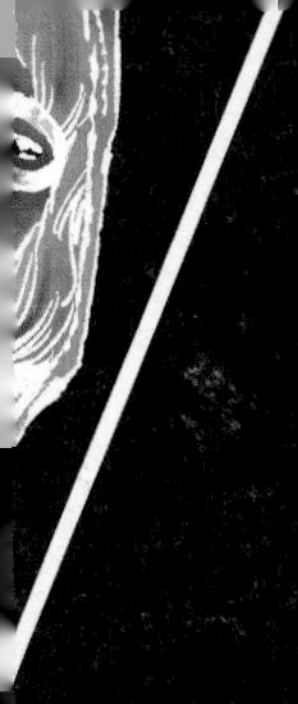

CROSSOVER™

THE 10-CENT PLAGUE 2

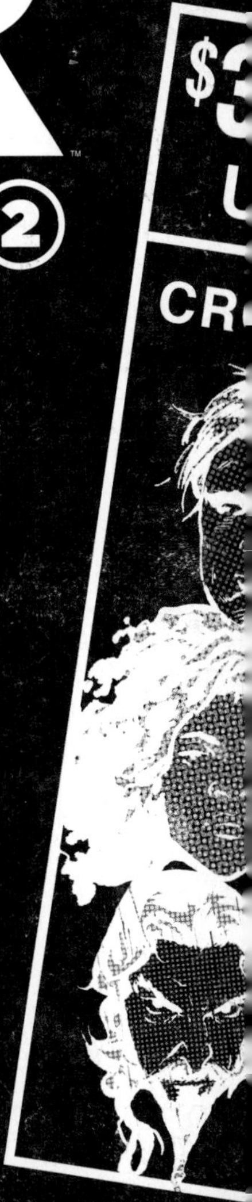

$3

DONNY CATES
STORY

GEOFF SHAW
ART

DEE CUNNIFFE
COLORS

JOHN J. HILL
LETTERS & DESIGN

MARK WAID
STORY EDITS

INTERLUDE

CHIP ZDARSKY
STORY

PHIL HESTER
PENCILS

ANDE PARKS
INKS

CHAPTER 3 (pgs 12-17)

BRIAN MICHAEL BENDIS
STORY

MICHAEL AVON OEMING
ART

NICK FILARDI
COLORS

CHAPTER 5 (pgs 1-10)

ROBERT KIRKMAN
STORY

PHIL HESTER
PENCILS

KLAUS JANSON
INKS

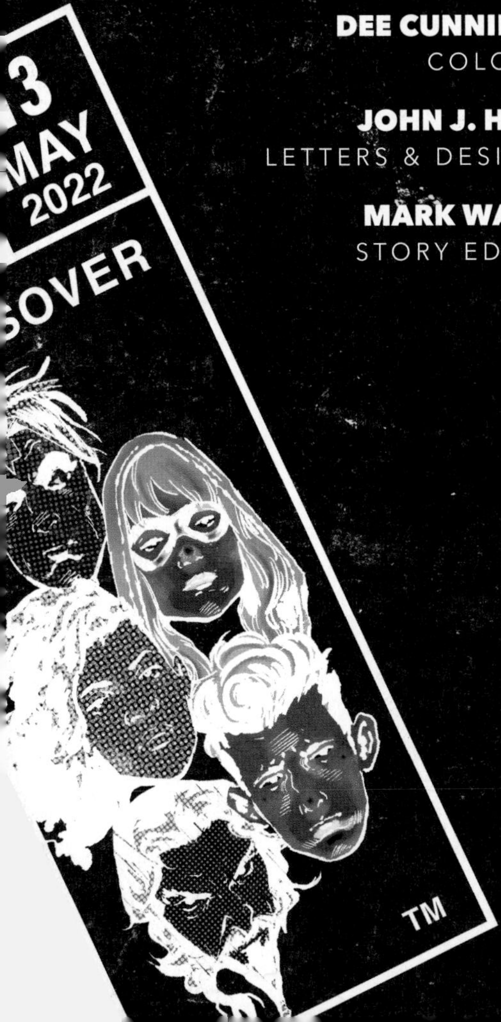

3
MAY
2022
TM

Collected edition cover by
GEOFF SHAW w/**DEE CUNNIFFE**

IMAGE COMICS, INC.

CROSSOVER VOL. 2. First printing. June 2022. Published by Image Comics, Inc. Office of publication: PO BOX 14457, Portland, OR 97293. Copyright © 2022 Donny Cates & Geoff Shaw. All rights reserved. Contains material originally published in single magazine form as CROSSOVER #7-13. "CROSSOVER," its logos, and the likenesses of all characters herein are trademarks of Donny Cates & Geoff Shaw, unless otherwise noted. "Atomahawk" and the likenesses of all associated characters herein are TM & © 2022 Donny Cates & Ian Bederman. All rights reserved. "God Country" and the likenesses of all associated characters herein are TM & © 2022 Donny Cates & Geoff Shaw. All rights reserved. "The Paybacks" and the likenesses of all associated characters herein are TM & © 2022 Eliot Rahal, Donny Cates & Geoff Shaw. All rights reserved. "Buzzkill," and the likenesses of all associated characters herein are TM & © 2022 Mark Reznicek, Donny Cates & Geoff Shaw. All rights reserved. "The Ghost Fleet" and the likenesses of all associated characters herein are TM & © 2022 Donny Cates. All rights reserved. Dave Murray, Steve Murray and Chip Zdarsky TM & © 2022 Zdarsco, Inc. All rights reserved. "Madman" and the likenesses of all associated characters herein are TM & © 2022 Michael Allred. All rights reserved. "Powers" and the likenesses of all associated characters herein are TM & © 2022 Jinxworld, Inc. All rights reserved. "The Darkness" and the likenesses of all associated characters herein are TM & © 2022 Top Cow Productions, Inc. All rights reserved. "The Walking Dead," "Negan," and the likenesses of all associated characters herein are TM & © 2022 Robert Kirkman, LLC. All rights reserved. "Image" and the Image Comics logos are registered trademarks of Image Comics, Inc. No part of this publication may be reproduced or transmitted, in any form or by any means (except for short excerpts for journalistic or review purposes), without the express written permission of Donny Cates & Geoff Shaw, or Image Comics, Inc. All names, characters, events, and locales in this publication are entirely fictional. Any resemblance to actual persons (living or dead), events, or places, without satirical intent, is coincidental. Printed in the USA. For international rights, contact: foreignlicensing@imagecomics.com. 978-1-5343-1928-8.

IMAGECOMICS.COM

BRIAN MICHAEL BENDIS

CROSSOVER! POWERS! FINALLY! JOY!

Originally appeared in the JINXWORLD newsletter on 2.3.22
ATTENTION: SPOILERS! *You may want to swing back around and read this later!*

So I sat on this newsletter for a few weeks because of spoilers. And I'm glad I did. Firstly because it's a big **CROSSOVER** day but I'll get to the other reasons why in a minute.

Donny Cates and Geoff Shaw, fellow creators and sub-stack-arinos, have a very cool comic called **CROSSOVER**. The pitch: comic book universes have invaded 'the real world' and now comic book creators are being murdered.

Like ya do.

It's a brilliant bit of madness. It's up there with Brubaker's *Scene of a Crime* and *Buckaroo Banzai* on the list of things I wish I thought of.

(Donny, there's your trade paperback quote, if you want it :-))

Early in the pandemic, when I couldn't understand what anyone was saying, Donny called and asked for permission to use *Powers* universe characters in this new book that did not exist yet. I asked: the Eisner Award-winning, multi-graphic novel, generation-spanning cops and capes odyssey, *POWERS*? Donny sighed- almost as if he immediately regretted calling. He sighed. For a while. And then said: yup.

I was very happy Mike and I were in a position to say yes.

I love stuff like this. There's a grand history to it in comics. *Powers* was already part of that grand tradition.

I know we now live in a time where you see a lot of IP crossing-over but that IP crossover is usually in service of a corporate agenda or whatever the hell *Ready Player One* was. BUT in the high-flying jet set lifestyle of creator owned comics, it's just friends and peers lending each other their toys. It's genuinely cool.

Waaaaaay back, in our very first storyline *Powers: Who Killed Retro Girl?* we had dozens of independent comic character cameos of the day.

Each one a favor- sometimes from a stranger. A fellow creator happy to help have genuine comic book fun. Now some TWENTY years later it was our turn to pay the favor forward.

It is a wonderful and unique treat for Mike and I to see *Powers* interpreted by others. Geoff is a crazy talented person.

Once the book got rolling, Donny reached out again because they now had guest star creators coming in to jam on the book as well, people like Chip Zdarsky. Which I was told is not a made-up name and is a real person. Would Mike and I be able to reunite for a *Powers* sequence that takes place inside the **CROSSOVER** universe?

Could we do a sequence where Mike and I are interrogated by our *Powers* leads, homicide detectives Christian Walker and Deena Pilgrim, over the deaths of our peers?

I said yes. Donny's enthusiasm for where this is going was a nice break in my pandemic stress of the day.

I called Mike. Mike had already finished drawing it before I finished explaining it to him… because that's our relationship. And we even had *Powers* alumnus color genius Nick Filardi come back in and give it that authentic pixel spit and polish.

A little behind-the-scenes: I wrote this terrible joke about a bunch of people I honestly don't REALLY know. We all know each other professionally but they're actually mostly friends of friends of mine. None of this is funny if they don't think it's funny. So I had Donny make sure that Scott signed off on this. And then I double-checked. He did.

I'm glad I waited to spotlight this because some of you did not know it was us doing us. Some thought that Geoff had really nailed it… which he probably could, but no.

Also, a few people wrote us worried that somehow we didn't know about it. That they had done this without permission. Because Mike and I kept it hush, some took our silence as something is wrong. Nope! All preplanned and approved.

(For the record, because I do see this is a growing concern out there, you can't just use other people's characters. I know there are some content creators out there who think they can but they get a rude awakening in the form of a legal notice with a mouse head silhouette on it. Create something new. It's fun.)

Hey, if this **CROSSOVER** *POWERS* crossover was your first introduction to *Powers*, or if you fall into the category of people who heard about *Powers* and always meant to binge it, Dark Horse is now the publisher of the entire *Powers* library. Like the POWERS 20TH ANNIVERSARY GRAPHIC NOVEL: THE BEST EVER which is, oh my God, just coming back in print in this beautiful new softcover edition.

Anyway, as I said, I love shit like this and we were honored to be part of it. Thanks Donny.

From my perpetual state of gratitude

BENDIS!

THE 10-CENT PLAGUE

INTERLUDE

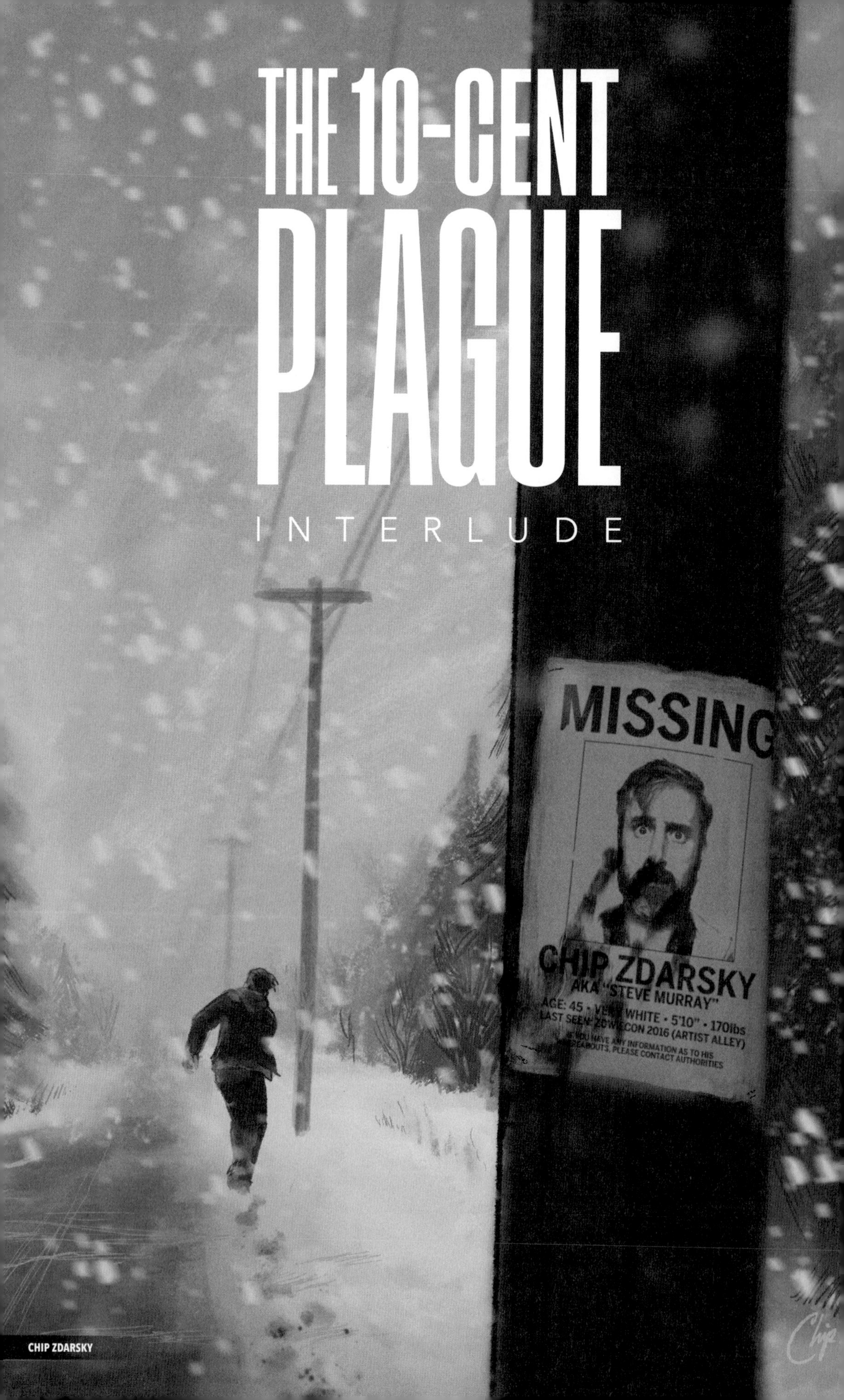

MISSING
CHIP ZDARSKY
AKA "STEVE MURRAY"
AGE: 45 • WHITE • 5'10" • 170lbs
LAST SEEN: CON 2016 (ARTIST ALLEY)
INFORMATION AS TO HIS
PLEASE CONTACT AUTHORITIES

CHIP ZDARSKY

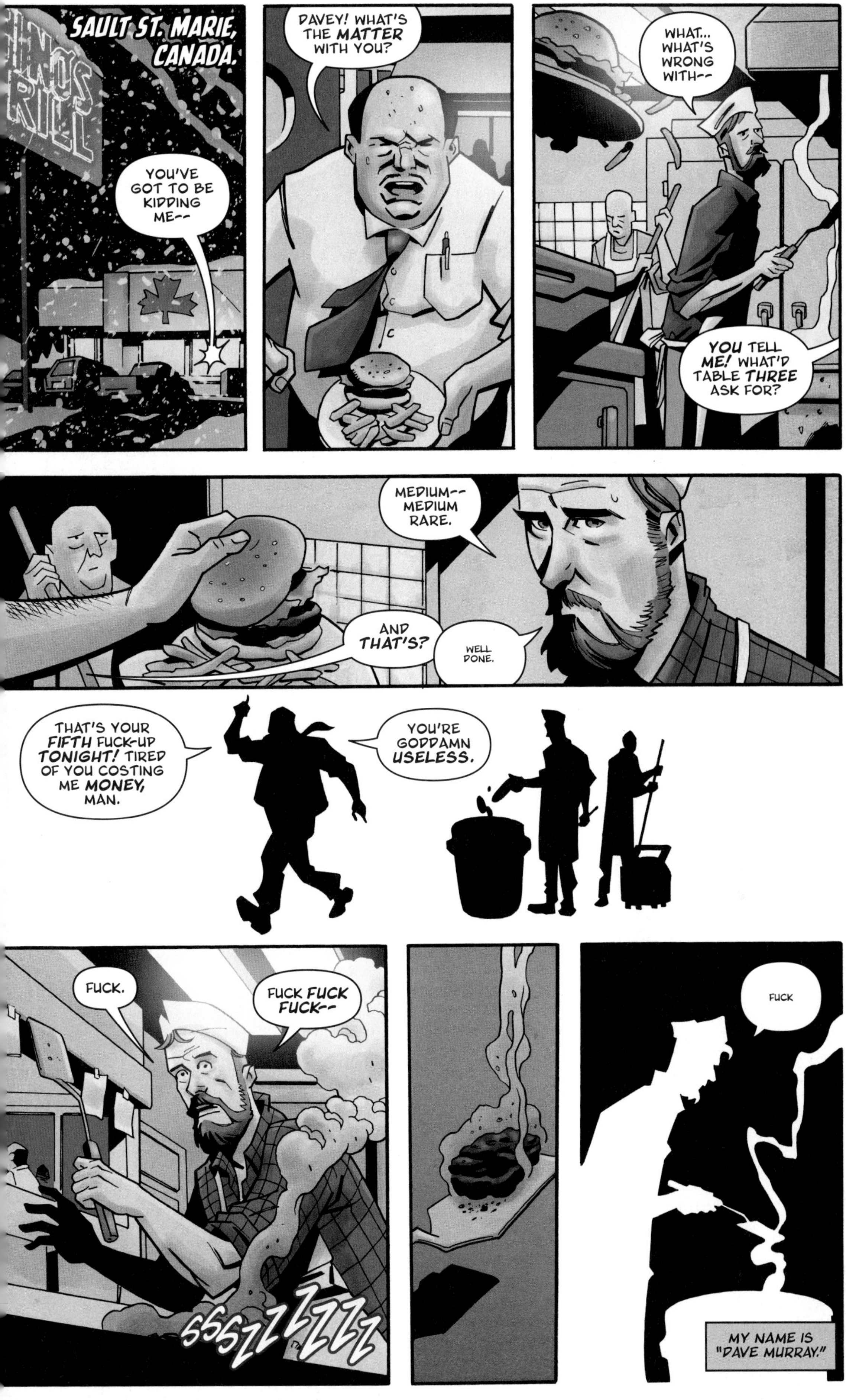
SAULT ST. MARIE, CANADA.
YOU'VE GOT TO BE KIDDING ME--
DAVEY! WHAT'S THE MATTER WITH YOU?
WHAT... WHAT'S WRONG WITH--
YOU TELL ME! WHAT'D TABLE THREE ASK FOR?
MEDIUM-- MEDIUM RARE.
AND THAT'S?
WELL DONE.
THAT'S YOUR FIFTH FUCK-UP TONIGHT! TIRED OF YOU COSTING ME MONEY, MAN.
YOU'RE GODDAMN USELESS.
FUCK.
FUCK FUCK FUCK--
SSSZZZZZZ
FUCK
MY NAME IS "DAVE MURRAY."

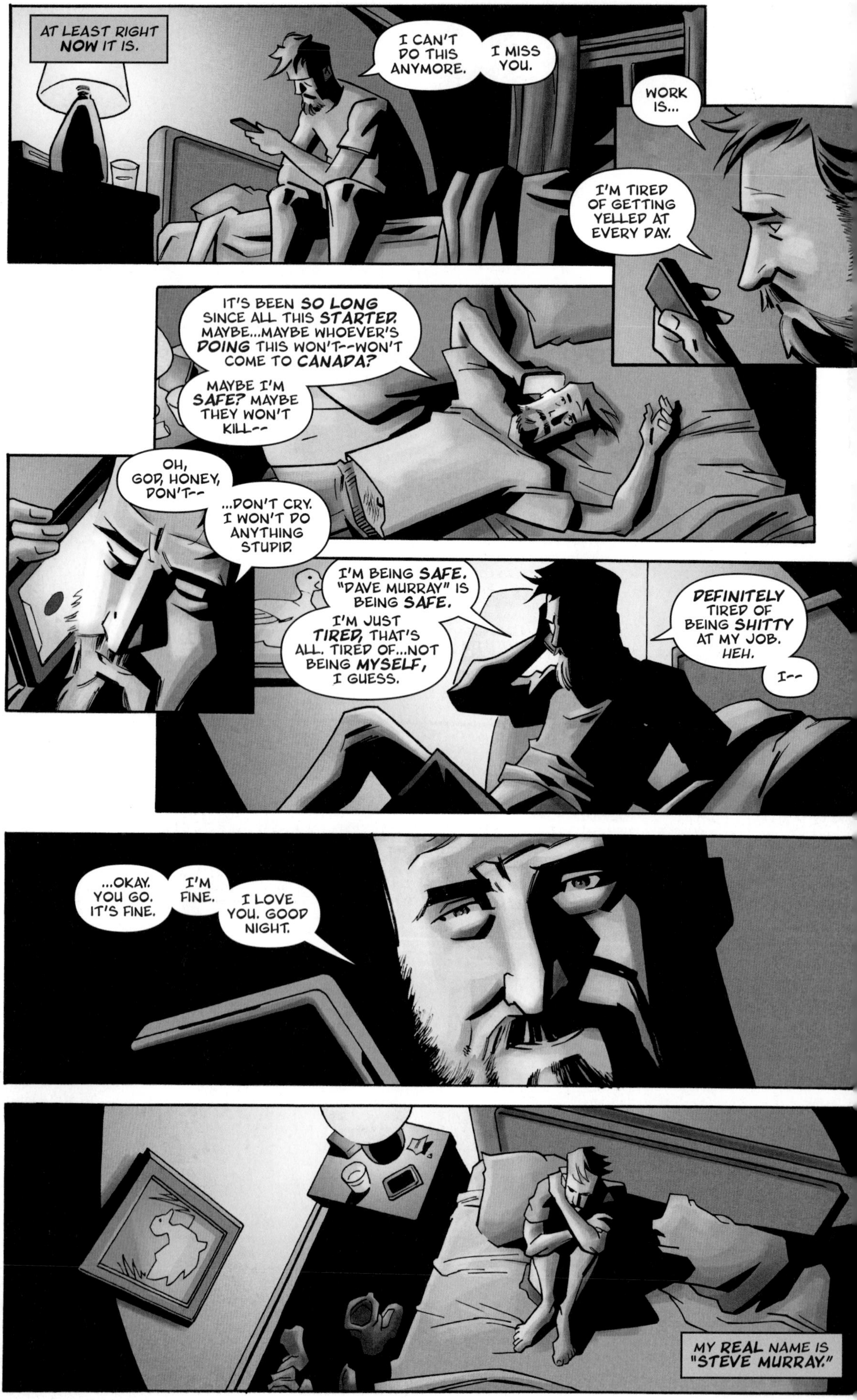
AT LEAST RIGHT NOW IT IS.
I CAN'T DO THIS ANYMORE.
I MISS YOU.
WORK IS...
I'M TIRED OF GETTING YELLED AT EVERY DAY.
IT'S BEEN SO LONG SINCE ALL THIS STARTED. MAYBE...MAYBE WHOEVER'S DOING THIS WON'T--WON'T COME TO CANADA?
MAYBE I'M SAFE? MAYBE THEY WON'T KILL--
OH, GOD, HONEY, DON'T--
...DON'T CRY. I WON'T DO ANYTHING STUPID.
I'M BEING SAFE. "DAVE MURRAY" IS BEING SAFE.
I'M JUST TIRED, THAT'S ALL. TIRED OF...NOT BEING MYSELF, I GUESS.
DEFINITELY TIRED OF BEING SHITTY AT MY JOB. HEH.
I--
...OKAY. YOU GO. IT'S FINE.
I'M FINE.
I LOVE YOU. GOOD NIGHT.
MY REAL NAME IS "STEVE MURRAY."

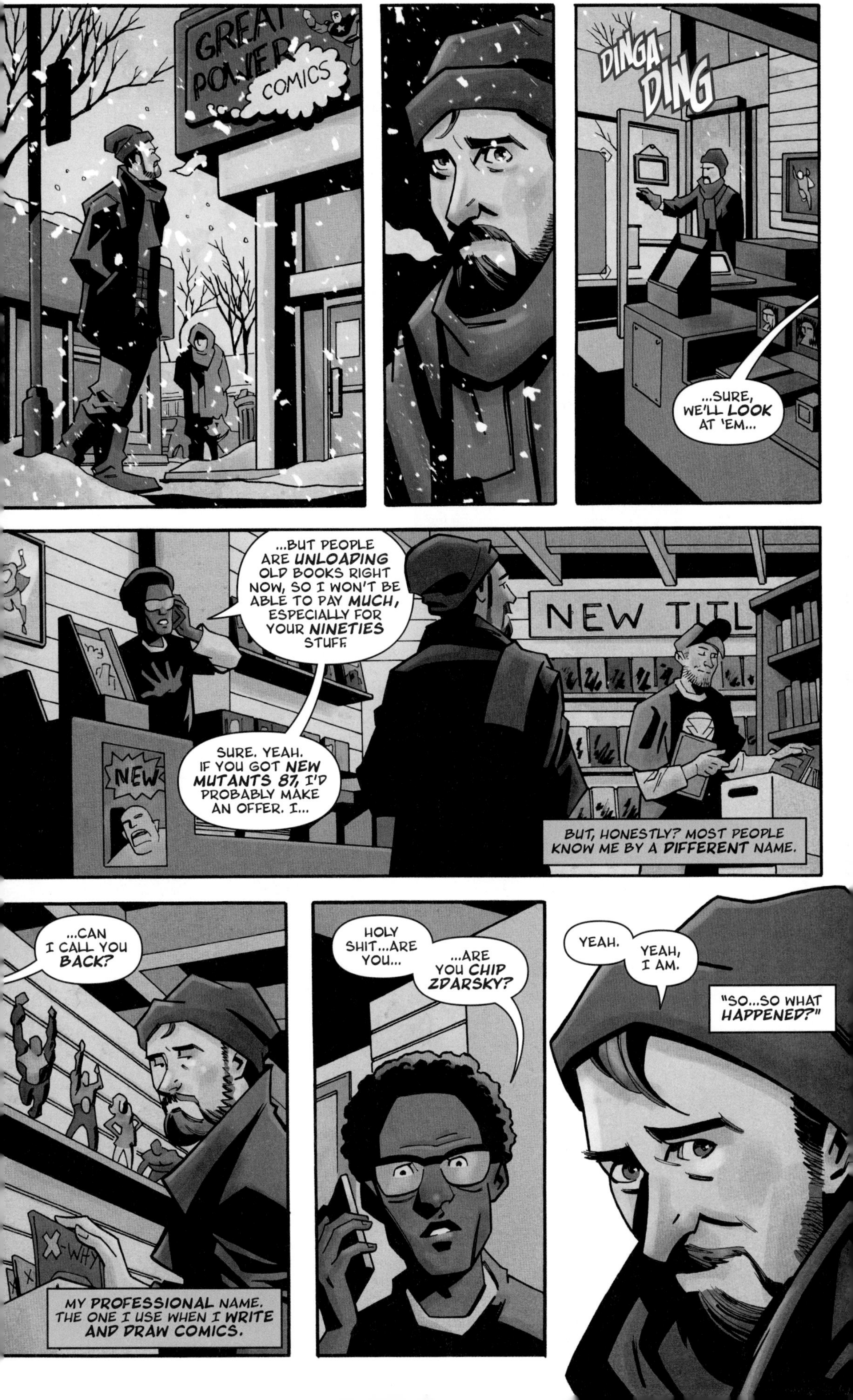

GREAT POWER COMICS
DINGA DING
...SURE, WE'LL LOOK AT 'EM...
...BUT PEOPLE ARE UNLOADING OLD BOOKS RIGHT NOW, SO I WON'T BE ABLE TO PAY MUCH, ESPECIALLY FOR YOUR NINETIES STUFF.
SURE. YEAH. IF YOU GOT NEW MUTANTS 87, I'D PROBABLY MAKE AN OFFER. I...
NEW TITL
NEW
BUT, HONESTLY? MOST PEOPLE KNOW ME BY A DIFFERENT NAME.
...CAN I CALL YOU BACK?
X-WHY
MY PROFESSIONAL NAME. THE ONE I USE WHEN I WRITE AND DRAW COMICS.
HOLY SHIT...ARE YOU...
...ARE YOU CHIP ZDARSKY?
YEAH.
YEAH, I AM.
"SO...SO WHAT HAPPENED?"

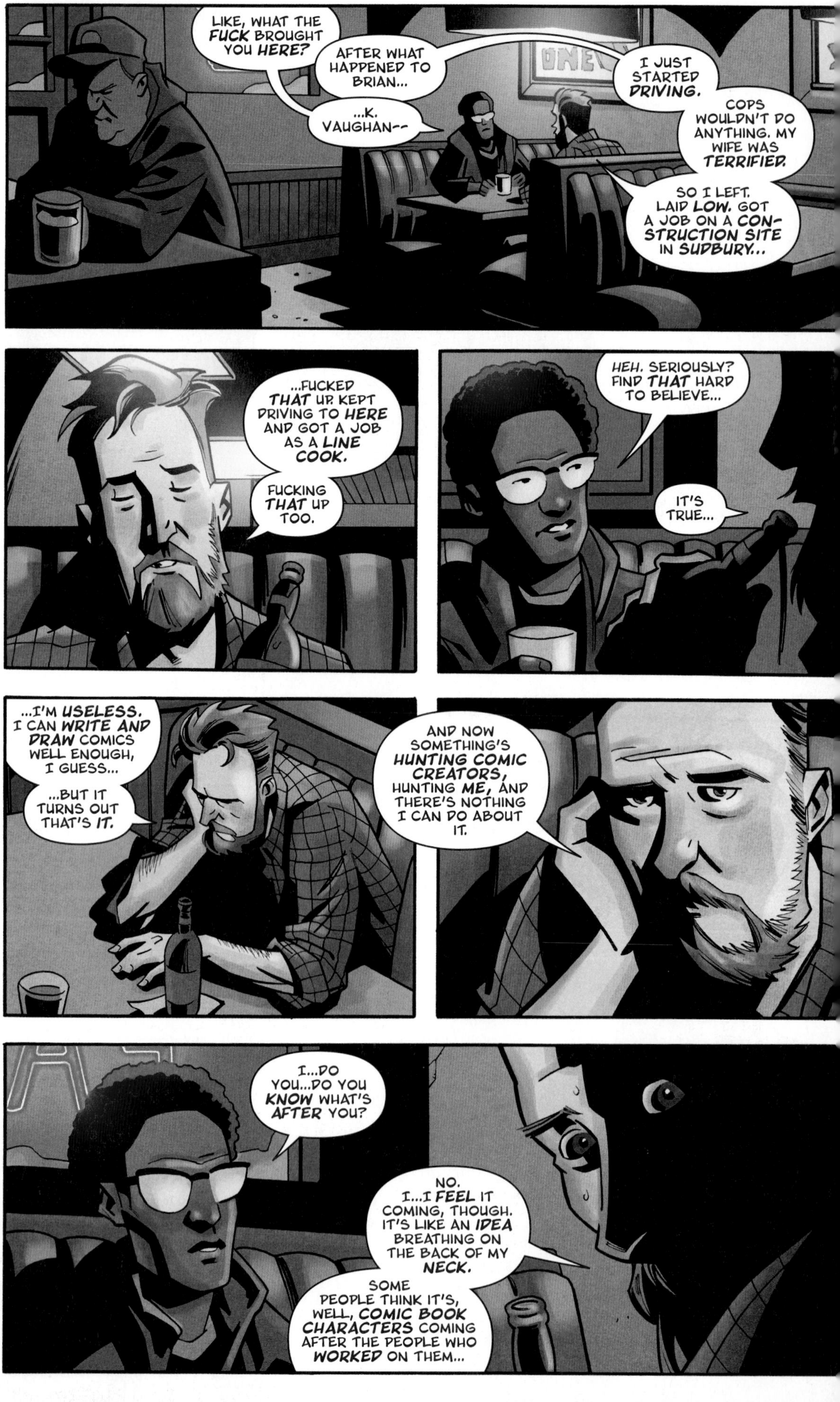
LIKE, WHAT THE FUCK BROUGHT YOU HERE?
AFTER WHAT HAPPENED TO BRIAN...
...K. VAUGHAN--
I JUST STARTED DRIVING.
COPS WOULDN'T DO ANYTHING. MY WIFE WAS TERRIFIED.
SO I LEFT. LAID LOW. GOT A JOB ON A CON-STRUCTION SITE IN SUDBURY...
...FUCKED THAT UP. KEPT DRIVING TO HERE AND GOT A JOB AS A LINE COOK.
FUCKING THAT UP TOO.
HEH. SERIOUSLY? FIND THAT HARD TO BELIEVE...
IT'S TRUE...
...I'M USELESS. I CAN WRITE AND DRAW COMICS WELL ENOUGH, I GUESS...
...BUT IT TURNS OUT THAT'S IT.
AND NOW SOMETHING'S HUNTING COMIC CREATORS, HUNTING ME, AND THERE'S NOTHING I CAN DO ABOUT IT.
I...DO YOU...DO YOU KNOW WHAT'S AFTER YOU?
NO. I...I FEEL IT COMING, THOUGH. IT'S LIKE AN IDEA BREATHING ON THE BACK OF MY NECK.
SOME PEOPLE THINK IT'S, WELL, COMIC BOOK CHARACTERS COMING AFTER THE PEOPLE WHO WORKED ON THEM...

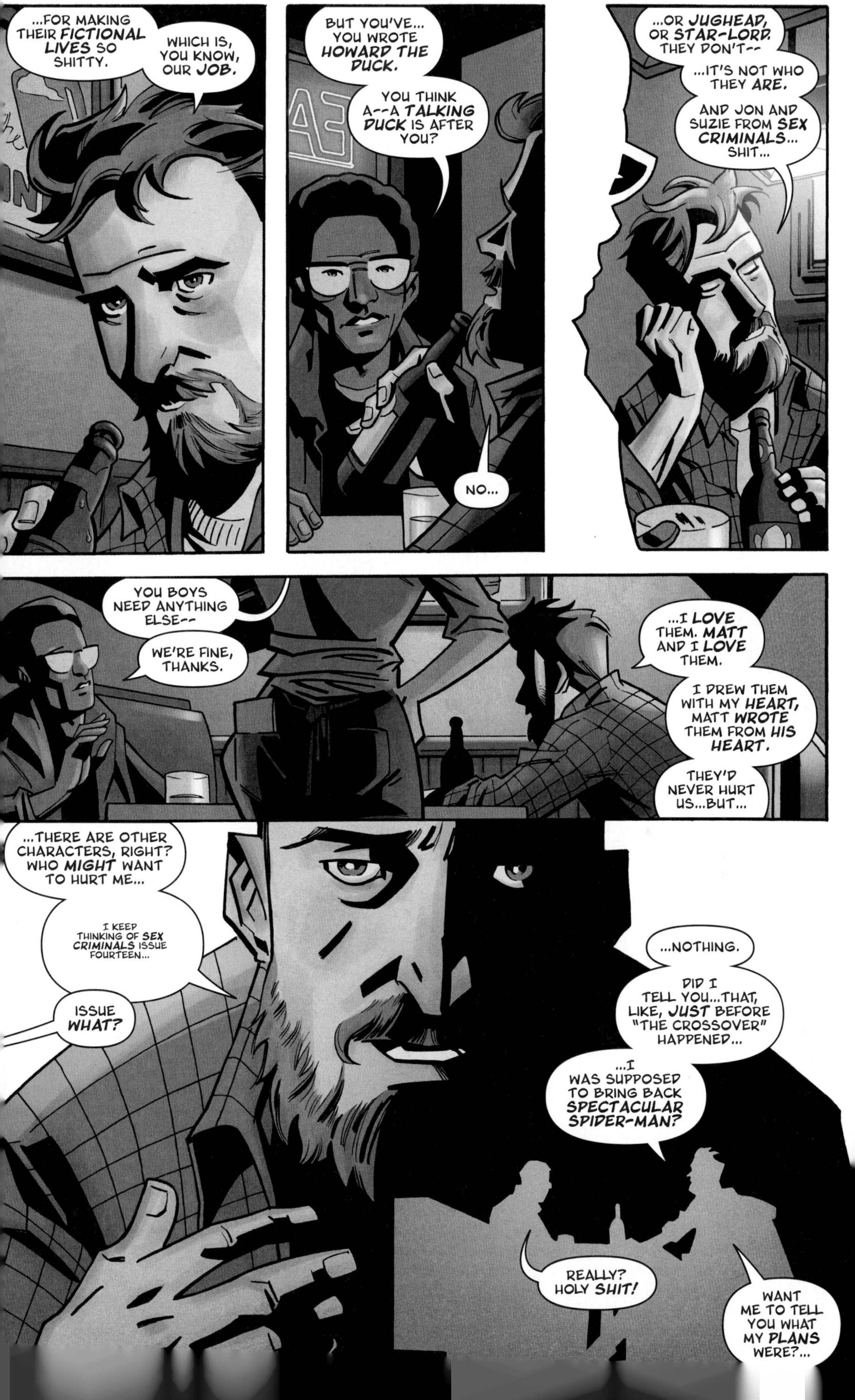

...FOR MAKING THEIR FICTIONAL LIVES SO SHITTY.
WHICH IS, YOU KNOW, OUR JOB.
BUT YOU'VE... YOU WROTE HOWARD THE DUCK.
YOU THINK A--A TALKING DUCK IS AFTER YOU?
NO...
...OR JUGHEAD, OR STAR-LORD. THEY DON'T--
...IT'S NOT WHO THEY ARE.
AND JON AND SUZIE FROM SEX CRIMINALS... SHIT...
YOU BOYS NEED ANYTHING ELSE--
WE'RE FINE, THANKS.
...I LOVE THEM. MATT AND I LOVE THEM.
I DREW THEM WITH MY HEART, MATT WROTE THEM FROM HIS HEART.
THEY'D NEVER HURT US...BUT...
...THERE ARE OTHER CHARACTERS, RIGHT? WHO MIGHT WANT TO HURT ME...
I KEEP THINKING OF SEX CRIMINALS ISSUE FOURTEEN...
ISSUE WHAT?
...NOTHING.
DID I TELL YOU...THAT, LIKE, JUST BEFORE "THE CROSSOVER" HAPPENED...
...I WAS SUPPOSED TO BRING BACK SPECTACULAR SPIDER-MAN?
REALLY? HOLY SHIT!
WANT ME TO TELL YOU WHAT MY PLANS WERE?...

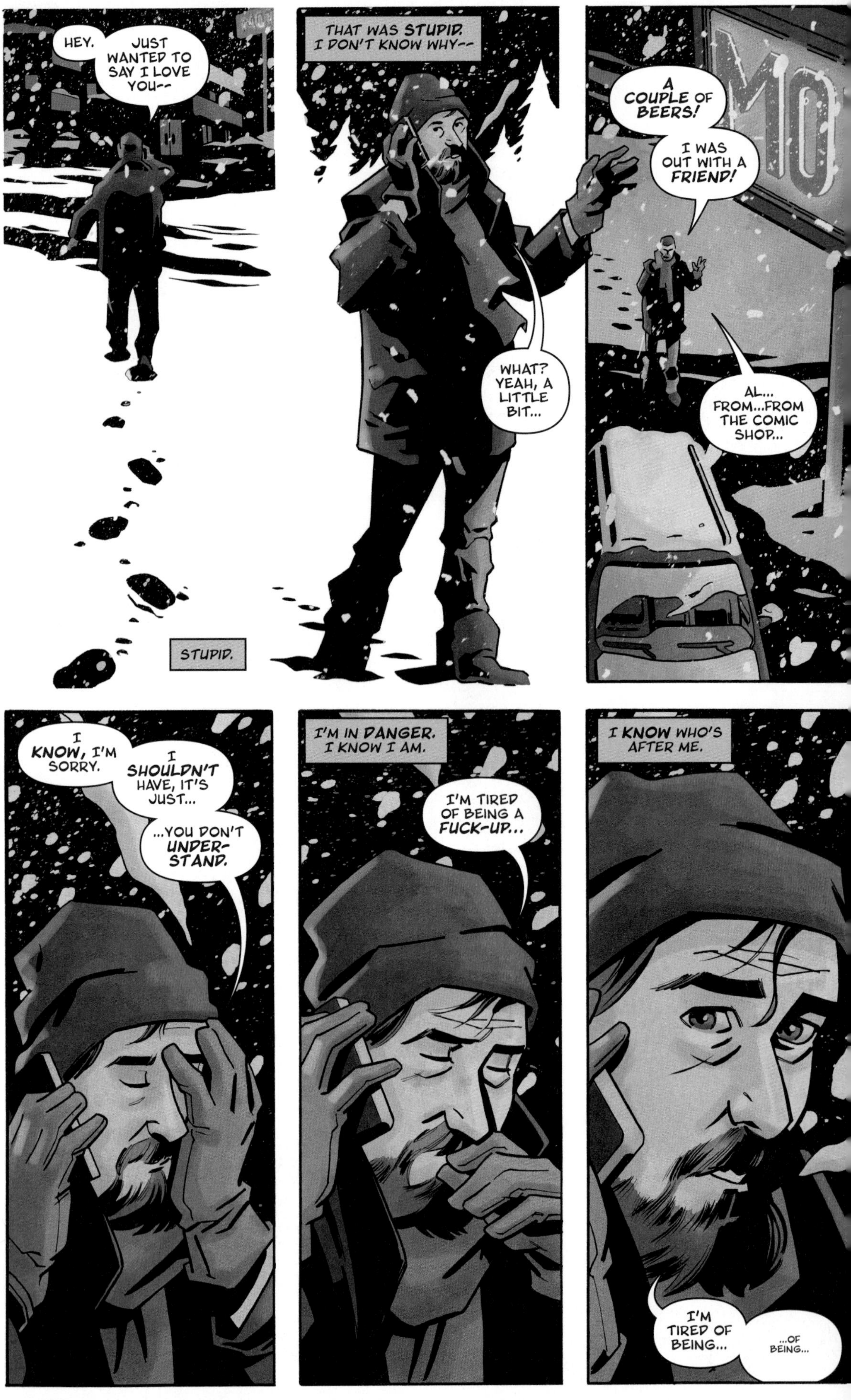
HEY.
JUST WANTED TO SAY I LOVE YOU--
STUPID.
THAT WAS STUPID. I DON'T KNOW WHY--
WHAT? YEAH, A LITTLE BIT...
A COUPLE OF BEERS!
I WAS OUT WITH A FRIEND!
AL... FROM...FROM THE COMIC SHOP...
I KNOW, I'M SORRY.
I SHOULDN'T HAVE, IT'S JUST...
...YOU DON'T UNDER-STAND.
I'M IN DANGER. I KNOW I AM.
I'M TIRED OF BEING A FUCK-UP...
I KNOW WHO'S AFTER ME.
I'M TIRED OF BEING...
...OF BEING...

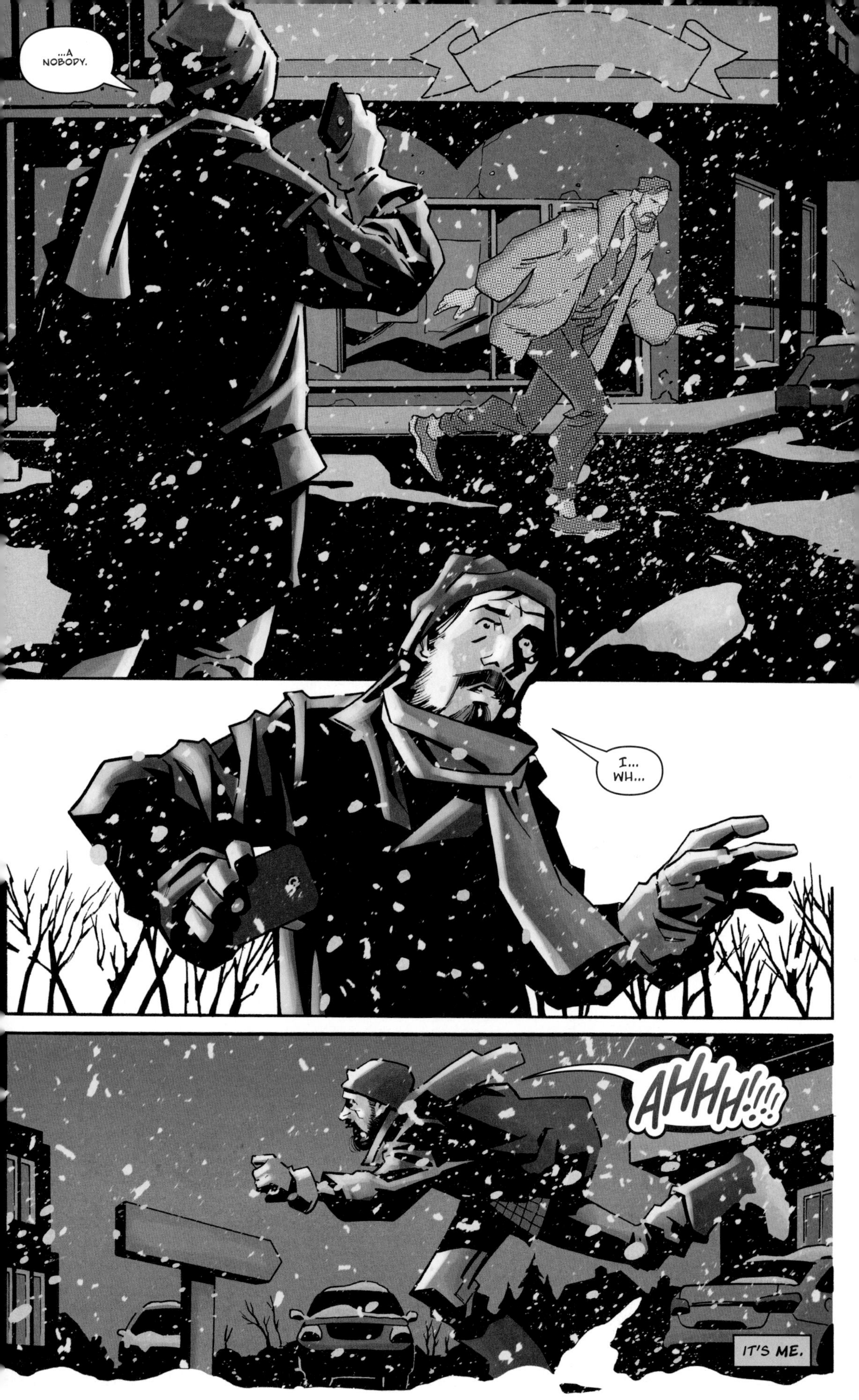

...A NOBODY.
I... WH...
AHHH!!!!
IT'S ME.

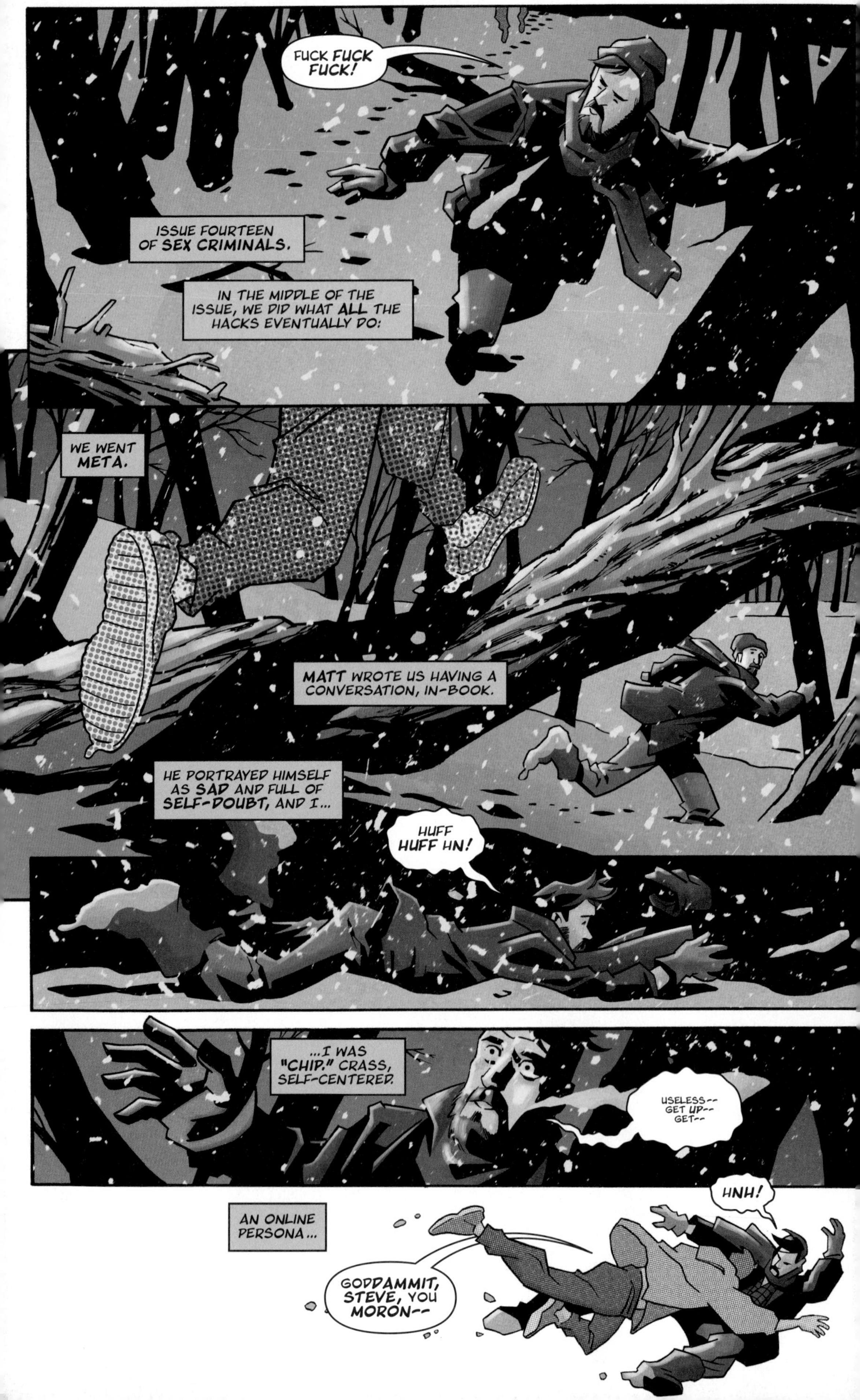

FUCK FUCK FUCK!
ISSUE FOURTEEN OF SEX CRIMINALS.
IN THE MIDDLE OF THE ISSUE, WE DID WHAT ALL THE HACKS EVENTUALLY DO:
WE WENT META.
MATT WROTE US HAVING A CONVERSATION, IN-BOOK.
HE PORTRAYED HIMSELF AS SAD AND FULL OF SELF-DOUBT, AND I...
HUFF HUFF HN!
...I WAS "CHIP." CRASS, SELF-CENTERED.
USELESS-- GET UP-- GET--
AN ONLINE PERSONA...
HNH!
GODDAMMIT, STEVE, YOU MORON--

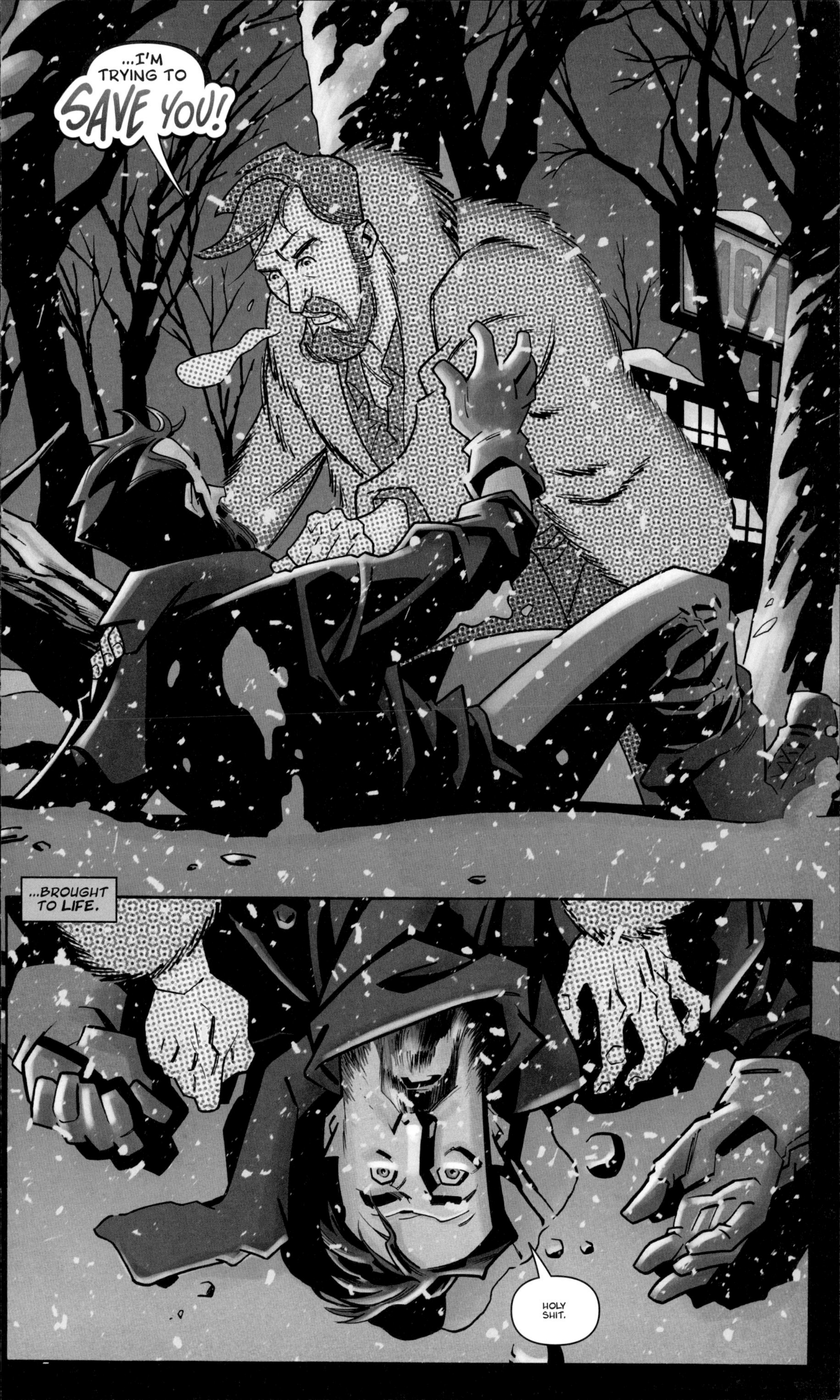
...I'M TRYING TO SAVE YOU!
...BROUGHT TO LIFE.
HOLY SHIT.

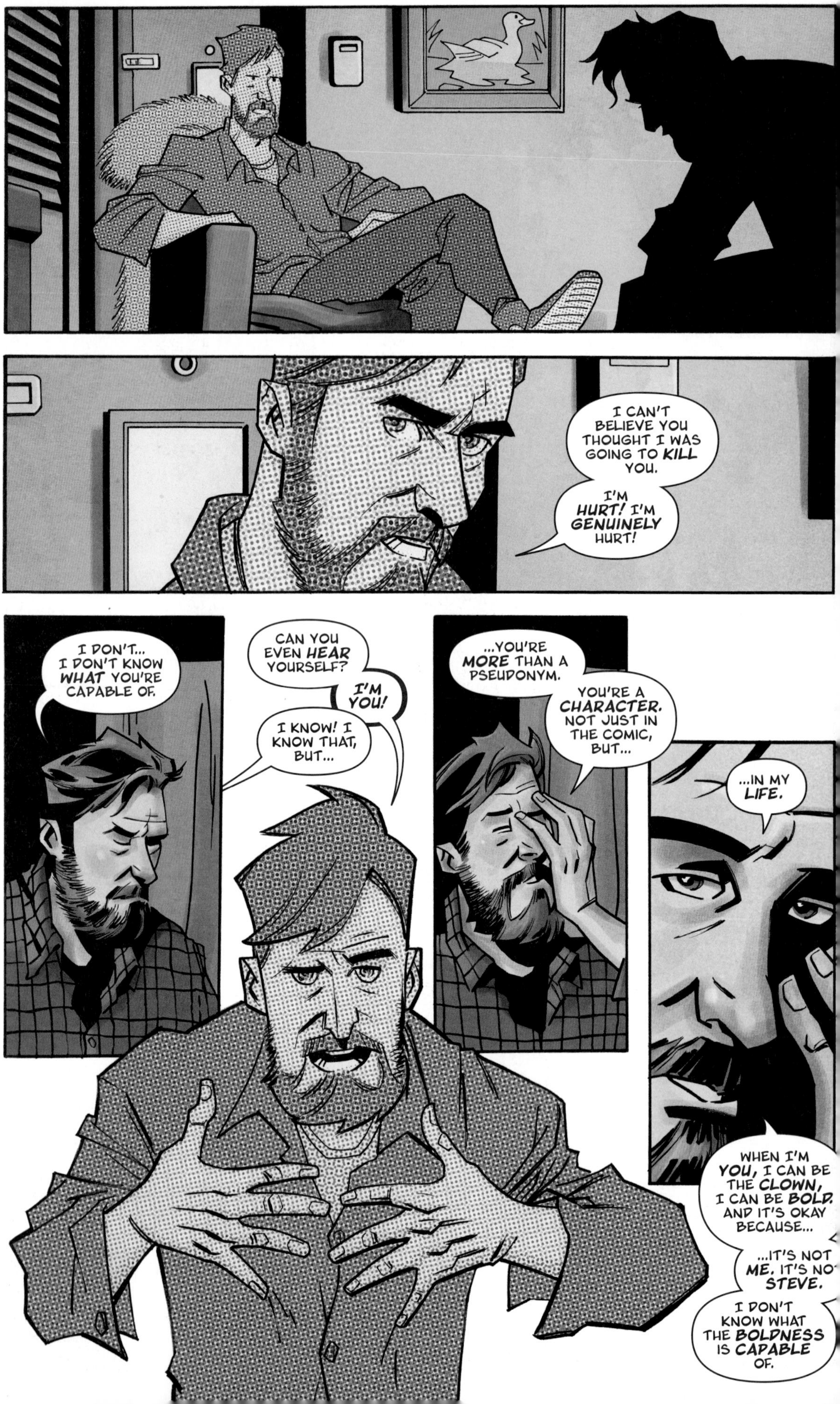
I CAN'T BELIEVE YOU THOUGHT I WAS GOING TO KILL YOU.
I'M HURT! I'M GENUINELY HURT!
I DON'T... I DON'T KNOW WHAT YOU'RE CAPABLE OF.
CAN YOU EVEN HEAR YOURSELF?
I'M YOU!
I KNOW! I KNOW THAT, BUT...
...YOU'RE MORE THAN A PSEUDONYM.
YOU'RE A CHARACTER. NOT JUST IN THE COMIC, BUT...
...IN MY LIFE.
WHEN I'M YOU, I CAN BE THE CLOWN, I CAN BE BOLD. AND IT'S OKAY BECAUSE...
...IT'S NOT ME. IT'S NO STEVE.
I DON'T KNOW WHAT THE BOLDNESS IS CAPABLE OF.

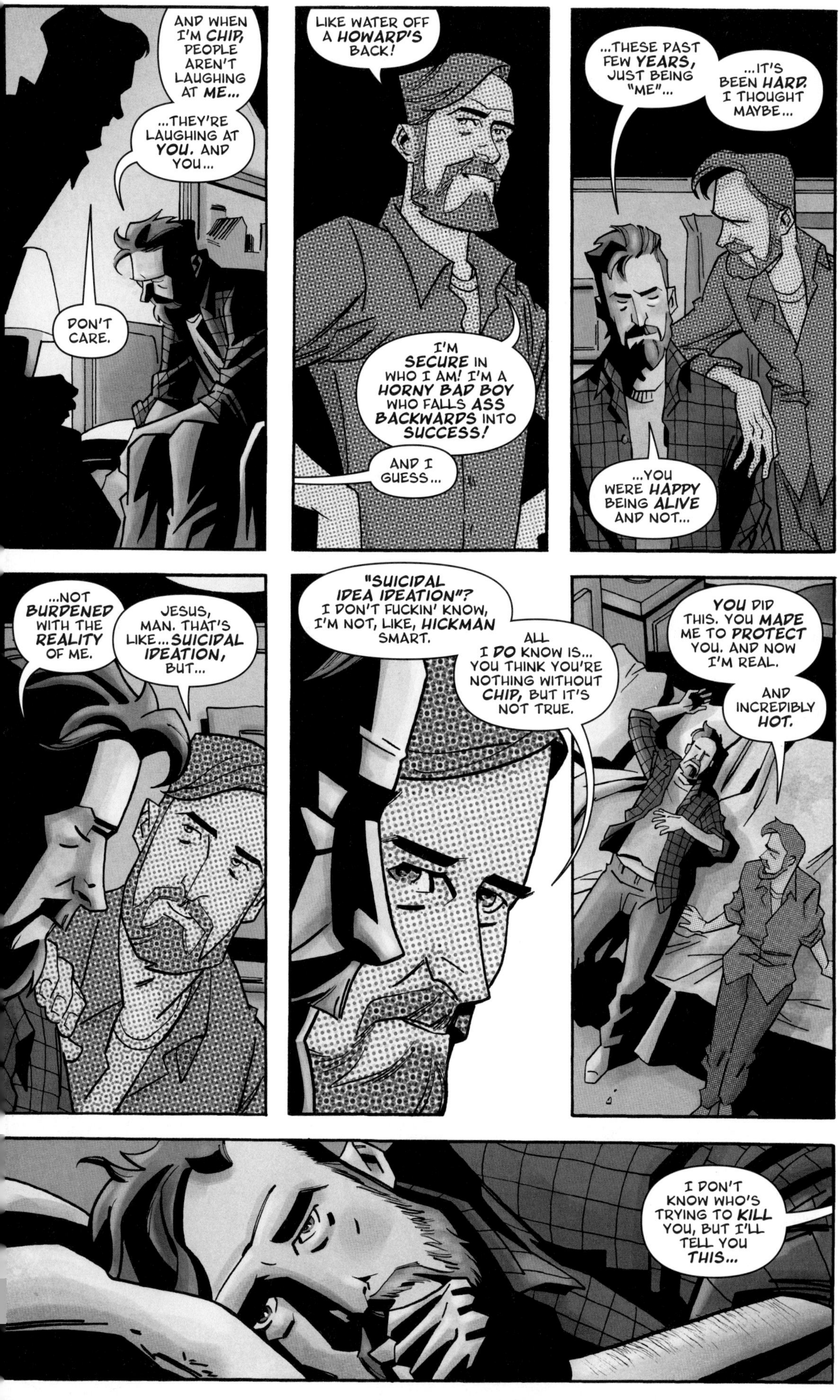
AND WHEN I'M CHIP, PEOPLE AREN'T LAUGHING AT ME...
...THEY'RE LAUGHING AT YOU. AND YOU...
DON'T CARE.
LIKE WATER OFF A HOWARD'S BACK!
I'M SECURE IN WHO I AM! I'M A HORNY BAD BOY WHO FALLS ASS BACKWARDS INTO SUCCESS!
AND I GUESS...
...THESE PAST FEW YEARS, JUST BEING "ME"...
...IT'S BEEN HARD. I THOUGHT MAYBE...
...YOU WERE HAPPY BEING ALIVE AND NOT...
...NOT BURDENED WITH THE REALITY OF ME.
JESUS, MAN. THAT'S LIKE... SUICIDAL IDEATION, BUT...
"SUICIDAL IDEA IDEATION"? I DON'T FUCKIN' KNOW, I'M NOT, LIKE, HICKMAN SMART.
ALL I DO KNOW IS... YOU THINK YOU'RE NOTHING WITHOUT CHIP, BUT IT'S NOT TRUE.
YOU DID THIS. YOU MADE ME TO PROTECT YOU. AND NOW I'M REAL.
AND INCREDIBLY HOT.
I DON'T KNOW WHO'S TRYING TO KILL YOU, BUT I'LL TELL YOU THIS...

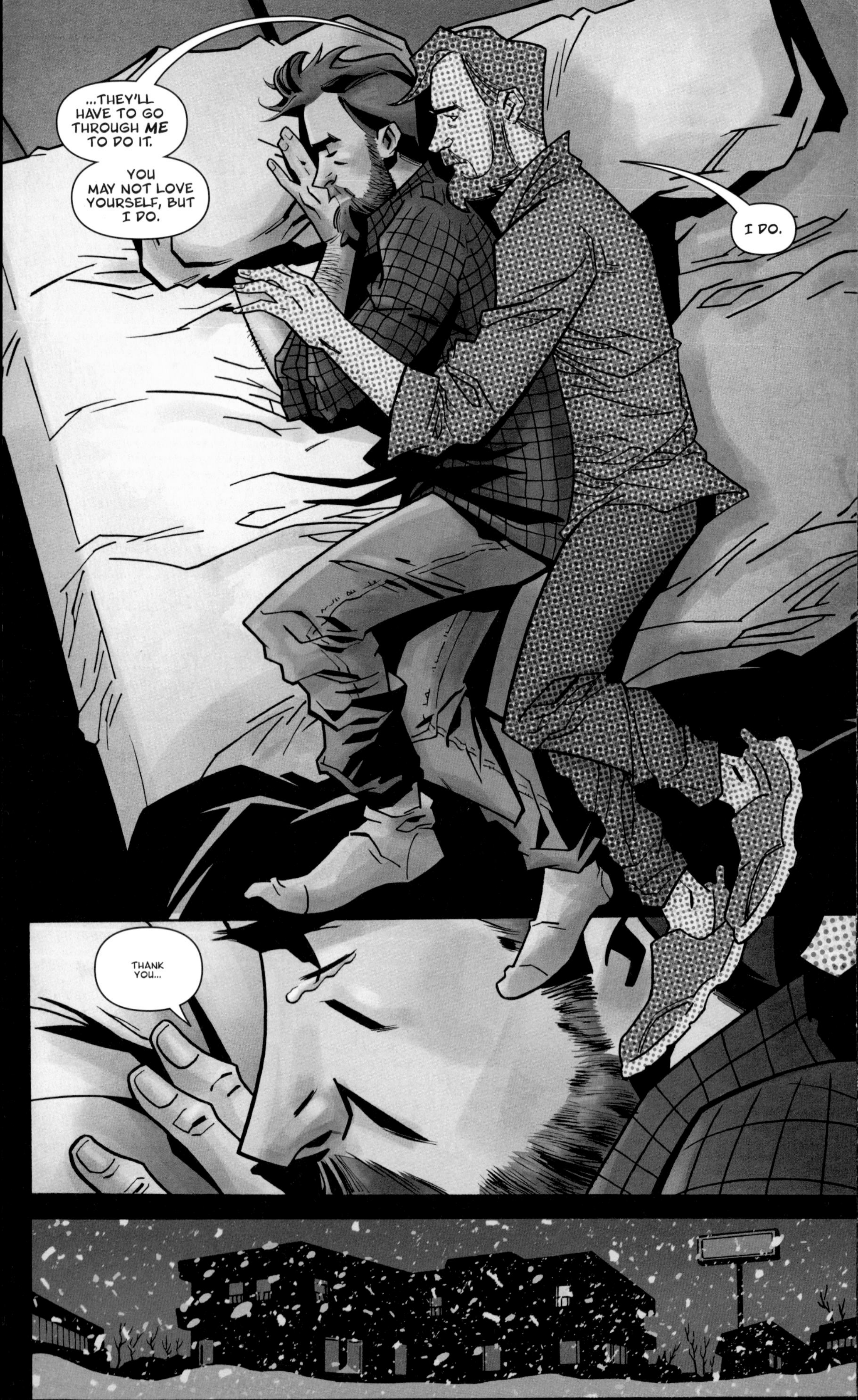
...THEY'LL HAVE TO GO THROUGH **ME** TO DO IT.
YOU MAY NOT LOVE YOURSELF, BUT I DO.
I DO.
THANK YOU...

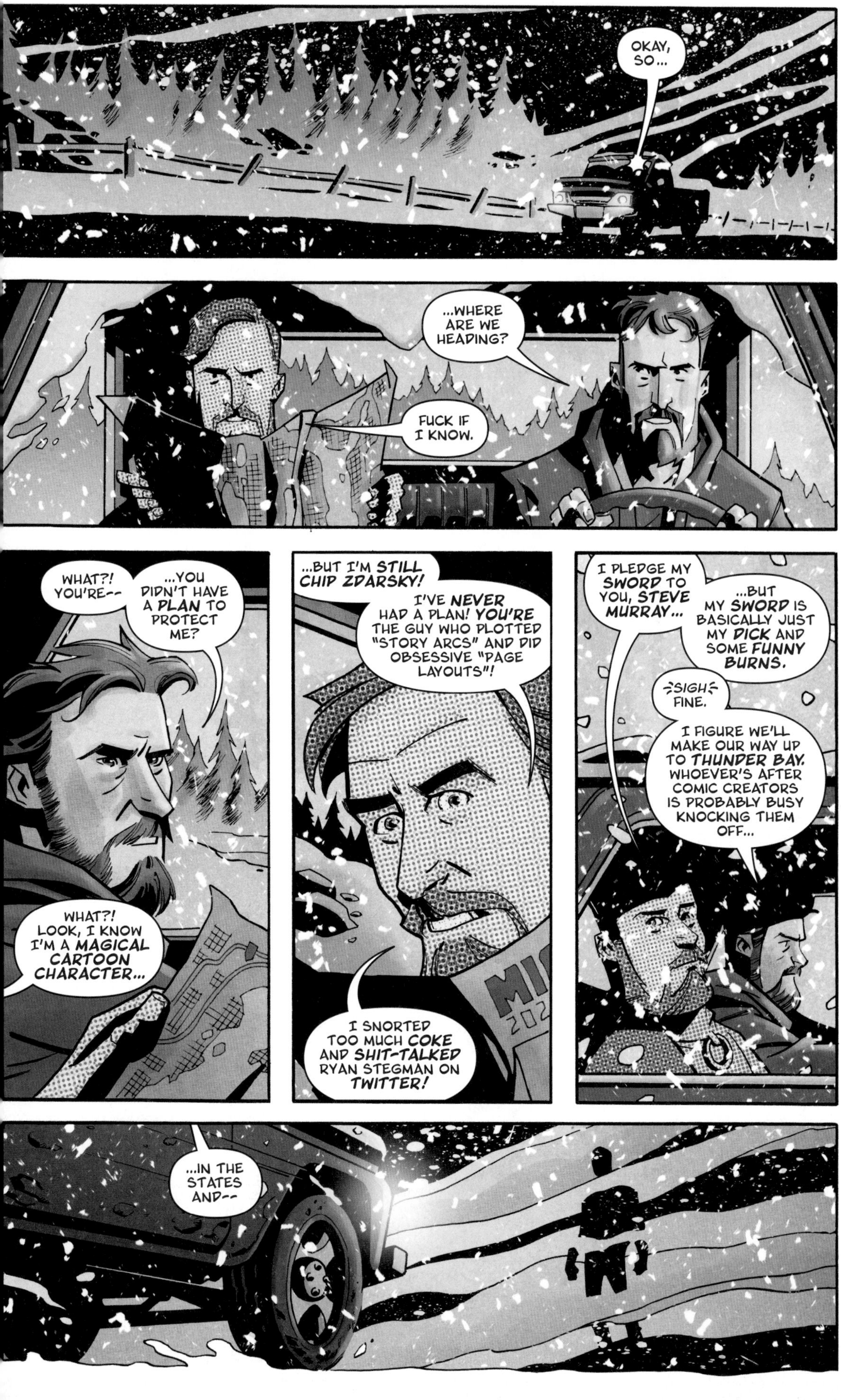

OKAY, SO...
...WHERE ARE WE HEADING?
FUCK IF I KNOW.
WHAT?! YOU'RE--
...YOU DIDN'T HAVE A PLAN TO PROTECT ME?
WHAT?! LOOK, I KNOW I'M A MAGICAL CARTOON CHARACTER...
...BUT I'M STILL CHIP ZDARSKY!
I'VE NEVER HAD A PLAN! YOU'RE THE GUY WHO PLOTTED "STORY ARCS" AND DID OBSESSIVE "PAGE LAYOUTS"!
I SNORTED TOO MUCH COKE AND SHIT-TALKED RYAN STEGMAN ON TWITTER!
I PLEDGE MY SWORD TO YOU, STEVE MURRAY...
...BUT MY SWORD IS BASICALLY JUST MY DICK AND SOME FUNNY BURNS.
SIGH
FINE.
I FIGURE WE'LL MAKE OUR WAY UP TO THUNDER BAY. WHOEVER'S AFTER COMIC CREATORS IS PROBABLY BUSY KNOCKING THEM OFF...
...IN THE STATES AND--

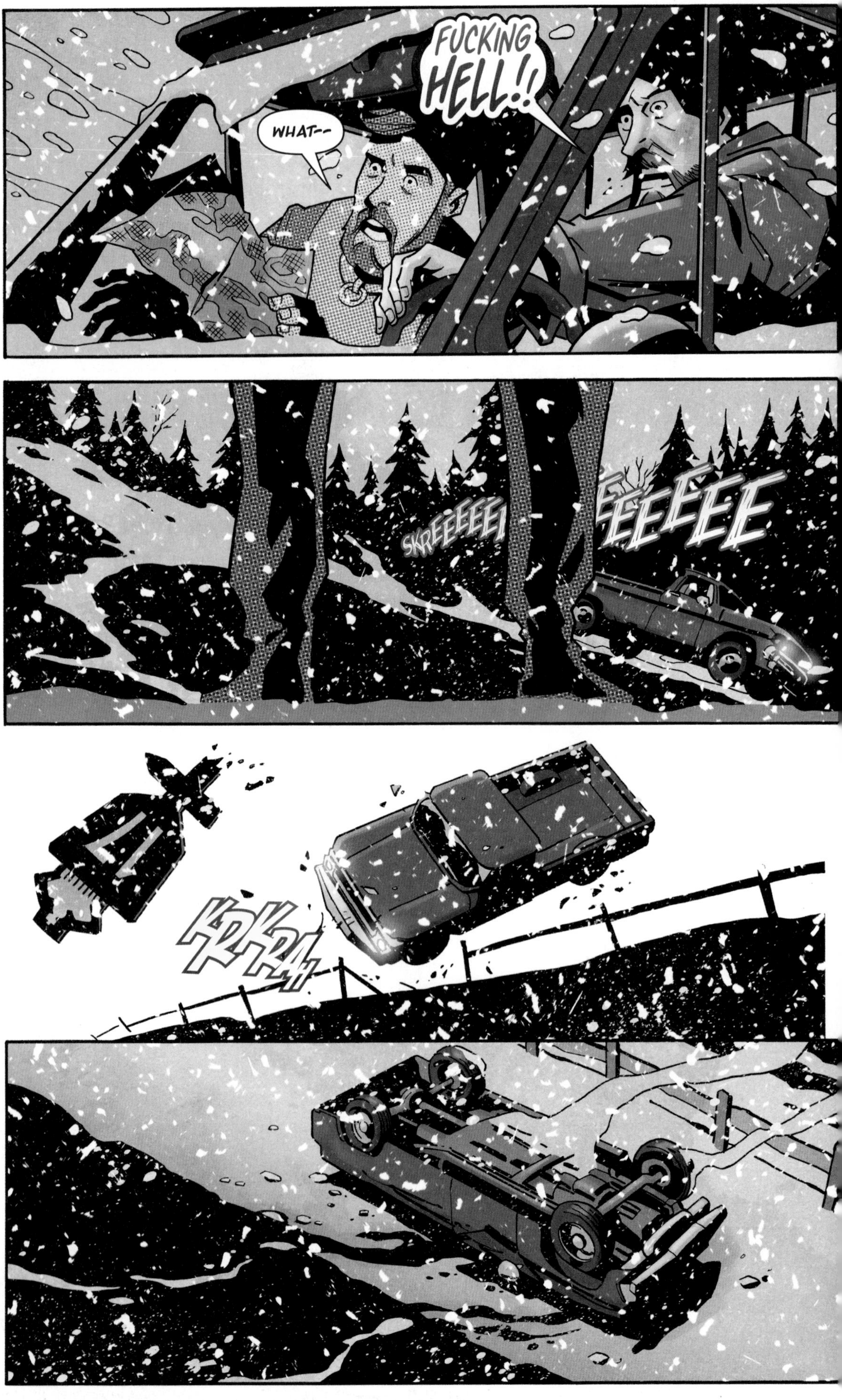
WHAT--
FUCKING HELL!!
SKREEEEEEEEEEEEE
KRKRA

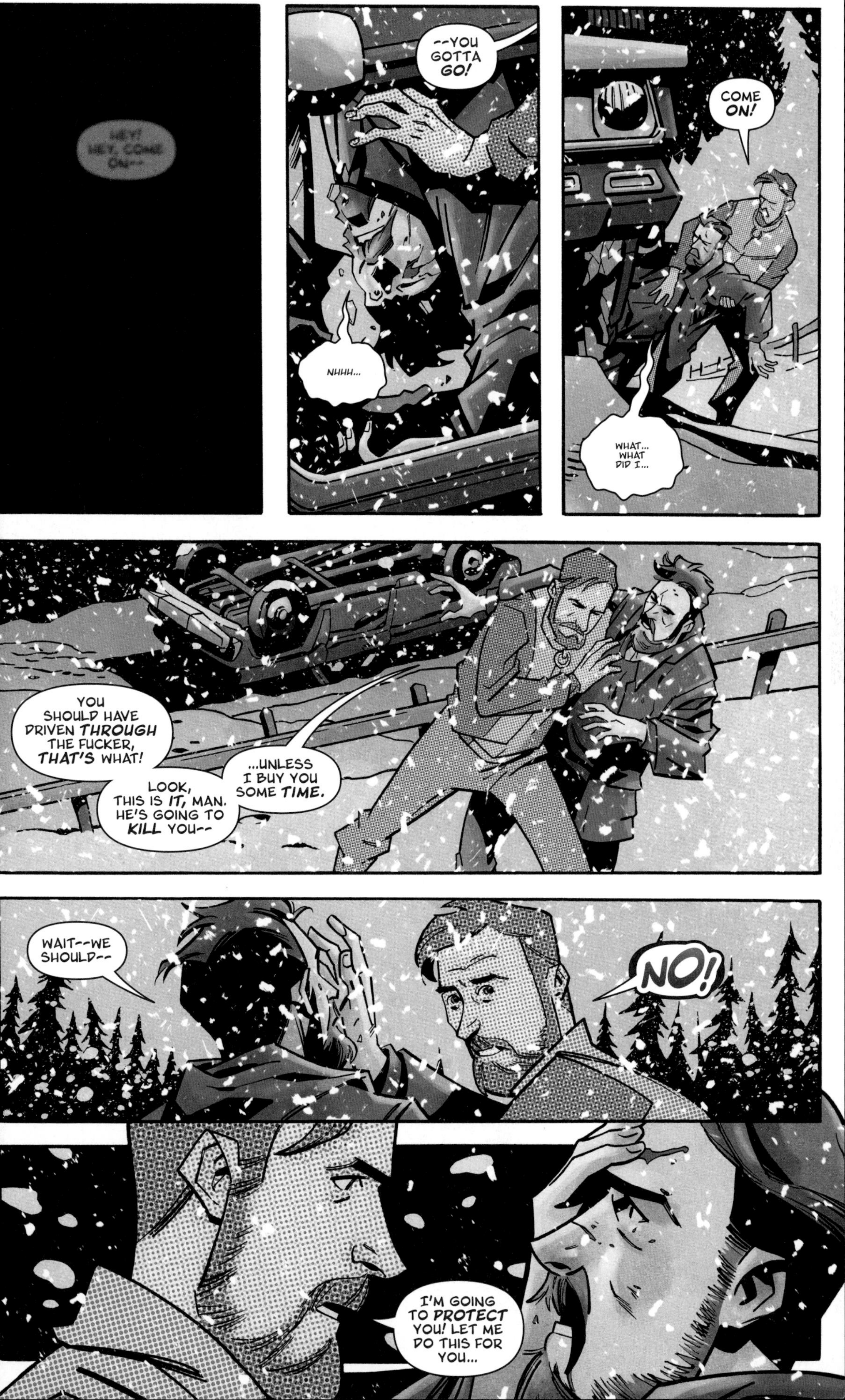
HEY! HEY, COME ON--
--YOU GOTTA GO!
NHHH...
COME ON!
WHAT... WHAT DID I...
YOU SHOULD HAVE DRIVEN THROUGH THE FUCKER, THAT'S WHAT!
LOOK, THIS IS IT, MAN. HE'S GOING TO KILL YOU--
...UNLESS I BUY YOU SOME TIME.
WAIT--WE SHOULD--
NO!
I'M GOING TO PROTECT YOU! LET ME DO THIS FOR YOU...

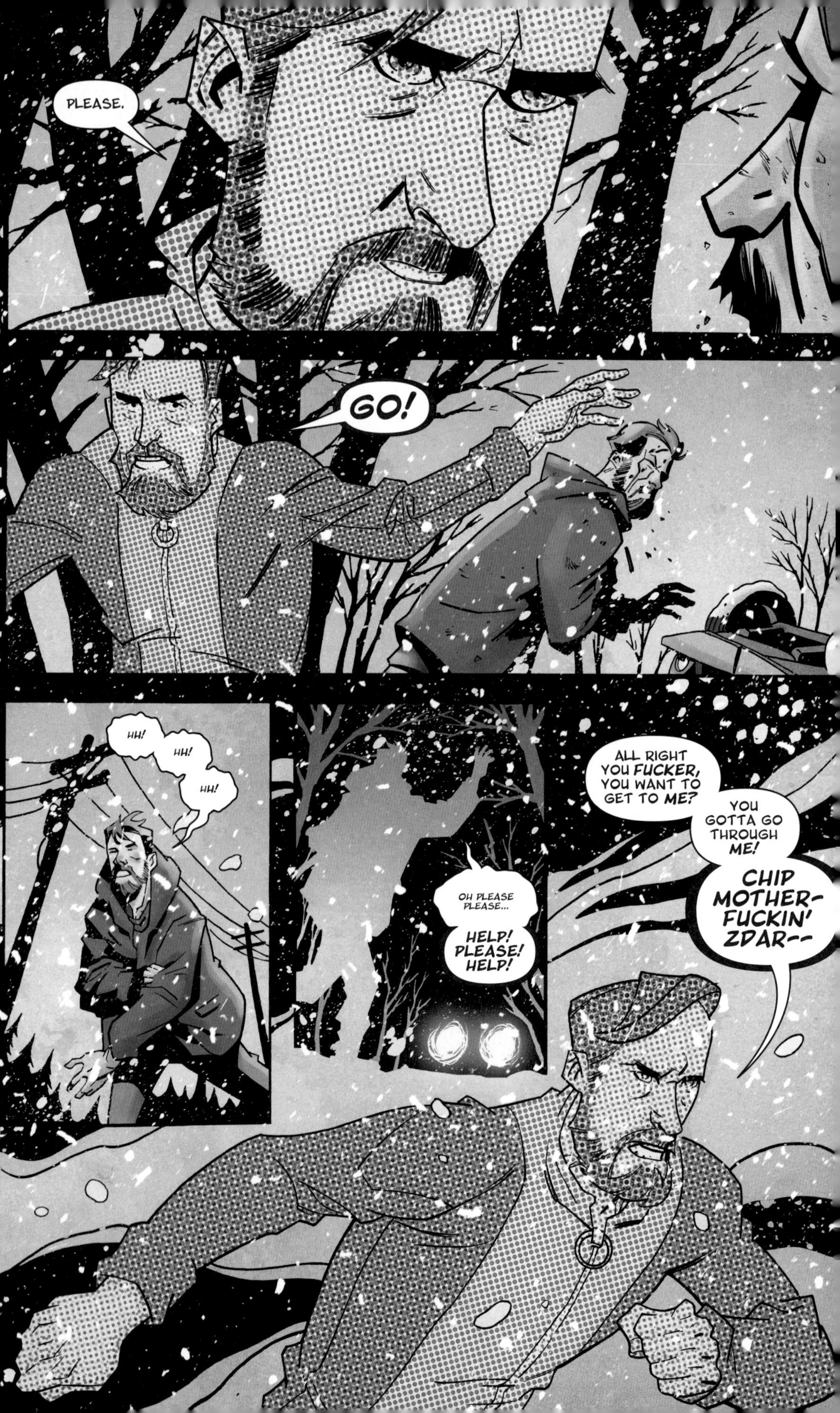
PLEASE.
GO!
HH!
HH!
HH!
OH PLEASE PLEASE...
HELP! PLEASE! HELP!
ALL RIGHT YOU FUCKER, YOU WANT TO GET TO ME?
YOU GOTTA GO THROUGH ME!
CHIP MOTHER-FUCKIN' ZDAR--

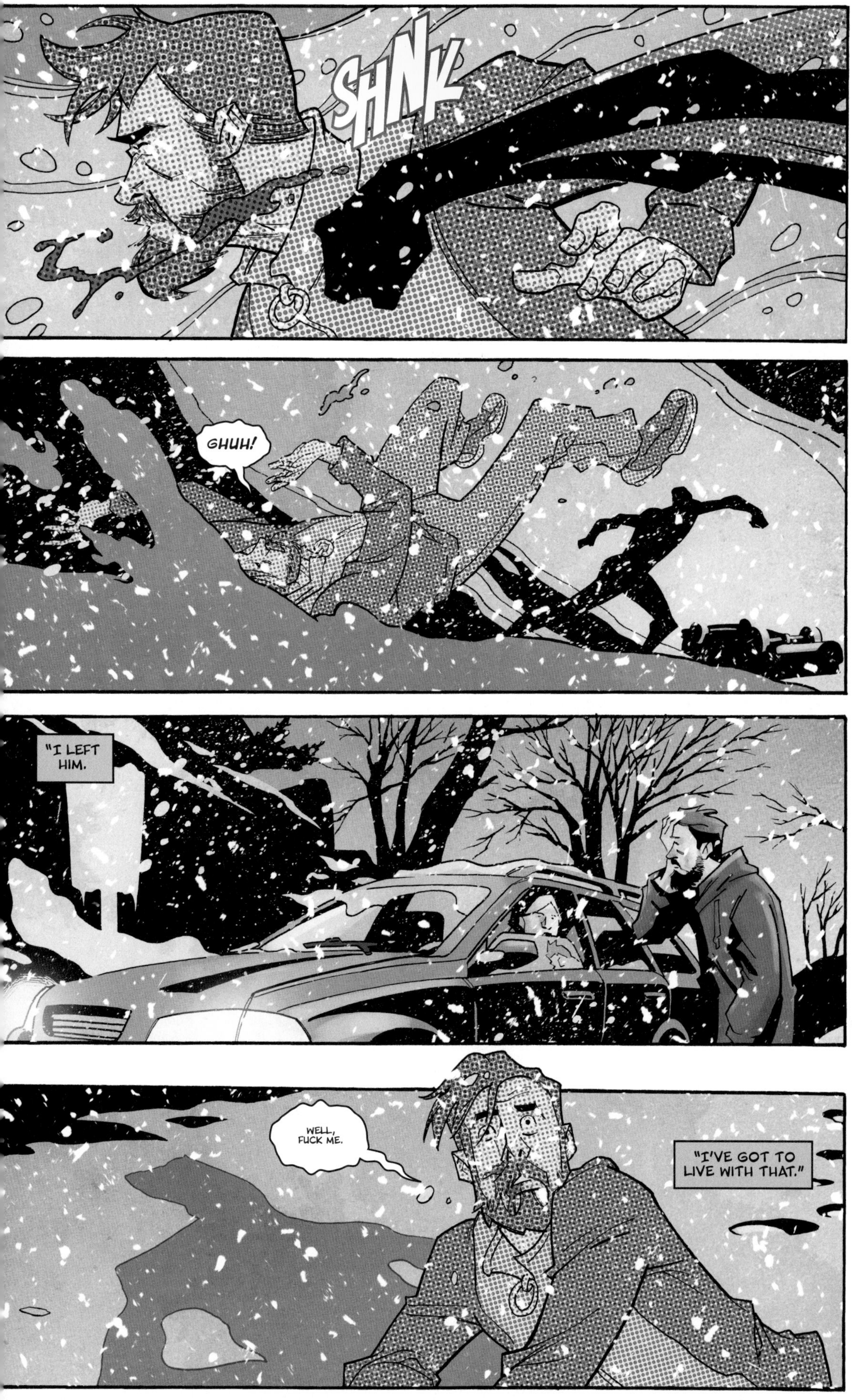
SHNK
GHUH!
"I LEFT HIM.
WELL, FUCK ME.
"I'VE GOT TO LIVE WITH THAT."

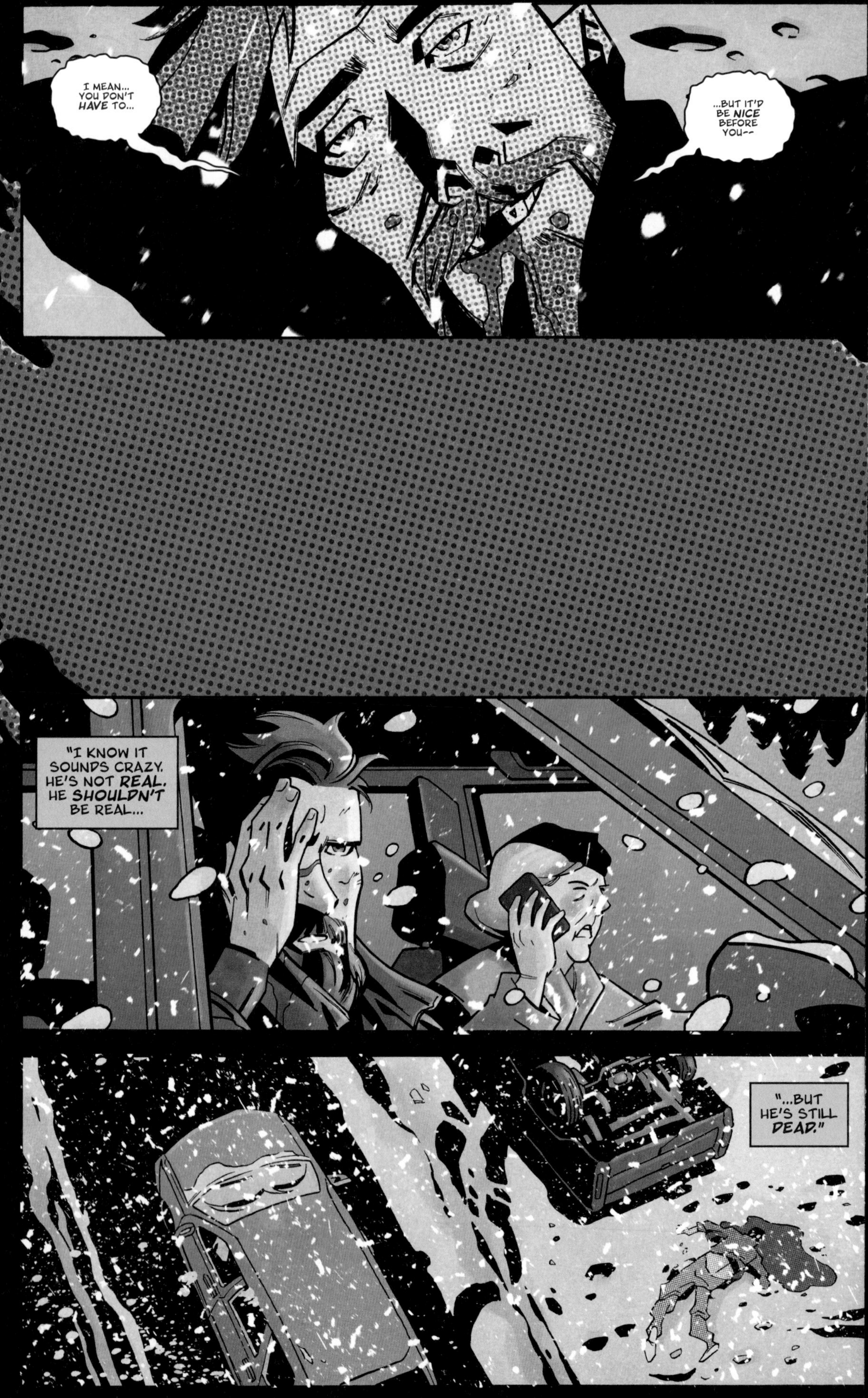

I MEAN... YOU DON'T HAVE TO...
...BUT IT'D BE NICE BEFORE YOU--
"I KNOW IT SOUNDS CRAZY. HE'S NOT REAL. HE SHOULDN'T BE REAL...
"...BUT HE'S STILL DEAD."

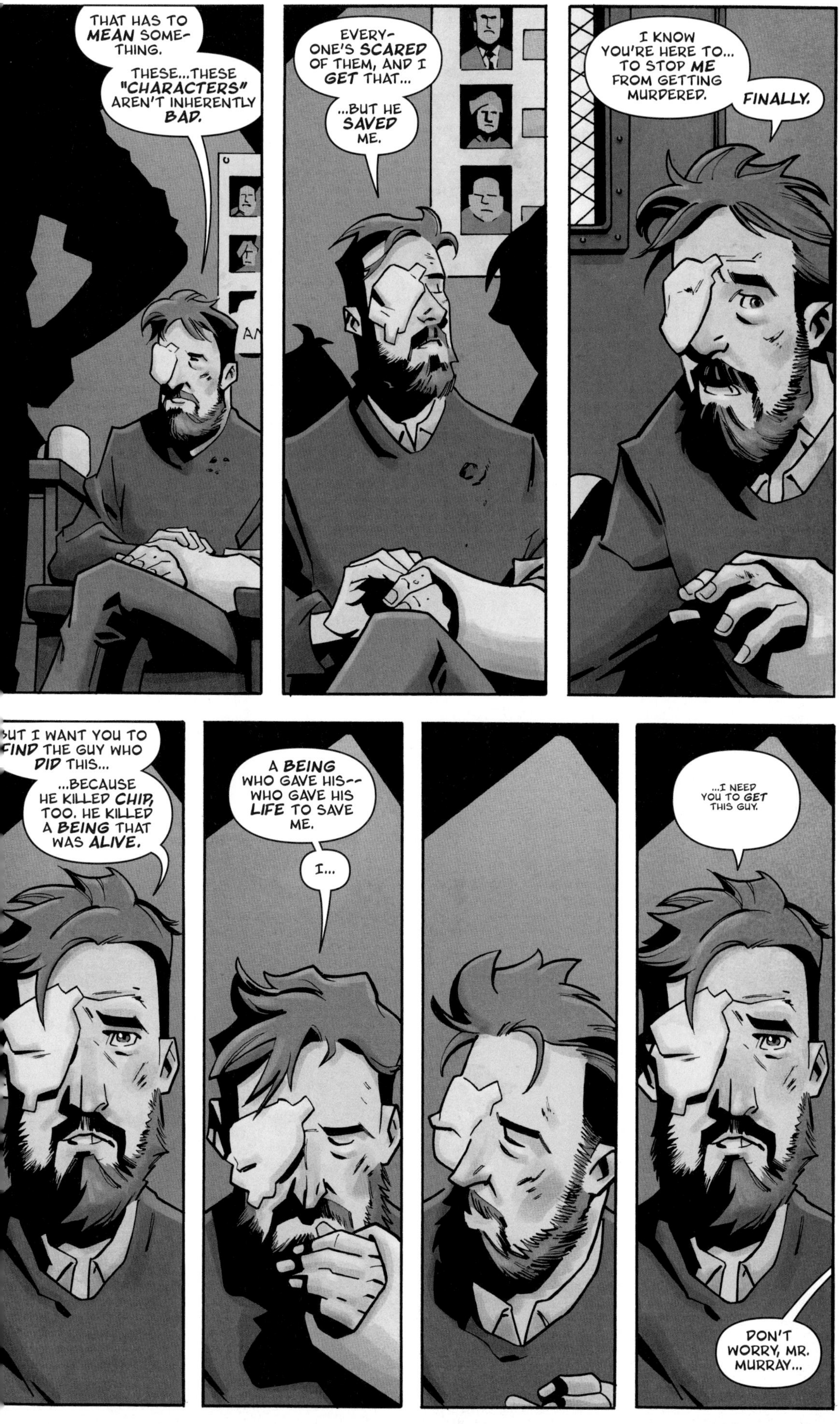
THAT HAS TO MEAN SOMETHING.
THESE...THESE "CHARACTERS" AREN'T INHERENTLY BAD.
EVERYONE'S SCARED OF THEM, AND I GET THAT...
...BUT HE SAVED ME.
I KNOW YOU'RE HERE TO... TO STOP ME FROM GETTING MURDERED.
FINALLY.
BUT I WANT YOU TO FIND THE GUY WHO DID THIS...
...BECAUSE HE KILLED CHIP, TOO. HE KILLED A BEING THAT WAS ALIVE.
A BEING WHO GAVE HIS-- WHO GAVE HIS LIFE TO SAVE ME.
I...
...I NEED YOU TO GET THIS GUY.
DON'T WORRY, MR. MURRAY...

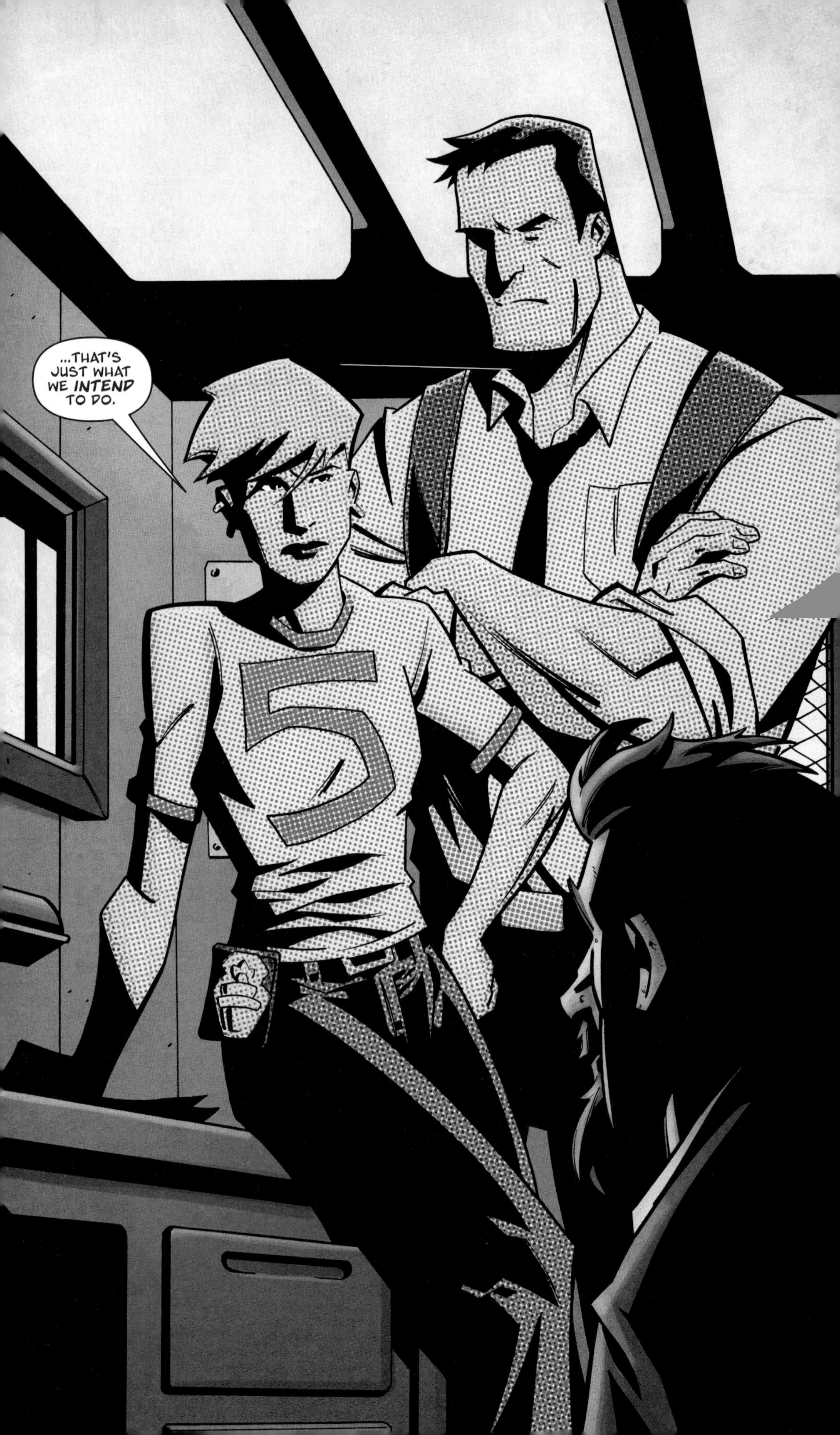
...THAT'S JUST WHAT WE INTEND TO DO.

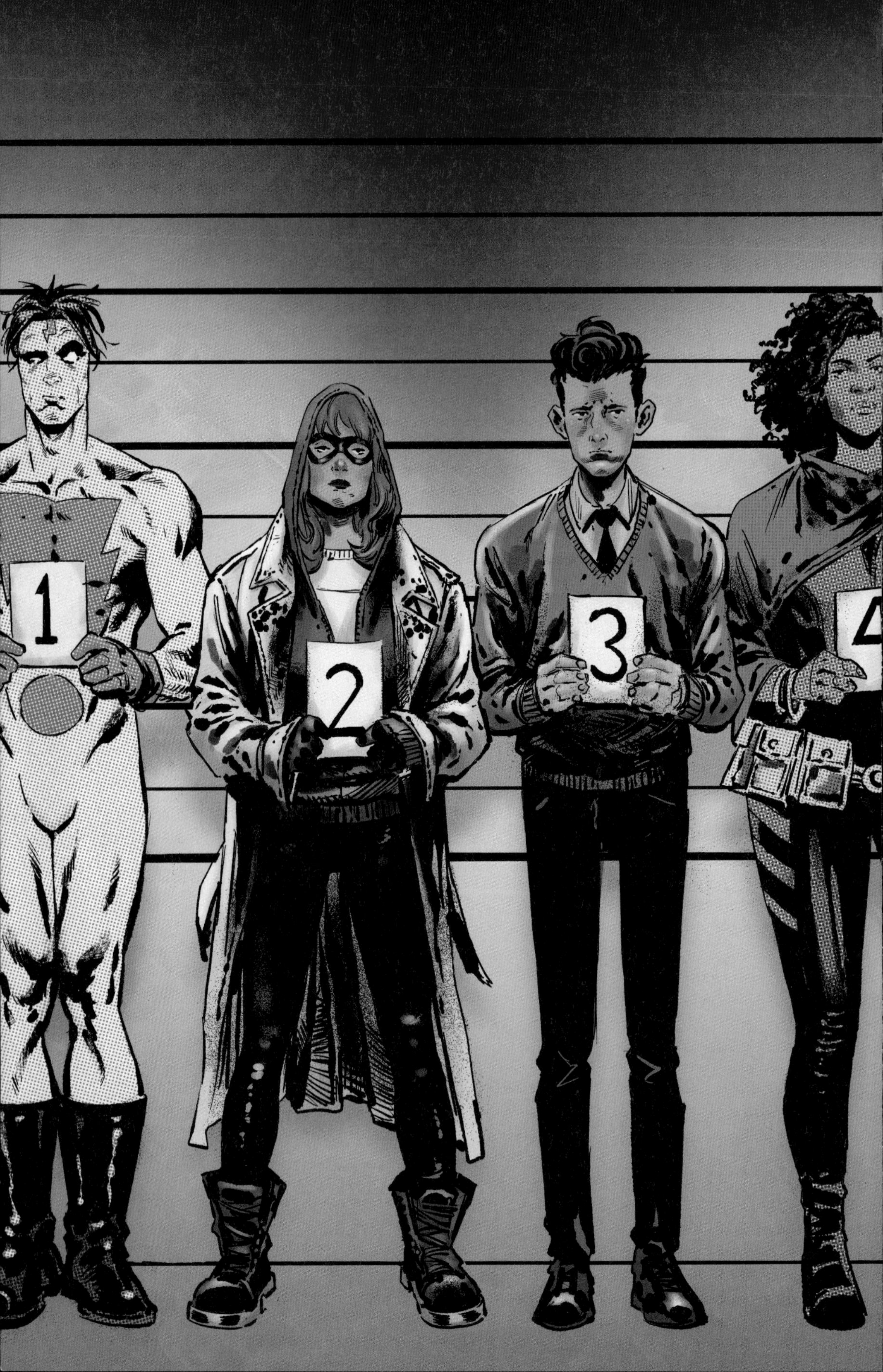
1
2
3
4

THE 10-CENT PLAGUE

PLAGUE

CHAPTER ONE

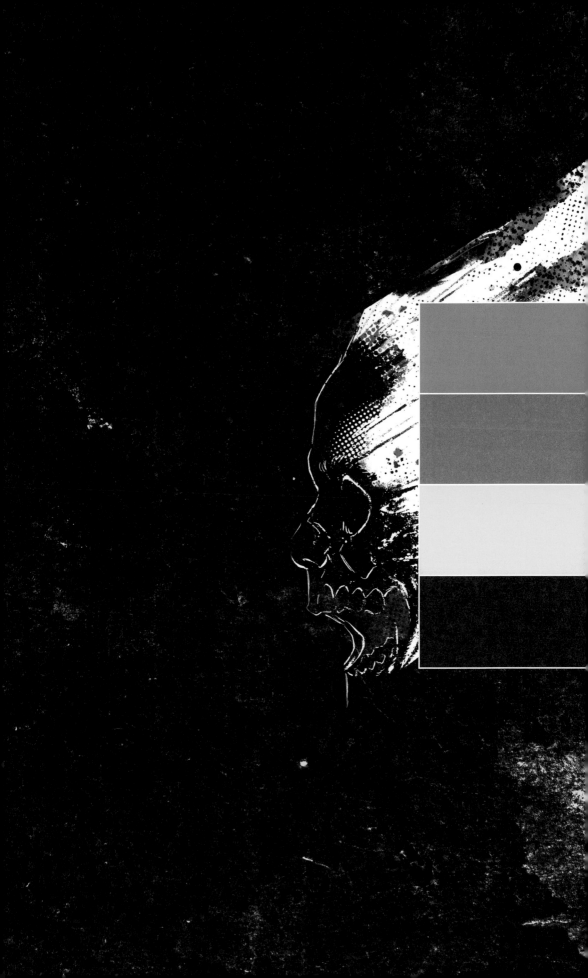

PREVIOUSLY IN

CROSSOVER...

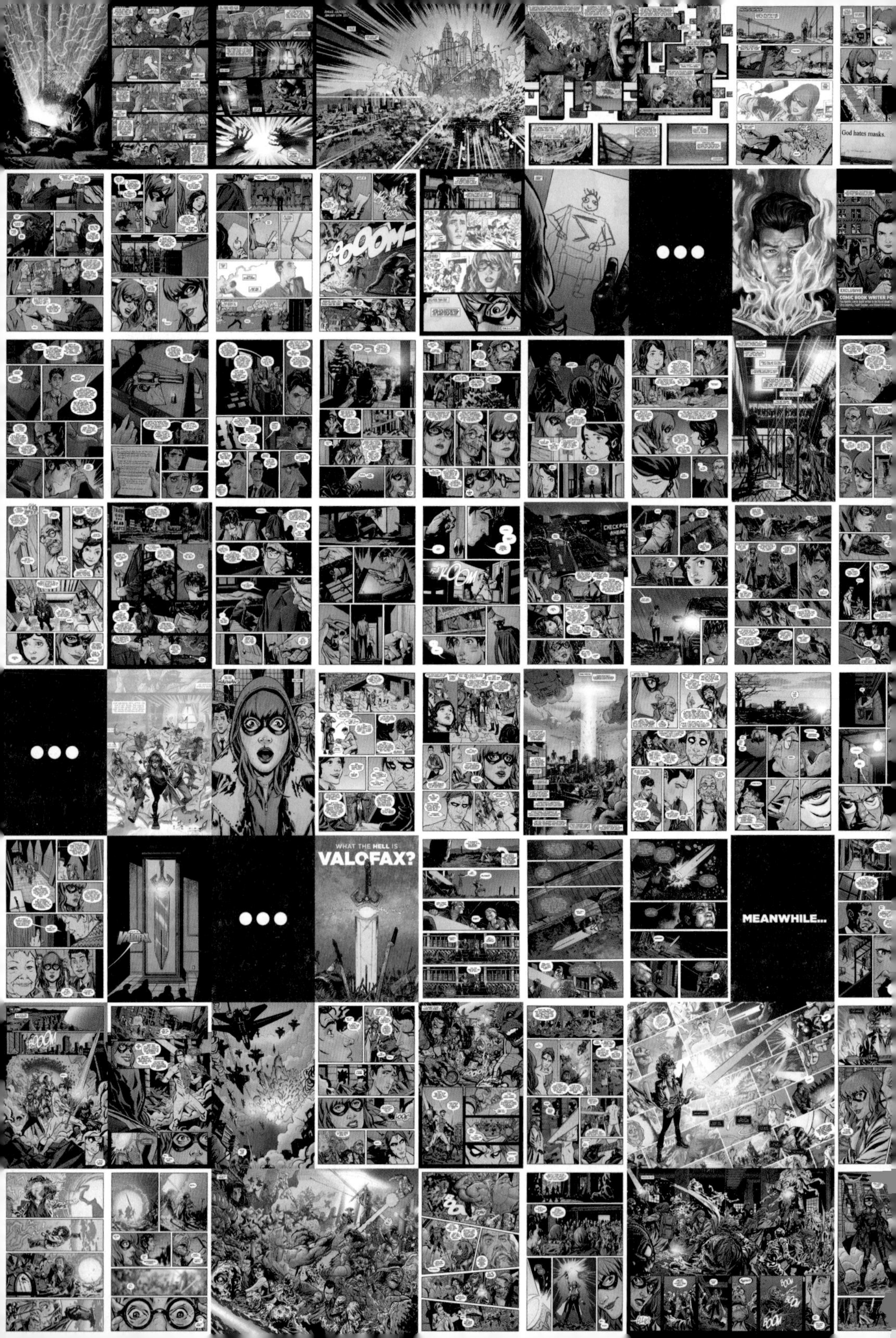
God hates masks.
EXCLUSIVE
COMIC BOOK WRITER FO
WHAT THE HELL IS
VALOFAX?
MEANWHILE...

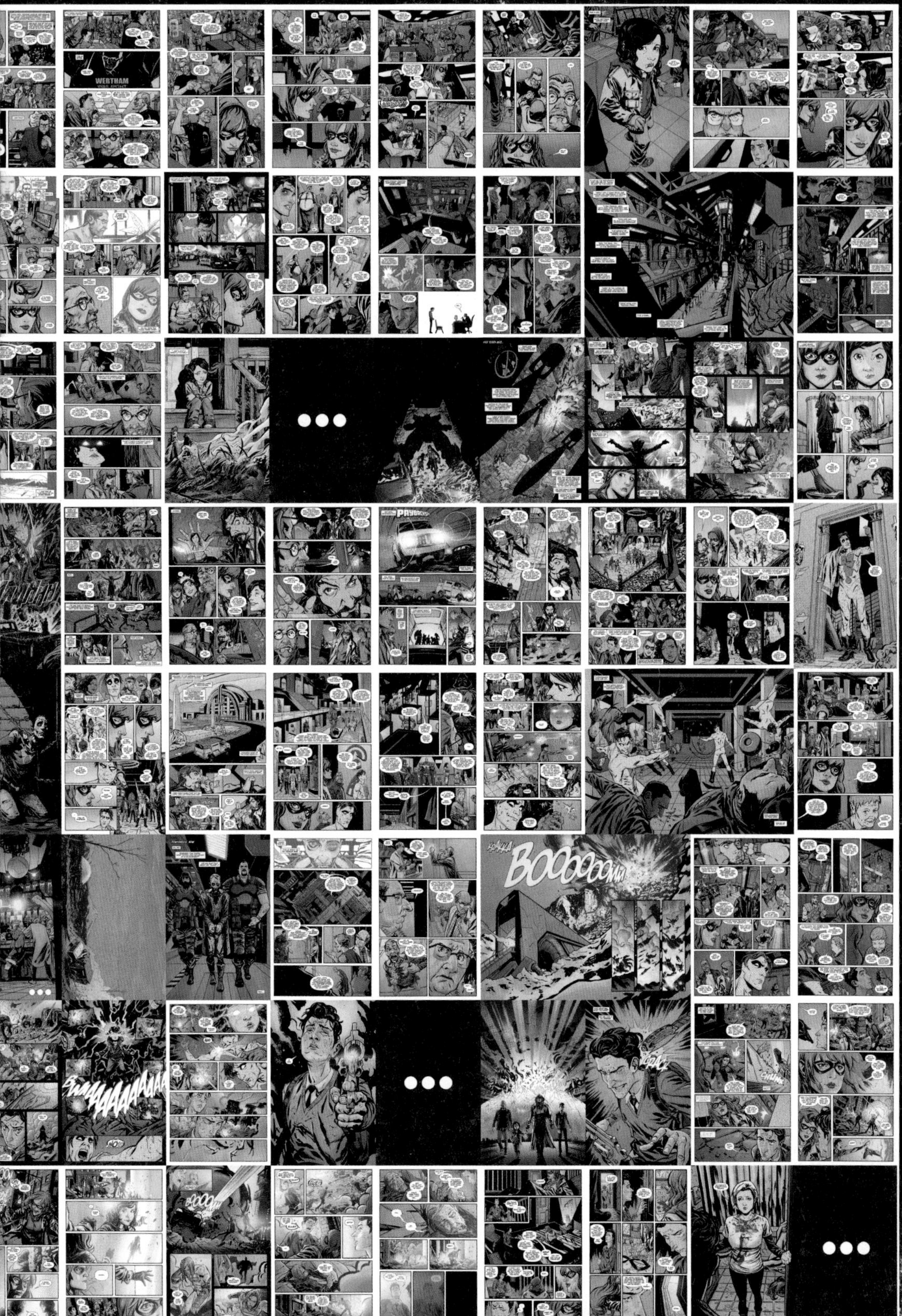
WERTHAM

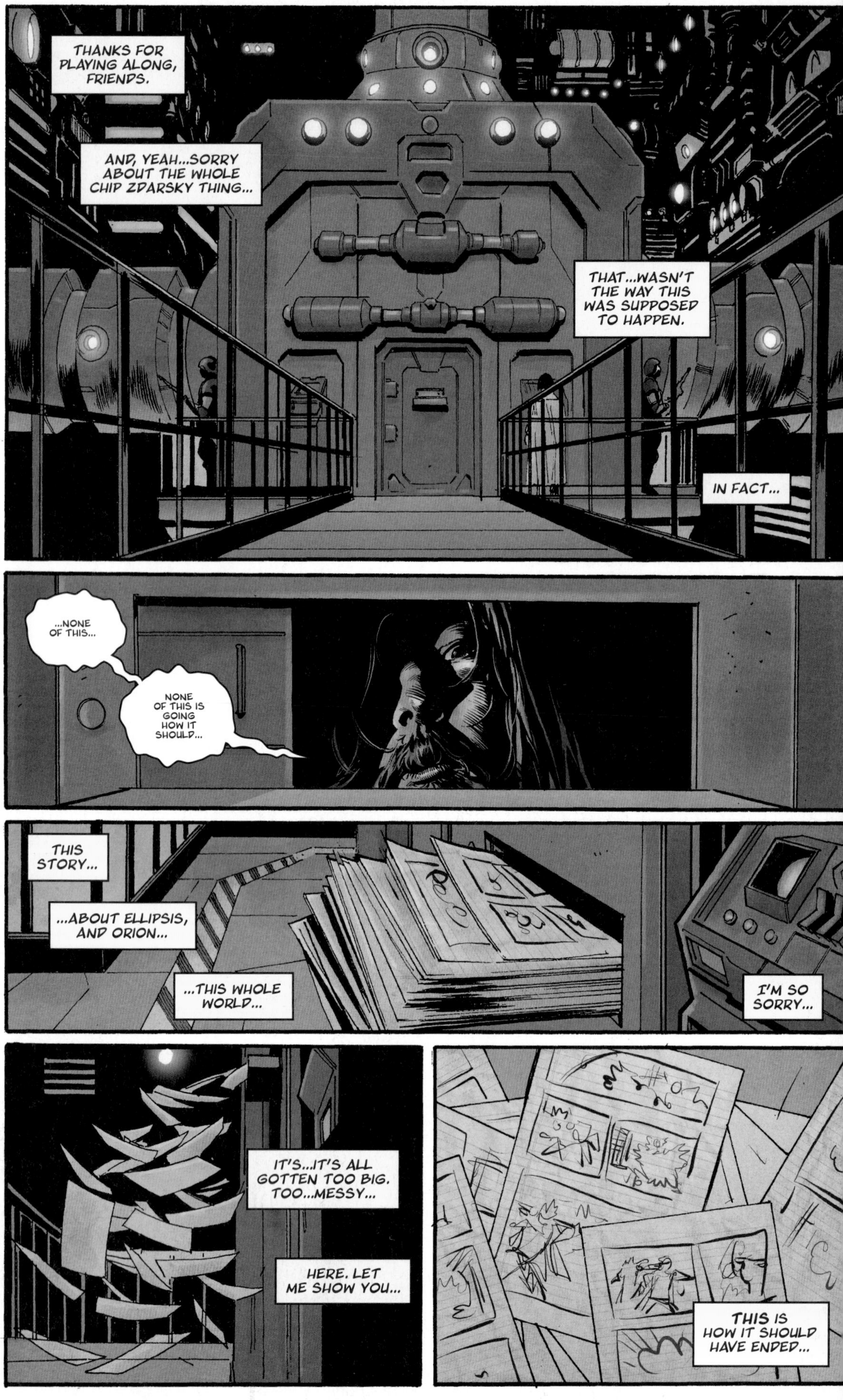
THANKS FOR PLAYING ALONG, FRIENDS.
AND, YEAH...SORRY ABOUT THE WHOLE CHIP ZDARSKY THING...
THAT...WASN'T THE WAY THIS WAS SUPPOSED TO HAPPEN.
IN FACT...
...NONE OF THIS...
NONE OF THIS IS GOING HOW IT SHOULD...
THIS STORY...
...ABOUT ELLIPSIS, AND ORION...
...THIS WHOLE WORLD...
I'M SO SORRY...
IT'S...IT'S ALL GOTTEN TOO BIG. TOO...MESSY...
HERE. LET ME SHOW YOU...
THIS IS HOW IT SHOULD HAVE ENDED...

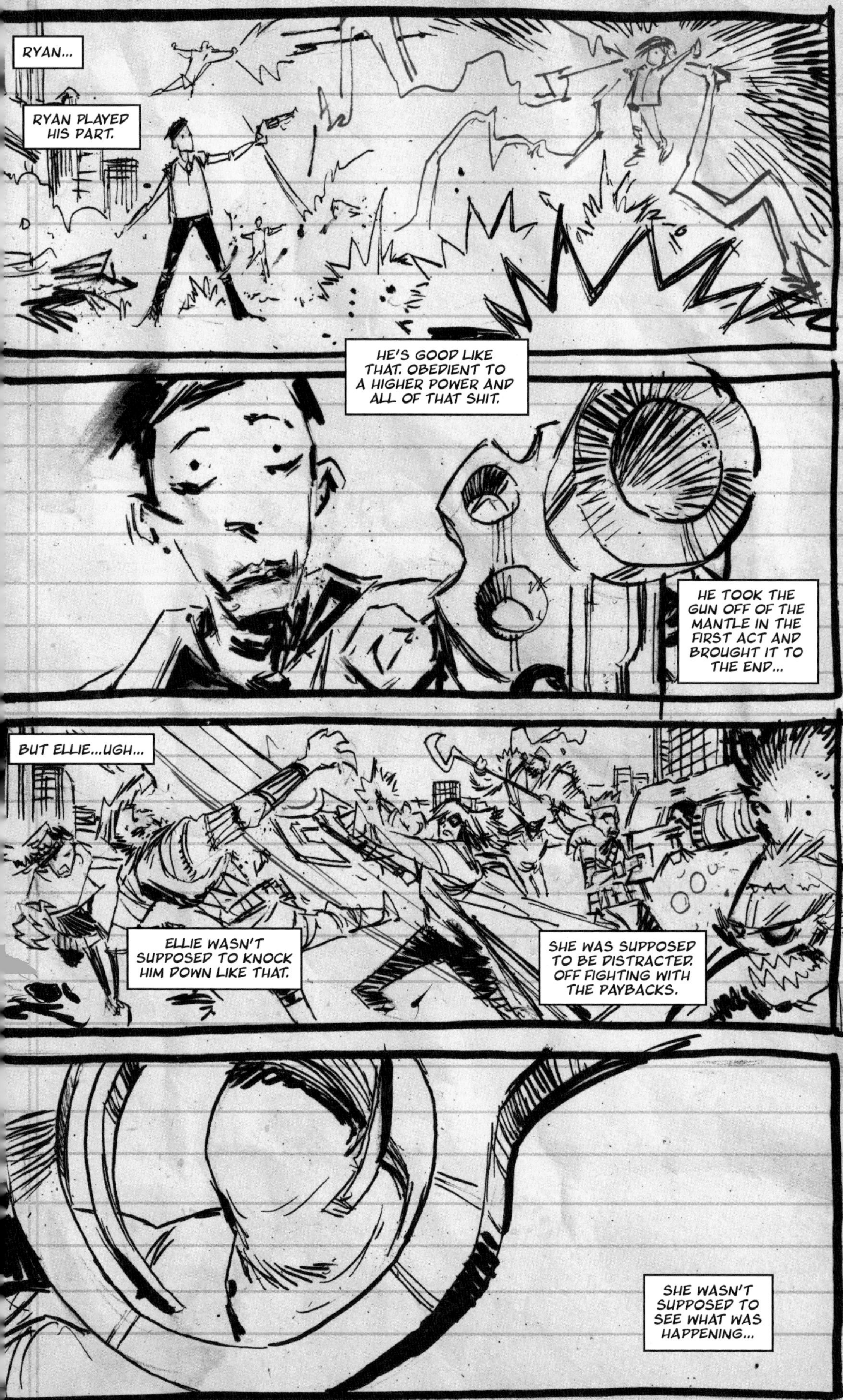
RYAN...
RYAN PLAYED HIS PART.
HE'S GOOD LIKE THAT. OBEDIENT TO A HIGHER POWER AND ALL OF THAT SHIT.
HE TOOK THE GUN OFF OF THE MANTLE IN THE FIRST ACT AND BROUGHT IT TO THE END...
BUT ELLIE...UGH...
ELLIE WASN'T SUPPOSED TO KNOCK HIM DOWN LIKE THAT.
SHE WAS SUPPOSED TO BE DISTRACTED. OFF FIGHTING WITH THE PAYBACKS.
SHE WASN'T SUPPOSED TO SEE WHAT WAS HAPPENING...

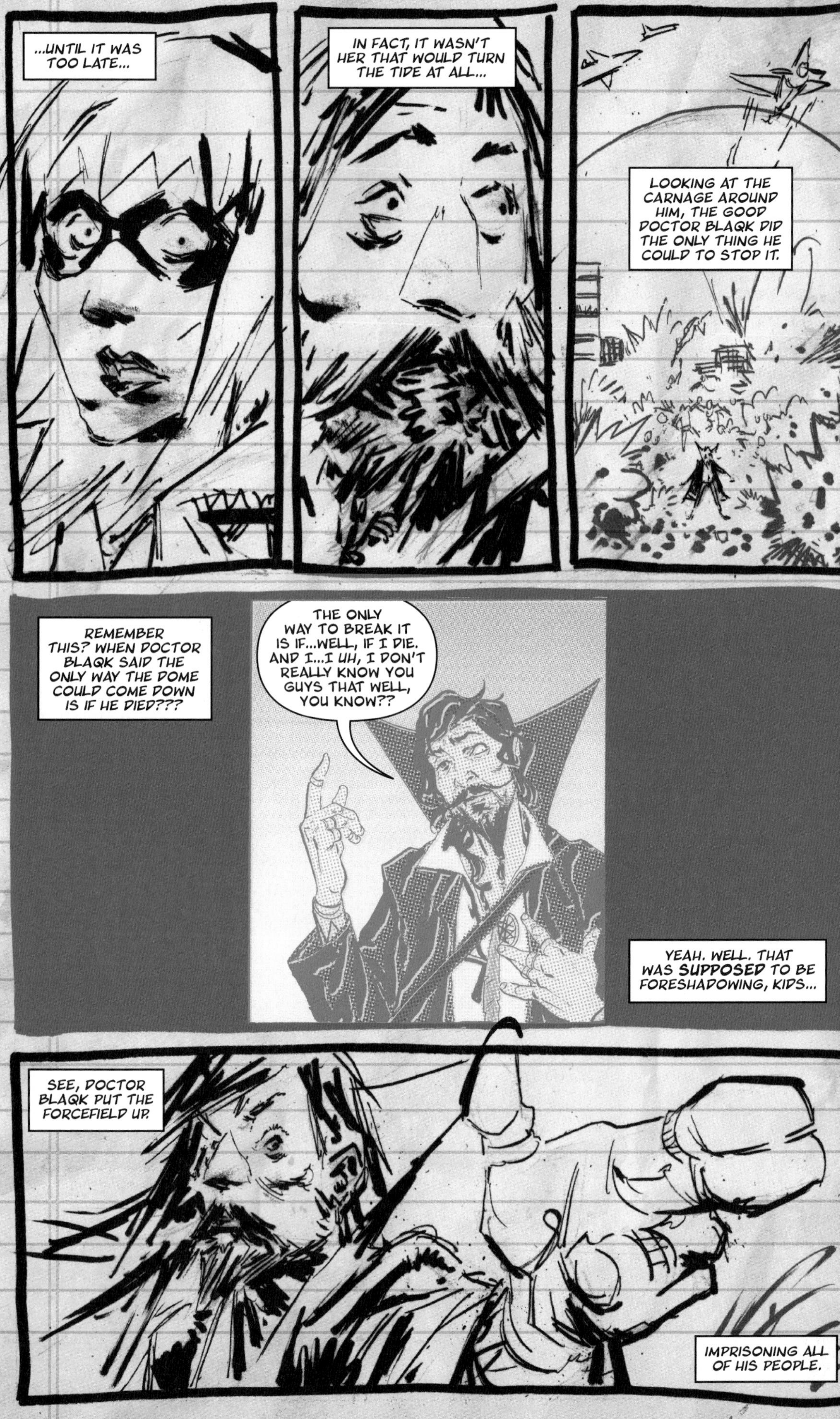
...UNTIL IT WAS TOO LATE...
IN FACT, IT WASN'T HER THAT WOULD TURN THE TIDE AT ALL...
LOOKING AT THE CARNAGE AROUND HIM, THE GOOD DOCTOR BLAQK DID THE ONLY THING HE COULD TO STOP IT.
REMEMBER THIS? WHEN DOCTOR BLAQK SAID THE ONLY WAY THE DOME COULD COME DOWN IS IF HE DIED???
THE ONLY WAY TO BREAK IT IS IF...WELL, IF I DIE. AND I...I UH, I DON'T REALLY KNOW YOU GUYS THAT WELL, YOU KNOW??
YEAH. WELL. THAT WAS SUPPOSED TO BE FORESHADOWING, KIDS...
SEE, DOCTOR BLAQK PUT THE FORCEFIELD UP.
IMPRISONING ALL OF HIS PEOPLE.

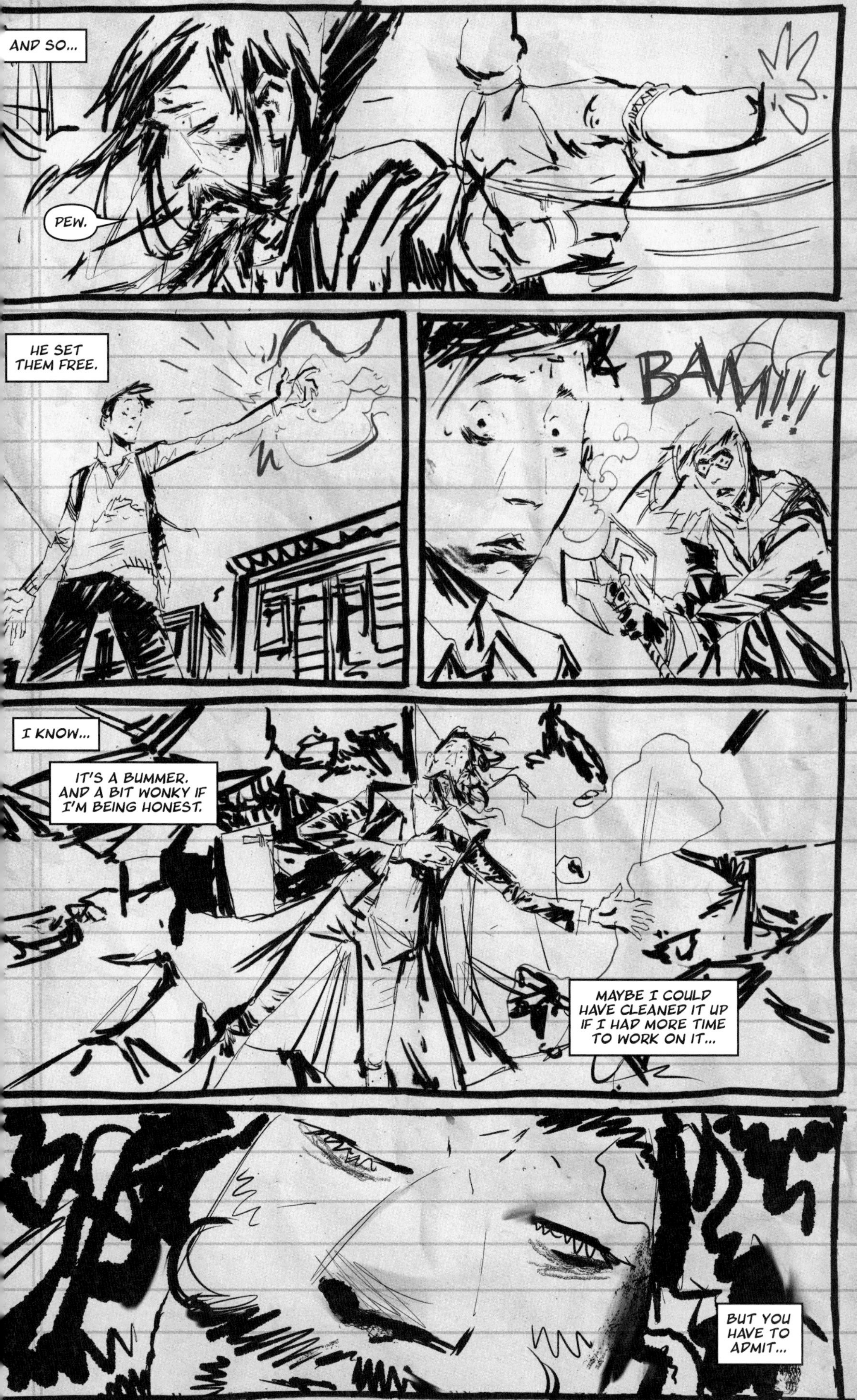
AND SO...
PEW.
HE SET THEM FREE.
BAM!!!
I KNOW...
IT'S A BUMMER. AND A BIT WONKY IF I'M BEING HONEST.
MAYBE I COULD HAVE CLEANED IT UP IF I HAD MORE TIME TO WORK ON IT...
BUT YOU HAVE TO ADMIT...

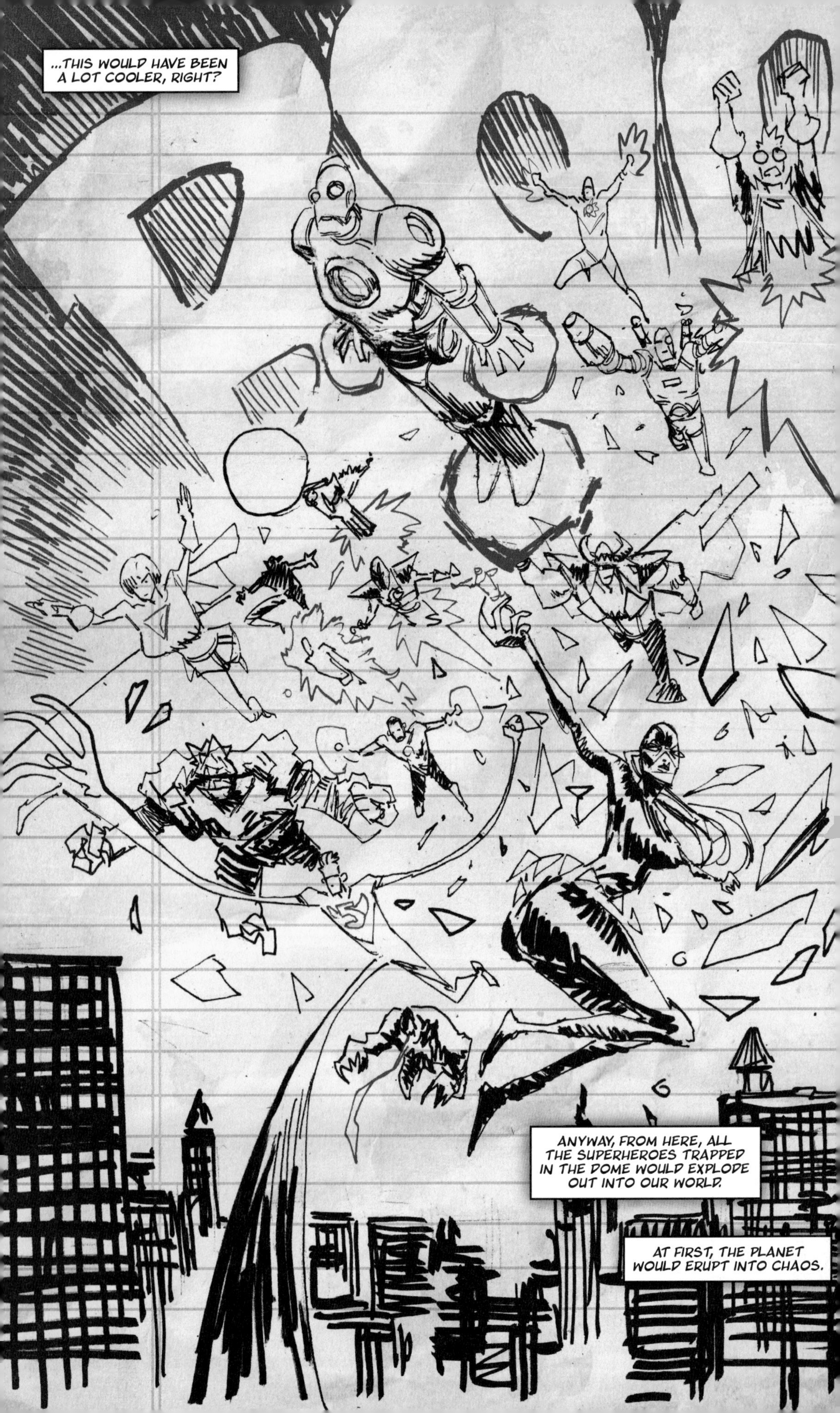
...THIS WOULD HAVE BEEN A LOT COOLER, RIGHT?
ANYWAY, FROM HERE, ALL THE SUPERHEROES TRAPPED IN THE DOME WOULD EXPLODE OUT INTO OUR WORLD.
AT FIRST, THE PLANET WOULD ERUPT INTO CHAOS.

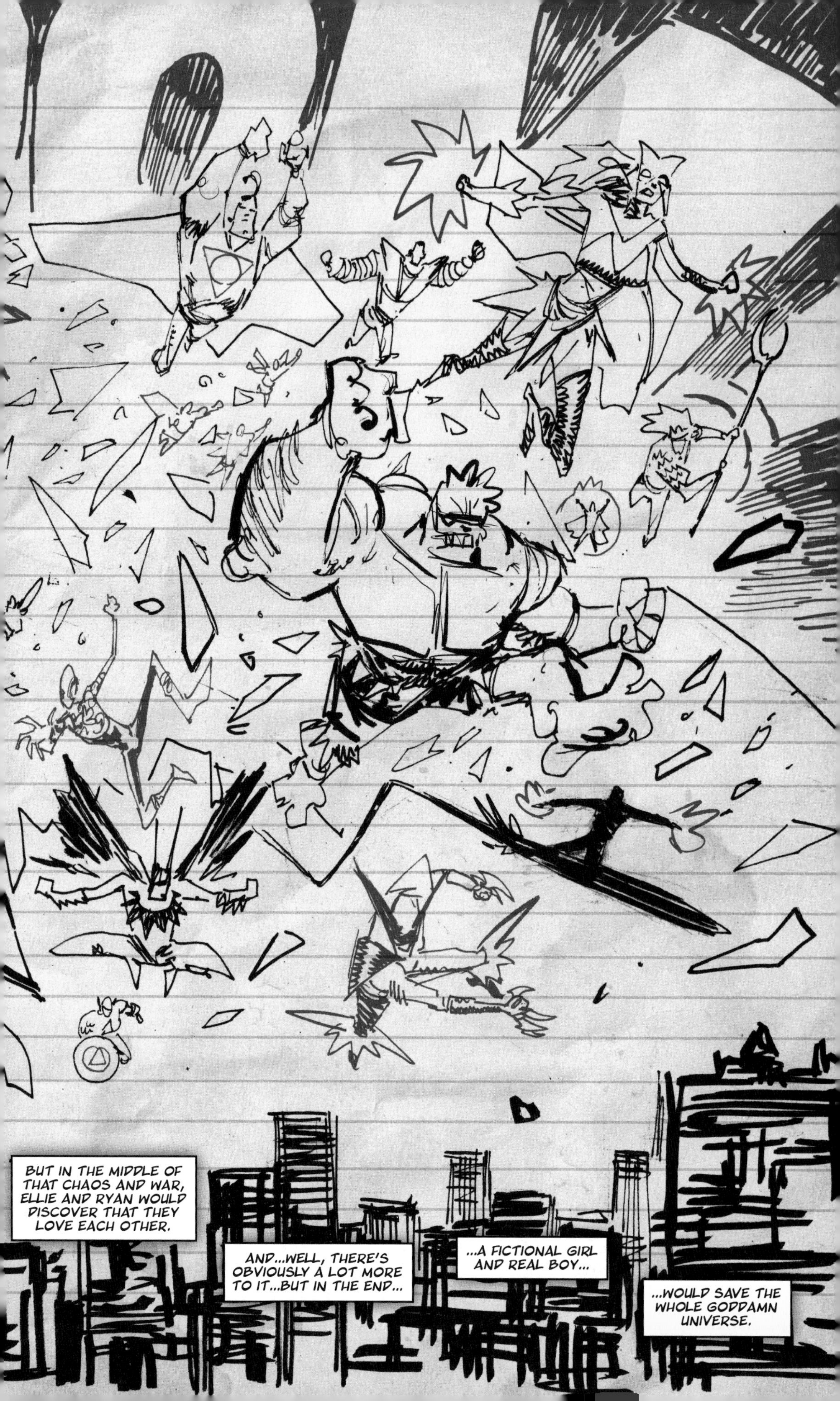

BUT IN THE MIDDLE OF THAT CHAOS AND WAR, ELLIE AND RYAN WOULD DISCOVER THAT THEY LOVE EACH OTHER.
AND...WELL, THERE'S OBVIOUSLY A LOT MORE TO IT...BUT IN THE END...
...A FICTIONAL GIRL AND REAL BOY...
...WOULD SAVE THE WHOLE GODDAMN UNIVERSE.

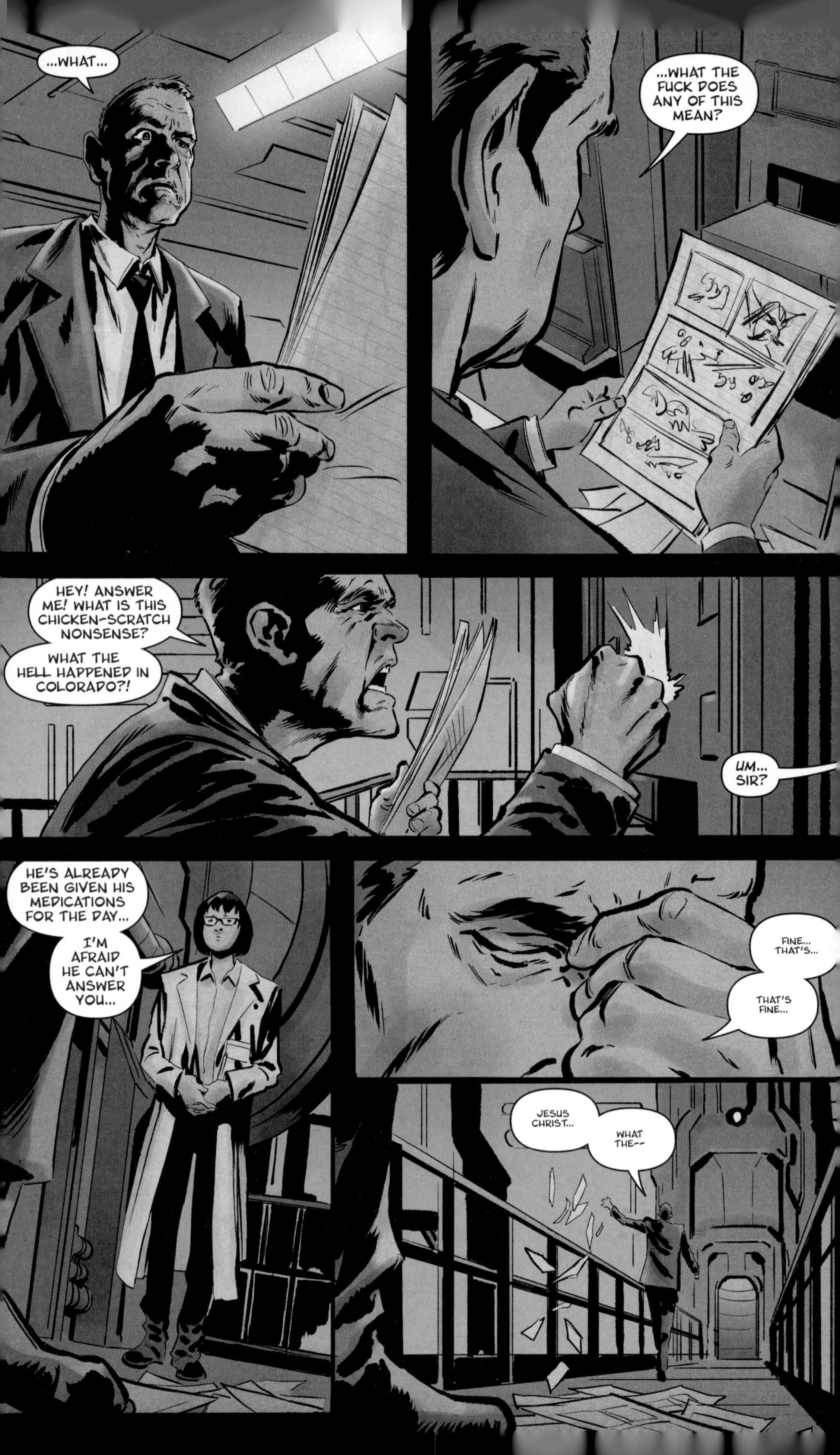

...WHAT...
...WHAT THE FUCK DOES ANY OF THIS MEAN?
HEY! ANSWER ME! WHAT IS THIS CHICKEN-SCRATCH NONSENSE?
WHAT THE HELL HAPPENED IN COLORADO?!
UM... SIR?
HE'S ALREADY BEEN GIVEN HIS MEDICATIONS FOR THE DAY...
I'M AFRAID HE CAN'T ANSWER YOU...
FINE... THAT'S...
THAT'S FINE...
JESUS CHRIST...
WHAT THE--

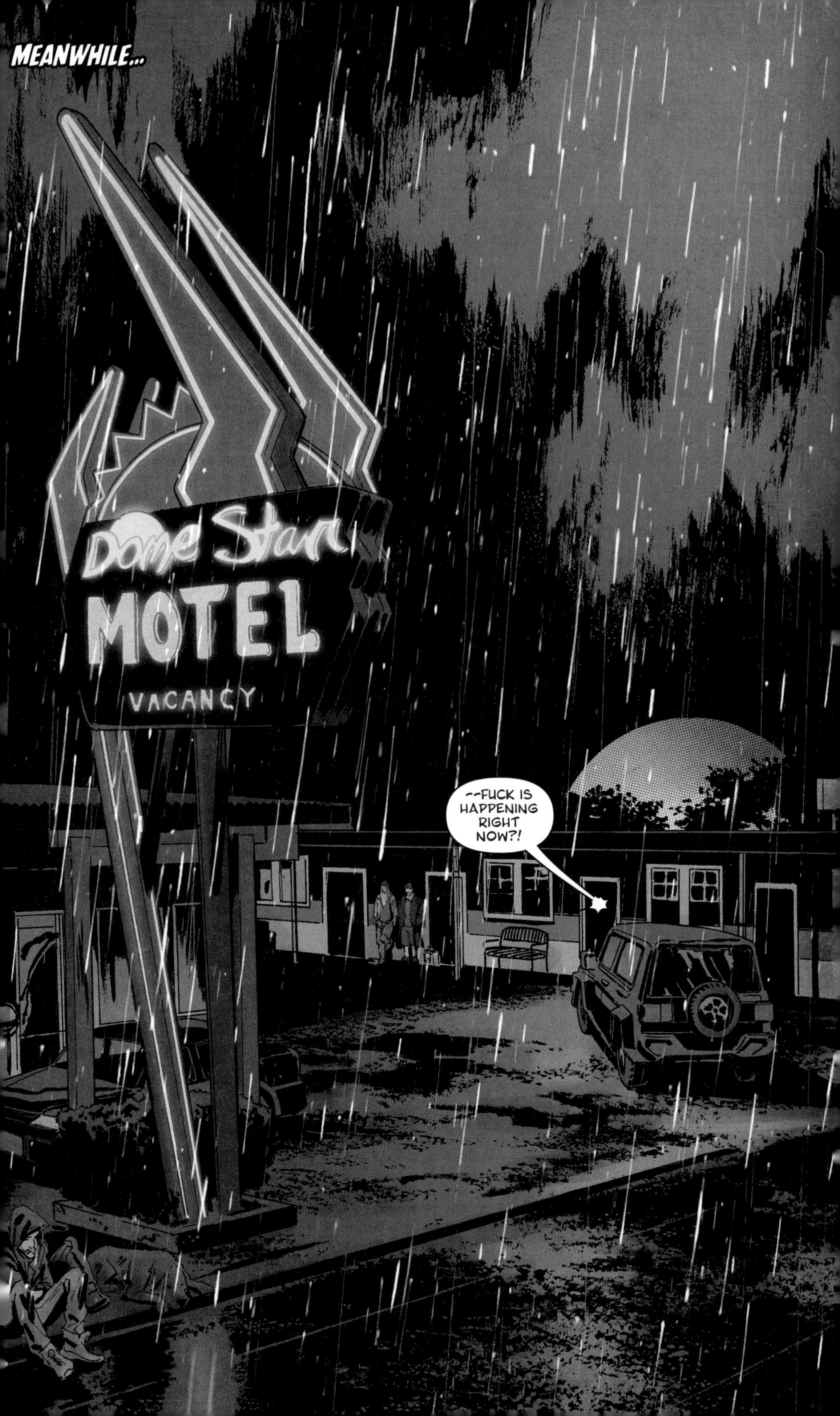
MEANWHILE...
Dome Star
MOTEL
VACANCY
--FUCK IS HAPPENING RIGHT NOW?!

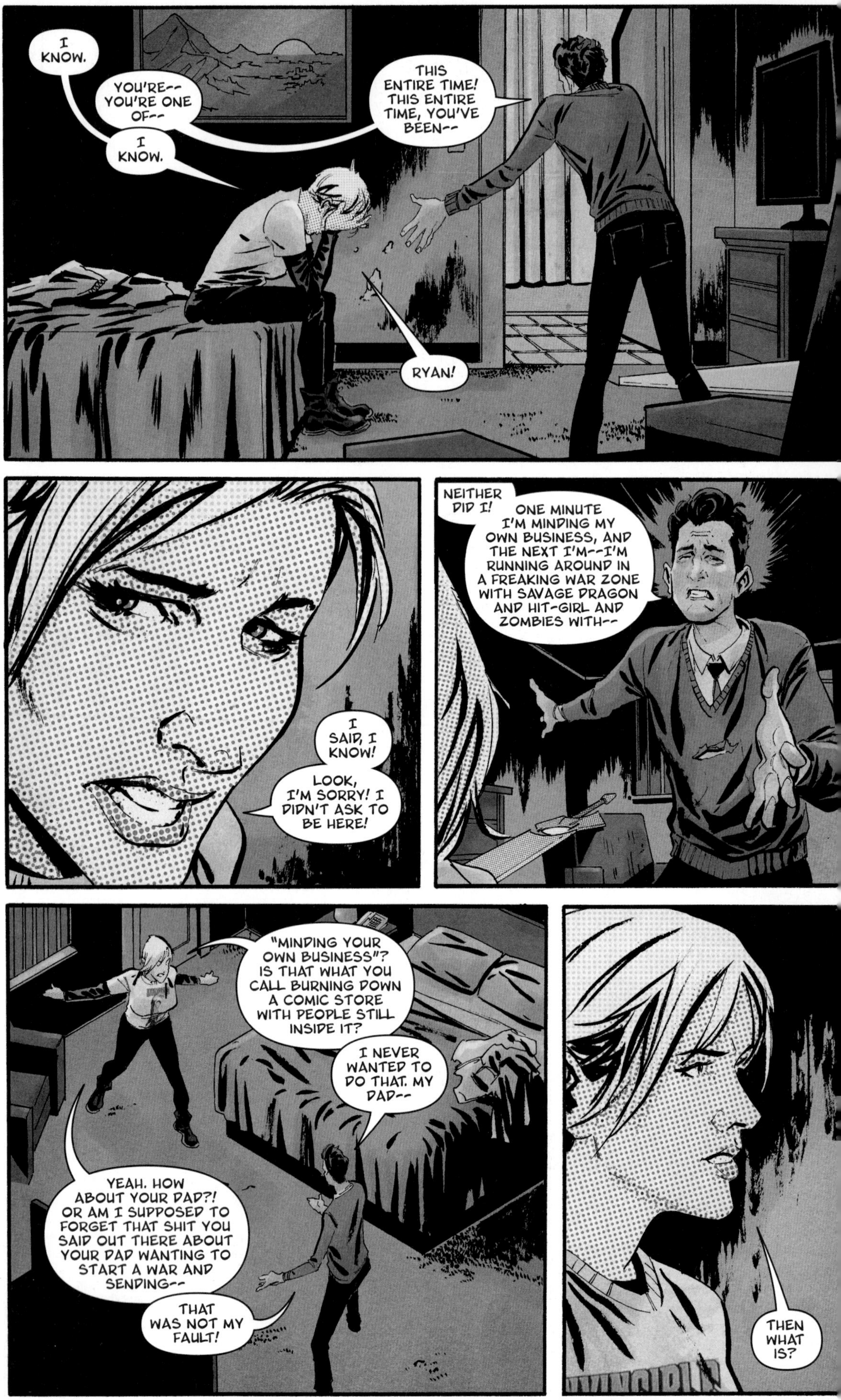
THIS ENTIRE TIME! THIS ENTIRE TIME, YOU'VE BEEN--
YOU'RE-- YOU'RE ONE OF--
I KNOW.
I KNOW.
RYAN!
I SAID, I KNOW!
LOOK, I'M SORRY! I DIDN'T ASK TO BE HERE!
NEITHER DID I!
ONE MINUTE I'M MINDING MY OWN BUSINESS, AND THE NEXT I'M--I'M RUNNING AROUND IN A FREAKING WAR ZONE WITH SAVAGE DRAGON AND HIT-GIRL AND ZOMBIES WITH--
"MINDING YOUR OWN BUSINESS"? IS THAT WHAT YOU CALL BURNING DOWN A COMIC STORE WITH PEOPLE STILL INSIDE IT?
I NEVER WANTED TO DO THAT. MY DAD--
YEAH. HOW ABOUT YOUR DAD?! OR AM I SUPPOSED TO FORGET THAT SHIT YOU SAID OUT THERE ABOUT YOUR DAD WANTING TO START A WAR AND SENDING--
THAT WAS NOT MY FAULT!
THEN WHAT IS?

WHAT?

YOU DIDN'T WANT TO BURN THE COMIC SHOP DOWN, BUT YOU DID.

YOU DIDN'T WANT TO KILL AVA, BUT YOU POINTED A GUN AT HER, ANYWAY.

YOU KNEW YOUR DAD WAS GOING TO DO WHAT HE DID, BUT YOU DIDN'T DO ANYTHING ABOUT IT.

YOU ASKED ME TO TRUST YOU.

BUT NEITHER OF US HAS ANY IDEA WHO YOU ARE.

I'M...I'M NOT A BAD PERSON.

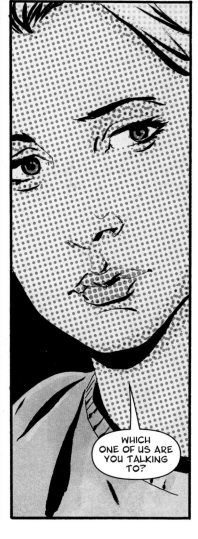

WHICH ONE OF US ARE YOU TALKING TO?

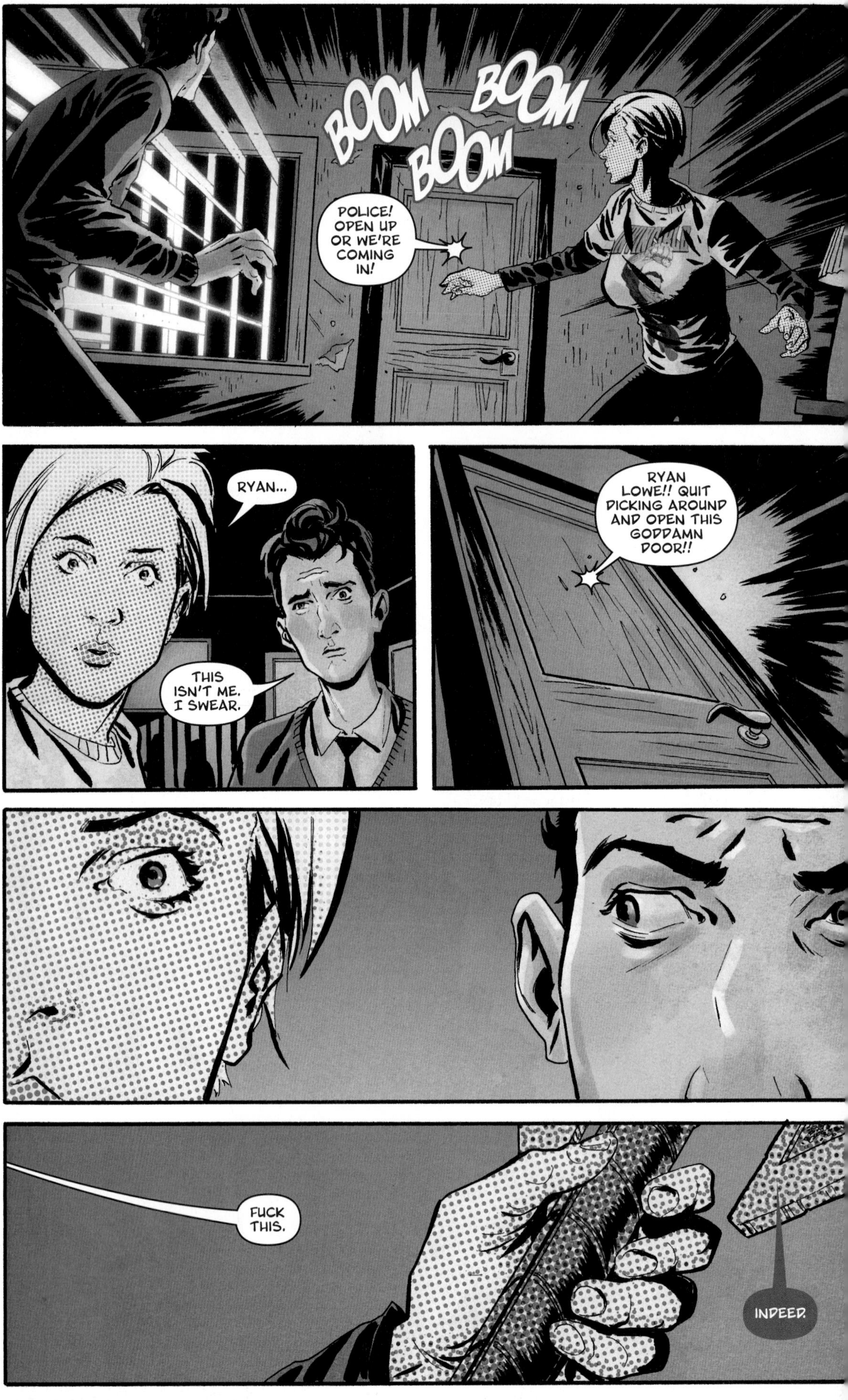
BOOM BOOM BOOM
POLICE! OPEN UP OR WE'RE COMING IN!
RYAN...
THIS ISN'T ME. I SWEAR.
RYAN LOWE!! QUIT DICKING AROUND AND OPEN THIS GODDAMN DOOR!!
FUCK THIS.
INDEED.

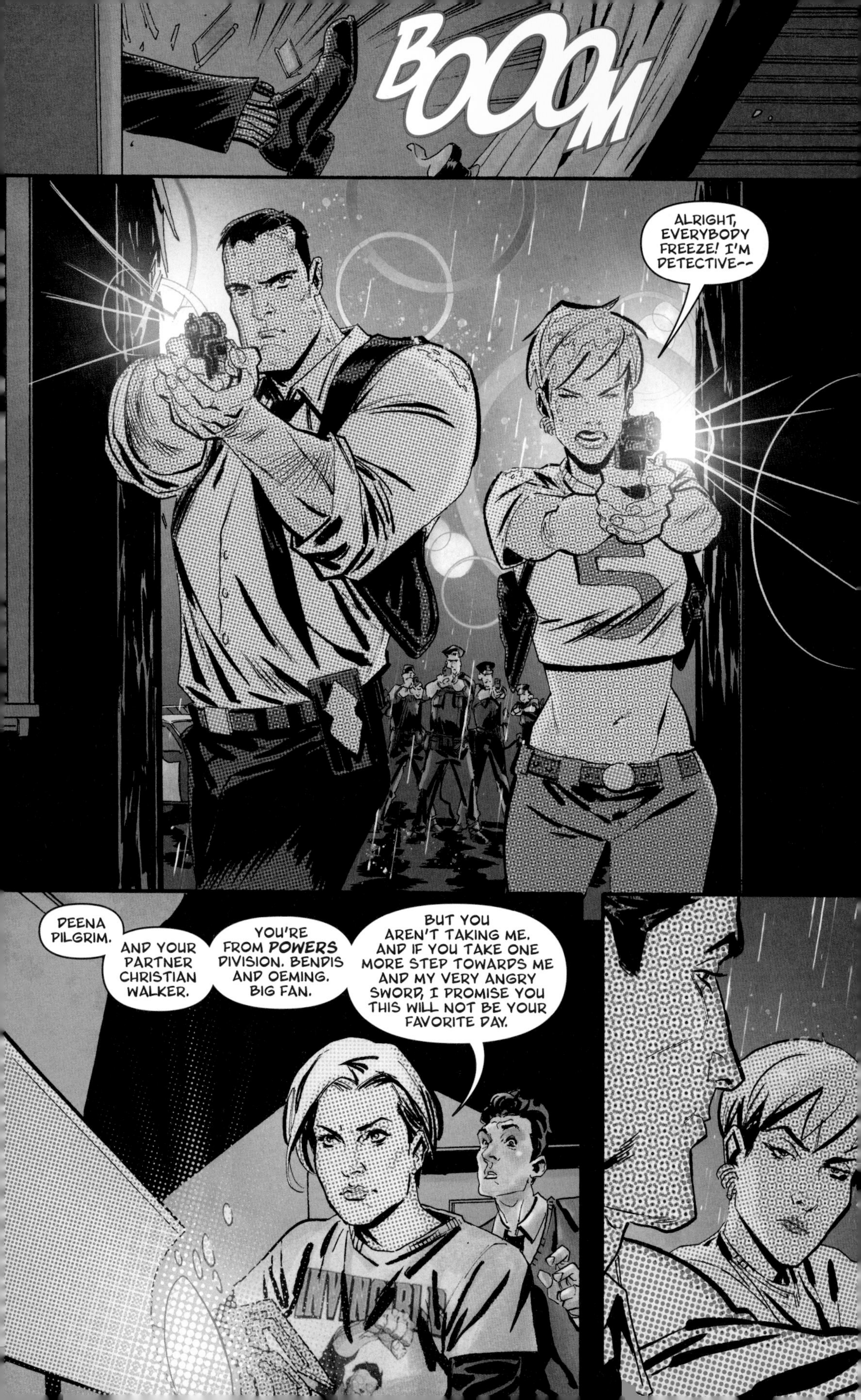
BOOOM
ALRIGHT, EVERYBODY FREEZE! I'M DETECTIVE--
DEENA PILGRIM.
AND YOUR PARTNER CHRISTIAN WALKER.
YOU'RE FROM POWERS DIVISION. BENDIS AND OEMING. BIG FAN.
BUT YOU AREN'T TAKING ME. AND IF YOU TAKE ONE MORE STEP TOWARDS ME AND MY VERY ANGRY SWORD, I PROMISE YOU THIS WILL NOT BE YOUR FAVORITE DAY.

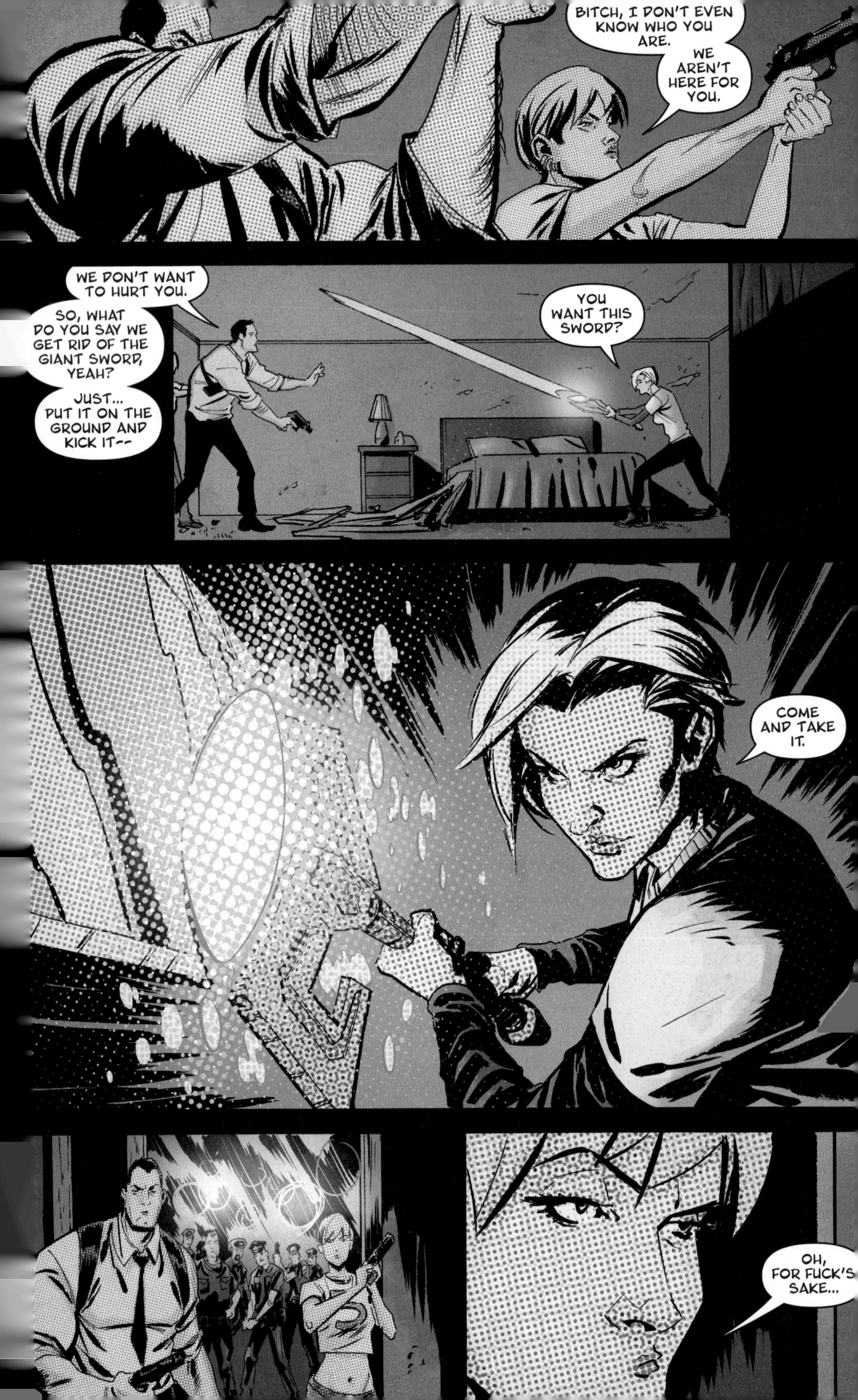
BITCH, I DON'T EVEN KNOW WHO YOU ARE.
WE AREN'T HERE FOR YOU.
WE DON'T WANT TO HURT YOU.
SO, WHAT DO YOU SAY WE GET RID OF THE GIANT SWORD, YEAH?
JUST... PUT IT ON THE GROUND AND KICK IT--
YOU WANT THIS SWORD?
COME AND TAKE IT.
OH, FOR FUCK'S SAKE...

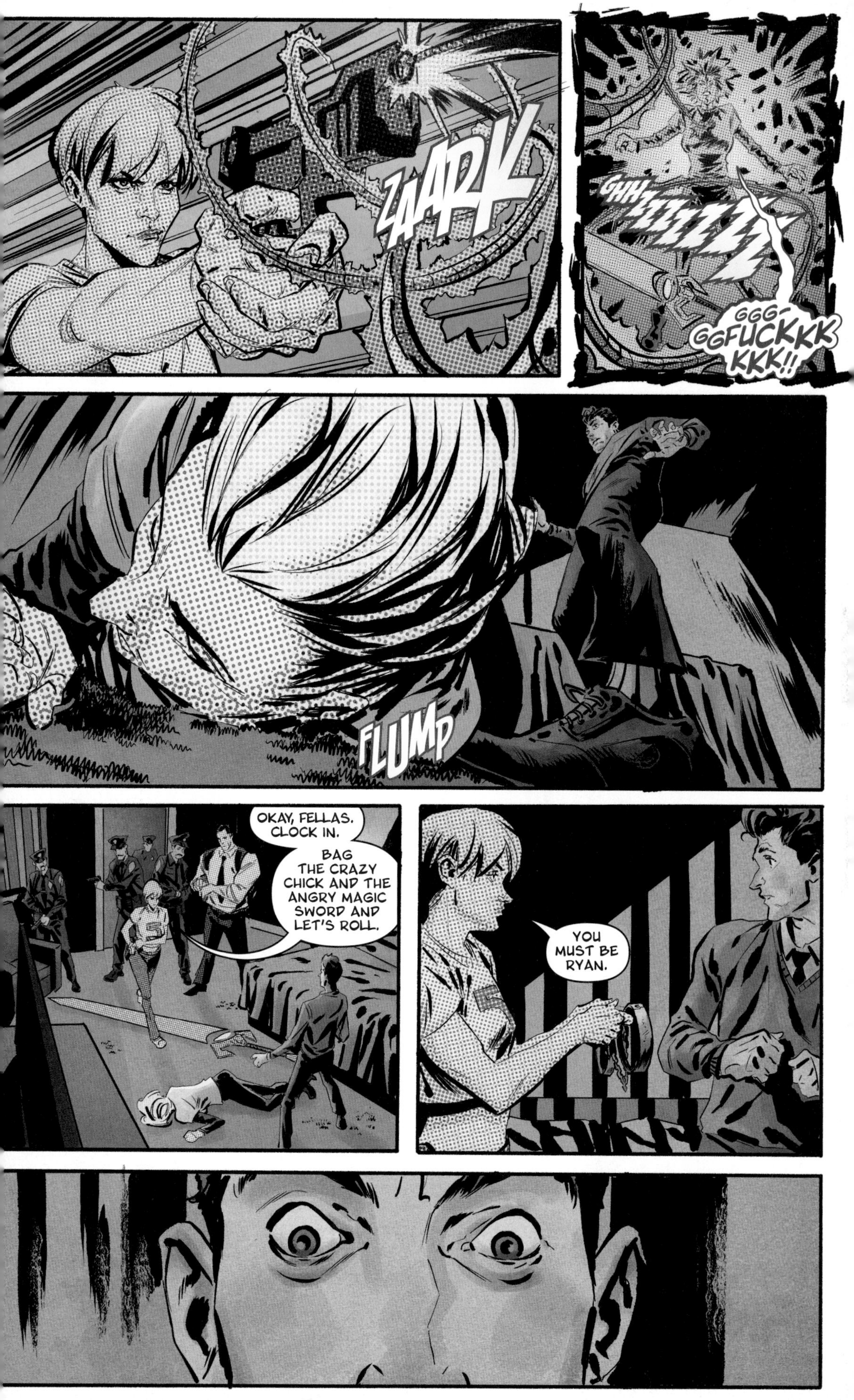
ZAARK
GHHZZZZZ
GGG-GGFUCKKKKKK!!
FLUMP
OKAY, FELLAS. CLOCK IN.
BAG THE CRAZY CHICK AND THE ANGRY MAGIC SWORD AND LET'S ROLL.
YOU MUST BE RYAN.

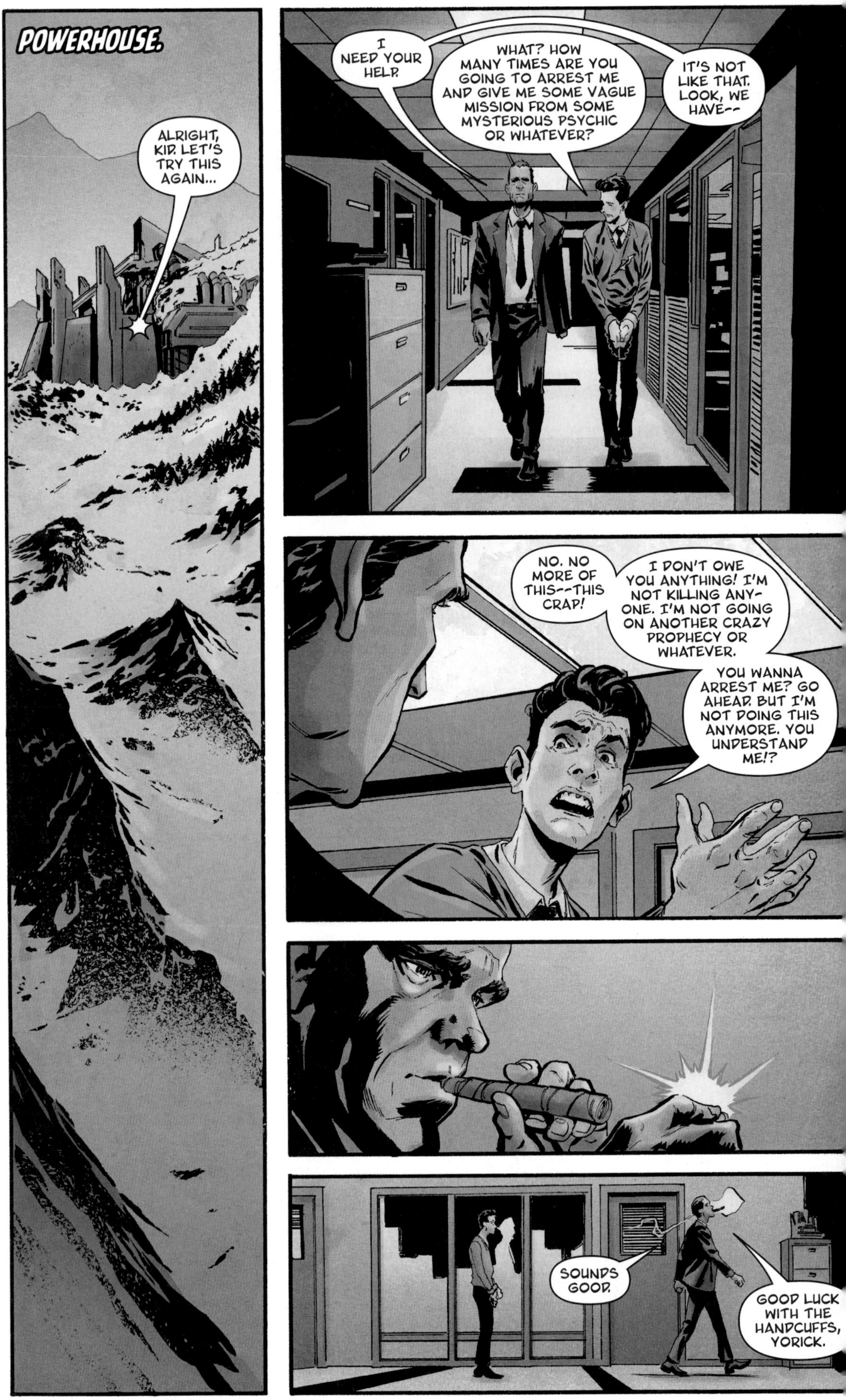
POWERHOUSE.
ALRIGHT, KID. LET'S TRY THIS AGAIN...
I NEED YOUR HELP.
WHAT? HOW MANY TIMES ARE YOU GOING TO ARREST ME AND GIVE ME SOME VAGUE MISSION FROM SOME MYSTERIOUS PSYCHIC OR WHATEVER?
IT'S NOT LIKE THAT. LOOK, WE HAVE--
NO. NO MORE OF THIS--THIS CRAP!
I DON'T OWE YOU ANYTHING! I'M NOT KILLING ANYONE. I'M NOT GOING ON ANOTHER CRAZY PROPHECY OR WHATEVER.
YOU WANNA ARREST ME? GO AHEAD. BUT I'M NOT DOING THIS ANYMORE. YOU UNDERSTAND ME!?
SOUNDS GOOD.
GOOD LUCK WITH THE HANDCUFFS, YORICK.

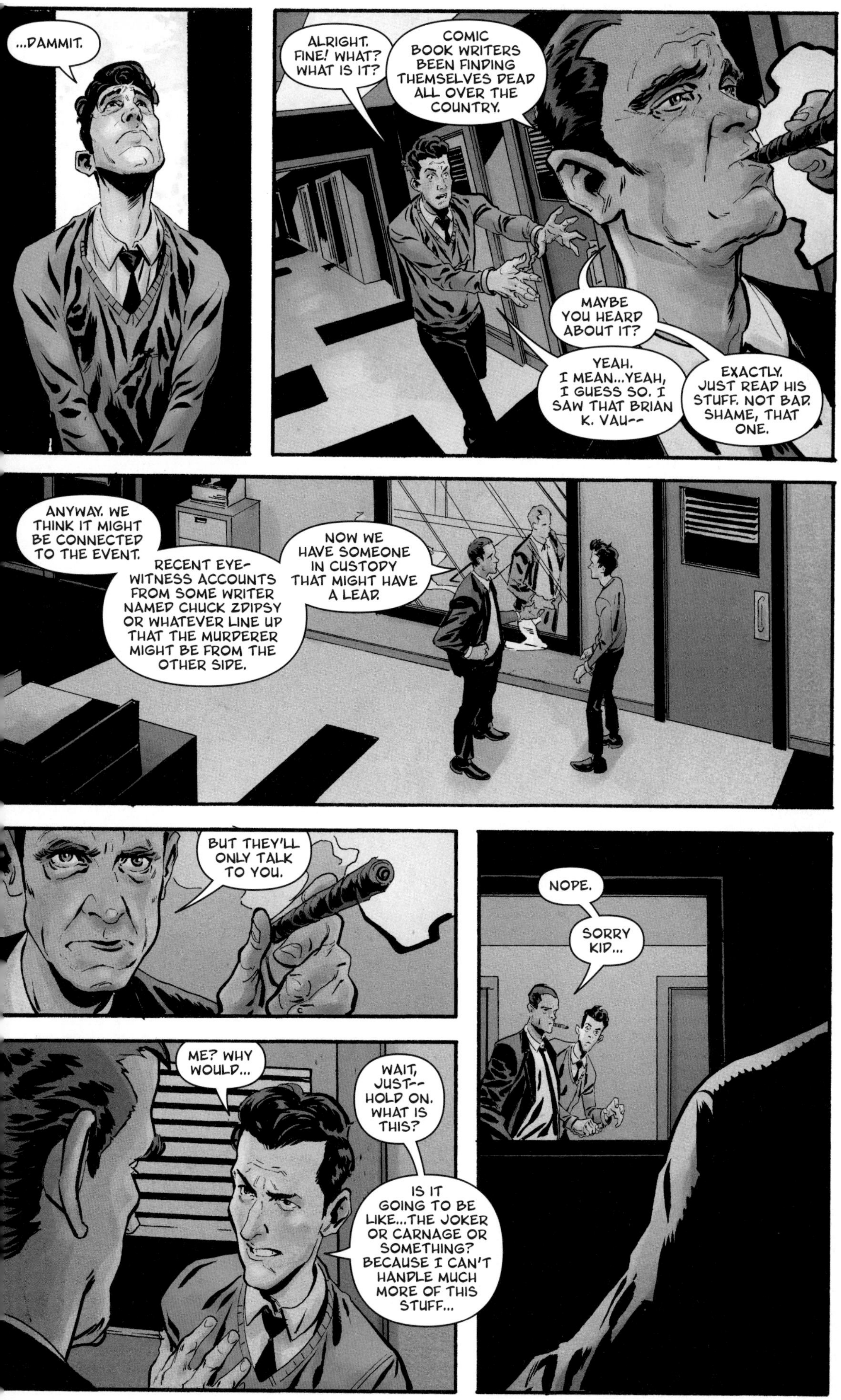

...DAMMIT.
ALRIGHT. FINE! WHAT? WHAT IS IT?
COMIC BOOK WRITERS BEEN FINDING THEMSELVES DEAD ALL OVER THE COUNTRY.
MAYBE YOU HEARD ABOUT IT?
YEAH. I MEAN...YEAH, I GUESS SO. I SAW THAT BRIAN K. VAU--
EXACTLY. JUST READ HIS STUFF. NOT BAD. SHAME, THAT ONE.
ANYWAY. WE THINK IT MIGHT BE CONNECTED TO THE EVENT.
RECENT EYE-WITNESS ACCOUNTS FROM SOME WRITER NAMED CHUCK ZDIPSY OR WHATEVER LINE UP THAT THE MURDERER MIGHT BE FROM THE OTHER SIDE.
NOW WE HAVE SOMEONE IN CUSTODY THAT MIGHT HAVE A LEAD.
BUT THEY'LL ONLY TALK TO YOU.
ME? WHY WOULD...
WAIT, JUST--HOLD ON. WHAT IS THIS?
IS IT GOING TO BE LIKE...THE JOKER OR CARNAGE OR SOMETHING? BECAUSE I CAN'T HANDLE MUCH MORE OF THIS STUFF...
NOPE.
SORRY KID...

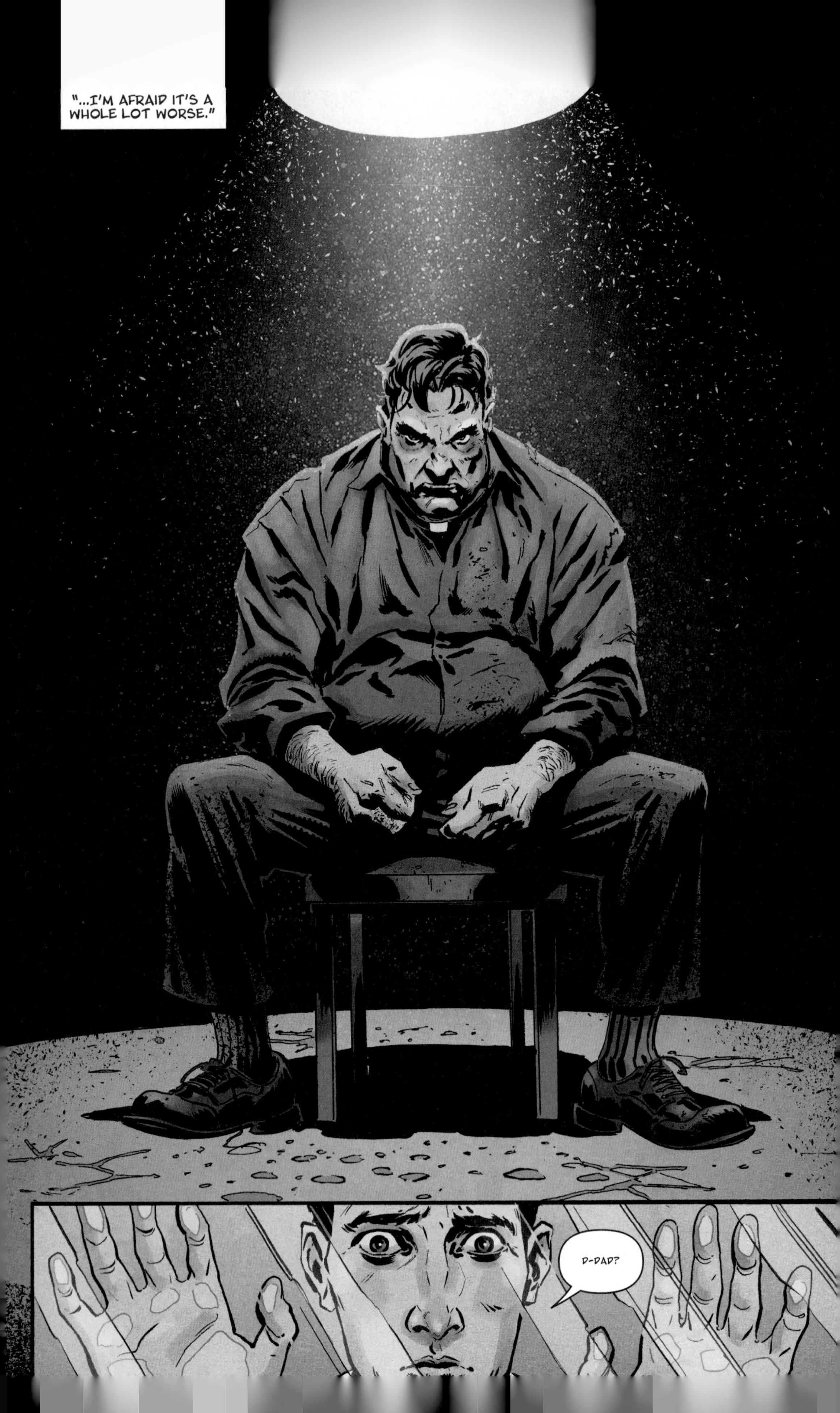
"...I'M AFRAID IT'S A WHOLE LOT WORSE."
D-DAD?

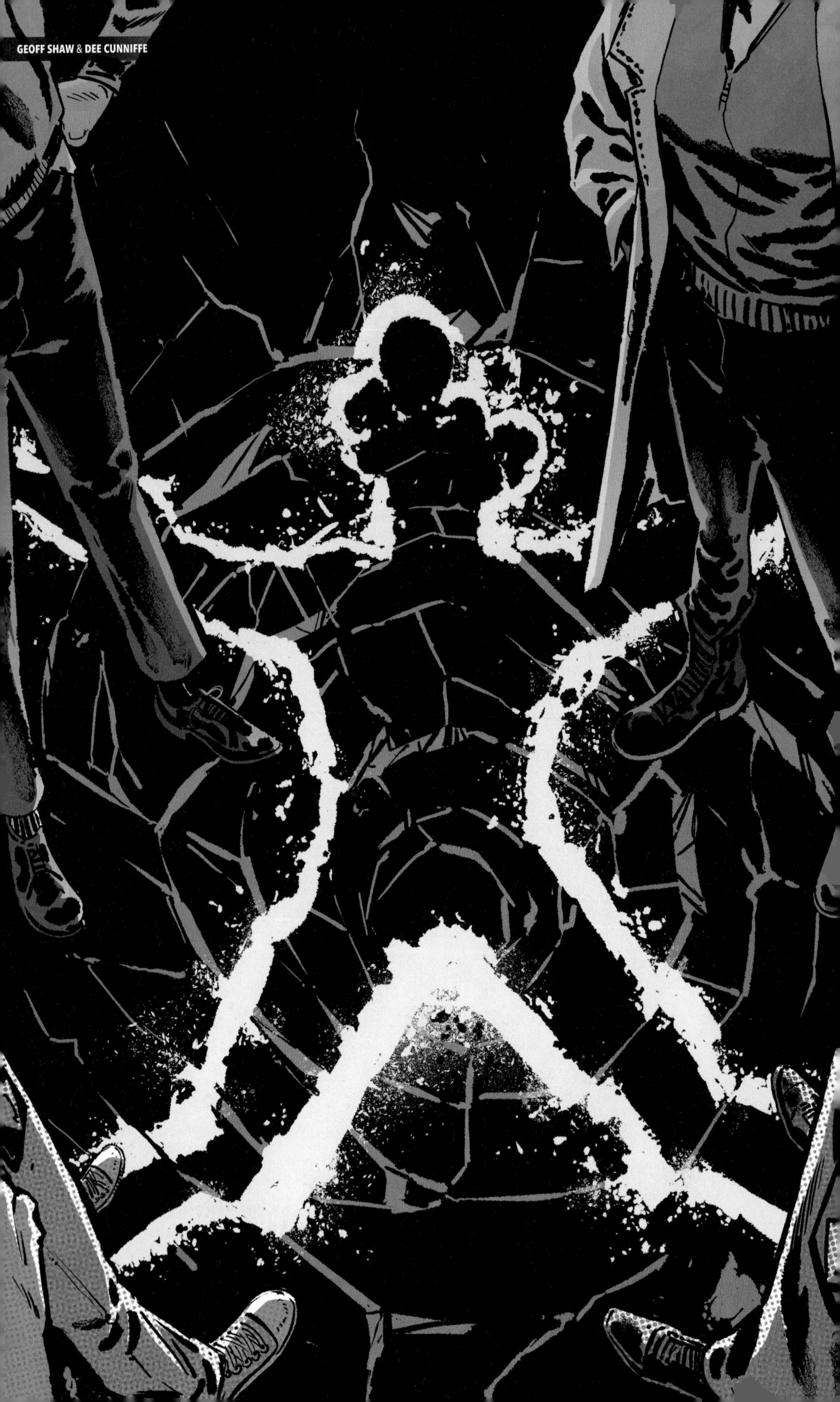

THE 10-CENT PLAGUE

CHAPTER TWO

•••

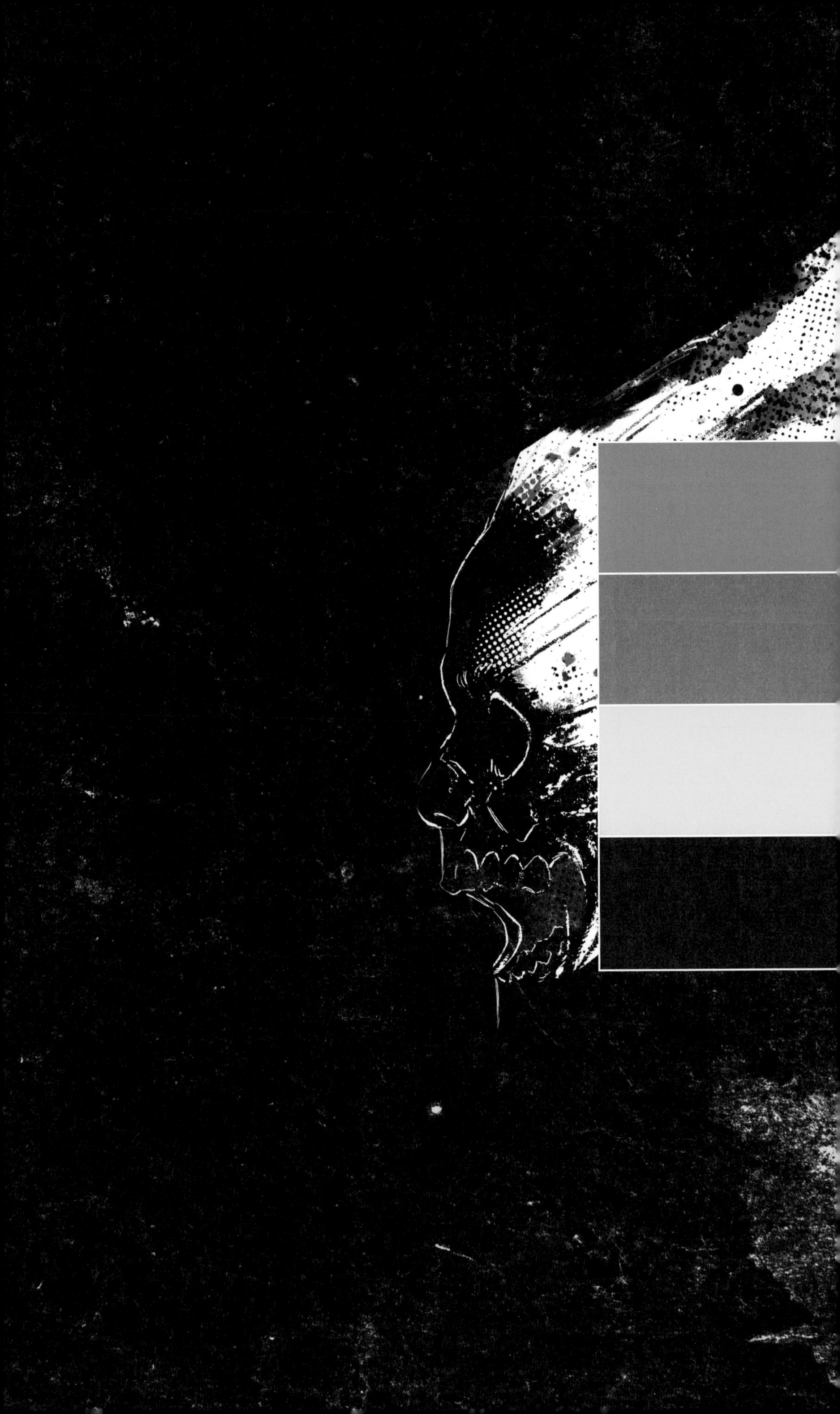

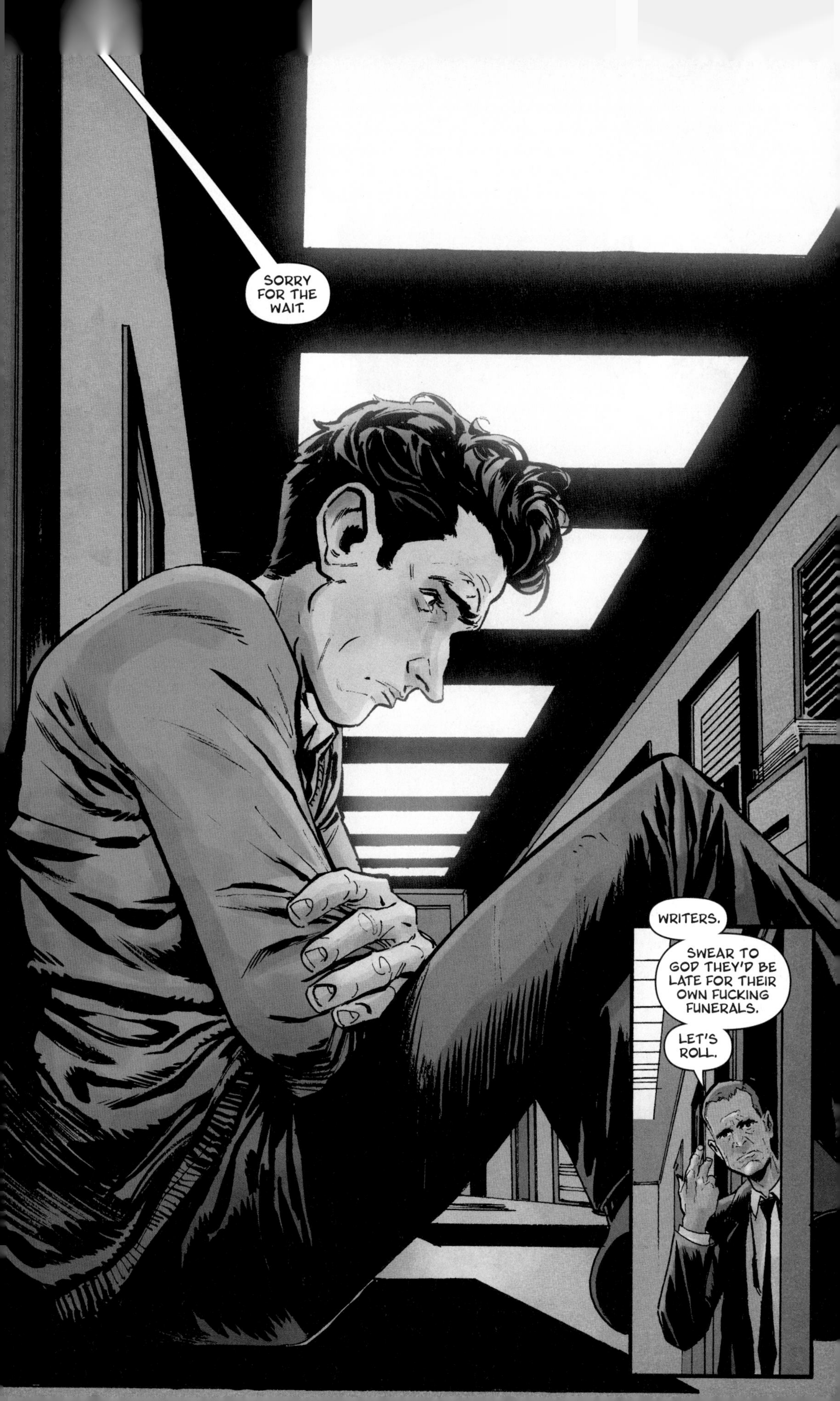

SORRY FOR THE WAIT.
WRITERS.
SWEAR TO GOD THEY'D BE LATE FOR THEIR OWN FUCKING FUNERALS.
LET'S ROLL.

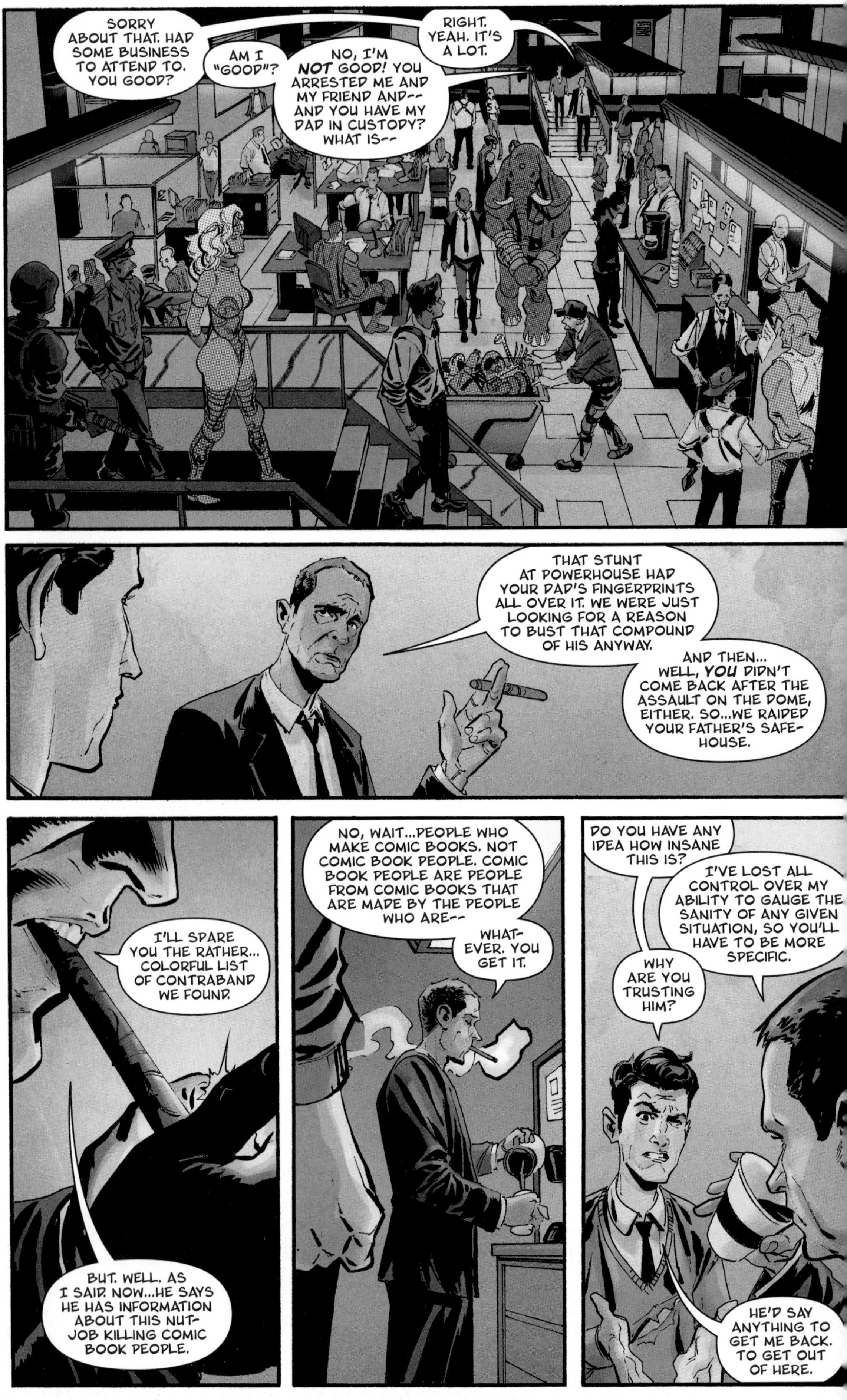
SORRY ABOUT THAT. HAD SOME BUSINESS TO ATTEND TO. YOU GOOD?
AM I "GOOD"?
NO, I'M NOT GOOD! YOU ARRESTED ME AND MY FRIEND AND-- AND YOU HAVE MY DAD IN CUSTODY? WHAT IS--
RIGHT. YEAH. IT'S A LOT.
THAT STUNT AT POWERHOUSE HAD YOUR DAD'S FINGERPRINTS ALL OVER IT. WE WERE JUST LOOKING FOR A REASON TO BUST THAT COMPOUND OF HIS ANYWAY.
AND THEN... WELL, YOU DIDN'T COME BACK AFTER THE ASSAULT ON THE DOME, EITHER. SO...WE RAIDED YOUR FATHER'S SAFE-HOUSE.
I'LL SPARE YOU THE RATHER... COLORFUL LIST OF CONTRABAND WE FOUND.
BUT. WELL. AS I SAID. NOW...HE SAYS HE HAS INFORMATION ABOUT THIS NUT-JOB KILLING COMIC BOOK PEOPLE.
NO, WAIT...PEOPLE WHO MAKE COMIC BOOKS. NOT COMIC BOOK PEOPLE. COMIC BOOK PEOPLE ARE PEOPLE FROM COMIC BOOKS THAT ARE MADE BY THE PEOPLE WHO ARE--
WHAT-EVER. YOU GET IT.
DO YOU HAVE ANY IDEA HOW INSANE THIS IS?
I'VE LOST ALL CONTROL OVER MY ABILITY TO GAUGE THE SANITY OF ANY GIVEN SITUATION, SO YOU'LL HAVE TO BE MORE SPECIFIC.
WHY ARE YOU TRUSTING HIM?
HE'D SAY ANYTHING TO GET ME BACK. TO GET OUT OF HERE.

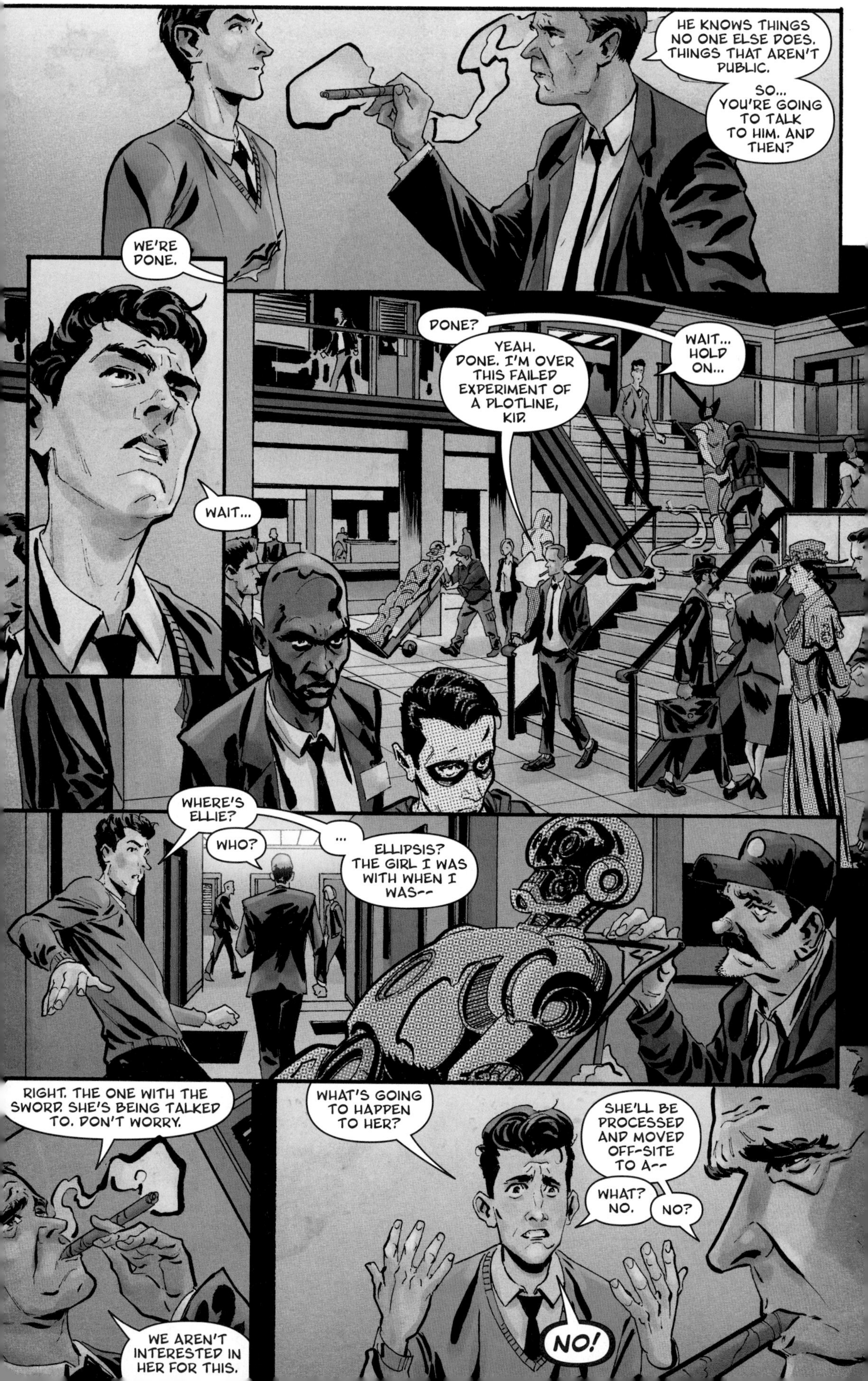
HE KNOWS THINGS NO ONE ELSE DOES. THINGS THAT AREN'T PUBLIC.
SO... YOU'RE GOING TO TALK TO HIM. AND THEN?
WE'RE DONE.
WAIT...
DONE?
YEAH. DONE. I'M OVER THIS FAILED EXPERIMENT OF A PLOTLINE, KID.
WAIT... HOLD ON...
WHERE'S ELLIE?
WHO?
...
ELLIPSIS? THE GIRL I WAS WITH WHEN I WAS--
RIGHT. THE ONE WITH THE SWORD. SHE'S BEING TALKED TO. DON'T WORRY.
WE AREN'T INTERESTED IN HER FOR THIS.
WHAT'S GOING TO HAPPEN TO HER?
SHE'LL BE PROCESSED AND MOVED OFF-SITE TO A--
WHAT? NO.
NO?
NO!

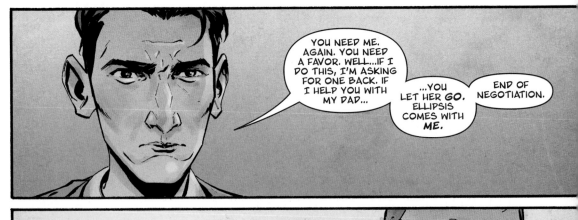

YOU NEED ME. AGAIN. YOU NEED A FAVOR. WELL...IF I DO THIS, I'M ASKING FOR ONE BACK. IF I HELP YOU WITH MY DAD...

...YOU LET HER *GO*. ELLIPSIS COMES WITH *ME*.

END OF NEGOTIATION.

ALRIGHT.

WAIT, REALLY?

SURE. WHAT, DO I GIVE A SHIT? I'M ALREADY TAKING ADVICE FROM A DELUSIONAL JUNKIE WRITER WHO THINKS HE'S A PROPHET, WORKING WITH TWO FICTIONAL COPS, AND TRYING TO STOP SOME CARTOON CHARACTER FROM KILLING NERDS.

I'M A LITTLE BEYOND THE PALE AS FAR AS GIVING A SHIT ABOUT SOME RANDOM GIRL.

THE SWORD STAYS HERE, THOUGH. AND THAT'S NOT UP FOR--

"WRITER WHO THINKS HE'S A PROPHET"...

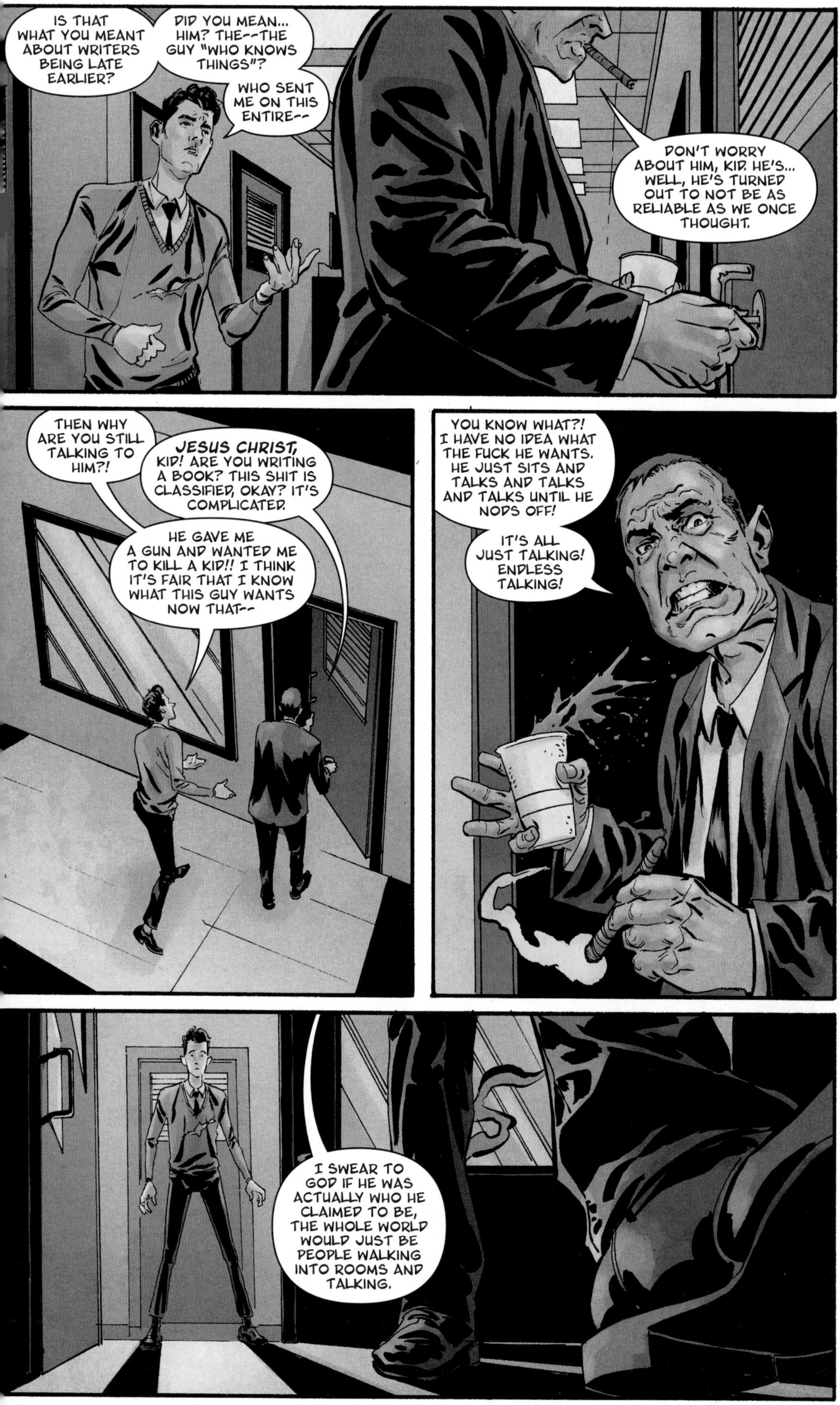
IS THAT WHAT YOU MEANT ABOUT WRITERS BEING LATE EARLIER?
DID YOU MEAN... HIM? THE--THE GUY "WHO KNOWS THINGS"?
WHO SENT ME ON THIS ENTIRE--
DON'T WORRY ABOUT HIM, KID. HE'S... WELL, HE'S TURNED OUT TO NOT BE AS RELIABLE AS WE ONCE THOUGHT.
THEN WHY ARE YOU STILL TALKING TO HIM?!
JESUS CHRIST, KID! ARE YOU WRITING A BOOK? THIS SHIT IS CLASSIFIED, OKAY? IT'S COMPLICATED.
HE GAVE ME A GUN AND WANTED ME TO KILL A KID!! I THINK IT'S FAIR THAT I KNOW WHAT THIS GUY WANTS NOW THAT--
YOU KNOW WHAT?! I HAVE NO IDEA WHAT THE FUCK HE WANTS. HE JUST SITS AND TALKS AND TALKS AND TALKS UNTIL HE NODS OFF!
IT'S ALL JUST TALKING! ENDLESS TALKING!
I SWEAR TO GOD IF HE WAS ACTUALLY WHO HE CLAIMED TO BE, THE WHOLE WORLD WOULD JUST BE PEOPLE WALKING INTO ROOMS AND TALKING.

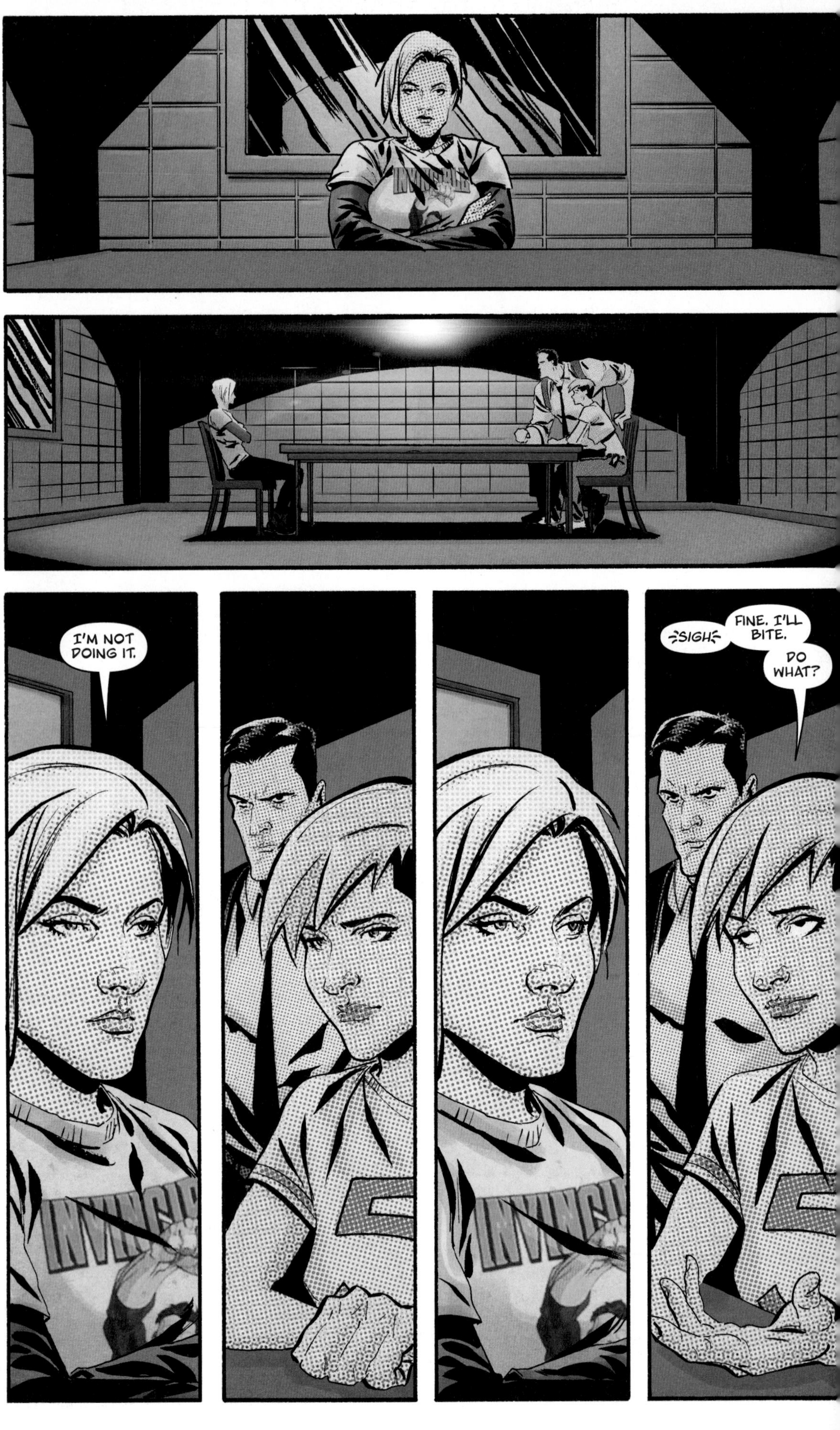
I'M NOT DOING IT.
SIGH
FINE. I'LL BITE.
DO WHAT?

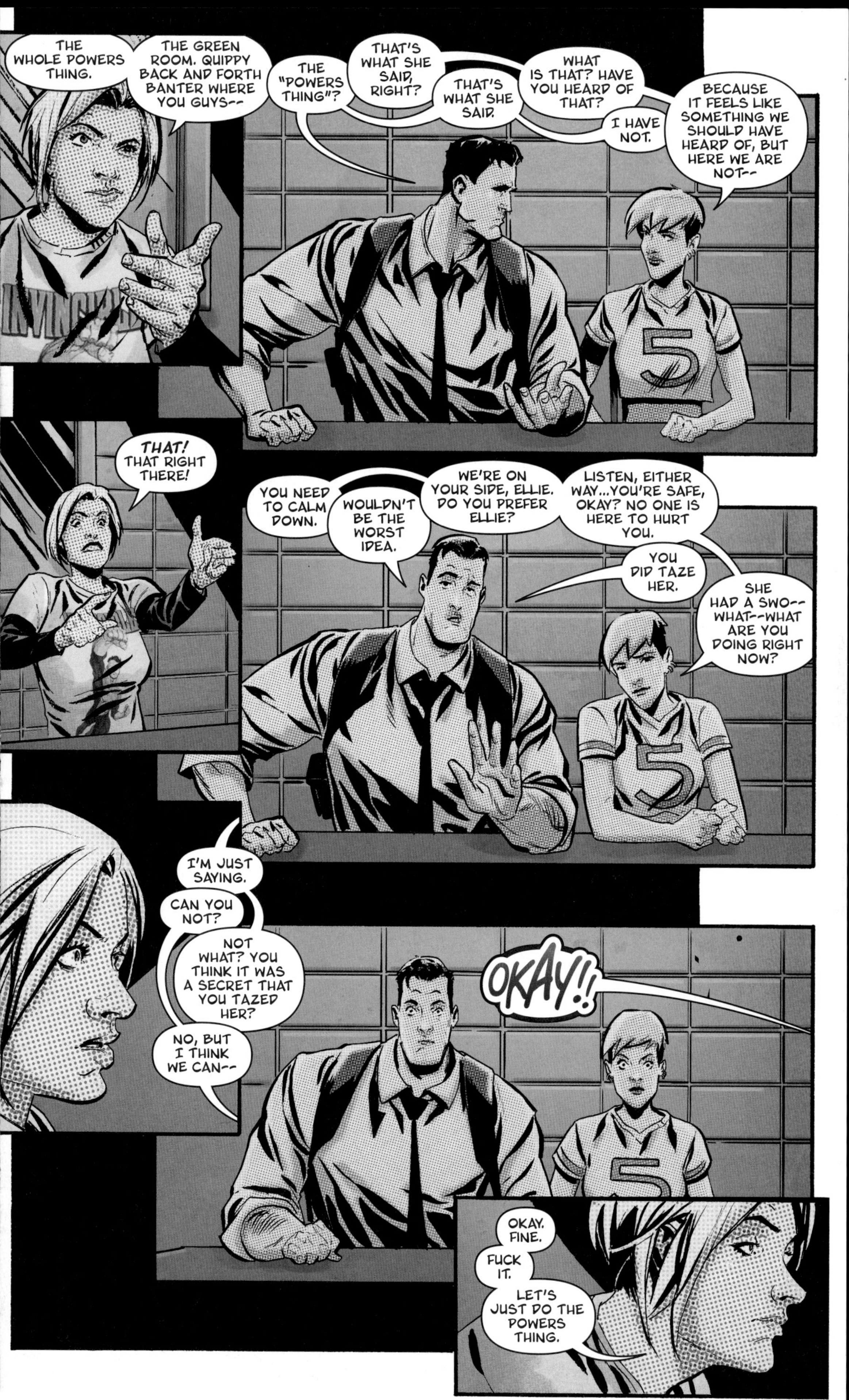
THE WHOLE POWERS THING.
THE GREEN ROOM. QUIPPY BACK AND FORTH BANTER WHERE YOU GUYS--
THE "POWERS THING"?
THAT'S WHAT SHE SAID, RIGHT?
THAT'S WHAT SHE SAID.
WHAT IS THAT? HAVE YOU HEARD OF THAT?
I HAVE NOT.
BECAUSE IT FEELS LIKE SOMETHING WE SHOULD HAVE HEARD OF, BUT HERE WE ARE NOT--
THAT! THAT RIGHT THERE!
YOU NEED TO CALM DOWN.
WOULDN'T BE THE WORST IDEA.
WE'RE ON YOUR SIDE, ELLIE. DO YOU PREFER ELLIE?
LISTEN, EITHER WAY...YOU'RE SAFE, OKAY? NO ONE IS HERE TO HURT YOU.
YOU DID TAZE HER.
SHE HAD A SWO--WHAT--WHAT ARE YOU DOING RIGHT NOW?
I'M JUST SAYING.
CAN YOU NOT?
NOT WHAT? YOU THINK IT WAS A SECRET THAT YOU TAZED HER?
NO, BUT I THINK WE CAN--
OKAY!!
OKAY. FINE.
FUCK IT.
LET'S JUST DO THE POWERS THING.

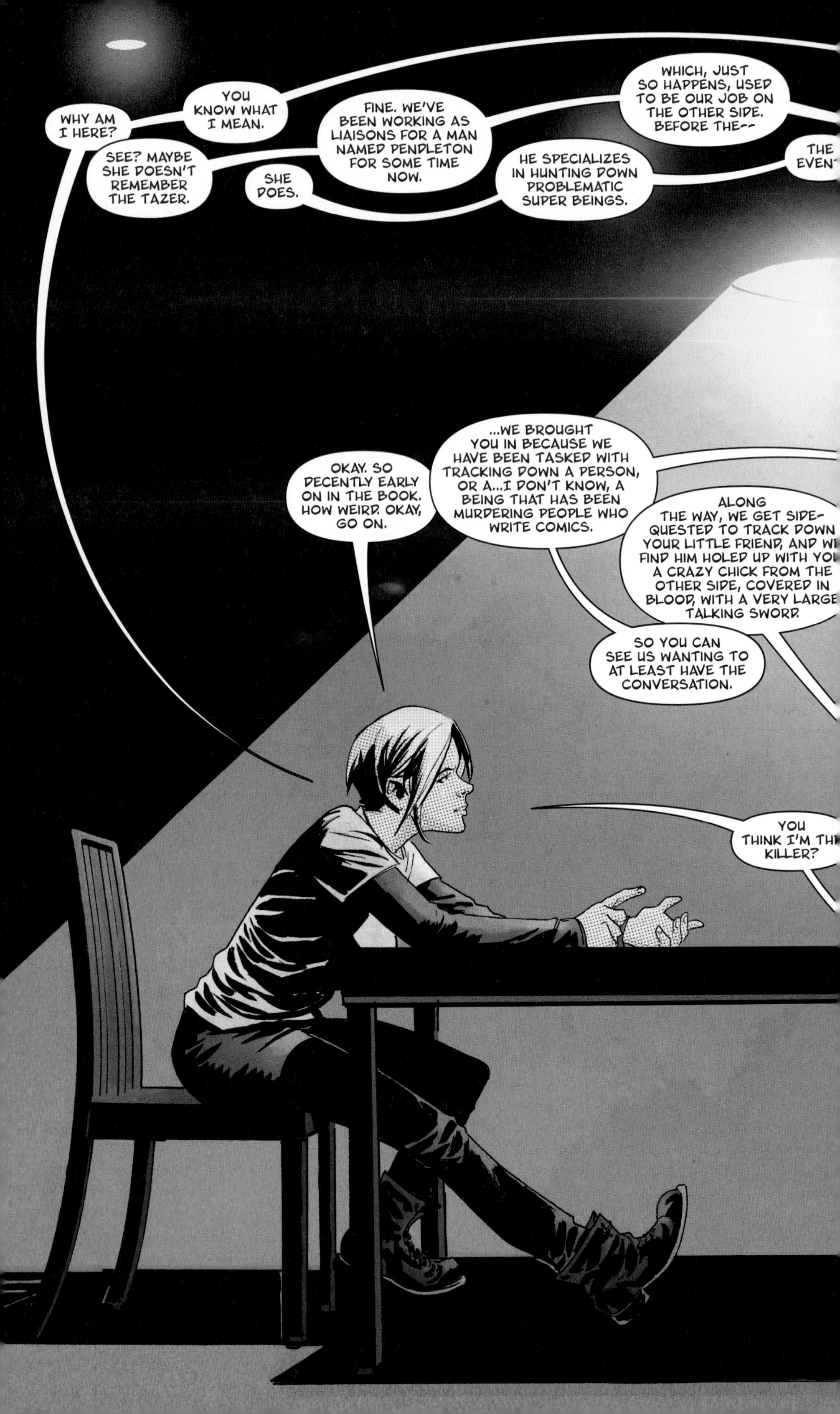
WHY AM I HERE?
YOU KNOW WHAT I MEAN.
SEE? MAYBE SHE DOESN'T REMEMBER THE TAZER.
SHE DOES.
FINE. WE'VE BEEN WORKING AS LIAISONS FOR A MAN NAMED PENDLETON FOR SOME TIME NOW.
HE SPECIALIZES IN HUNTING DOWN PROBLEMATIC SUPER BEINGS.
WHICH, JUST SO HAPPENS, USED TO BE OUR JOB ON THE OTHER SIDE. BEFORE THE--
THE EVEN
OKAY. SO DECENTLY EARLY ON IN THE BOOK. HOW WEIRD. OKAY, GO ON.
...WE BROUGHT YOU IN BECAUSE WE HAVE BEEN TASKED WITH TRACKING DOWN A PERSON, OR A...I DON'T KNOW, A BEING THAT HAS BEEN MURDERING PEOPLE WHO WRITE COMICS.
ALONG THE WAY, WE GET SIDE-QUESTED TO TRACK DOWN YOUR LITTLE FRIEND, AND WE FIND HIM HOLED UP WITH YOU A CRAZY CHICK FROM THE OTHER SIDE, COVERED IN BLOOD, WITH A VERY LARGE TALKING SWORD.
SO YOU CAN SEE US WANTING TO AT LEAST HAVE THE CONVERSATION.
YOU THINK I'M TH KILLER?

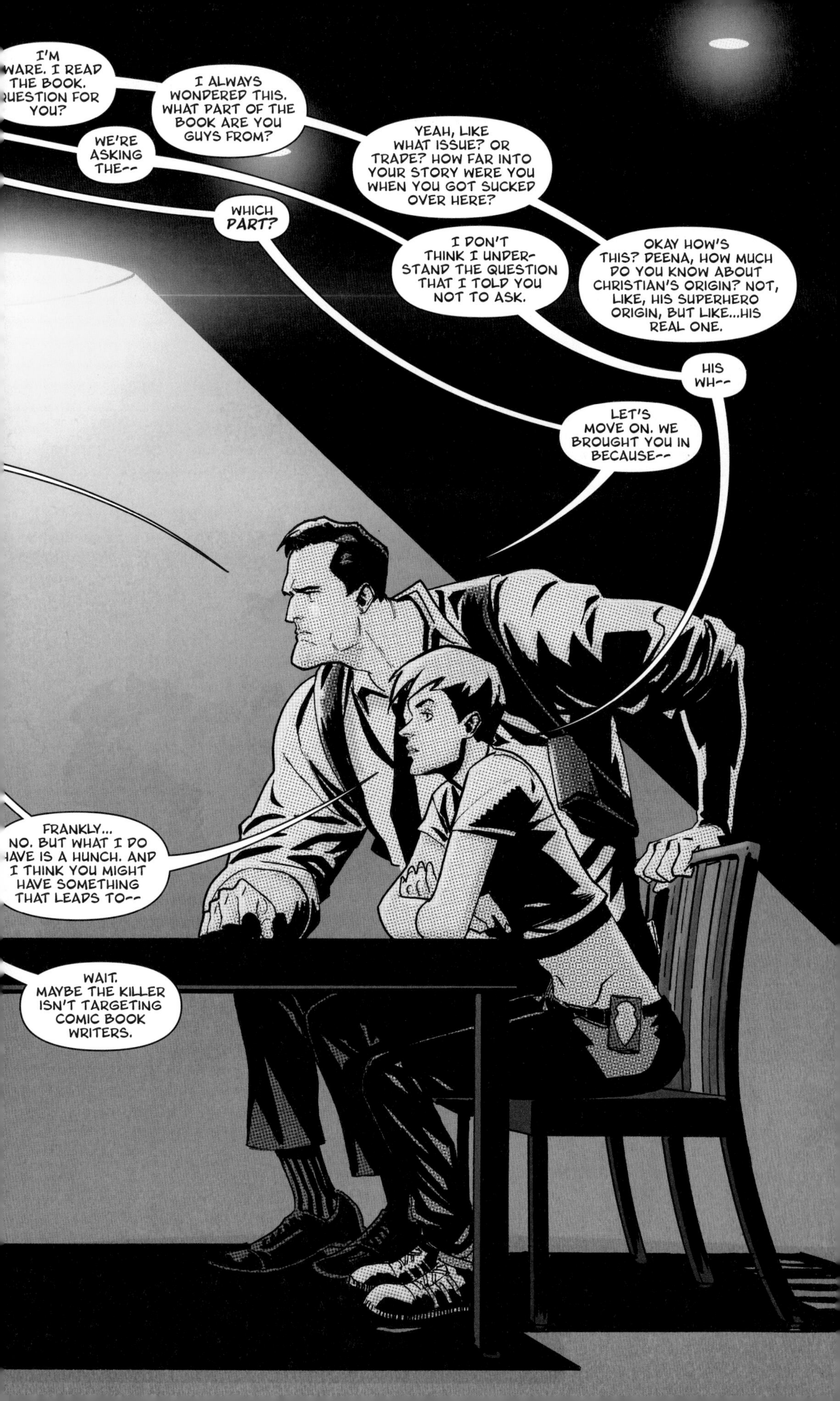
I'M
WARE. I READ THE BOOK. UESTION FOR YOU?
I ALWAYS WONDERED THIS. WHAT PART OF THE BOOK ARE YOU GUYS FROM?
WE'RE ASKING THE--
YEAH, LIKE WHAT ISSUE? OR TRADE? HOW FAR INTO YOUR STORY WERE YOU WHEN YOU GOT SUCKED OVER HERE?
WHICH *PART?*
I DON'T THINK I UNDERSTAND THE QUESTION THAT I TOLD YOU NOT TO ASK.
OKAY HOW'S THIS? DEENA, HOW MUCH DO YOU KNOW ABOUT CHRISTIAN'S ORIGIN? NOT, LIKE, HIS SUPERHERO ORIGIN, BUT LIKE...HIS REAL ONE.
HIS WH--
LET'S MOVE ON. WE BROUGHT YOU IN BECAUSE--
FRANKLY... NO. BUT WHAT I DO HAVE IS A HUNCH. AND I THINK YOU MIGHT HAVE SOMETHING THAT LEADS TO--
WAIT. MAYBE THE KILLER ISN'T TARGETING COMIC BOOK WRITERS.

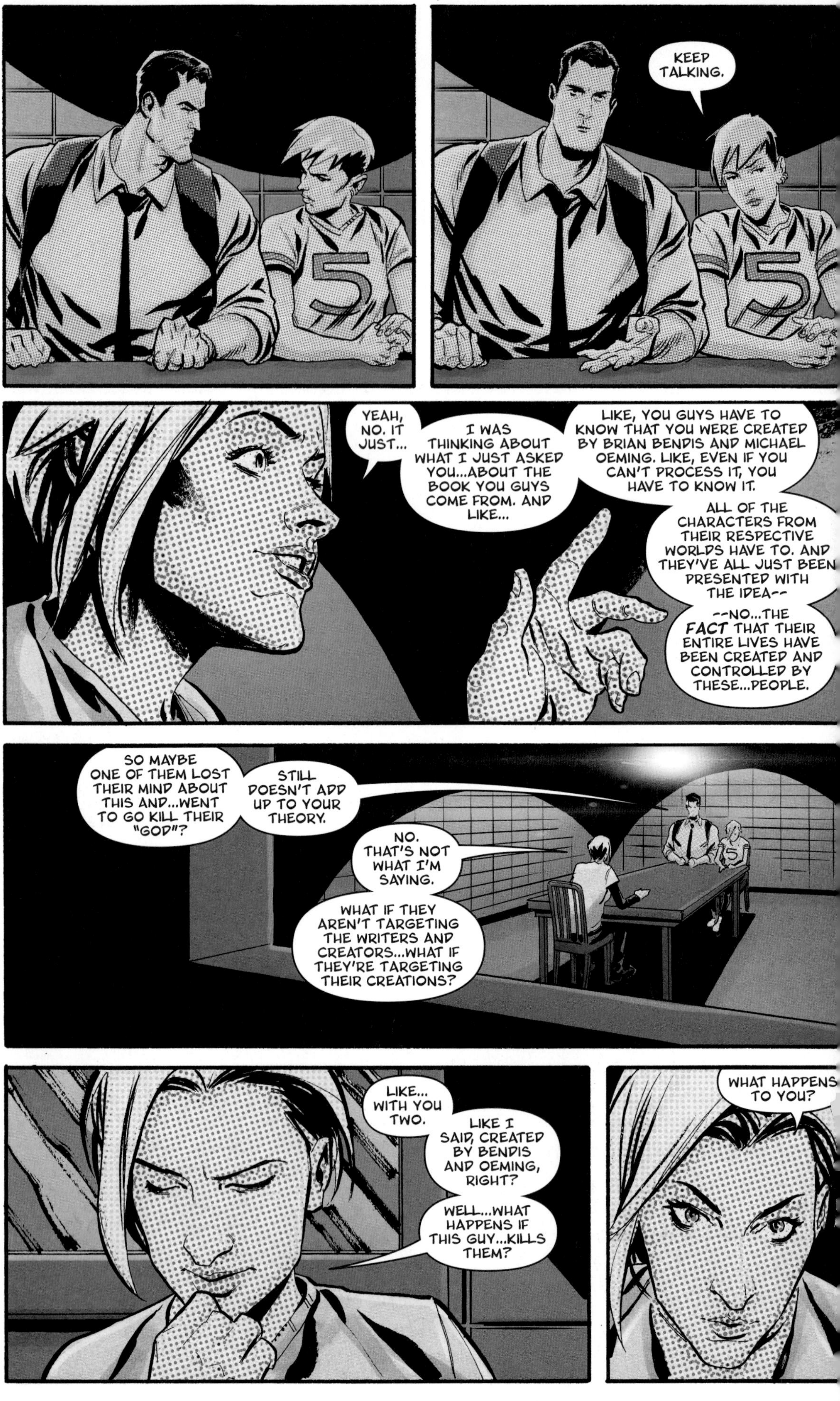
KEEP TALKING.
YEAH, NO. IT JUST...
I WAS THINKING ABOUT WHAT I JUST ASKED YOU...ABOUT THE BOOK YOU GUYS COME FROM. AND LIKE...
LIKE, YOU GUYS HAVE TO KNOW THAT YOU WERE CREATED BY BRIAN BENDIS AND MICHAEL OEMING. LIKE, EVEN IF YOU CAN'T PROCESS IT, YOU HAVE TO KNOW IT.
ALL OF THE CHARACTERS FROM THEIR RESPECTIVE WORLDS HAVE TO. AND THEY'VE ALL JUST BEEN PRESENTED WITH THE IDEA--
--NO...THE FACT THAT THEIR ENTIRE LIVES HAVE BEEN CREATED AND CONTROLLED BY THESE...PEOPLE.
SO MAYBE ONE OF THEM LOST THEIR MIND ABOUT THIS AND...WENT TO GO KILL THEIR "GOD"?
STILL DOESN'T ADD UP TO YOUR THEORY.
NO. THAT'S NOT WHAT I'M SAYING.
WHAT IF THEY AREN'T TARGETING THE WRITERS AND CREATORS...WHAT IF THEY'RE TARGETING THEIR CREATIONS?
LIKE... WITH YOU TWO.
LIKE I SAID, CREATED BY BENDIS AND OEMING, RIGHT?
WELL...WHAT HAPPENS IF THIS GUY...KILLS THEM?
WHAT HAPPENS TO YOU?

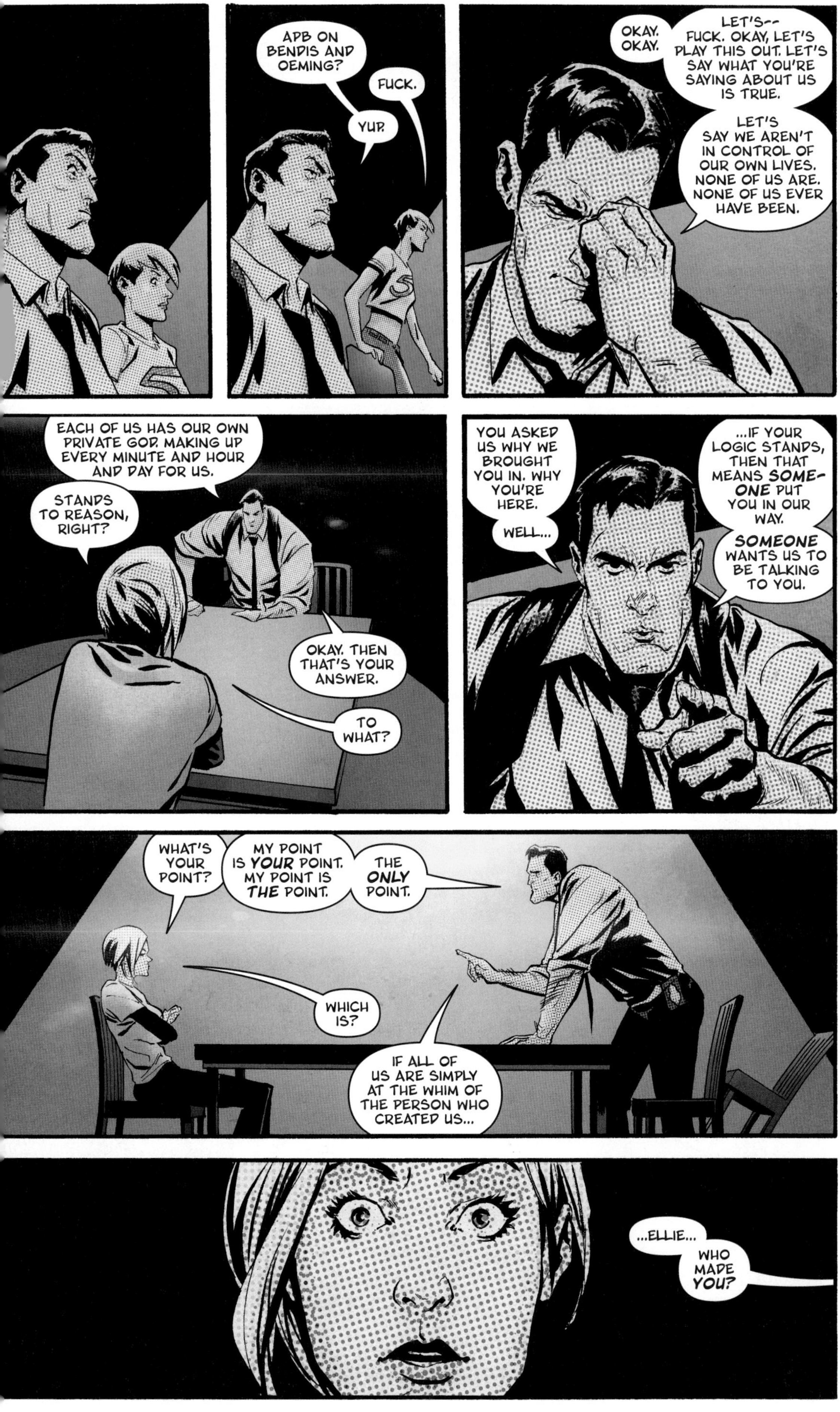
APB ON BENDIS AND OEMING?
YUP.
FUCK.
OKAY. OKAY.
LET'S-- FUCK. OKAY, LET'S PLAY THIS OUT. LET'S SAY WHAT YOU'RE SAYING ABOUT US IS TRUE.
LET'S SAY WE AREN'T IN CONTROL OF OUR OWN LIVES. NONE OF US ARE. NONE OF US EVER HAVE BEEN.
EACH OF US HAS OUR OWN PRIVATE GOD, MAKING UP EVERY MINUTE AND HOUR AND DAY FOR US.
STANDS TO REASON, RIGHT?
OKAY. THEN THAT'S YOUR ANSWER.
TO WHAT?
YOU ASKED US WHY WE BROUGHT YOU IN. WHY YOU'RE HERE.
WELL...
...IF YOUR LOGIC STANDS, THEN THAT MEANS **SOMEONE** PUT YOU IN OUR WAY.
SOMEONE WANTS US TO BE TALKING TO YOU.
WHAT'S YOUR POINT?
MY POINT IS **YOUR** POINT. MY POINT IS **THE** POINT.
THE **ONLY** POINT.
WHICH IS?
IF ALL OF US ARE SIMPLY AT THE WHIM OF THE PERSON WHO CREATED US...
...ELLIE...
WHO MADE **YOU?**

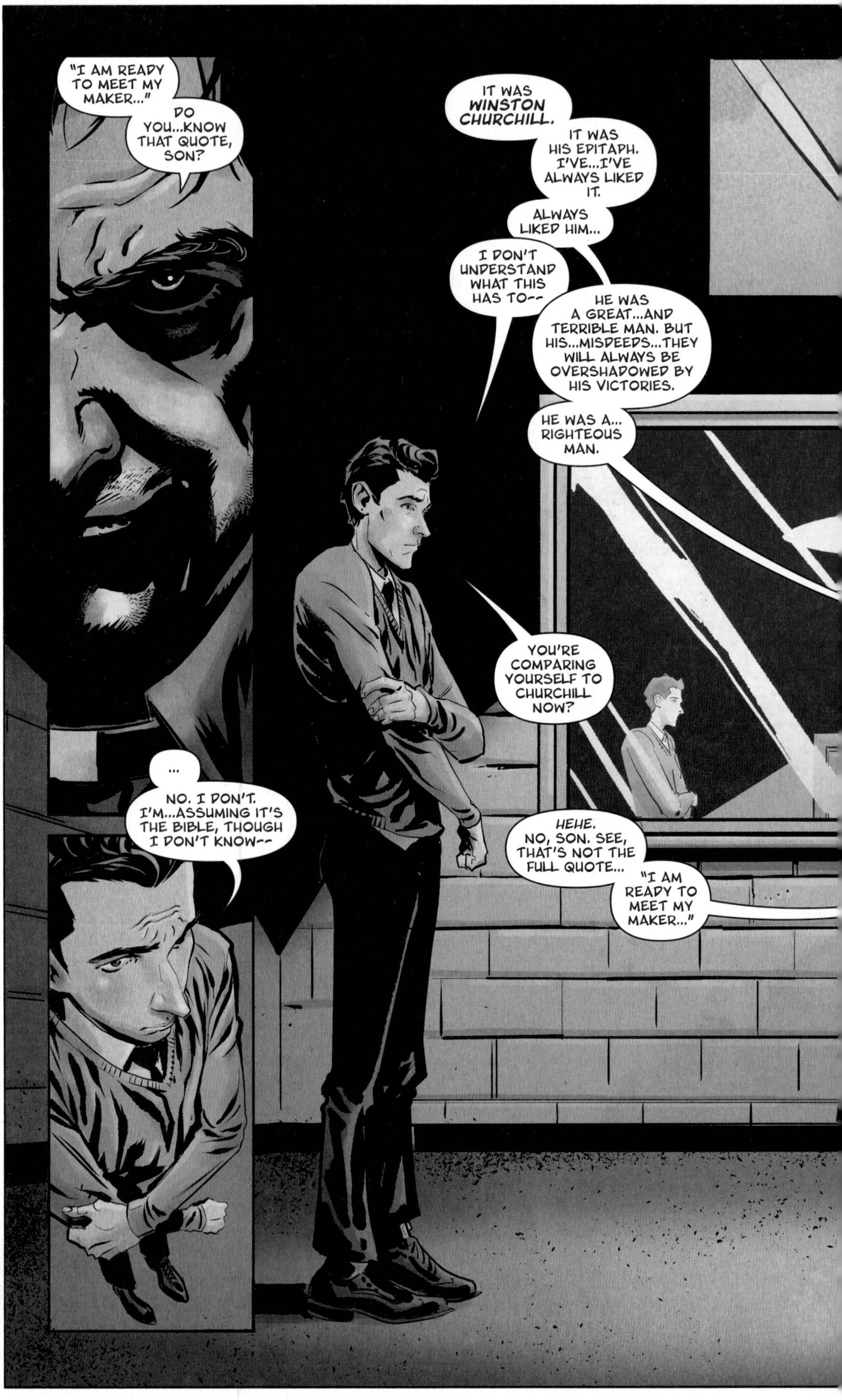
"I AM READY TO MEET MY MAKER..."
DO YOU...KNOW THAT QUOTE, SON?
...
NO. I DON'T. I'M...ASSUMING IT'S THE BIBLE, THOUGH I DON'T KNOW--
IT WAS WINSTON CHURCHILL.
IT WAS HIS EPITAPH. I'VE...I'VE ALWAYS LIKED IT.
ALWAYS LIKED HIM...
I DON'T UNDERSTAND WHAT THIS HAS TO--
HE WAS A GREAT...AND TERRIBLE MAN. BUT HIS...MISDEEDS...THEY WILL ALWAYS BE OVERSHADOWED BY HIS VICTORIES.
HE WAS A... RIGHTEOUS MAN.
YOU'RE COMPARING YOURSELF TO CHURCHILL NOW?
HEHE. NO, SON. SEE, THAT'S NOT THE FULL QUOTE...
"I AM READY TO MEET MY MAKER..."

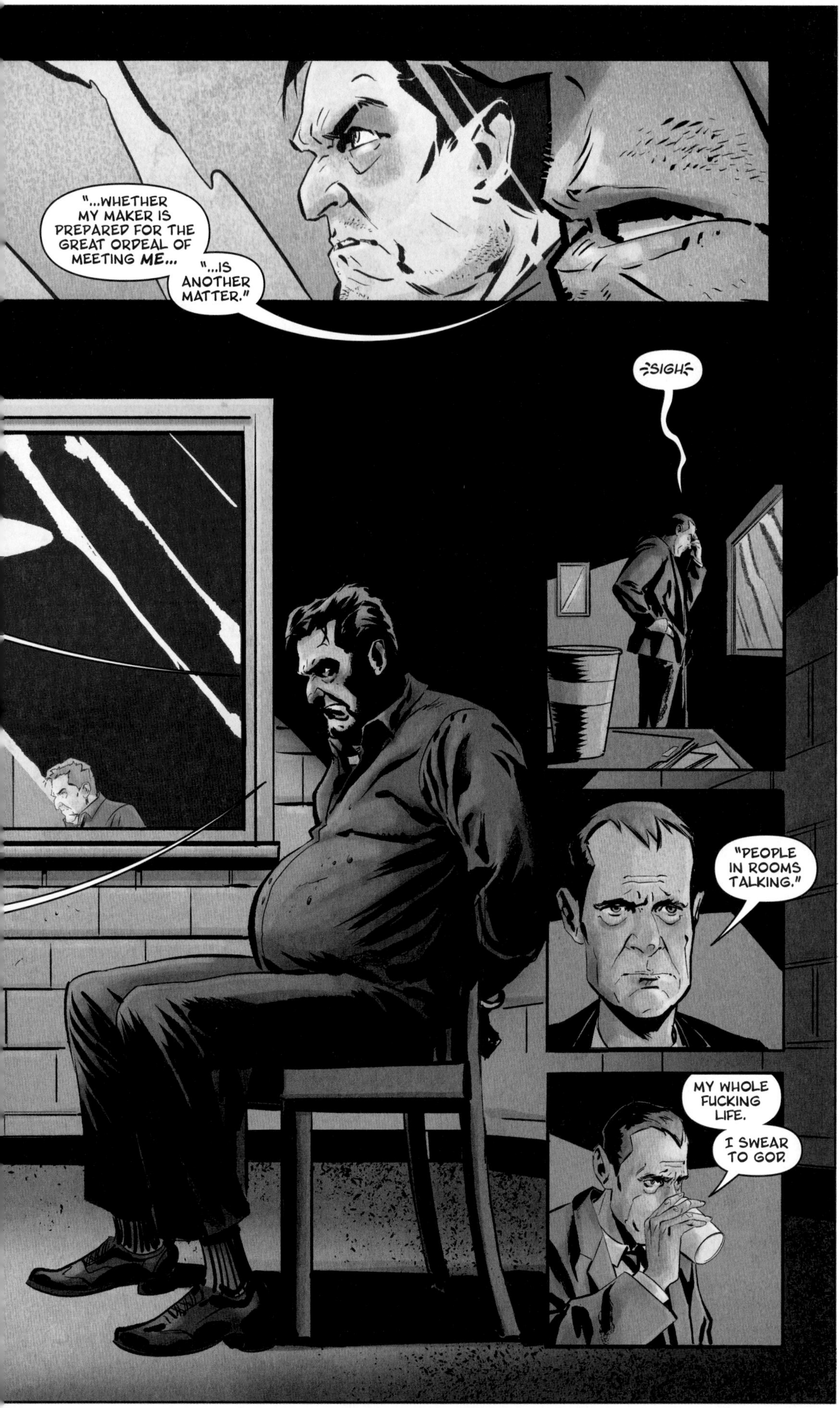
"...WHETHER MY MAKER IS PREPARED FOR THE GREAT ORDEAL OF MEETING **ME**...
"...IS ANOTHER MATTER."
SIGH
"PEOPLE IN ROOMS TALKING."
MY WHOLE FUCKING LIFE.
I SWEAR TO GOD.

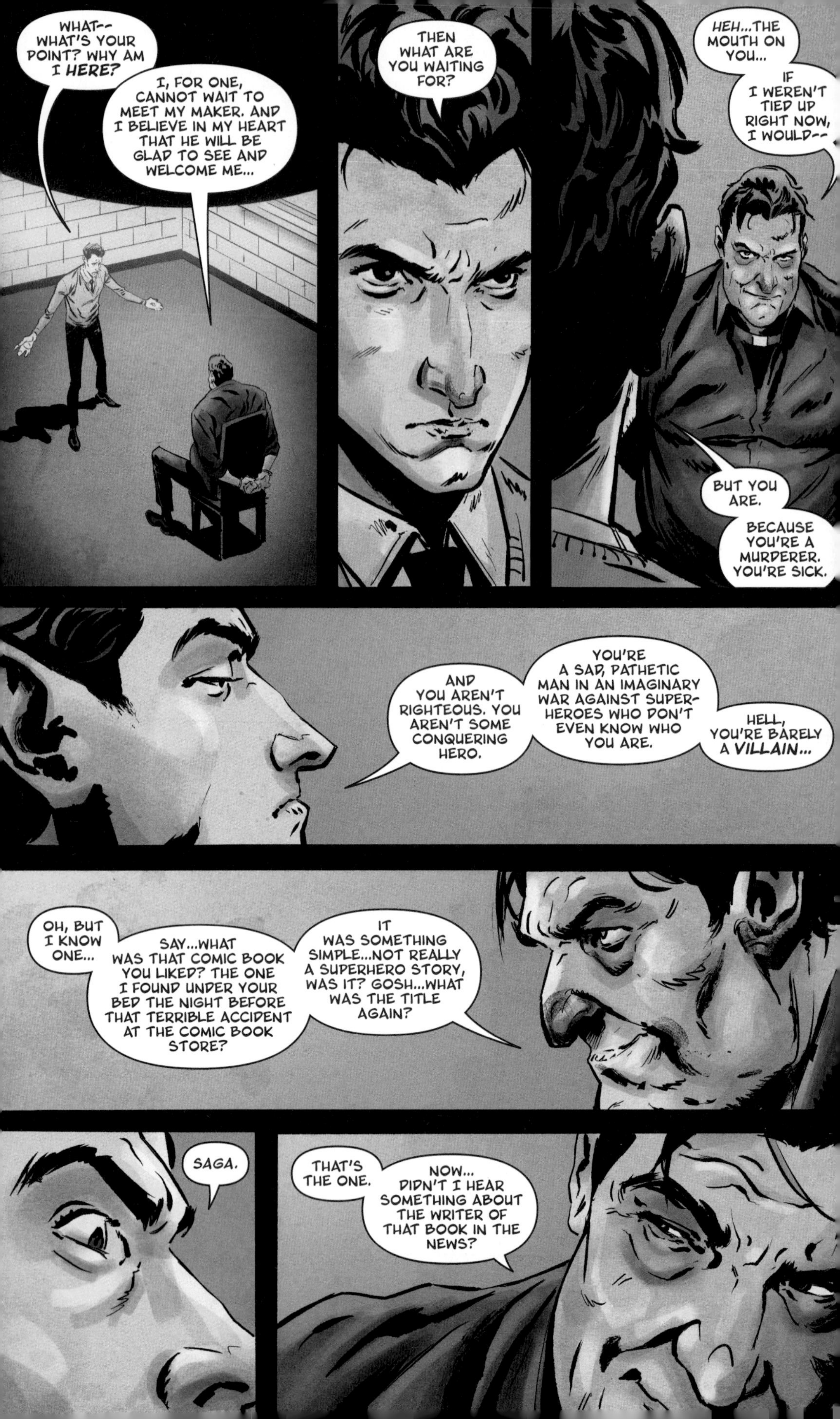
WHAT-- WHAT'S YOUR POINT? WHY AM I HERE?
I, FOR ONE, CANNOT WAIT TO MEET MY MAKER. AND I BELIEVE IN MY HEART THAT HE WILL BE GLAD TO SEE AND WELCOME ME...
THEN WHAT ARE YOU WAITING FOR?
HEH...THE MOUTH ON YOU...
IF I WEREN'T TIED UP RIGHT NOW, I WOULD--
BUT YOU ARE.
BECAUSE YOU'RE A MURDERER. YOU'RE SICK.
AND YOU AREN'T RIGHTEOUS. YOU AREN'T SOME CONQUERING HERO.
YOU'RE A SAD, PATHETIC MAN IN AN IMAGINARY WAR AGAINST SUPER-HEROES WHO DON'T EVEN KNOW WHO YOU ARE.
HELL, YOU'RE BARELY A VILLAIN...
OH, BUT I KNOW ONE...
SAY...WHAT WAS THAT COMIC BOOK YOU LIKED? THE ONE I FOUND UNDER YOUR BED THE NIGHT BEFORE THAT TERRIBLE ACCIDENT AT THE COMIC BOOK STORE?
IT WAS SOMETHING SIMPLE...NOT REALLY A SUPERHERO STORY, WAS IT? GOSH...WHAT WAS THE TITLE AGAIN?
SAGA.
THAT'S THE ONE.
NOW... DIDN'T I HEAR SOMETHING ABOUT THE WRITER OF THAT BOOK IN THE NEWS?

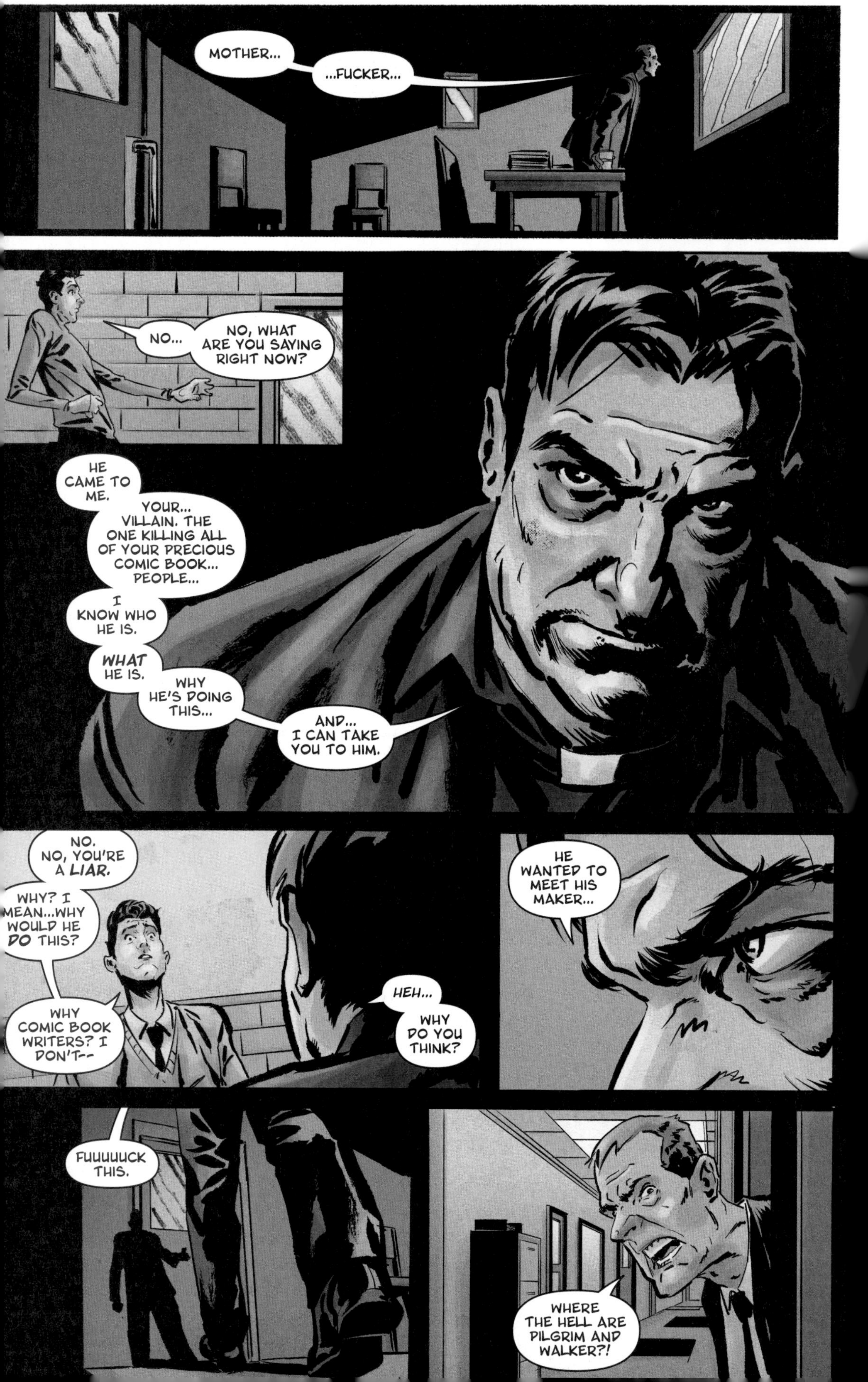
MOTHER...
...FUCKER...
NO...
NO, WHAT ARE YOU SAYING RIGHT NOW?
HE CAME TO ME.
YOUR... VILLAIN. THE ONE KILLING ALL OF YOUR PRECIOUS COMIC BOOK... PEOPLE...
I KNOW WHO HE IS.
WHAT HE IS.
WHY HE'S DOING THIS...
AND... I CAN TAKE YOU TO HIM.
NO. NO, YOU'RE A LIAR.
WHY? I MEAN...WHY WOULD HE DO THIS?
WHY COMIC BOOK WRITERS? I DON'T--
HEH...
WHY DO YOU THINK?
HE WANTED TO MEET HIS MAKER...
FUUUUUCK THIS.
WHERE THE HELL ARE PILGRIM AND WALKER?!

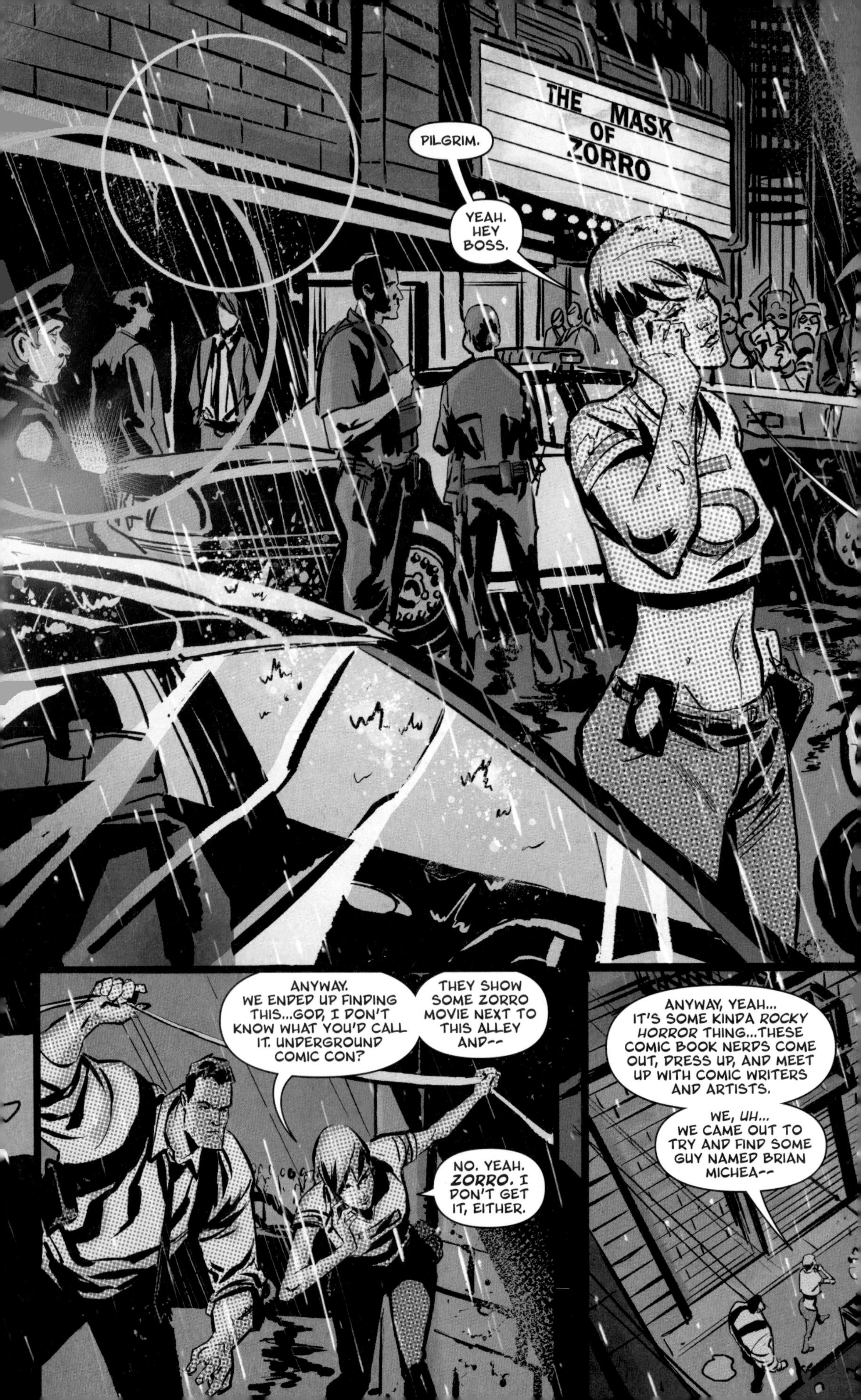
THE MASK OF ZORRO
PILGRIM.
YEAH. HEY BOSS.
ANYWAY. WE ENDED UP FINDING THIS...GOD, I DON'T KNOW WHAT YOU'D CALL IT. UNDERGROUND COMIC CON?
THEY SHOW SOME ZORRO MOVIE NEXT TO THIS ALLEY AND--
NO. YEAH. *ZORRO.* I DON'T GET IT, EITHER.
ANYWAY, YEAH... IT'S SOME KINDA *ROCKY HORROR* THING...THESE COMIC BOOK NERDS COME OUT, DRESS UP, AND MEET UP WITH COMIC WRITERS AND ARTISTS.
WE, *UH*... WE CAME OUT TO TRY AND FIND SOME GUY NAMED BRIAN MICHEA--

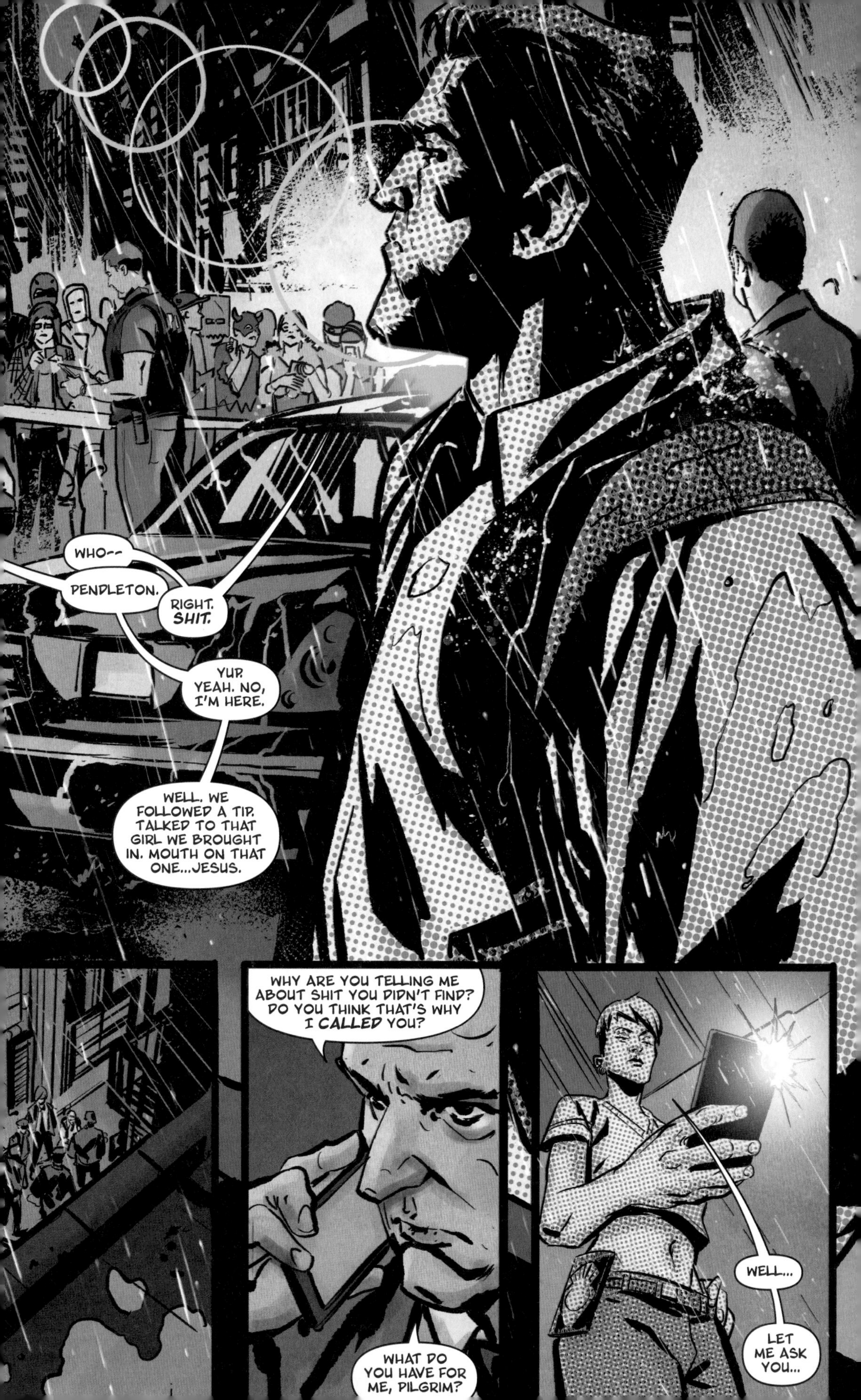
WHO--
PENDLETON.
RIGHT. SHIT.
YUP. YEAH. NO, I'M HERE.
WELL. WE FOLLOWED A TIP. TALKED TO THAT GIRL WE BROUGHT IN. MOUTH ON THAT ONE...JESUS.
WHY ARE YOU TELLING ME ABOUT SHIT YOU DIDN'T FIND? DO YOU THINK THAT'S WHY I CALLED YOU?
WHAT DO YOU HAVE FOR ME, PILGRIM?
WELL...
LET ME ASK YOU...

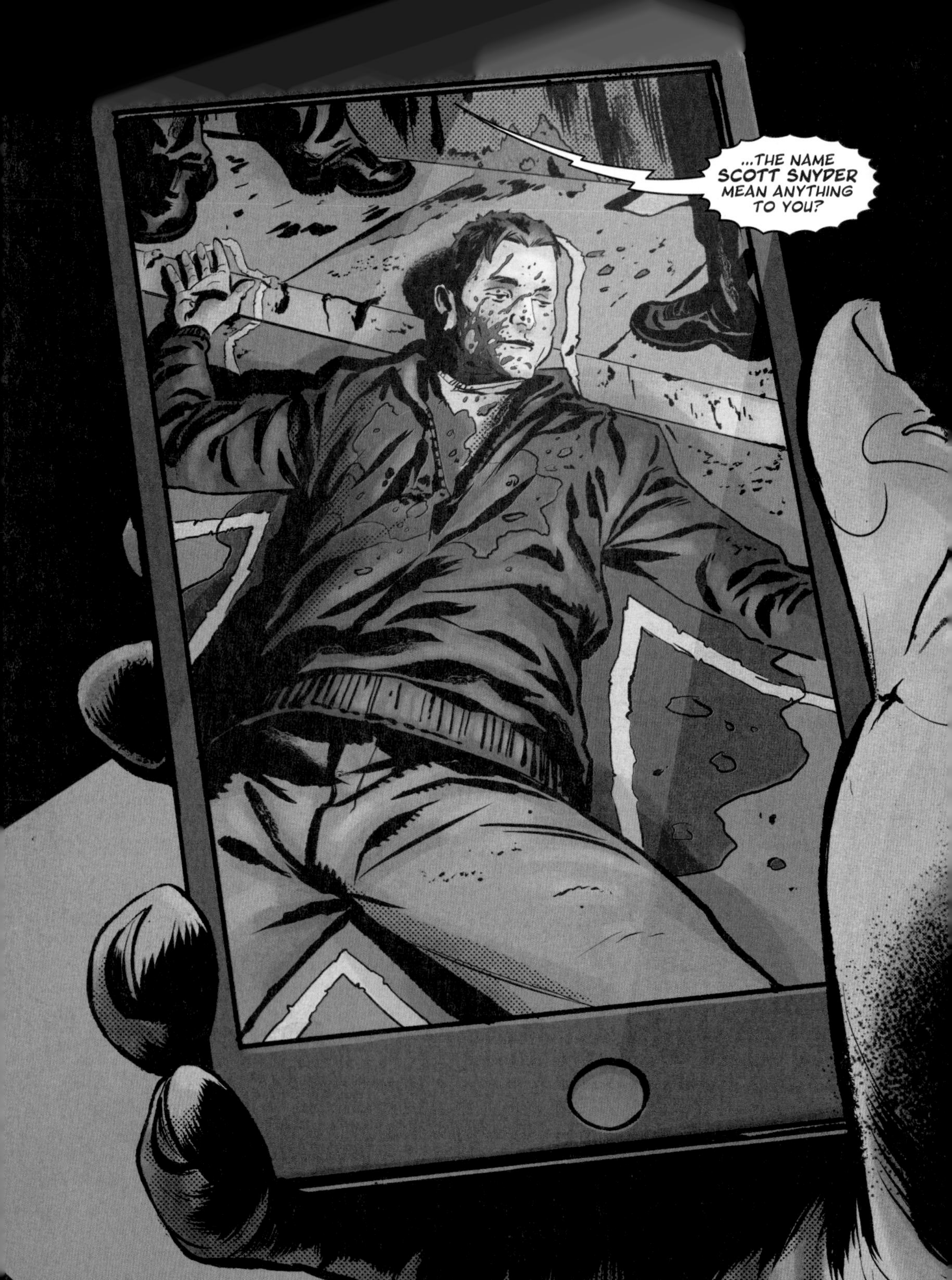
...THE NAME SCOTT SNYDER MEAN ANYTHING TO YOU?

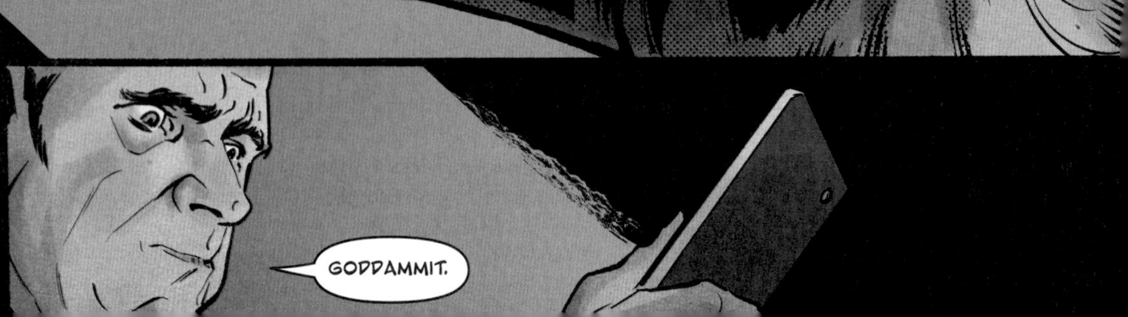
GODDAMMIT.

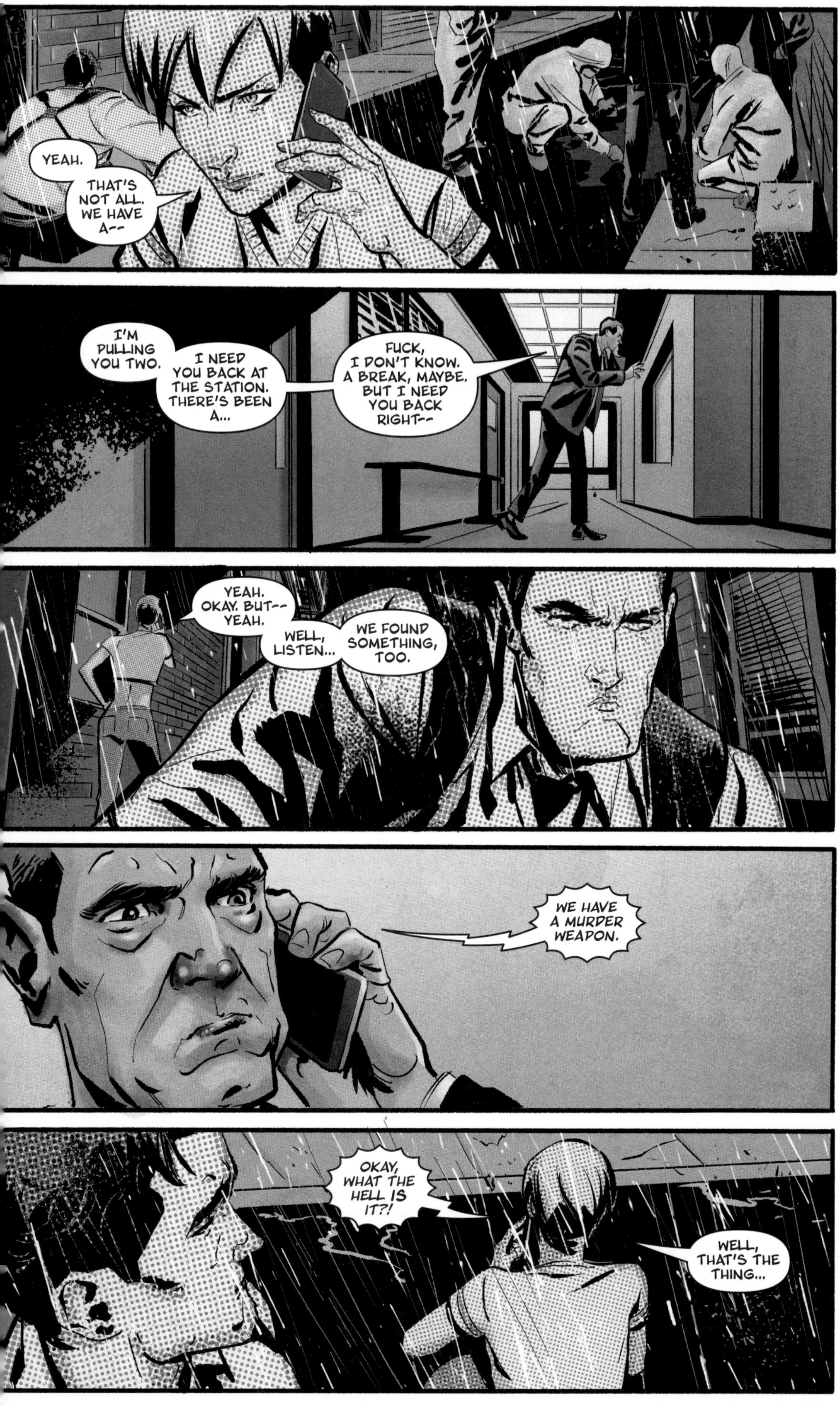
YEAH.
THAT'S NOT ALL. WE HAVE A--
I'M PULLING YOU TWO.
I NEED YOU BACK AT THE STATION. THERE'S BEEN A...
FUCK, I DON'T KNOW. A BREAK, MAYBE. BUT I NEED YOU BACK RIGHT--
YEAH. OKAY. BUT-- YEAH.
WELL, LISTEN...
WE FOUND SOMETHING, TOO.
WE HAVE A MURDER WEAPON.
OKAY, WHAT THE HELL IS IT?!
WELL, THAT'S THE THING...

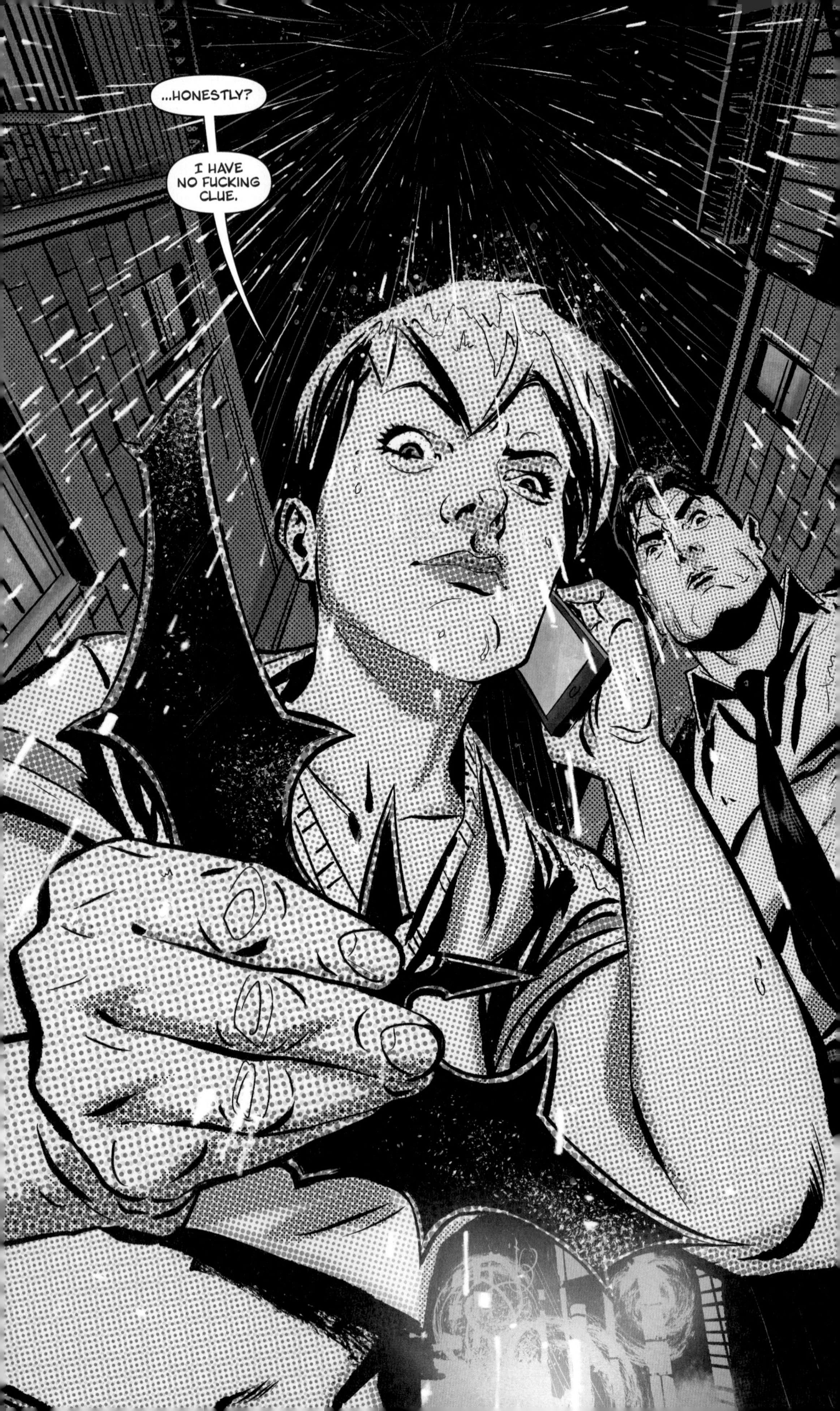
...HONESTLY?
I HAVE NO FUCKING CLUE.

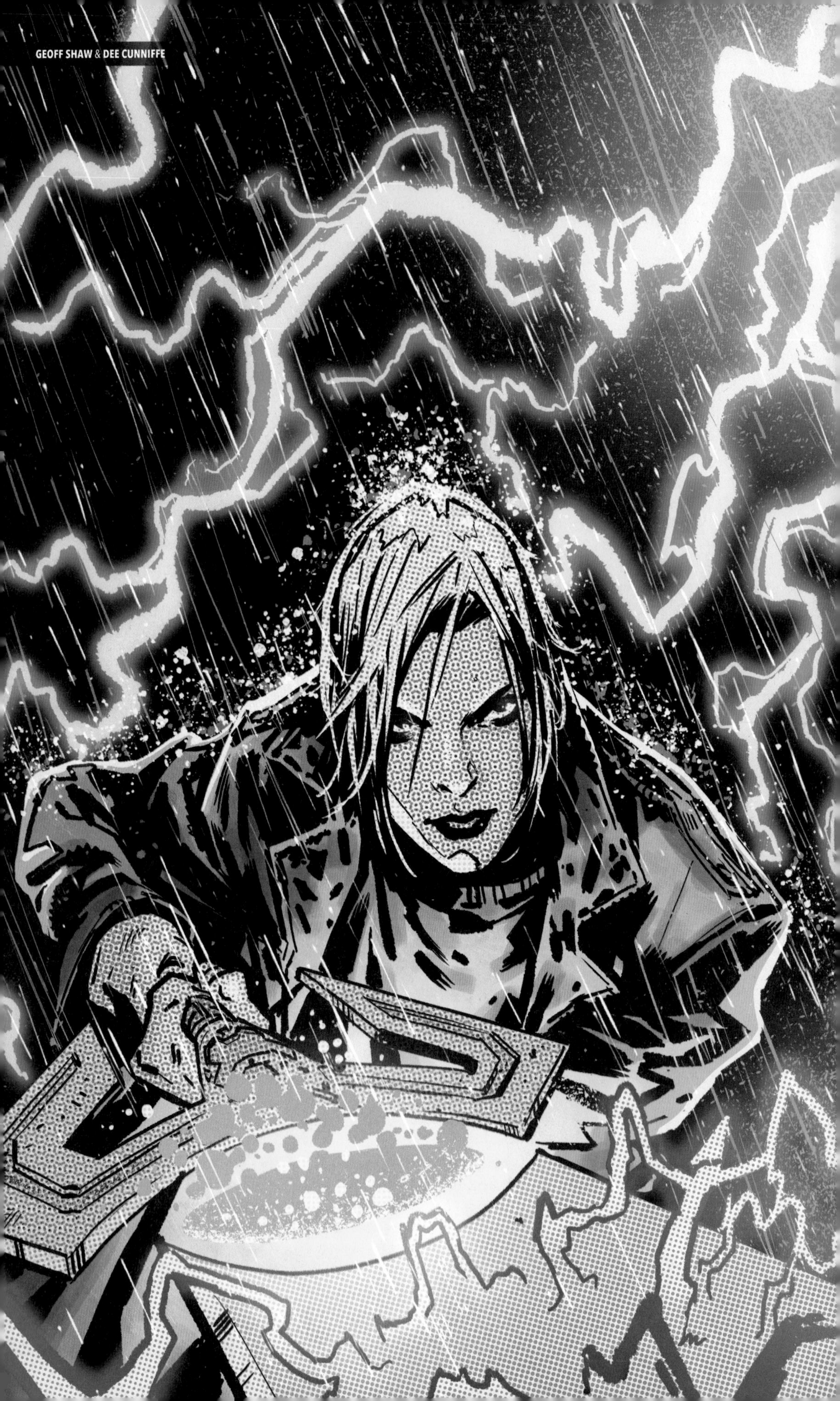
GEOFF SHAW & DEE CUNNIFFE

THE 10-CENT PLAGUE

CHAPTER THREE

...

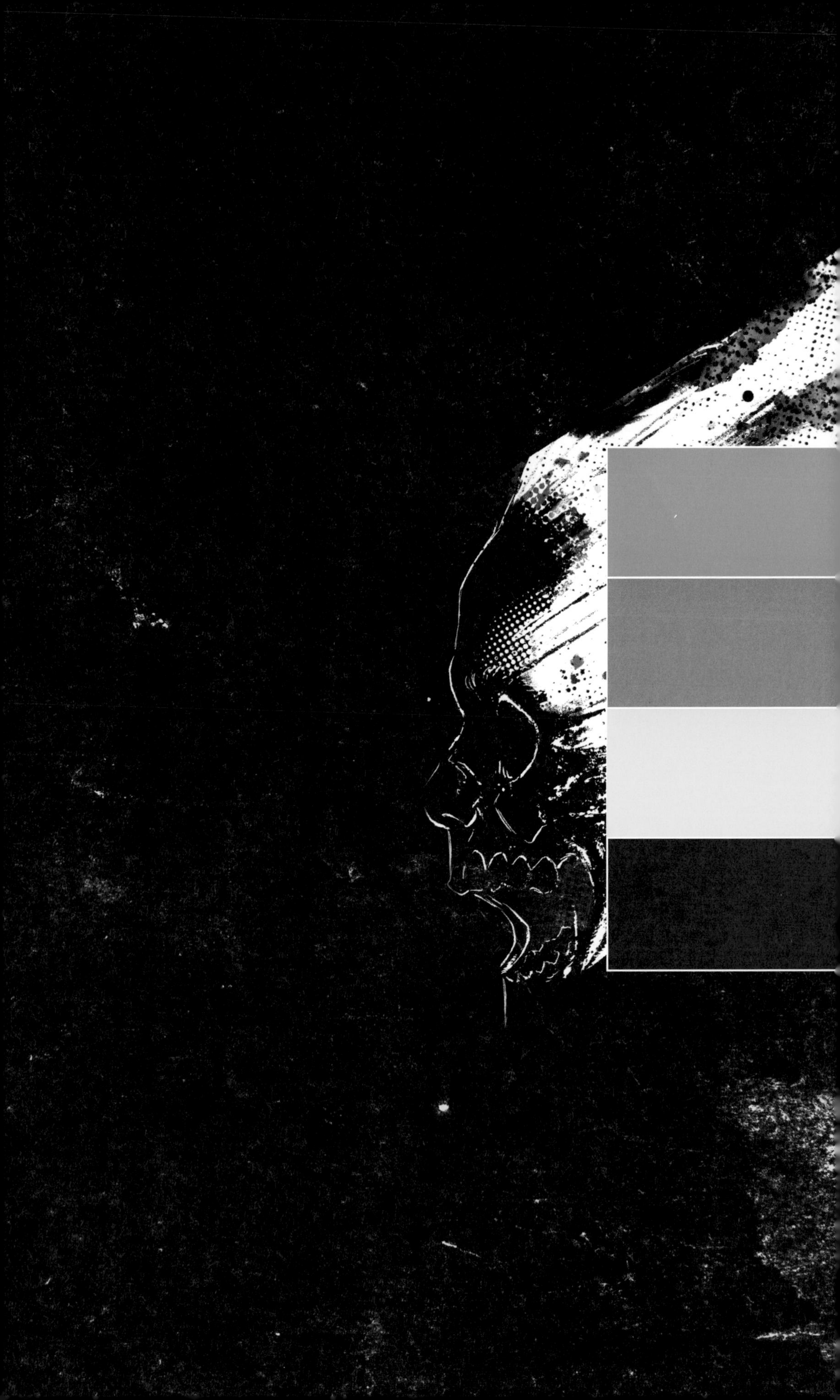

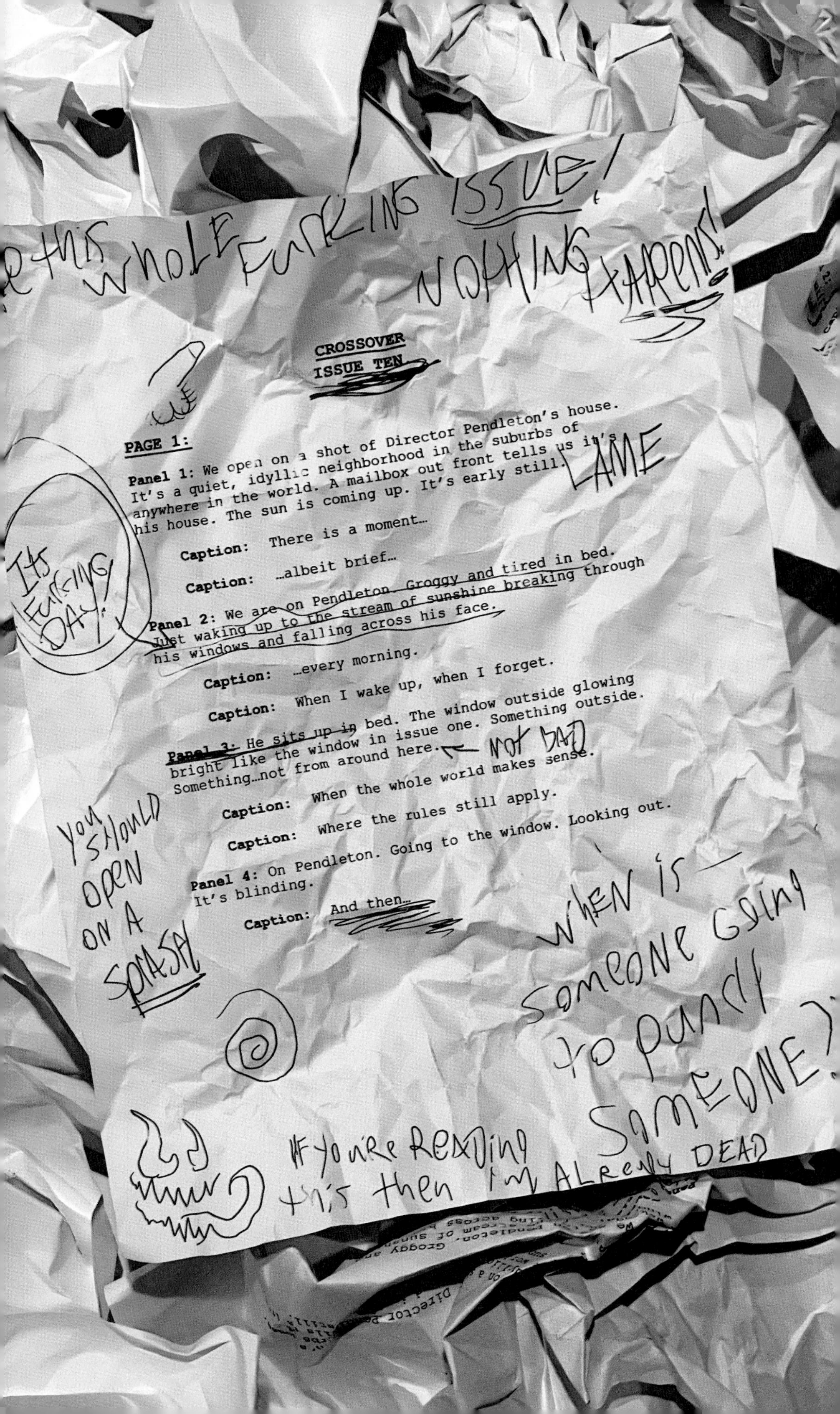

...e this whole fucking issue! Nothing happens!
CROSSOVER
ISSUE TEN
PAGE 1:
Panel 1: We open on a shot of Director Pendleton's house. It's a quiet, idyllic neighborhood in the suburbs of anywhere in the world. A mailbox out front tells us it's his house. The sun is coming up. It's early still.
LAME
Caption: There is a moment…
Caption: …albeit brief…
It's fucking day!
Panel 2: We are on Pendleton. Groggy and tired in bed. Just waking up to the stream of sunshine breaking through his windows and falling across his face.
Caption: …every morning.
Caption: When I wake up, when I forget.
Panel 3: He sits up in bed. The window outside glowing bright like the window in issue one. Something outside. Something…not from around here.
not bad
Caption: When the whole world makes sense.
Caption: Where the rules still apply.
You should open on a splash
Panel 4: On Pendleton. Going to the window. Looking out. It's blinding.
Caption: And then…
When is someone going to punch someone?
If you're reading this then I'm already dead

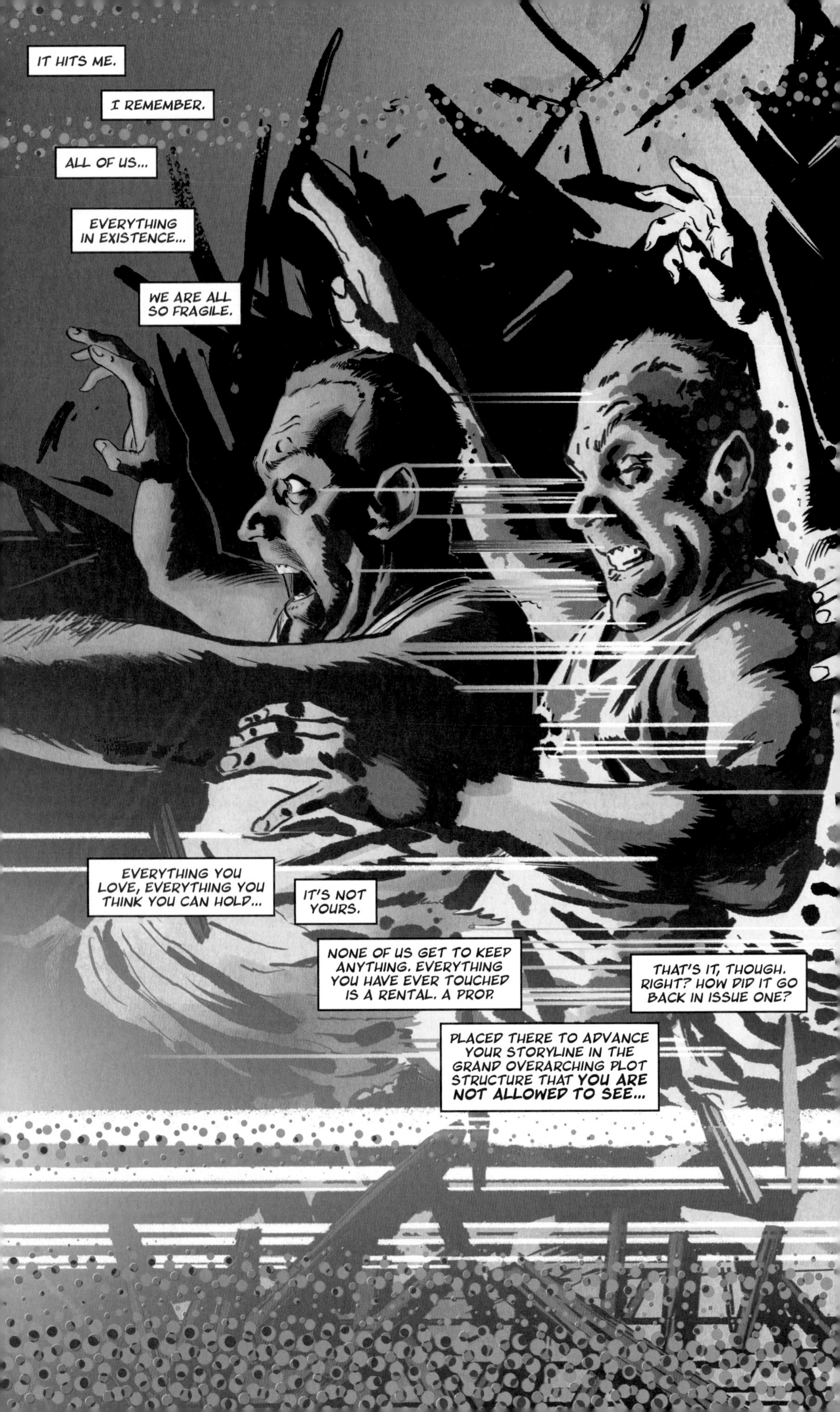
IT HITS ME.
I REMEMBER.
ALL OF US...
EVERYTHING IN EXISTENCE...
WE ARE ALL SO FRAGILE.
EVERYTHING YOU LOVE, EVERYTHING YOU THINK YOU CAN HOLD...
IT'S NOT YOURS.
NONE OF US GET TO KEEP ANYTHING. EVERYTHING YOU HAVE EVER TOUCHED IS A RENTAL. A PROP.
THAT'S IT, THOUGH. RIGHT? HOW DID IT GO BACK IN ISSUE ONE?
PLACED THERE TO ADVANCE YOUR STORYLINE IN THE GRAND OVERARCHING PLOT STRUCTURE THAT YOU ARE NOT ALLOWED TO SEE...

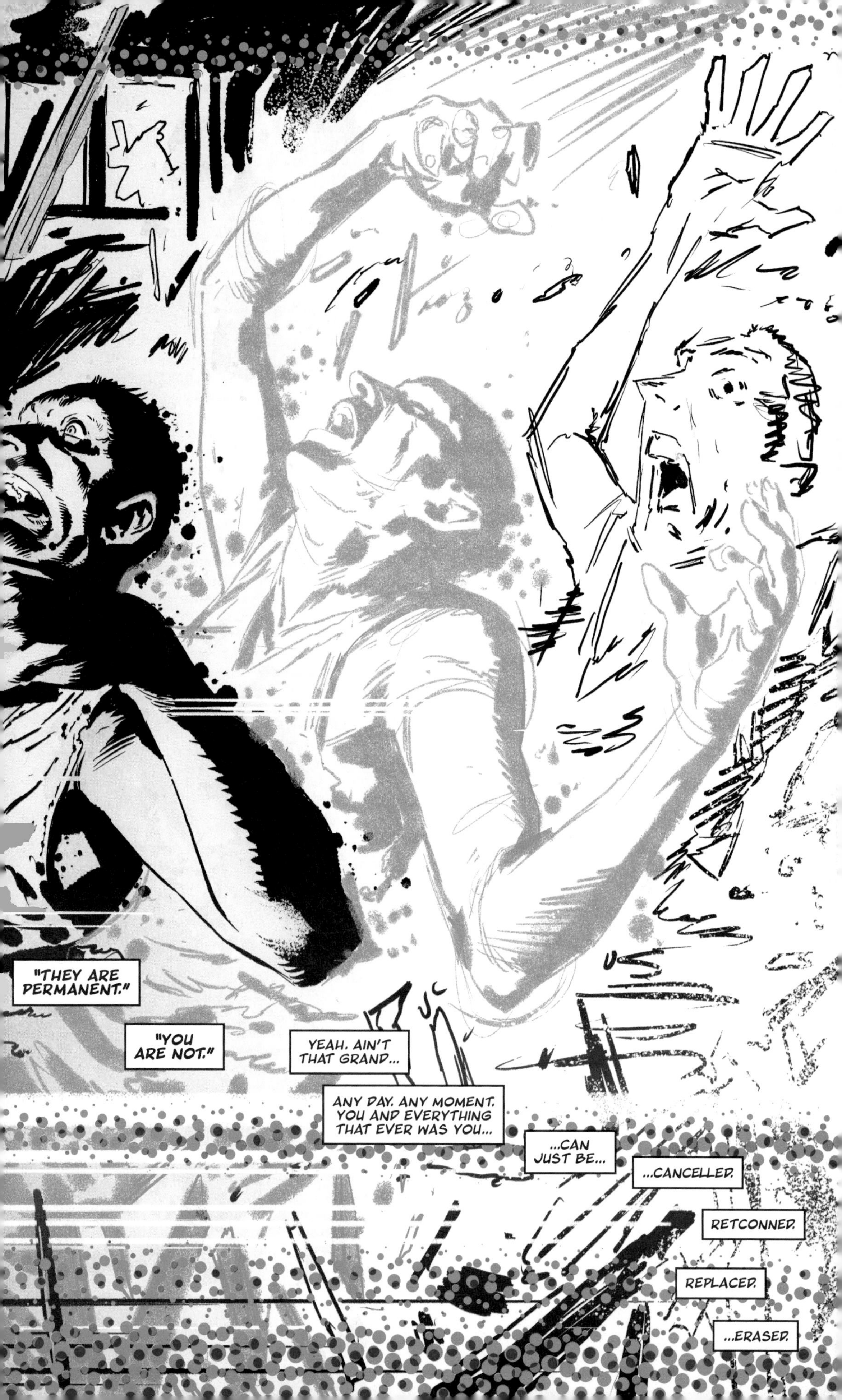

"THEY ARE PERMANENT."
"YOU ARE NOT."
YEAH. AIN'T THAT GRAND...
ANY DAY. ANY MOMENT. YOU AND EVERYTHING THAT EVER WAS YOU...
...CAN JUST BE...
...CANCELLED.
RETCONNED.
REPLACED.
...ERASED.

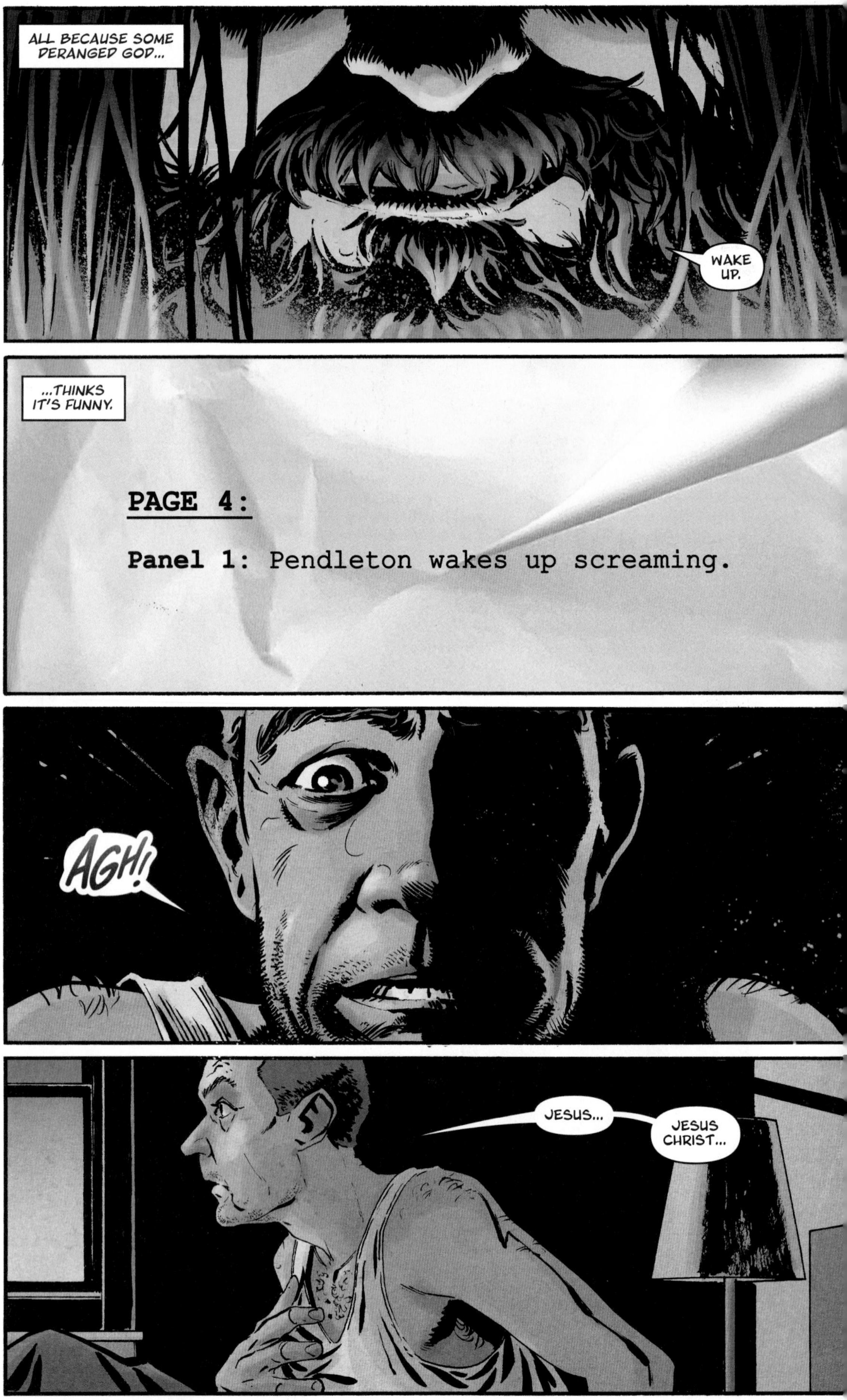
ALL BECAUSE SOME DERANGED GOD...
WAKE UP.
...THINKS IT'S FUNNY.
PAGE 4:
Panel 1: Pendleton wakes up screaming.
AGH!
JESUS...
JESUS CHRIST...

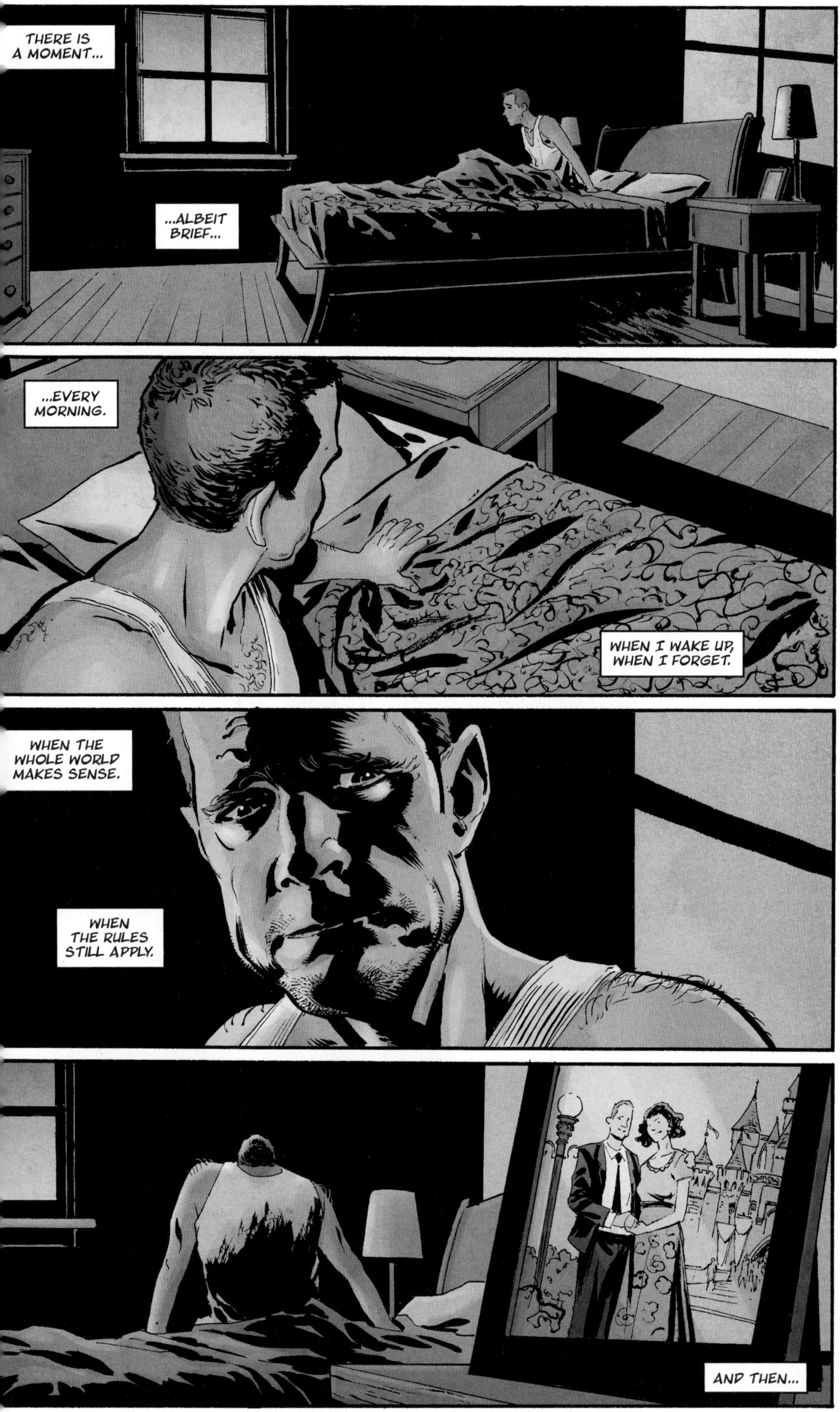
THERE IS A MOMENT...
...ALBEIT BRIEF...
...EVERY MORNING.
WHEN I WAKE UP, WHEN I FORGET.
WHEN THE WHOLE WORLD MAKES SENSE.
WHEN THE RULES STILL APPLY.
AND THEN...

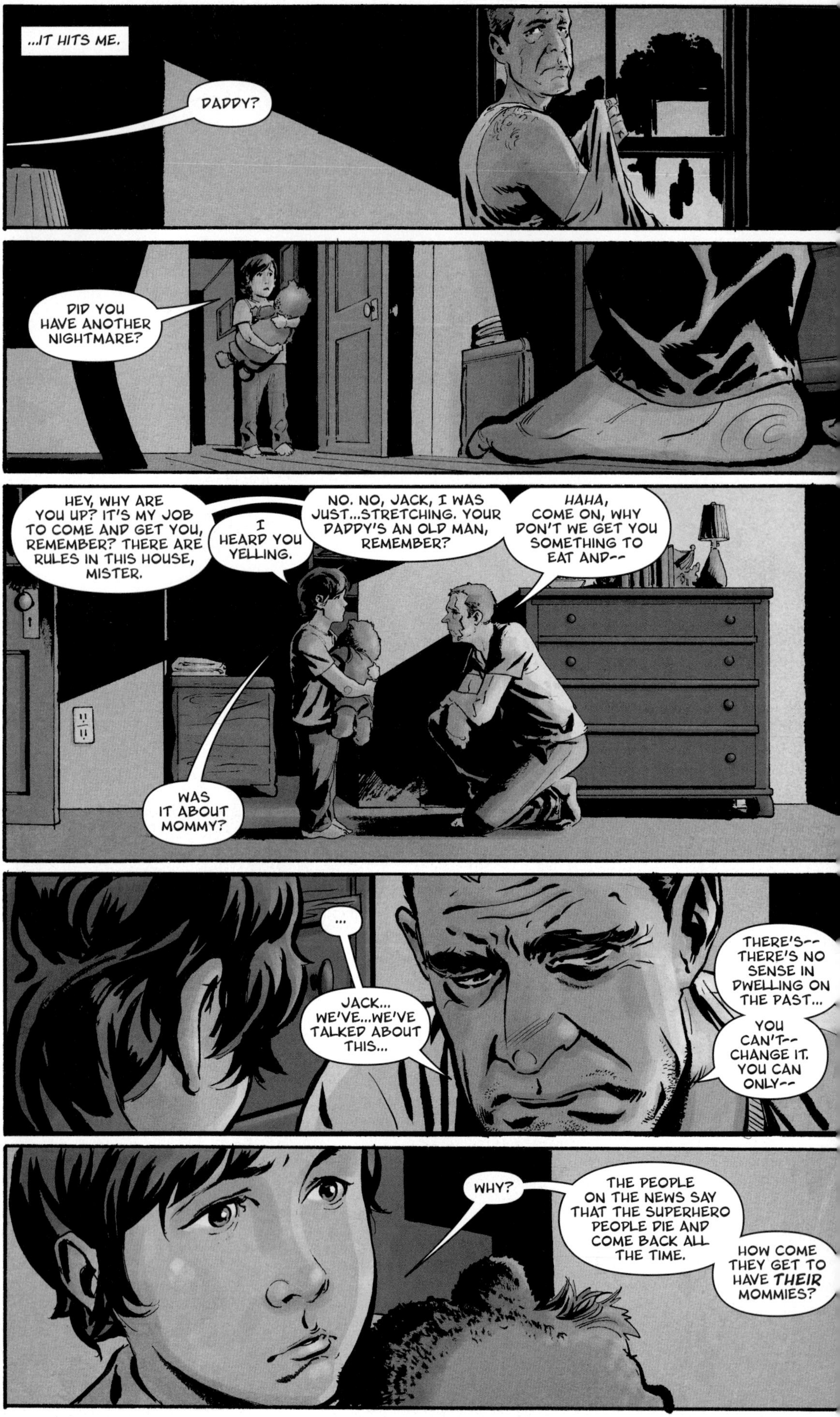
...IT HITS ME.
DADDY?
DID YOU HAVE ANOTHER NIGHTMARE?
HEY, WHY ARE YOU UP? IT'S MY JOB TO COME AND GET YOU, REMEMBER? THERE ARE RULES IN THIS HOUSE, MISTER.
I HEARD YOU YELLING.
NO. NO, JACK, I WAS JUST...STRETCHING. YOUR DADDY'S AN OLD MAN, REMEMBER?
HAHA, COME ON, WHY DON'T WE GET YOU SOMETHING TO EAT AND--
WAS IT ABOUT MOMMY?
...
JACK... WE'VE...WE'VE TALKED ABOUT THIS...
THERE'S-- THERE'S NO SENSE IN DWELLING ON THE PAST...
YOU CAN'T-- CHANGE IT. YOU CAN ONLY--
WHY?
THE PEOPLE ON THE NEWS SAY THAT THE SUPERHERO PEOPLE DIE AND COME BACK ALL THE TIME.
HOW COME THEY GET TO HAVE *THEIR* MOMMIES?

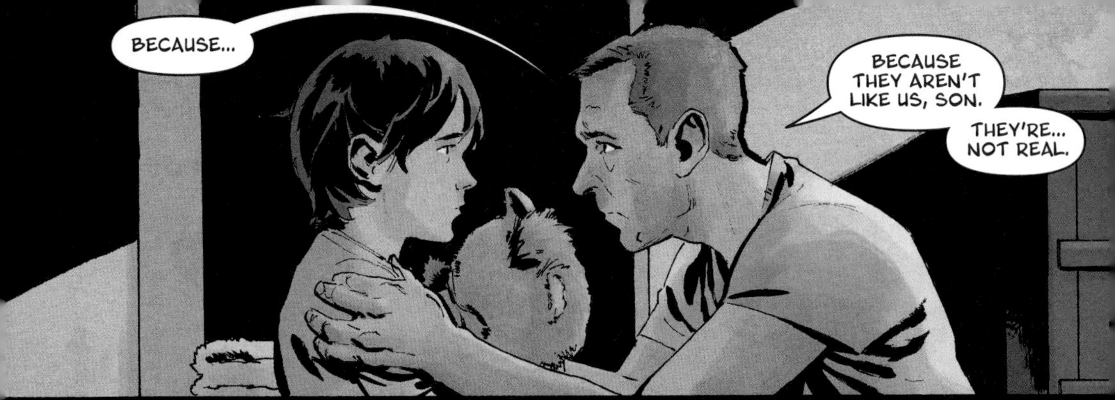
BECAUSE...
BECAUSE THEY AREN'T LIKE US, SON.
THEY'RE... NOT REAL.

Panel 3: Tight on Pendleton. Serious. Intense.

Pendleton: And we ARE.

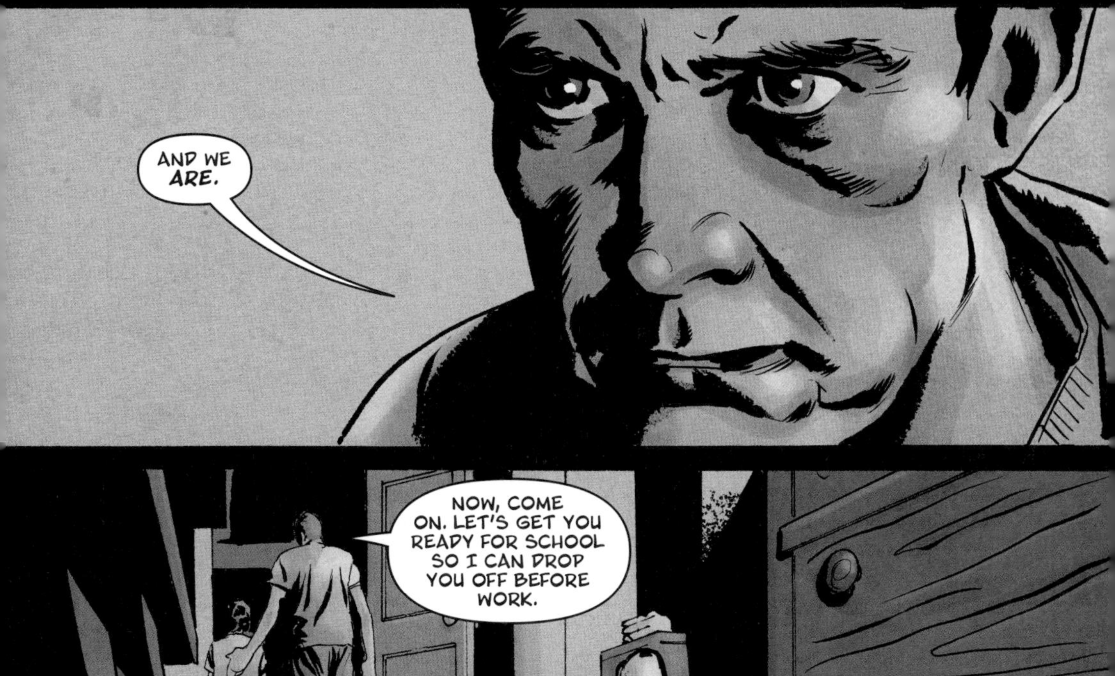
AND WE ***ARE.***

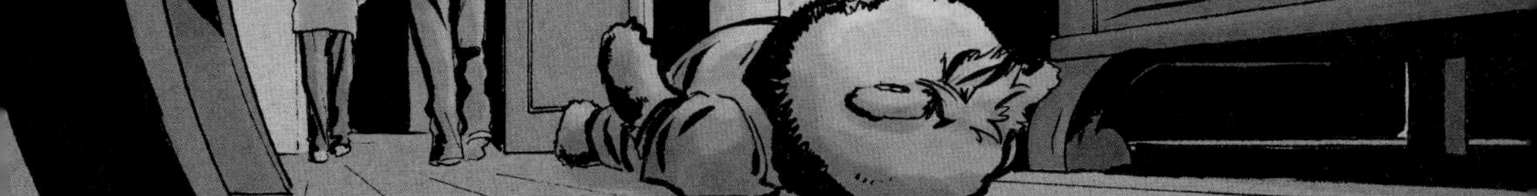
NOW, COME ON. LET'S GET YOU READY FOR SCHOOL SO I CAN DROP YOU OFF BEFORE WORK.

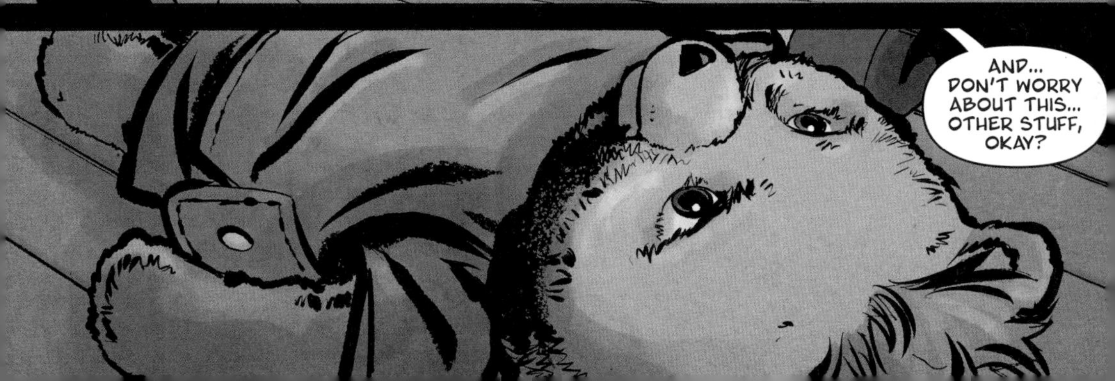
AND... DON'T WORRY ABOUT THIS... OTHER STUFF, OKAY?

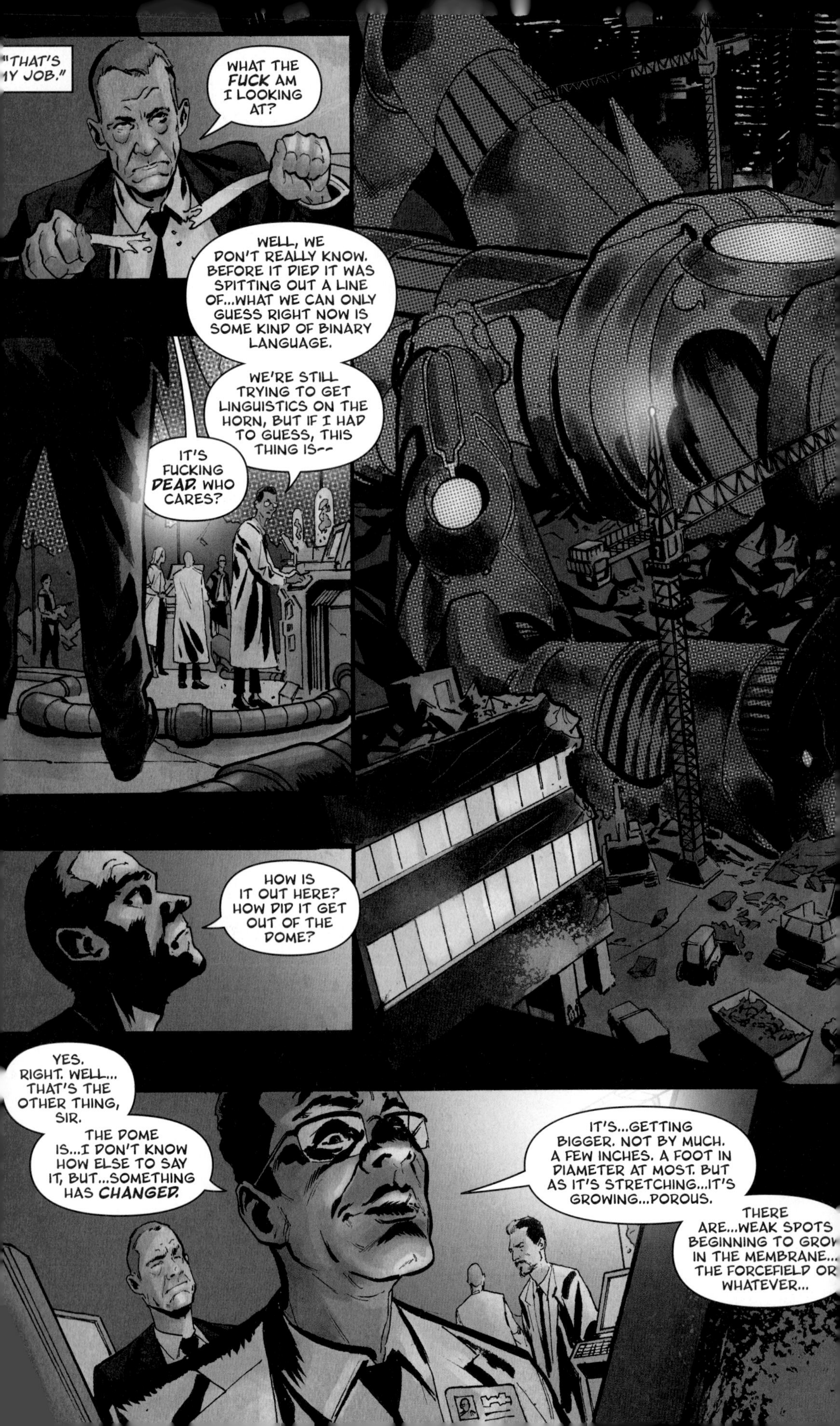
"THAT'S MY JOB."
WHAT THE FUCK AM I LOOKING AT?
WELL, WE DON'T REALLY KNOW. BEFORE IT DIED IT WAS SPITTING OUT A LINE OF...WHAT WE CAN ONLY GUESS RIGHT NOW IS SOME KIND OF BINARY LANGUAGE.
WE'RE STILL TRYING TO GET LINGUISTICS ON THE HORN, BUT IF I HAD TO GUESS, THIS THING IS--
IT'S FUCKING DEAD. WHO CARES?
HOW IS IT OUT HERE? HOW DID IT GET OUT OF THE DOME?
YES. RIGHT. WELL... THAT'S THE OTHER THING, SIR.
THE DOME IS...I DON'T KNOW HOW ELSE TO SAY IT, BUT...SOMETHING HAS CHANGED.
IT'S...GETTING BIGGER. NOT BY MUCH. A FEW INCHES. A FOOT IN DIAMETER AT MOST. BUT AS IT'S STRETCHING...IT'S GROWING...POROUS.
THERE ARE...WEAK SPOTS BEGINNING TO GROW IN THE MEMBRANE... THE FORCEFIELD OR WHATEVER...

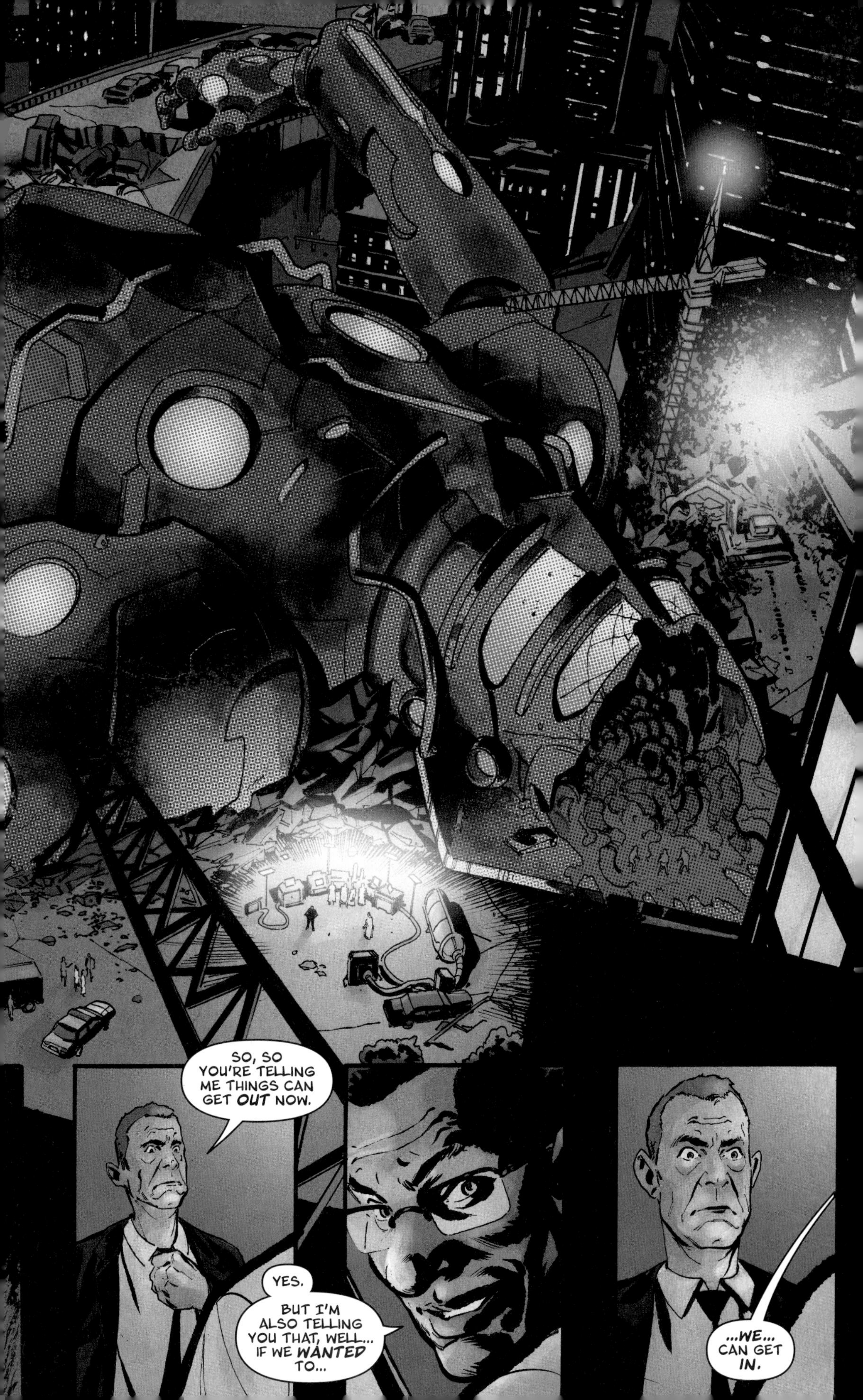
SO, SO YOU'RE TELLING ME THINGS CAN GET OUT NOW.
YES.
BUT I'M ALSO TELLING YOU THAT, WELL... IF WE WANTED TO...
...WE... CAN GET IN.

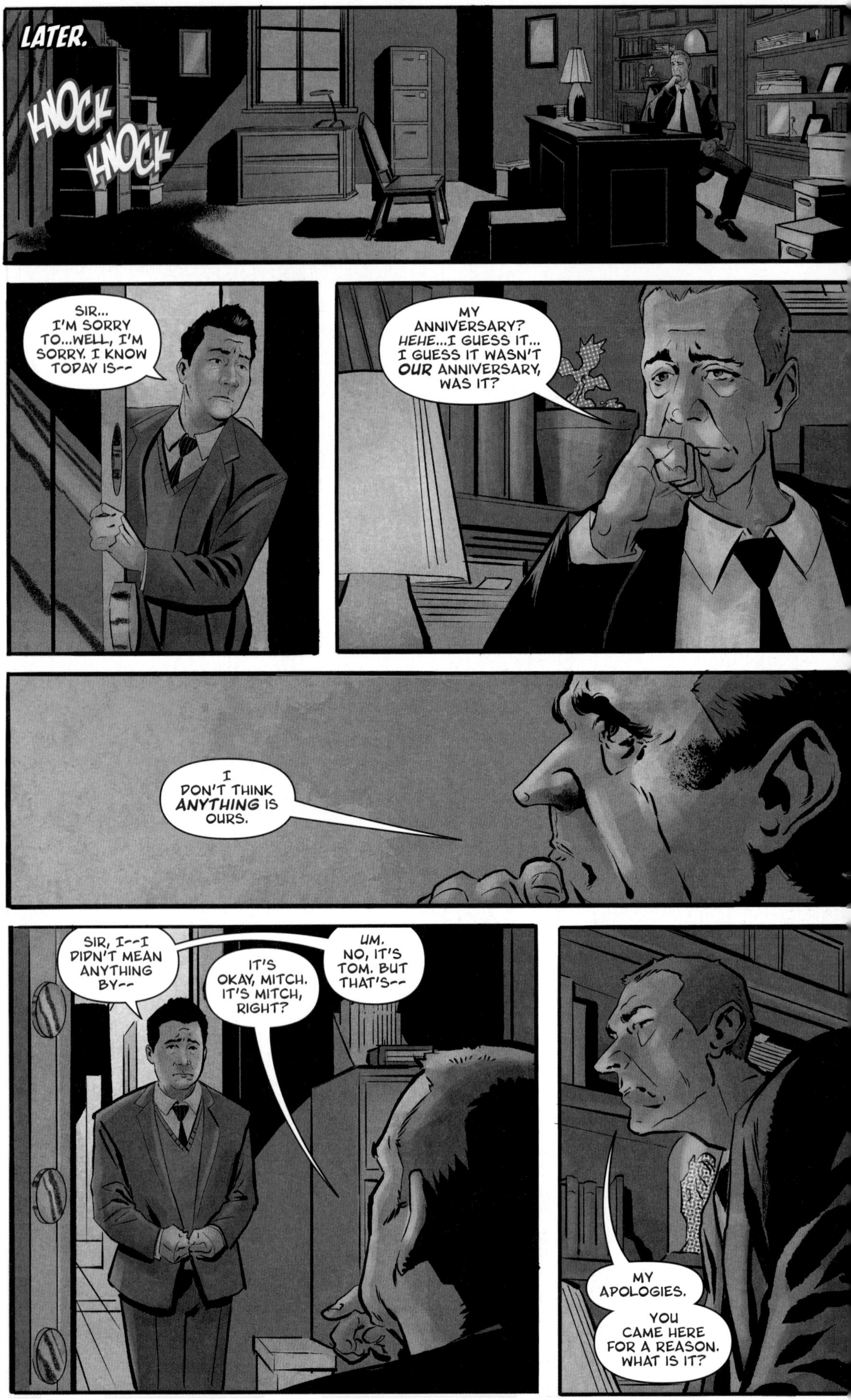
LATER.
KNOCK KNOCK
SIR... I'M SORRY TO...WELL, I'M SORRY. I KNOW TODAY IS--
MY ANNIVERSARY? HEHE...I GUESS IT... I GUESS IT WASN'T OUR ANNIVERSARY, WAS IT?
I DON'T THINK ANYTHING IS OURS.
SIR, I--I DIDN'T MEAN ANYTHING BY--
IT'S OKAY, MITCH. IT'S MITCH, RIGHT?
UM. NO, IT'S TOM. BUT THAT'S--
MY APOLOGIES.
YOU CAME HERE FOR A REASON. WHAT IS IT?

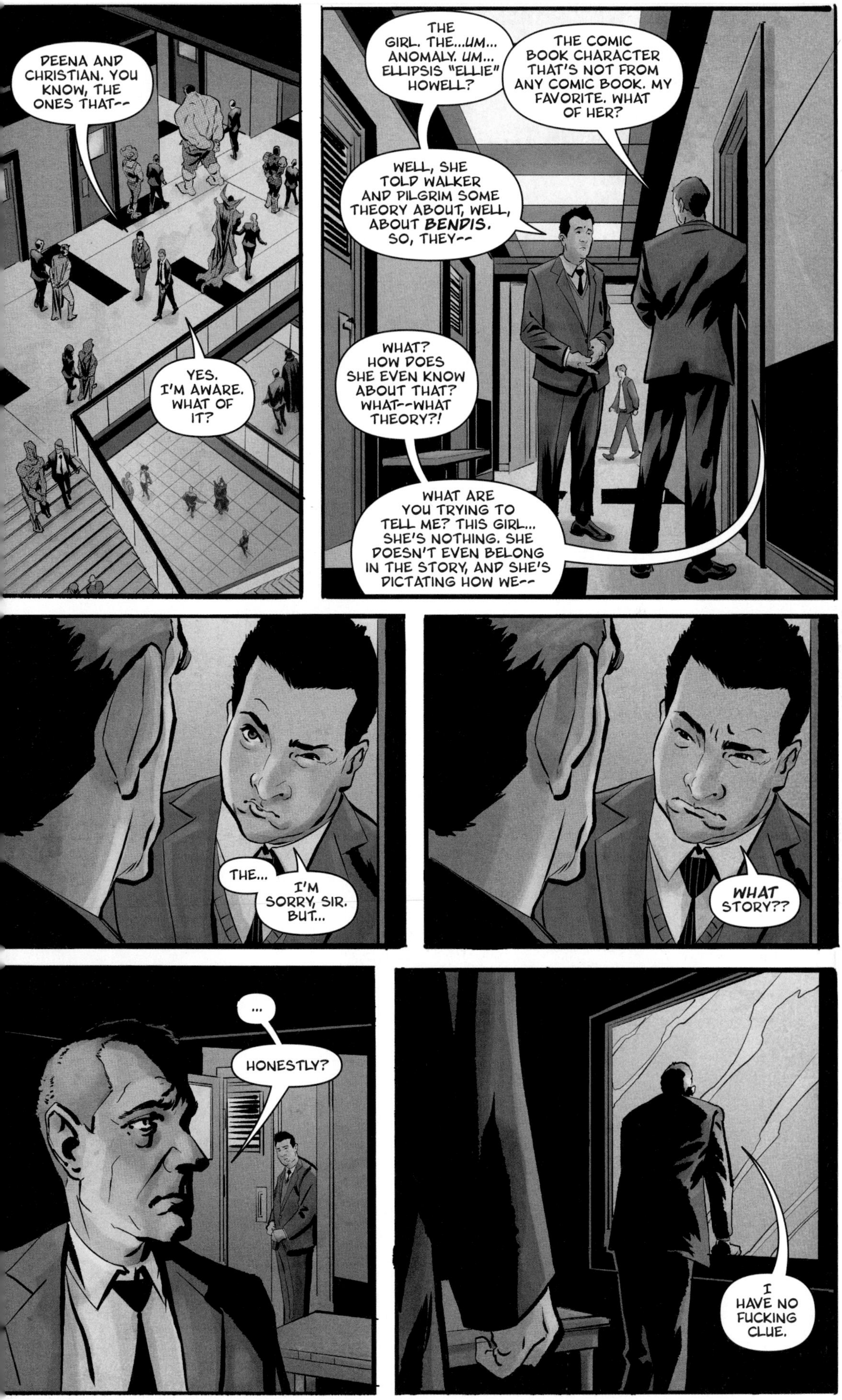
DEENA AND CHRISTIAN. YOU KNOW, THE ONES THAT--
YES. I'M AWARE. WHAT OF IT?
THE GIRL. THE...UM... ANOMALY. UM... ELLIPSIS "ELLIE" HOWELL?
THE COMIC BOOK CHARACTER THAT'S NOT FROM ANY COMIC BOOK. MY FAVORITE. WHAT OF HER?
WELL, SHE TOLD WALKER AND PILGRIM SOME THEORY ABOUT, WELL, ABOUT BENDIS. SO, THEY--
WHAT? HOW DOES SHE EVEN KNOW ABOUT THAT? WHAT--WHAT THEORY?!
WHAT ARE YOU TRYING TO TELL ME? THIS GIRL... SHE'S NOTHING. SHE DOESN'T EVEN BELONG IN THE STORY, AND SHE'S DICTATING HOW WE--
THE...
I'M SORRY, SIR. BUT...
WHAT STORY??
...
HONESTLY?
I HAVE NO FUCKING CLUE.

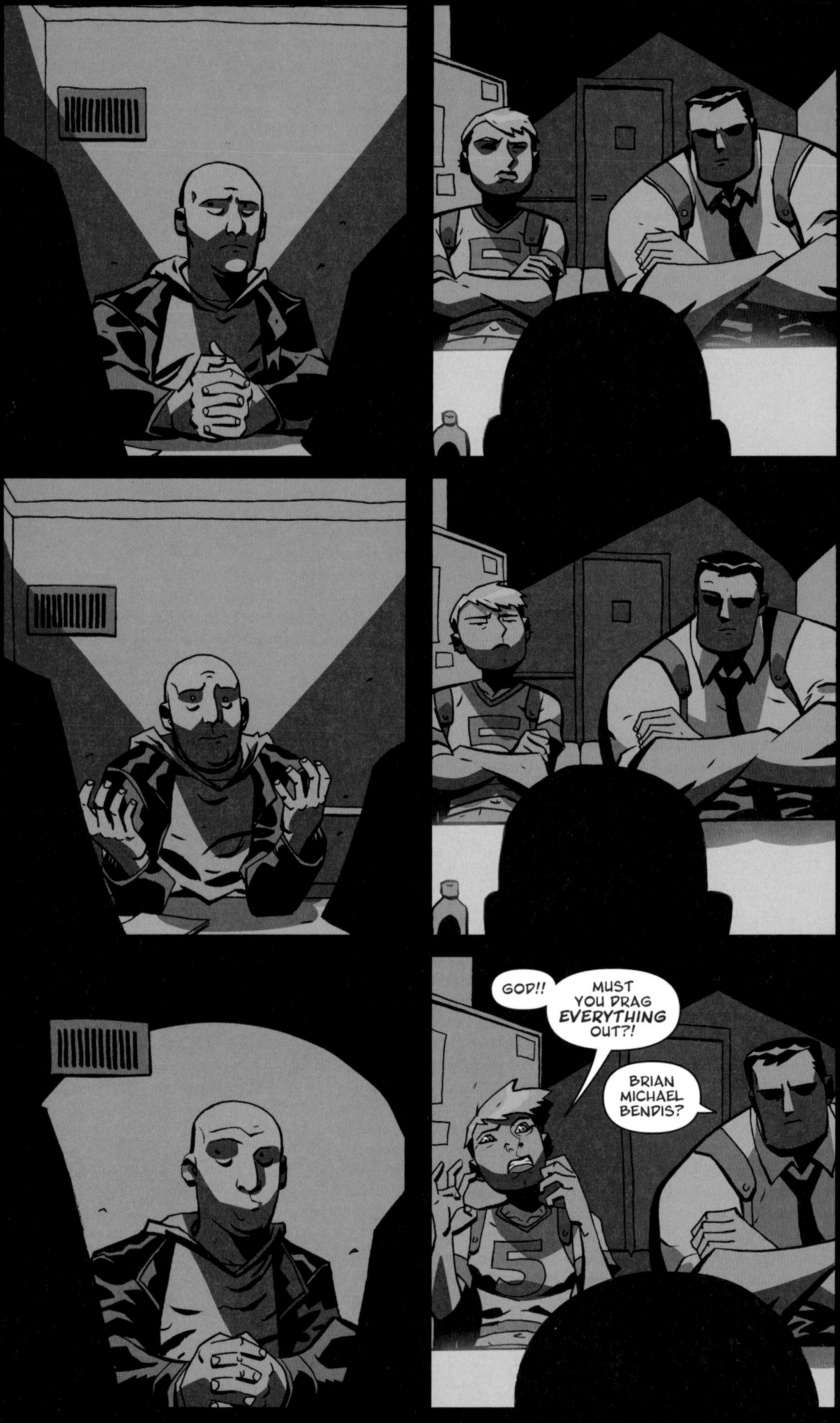
GOD!!
MUST YOU DRAG EVERYTHING OUT?!
BRIAN MICHAEL BENDIS?

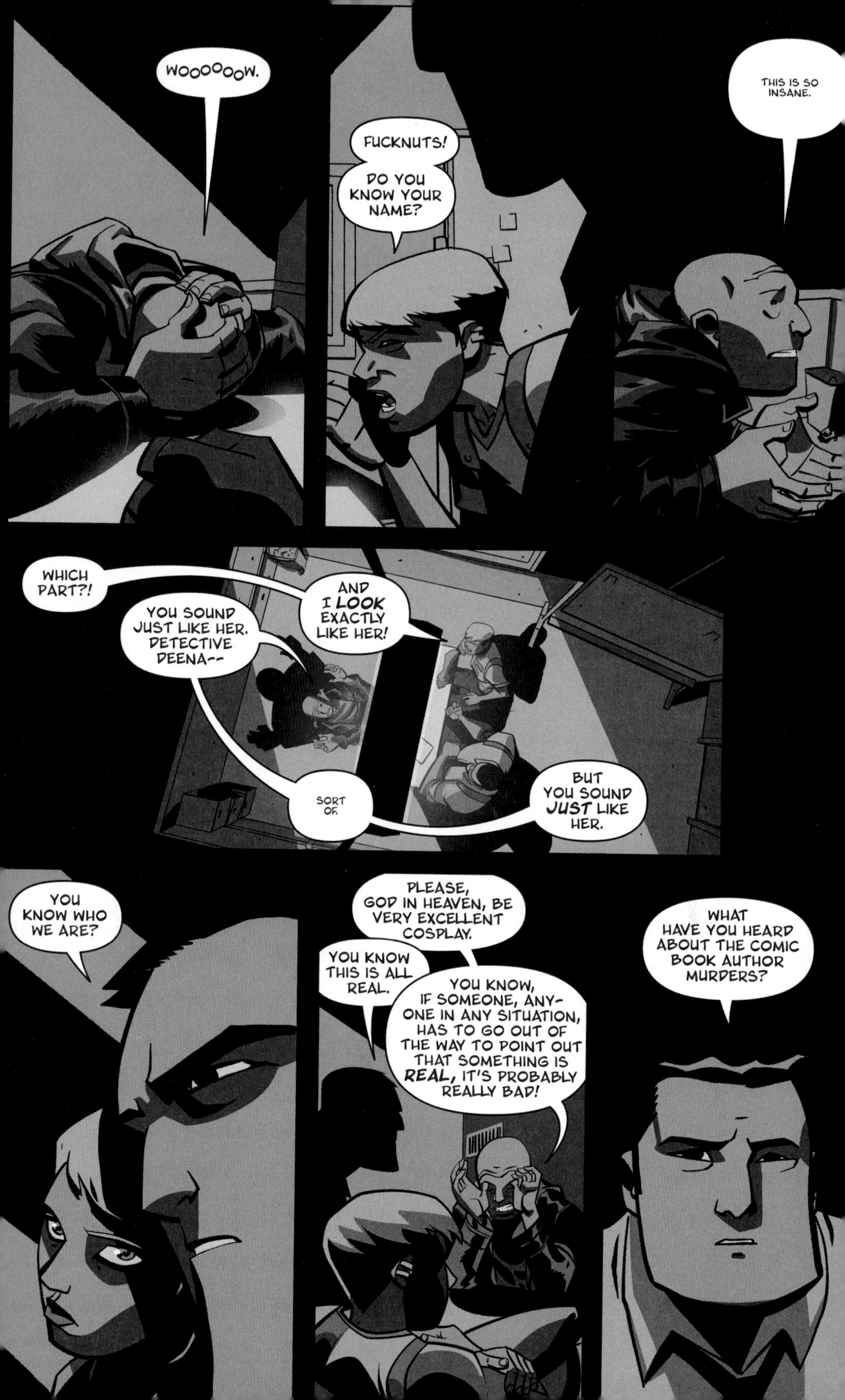
WOOOOOOW.
FUCKNUTS!
DO YOU KNOW YOUR NAME?
THIS IS SO INSANE.
WHICH PART?!
AND I LOOK EXACTLY LIKE HER!
YOU SOUND JUST LIKE HER. DETECTIVE DEENA--
SORT OF.
BUT YOU SOUND JUST LIKE HER.
YOU KNOW WHO WE ARE?
PLEASE, GOD IN HEAVEN, BE VERY EXCELLENT COSPLAY.
YOU KNOW THIS IS ALL REAL.
YOU KNOW, IF SOMEONE, ANY-ONE IN ANY SITUATION, HAS TO GO OUT OF THE WAY TO POINT OUT THAT SOMETHING IS REAL, IT'S PROBABLY REALLY BAD!
WHAT HAVE YOU HEARD ABOUT THE COMIC BOOK AUTHOR MURDERS?

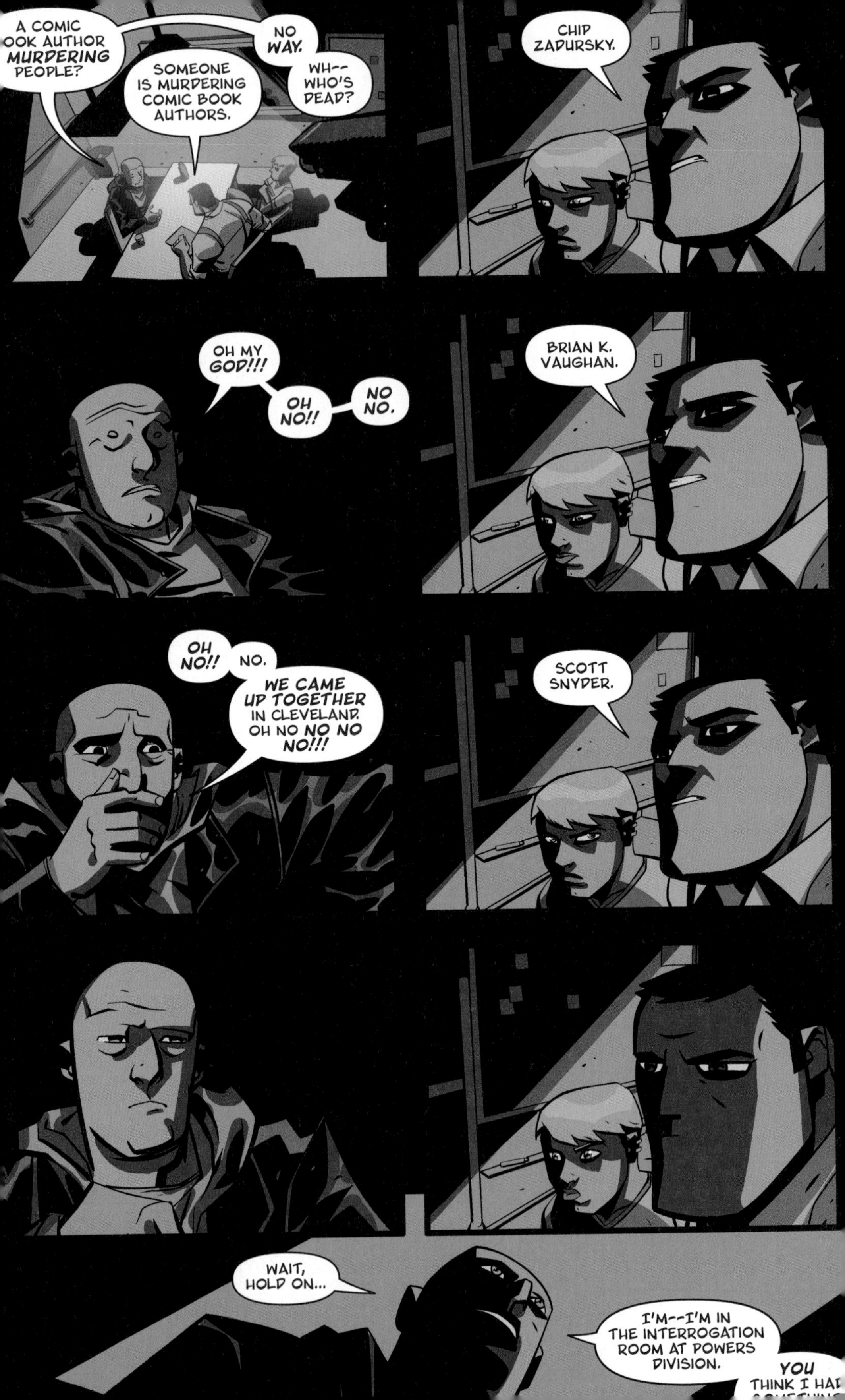
A COMIC OOK AUTHOR MURDERING PEOPLE?
NO WAY.
SOMEONE IS MURDERING COMIC BOOK AUTHORS.
WH-- WHO'S DEAD?
CHIP ZADURSKY.
OH MY GOD!!!
OH NO!!
NO NO.
BRIAN K. VAUGHAN.
OH NO!!
NO.
WE CAME UP TOGETHER IN CLEVELAND. OH NO NO NO NO!!!
SCOTT SNYDER.
WAIT, HOLD ON...
I'M--I'M IN THE INTERROGATION ROOM AT POWERS DIVISION.
YOU THINK I HA

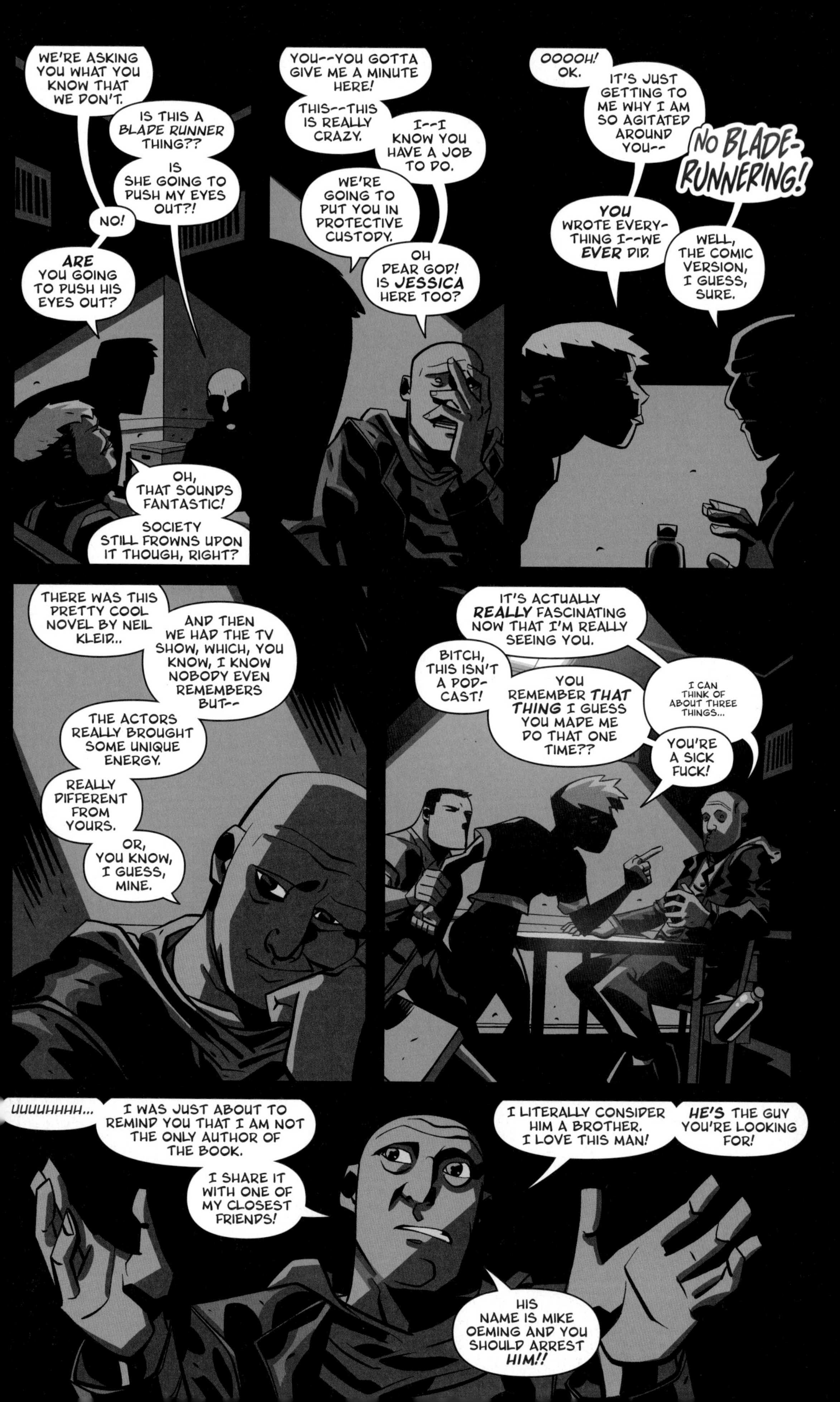
WE'RE ASKING YOU WHAT YOU KNOW THAT WE DON'T.
IS THIS A BLADE RUNNER THING??
IS SHE GOING TO PUSH MY EYES OUT?!
NO!
ARE YOU GOING TO PUSH HIS EYES OUT?
OH, THAT SOUNDS FANTASTIC!
SOCIETY STILL FROWNS UPON IT THOUGH, RIGHT?
YOU--YOU GOTTA GIVE ME A MINUTE HERE!
THIS--THIS IS REALLY CRAZY.
I--I KNOW YOU HAVE A JOB TO DO.
WE'RE GOING TO PUT YOU IN PROTECTIVE CUSTODY.
OH DEAR GOD! IS JESSICA HERE TOO?
OOOOH! OK.
IT'S JUST GETTING TO ME WHY I AM SO AGITATED AROUND YOU--
NO BLADE-RUNNERING!
YOU WROTE EVERY-THING I--WE EVER DID.
WELL, THE COMIC VERSION, I GUESS, SURE.
THERE WAS THIS PRETTY COOL NOVEL BY NEIL KLEID...
AND THEN WE HAD THE TV SHOW, WHICH, YOU KNOW, I KNOW NOBODY EVEN REMEMBERS BUT--
THE ACTORS REALLY BROUGHT SOME UNIQUE ENERGY.
REALLY DIFFERENT FROM YOURS.
OR, YOU KNOW, I GUESS, MINE.
IT'S ACTUALLY REALLY FASCINATING NOW THAT I'M REALLY SEEING YOU.
BITCH, THIS ISN'T A POD-CAST!
YOU REMEMBER THAT THING I GUESS YOU MADE ME DO THAT ONE TIME??
I CAN THINK OF ABOUT THREE THINGS...
YOU'RE A SICK FUCK!
UUUUHHHH...
I WAS JUST ABOUT TO REMIND YOU THAT I AM NOT THE ONLY AUTHOR OF THE BOOK.
I SHARE IT WITH ONE OF MY CLOSEST FRIENDS!
I LITERALLY CONSIDER HIM A BROTHER. I LOVE THIS MAN!
HE'S THE GUY YOU'RE LOOKING FOR!
HIS NAME IS MIKE OEMING AND YOU SHOULD ARREST HIM!!

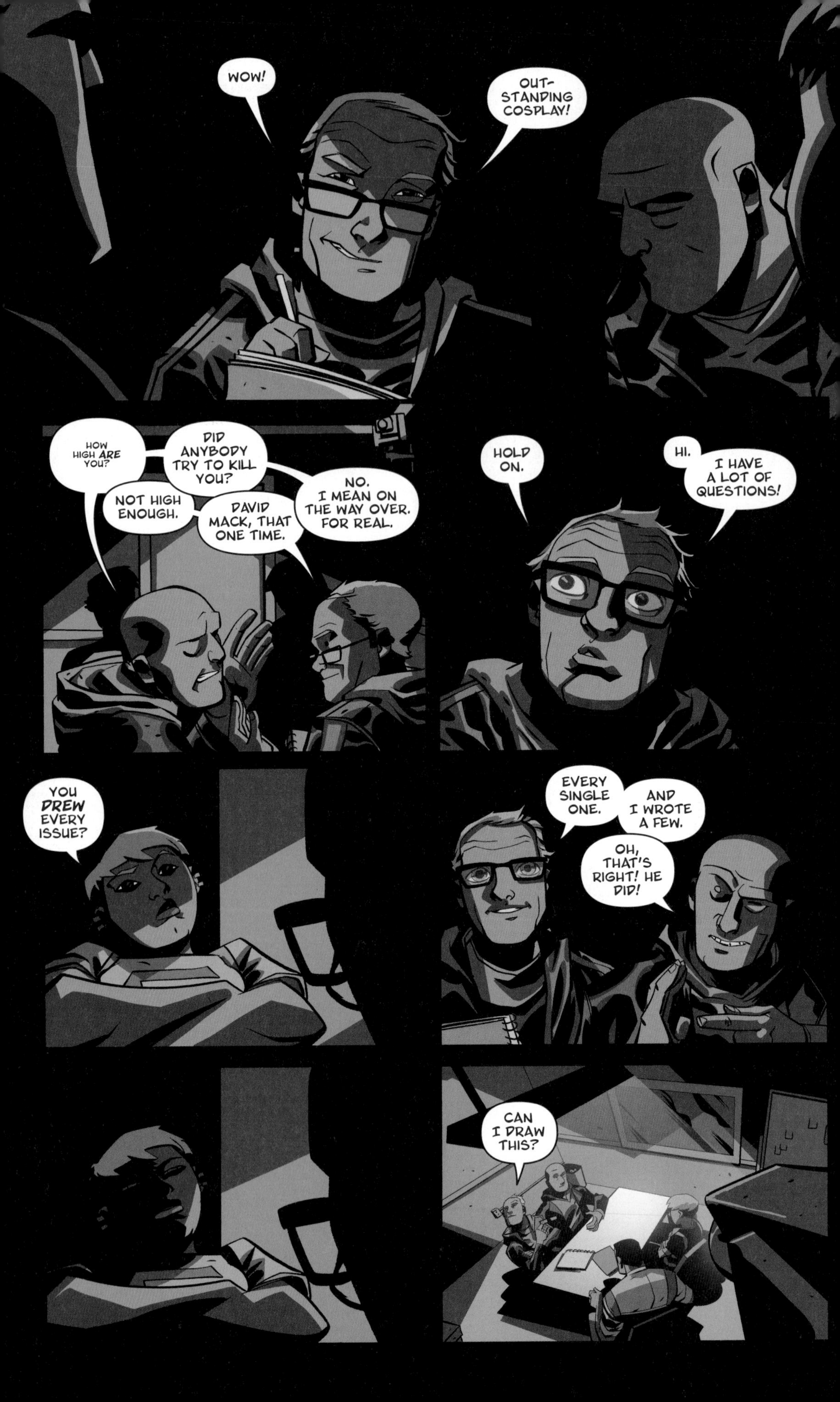
WOW!
OUT-STANDING COSPLAY!
HOW HIGH ARE YOU?
DID ANYBODY TRY TO KILL YOU?
NOT HIGH ENOUGH.
DAVID MACK, THAT ONE TIME.
NO. I MEAN ON THE WAY OVER. FOR REAL.
HOLD ON.
HI.
I HAVE A LOT OF QUESTIONS!
YOU DREW EVERY ISSUE?
EVERY SINGLE ONE.
AND I WROTE A FEW.
OH, THAT'S RIGHT! HE DID!
CAN I DRAW THIS?

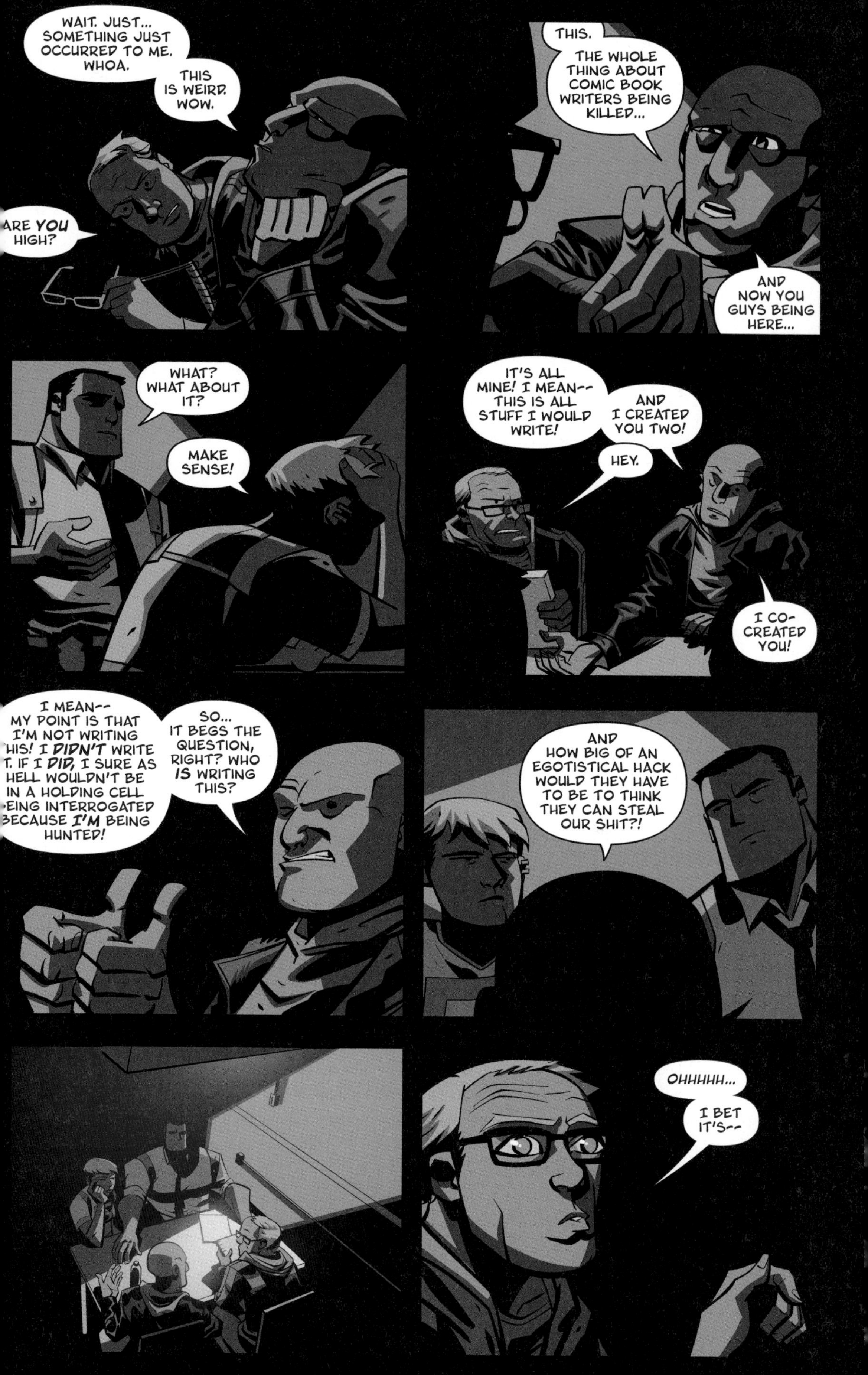

WAIT. JUST... SOMETHING JUST OCCURRED TO ME. WHOA.
THIS IS WEIRD. WOW.
ARE YOU HIGH?
THIS.
THE WHOLE THING ABOUT COMIC BOOK WRITERS BEING KILLED...
AND NOW YOU GUYS BEING HERE...
WHAT? WHAT ABOUT IT?
MAKE SENSE!
IT'S ALL MINE! I MEAN-- THIS IS ALL STUFF I WOULD WRITE!
AND I CREATED YOU TWO!
HEY.
I CO-CREATED YOU!
I MEAN-- MY POINT IS THAT I'M NOT WRITING THIS! I DIDN'T WRITE IT. IF I DID, I SURE AS HELL WOULDN'T BE IN A HOLDING CELL BEING INTERROGATED BECAUSE I'M BEING HUNTED!
SO... IT BEGS THE QUESTION, RIGHT? WHO IS WRITING THIS?
AND HOW BIG OF AN EGOTISTICAL HACK WOULD THEY HAVE TO BE TO THINK THEY CAN STEAL OUR SHIT?!
OHHHHH...
I BET IT'S--

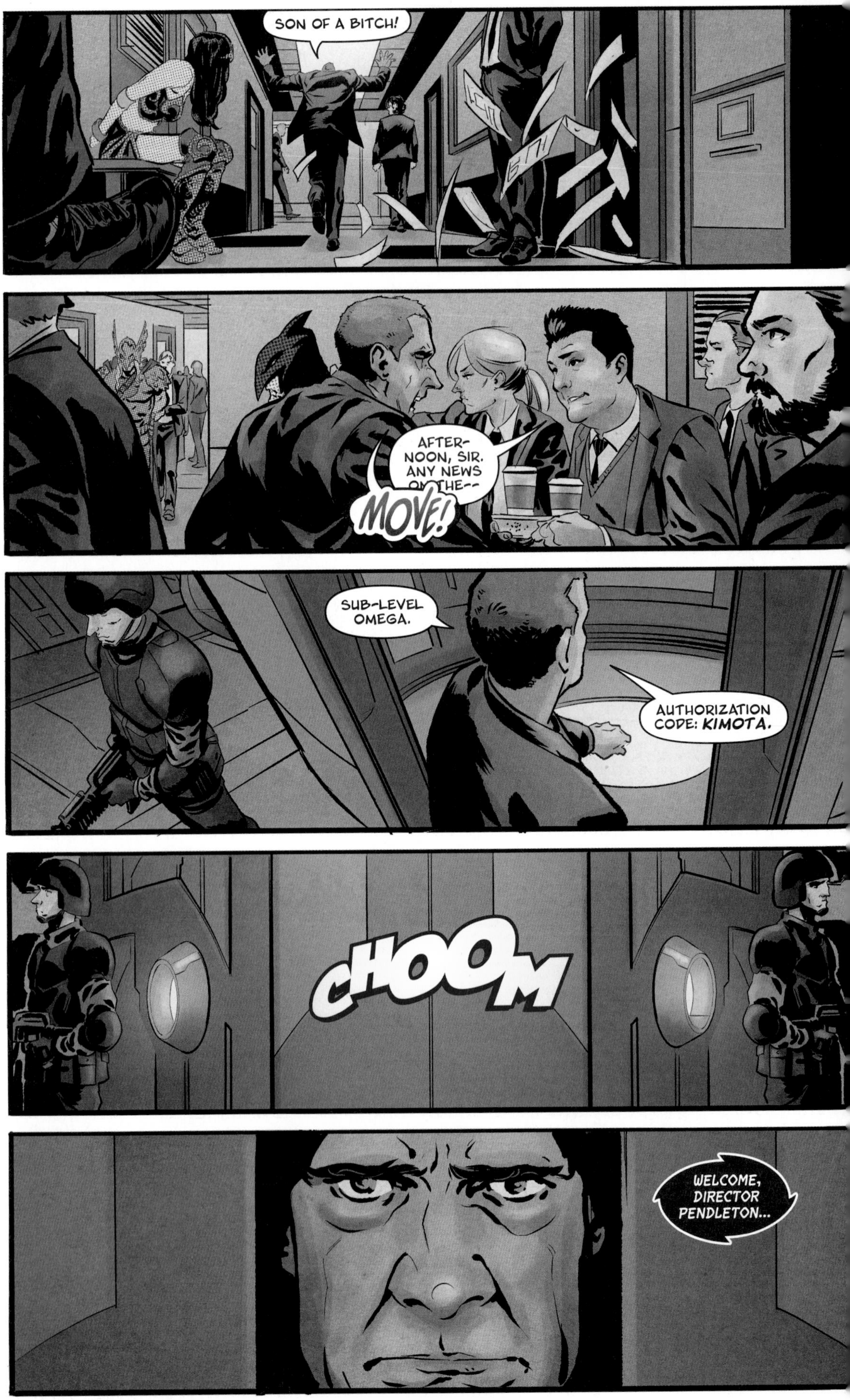

SON OF A BITCH!
AFTER-NOON, SIR. ANY NEWS ON THE--
MOVE!
SUB-LEVEL OMEGA.
AUTHORIZATION CODE: KIMOTA.
CHOOM
WELCOME, DIRECTOR PENDLETON...

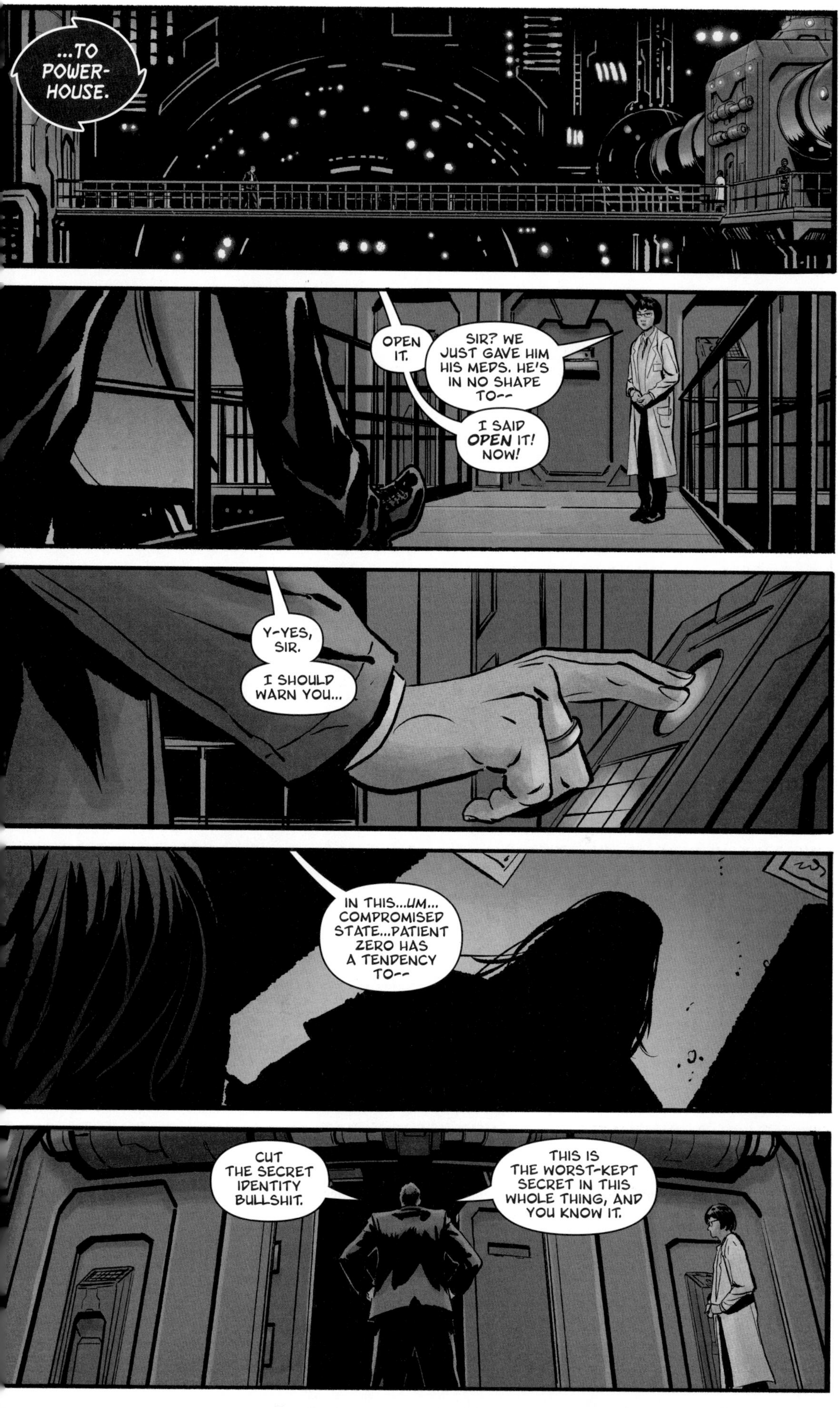
...TO POWER-HOUSE.
OPEN IT.
SIR? WE JUST GAVE HIM HIS MEDS. HE'S IN NO SHAPE TO--
I SAID **OPEN** IT! NOW!
Y-YES, SIR.
I SHOULD WARN YOU...
IN THIS...UM... COMPROMISED STATE...PATIENT ZERO HAS A TENDENCY TO--
CUT THE SECRET IDENTITY BULLSHIT.
THIS IS THE WORST-KEPT SECRET IN THIS WHOLE THING, AND YOU KNOW IT.

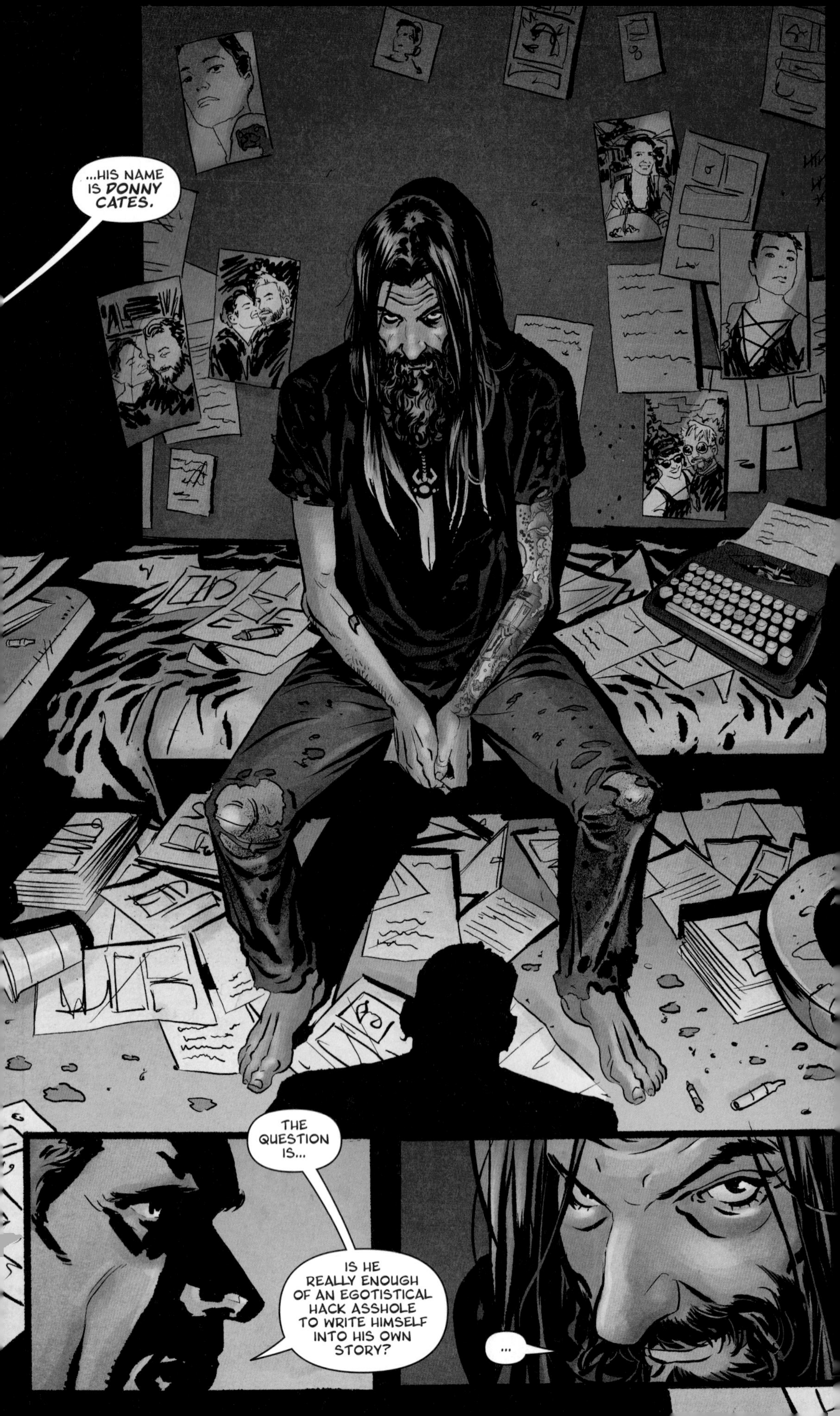
...HIS NAME IS DONNY CATES.
THE QUESTION IS...
IS HE REALLY ENOUGH OF AN EGOTISTICAL HACK ASSHOLE TO WRITE HIMSELF INTO HIS OWN STORY?
...

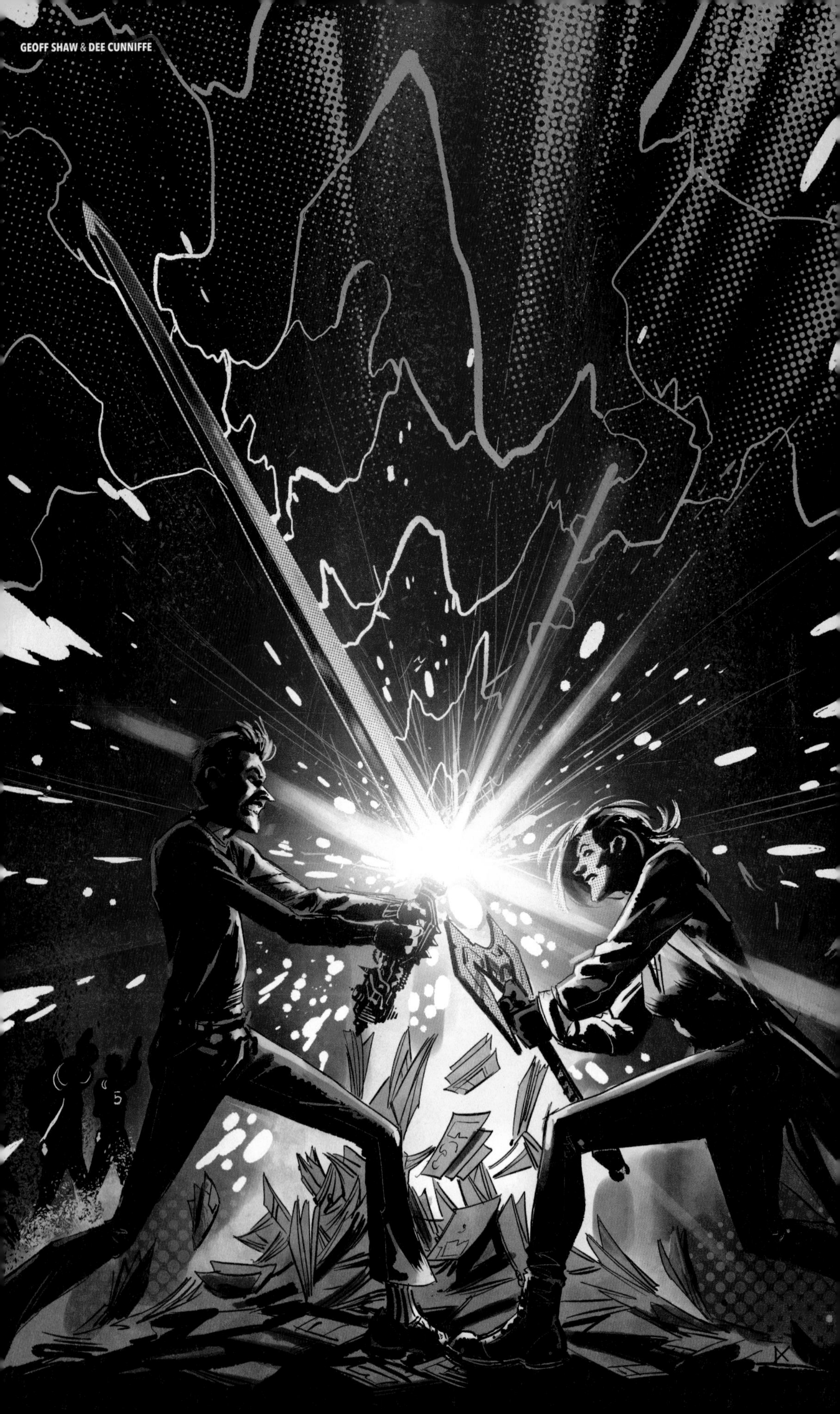
GEOFF SHAW & DEE CUNNIFFE

THE 10-CENT PLAGUE

CHAPTER FOUR

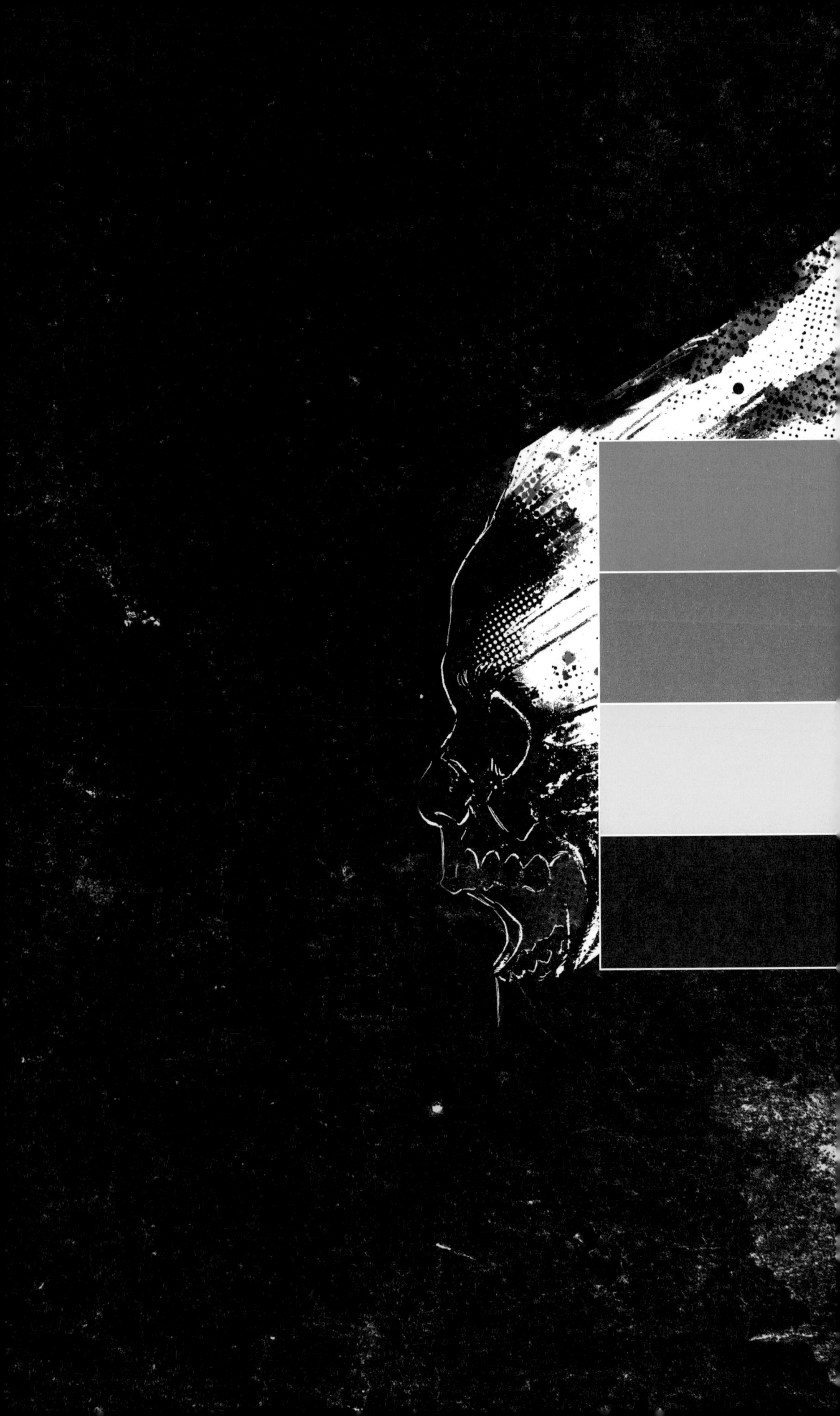

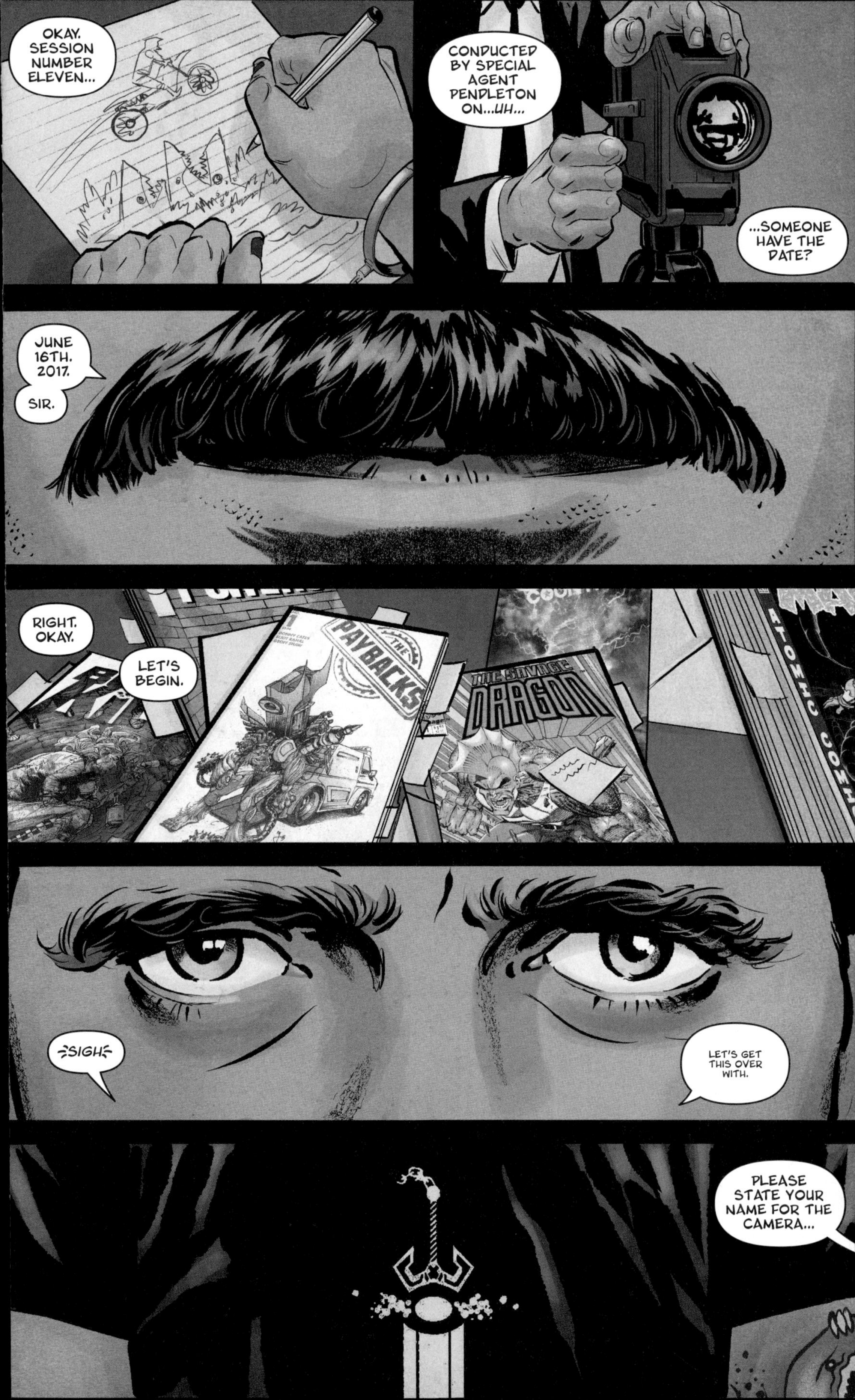
OKAY. SESSION NUMBER ELEVEN...
CONDUCTED BY SPECIAL AGENT PENDLETON ON...UH...
...SOMEONE HAVE THE DATE?
JUNE 16TH. 2017.
SIR.
RIGHT. OKAY.
LET'S BEGIN.
THE PAYBACKS
THE SAVAGE DRAGON
ATOMIC COMIC
SIGH
LET'S GET THIS OVER WITH.
PLEASE STATE YOUR NAME FOR THE CAMERA...

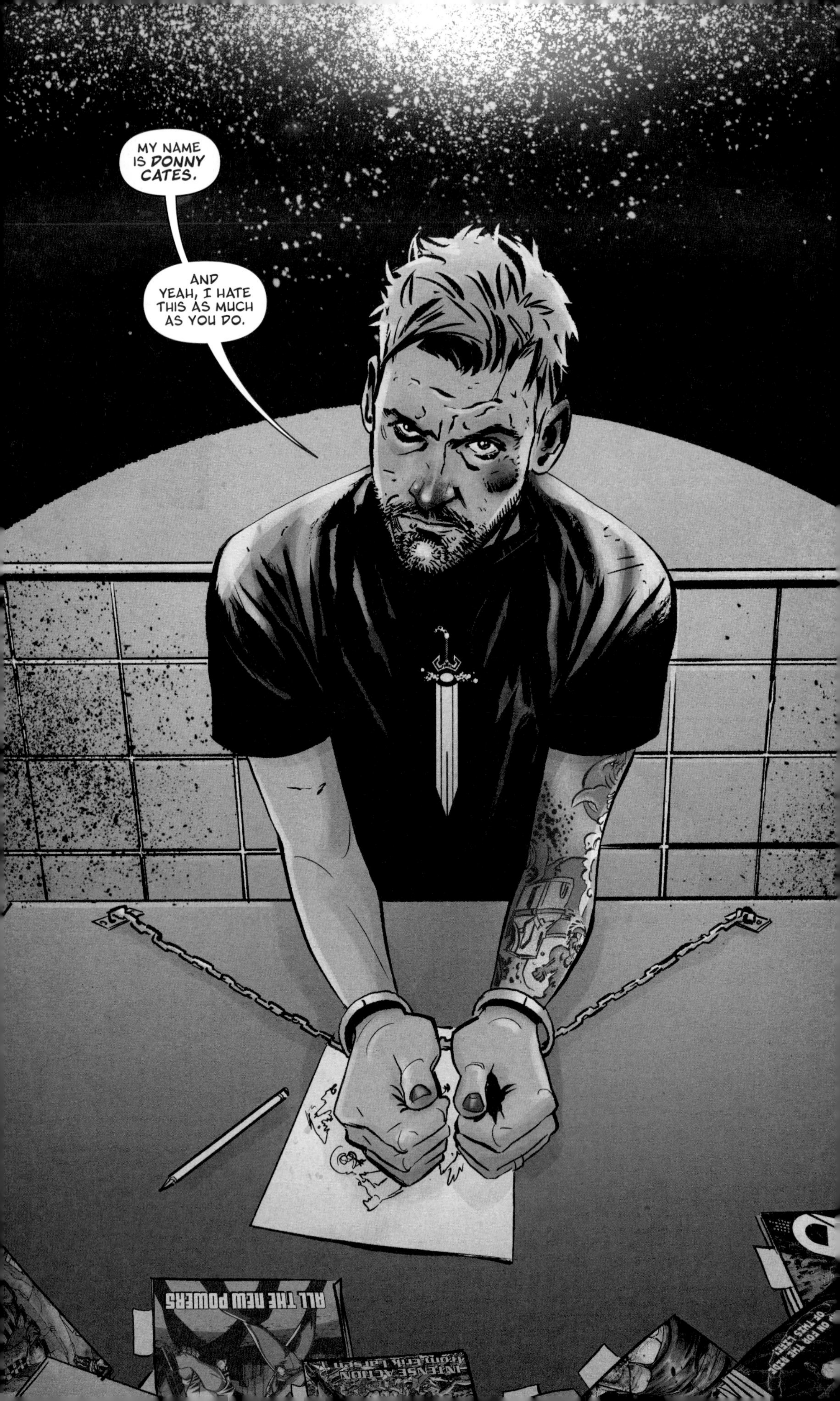
MY NAME IS DONNY CATES.
AND YEAH, I HATE THIS AS MUCH AS YOU DO.
ALL THE NEW POWERS

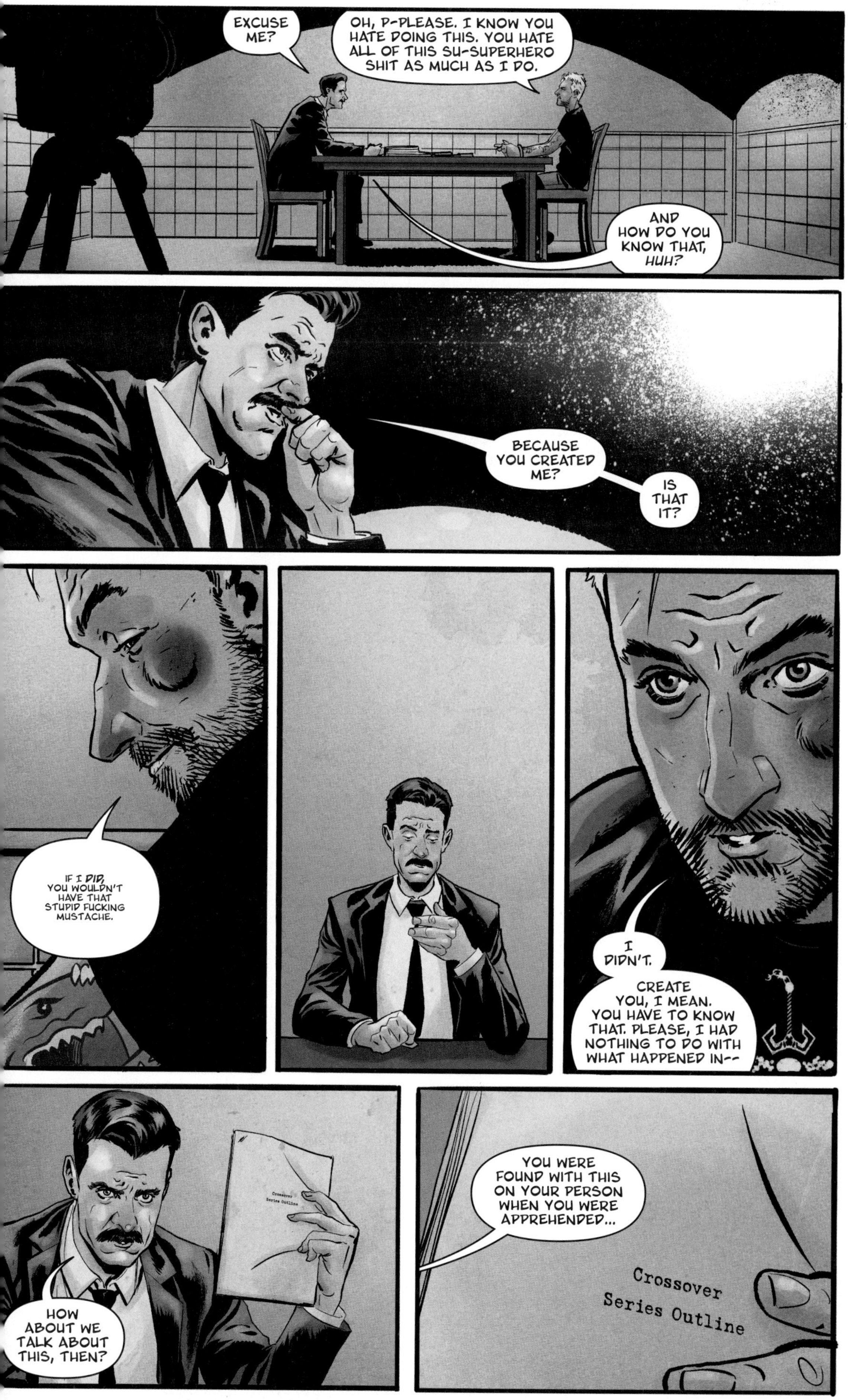
EXCUSE ME?
OH, P-PLEASE. I KNOW YOU HATE DOING THIS. YOU HATE ALL OF THIS SU-SUPERHERO SHIT AS MUCH AS I DO.
AND HOW DO YOU KNOW THAT, *HUH?*
BECAUSE YOU CREATED ME?
IS THAT IT?
IF I *DID,* YOU WOULDN'T HAVE THAT STUPID FUCKING MUSTACHE.
I DIDN'T.
CREATE YOU, I MEAN. YOU HAVE TO KNOW THAT. PLEASE, I HAD NOTHING TO DO WITH WHAT HAPPENED IN--
Crossover Series Outline
HOW ABOUT WE TALK ABOUT THIS, THEN?
YOU WERE FOUND WITH THIS ON YOUR PERSON WHEN YOU WERE APPREHENDED...
Crossover
Series Outline

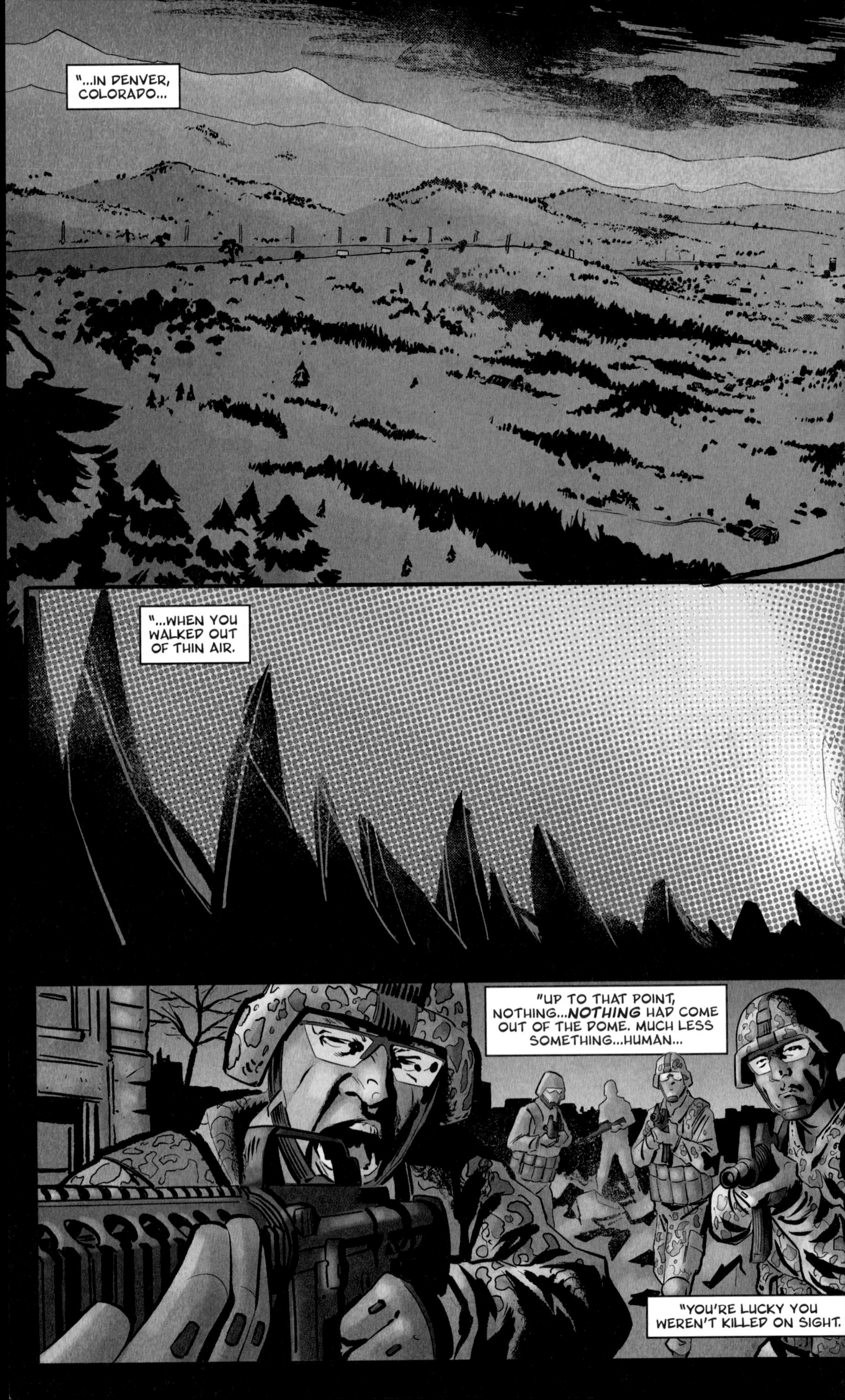
"...IN DENVER, COLORADO...
"...WHEN YOU WALKED OUT OF THIN AIR.
"UP TO THAT POINT, NOTHING...*NOTHING* HAD COME OUT OF THE DOME. MUCH LESS SOMETHING...HUMAN...
"YOU'RE LUCKY YOU WEREN'T KILLED ON SIGHT.

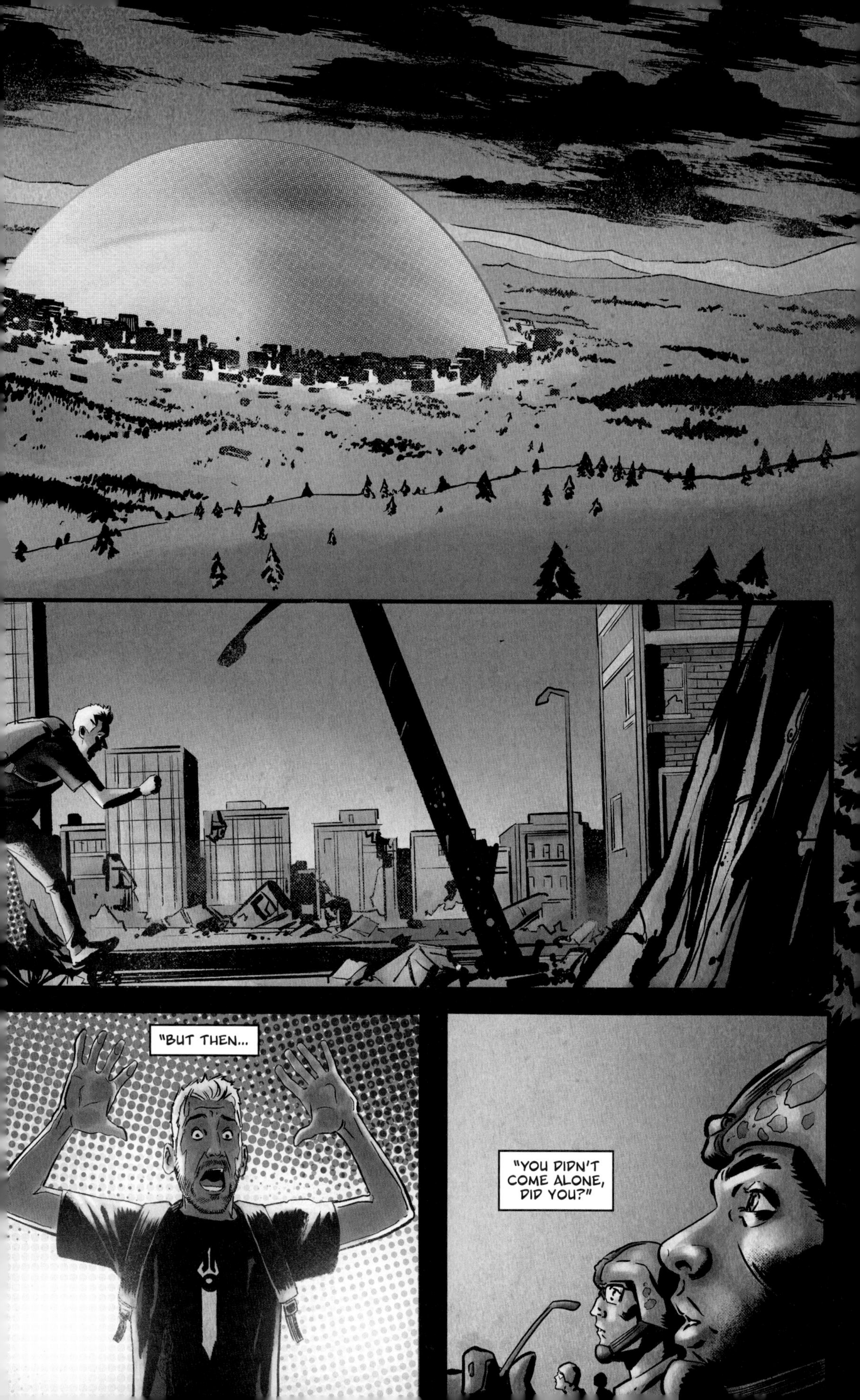
"BUT THEN...
"YOU DIDN'T
COME ALONE,
DID YOU?"

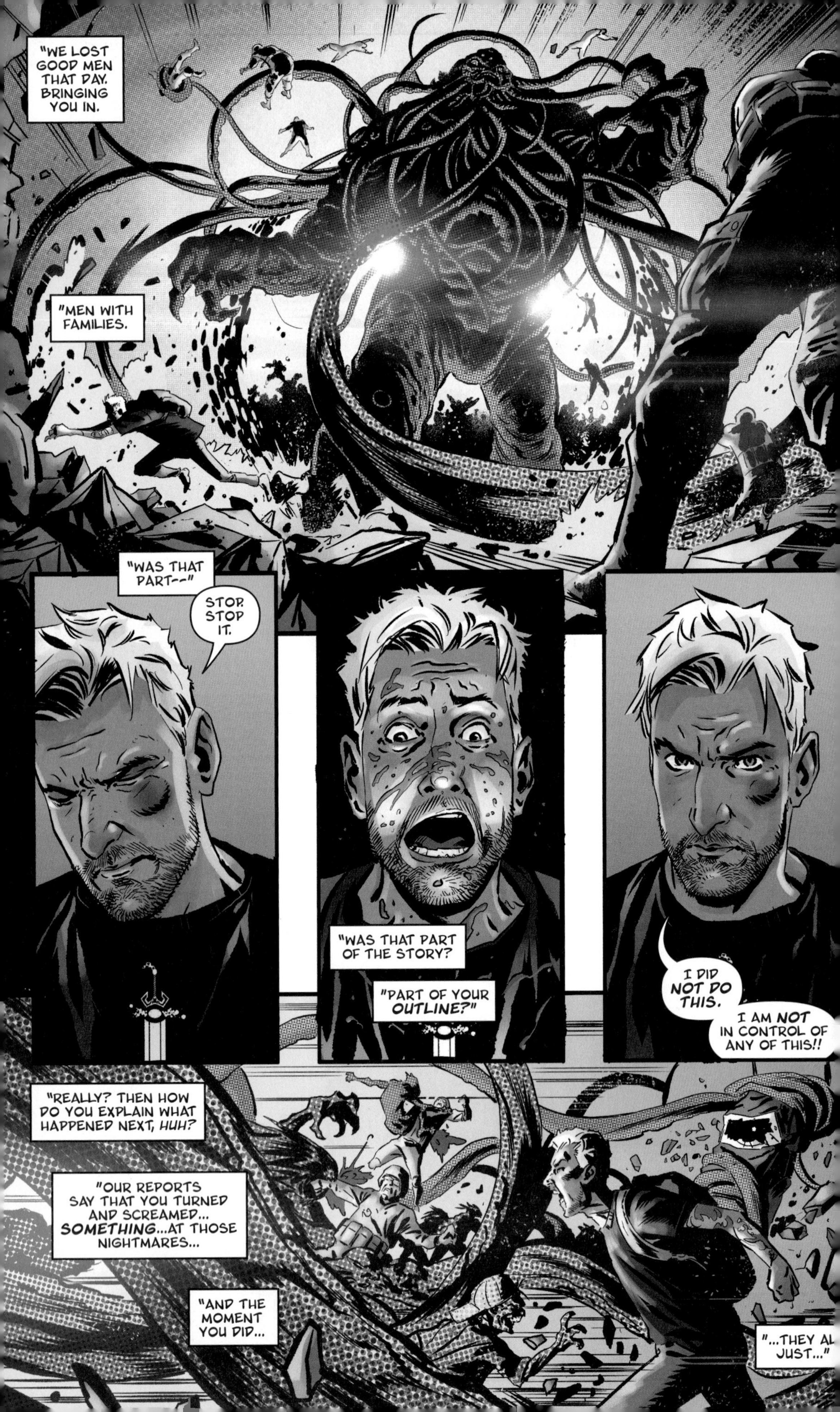
"WE LOST GOOD MEN THAT DAY. BRINGING YOU IN.
"MEN WITH FAMILIES.
"WAS THAT PART--"
STOP. STOP IT.
"WAS THAT PART OF THE STORY?
"PART OF YOUR *OUTLINE?*"
I DID **NOT DO THIS.**
I AM **NOT** IN CONTROL OF ANY OF THIS!!
"REALLY? THEN HOW DO YOU EXPLAIN WHAT HAPPENED NEXT, *HUH?*
"OUR REPORTS SAY THAT YOU TURNED AND SCREAMED... **SOMETHING**...AT THOSE NIGHTMARES...
"AND THE MOMENT YOU DID...
"...THEY AL JUST..."

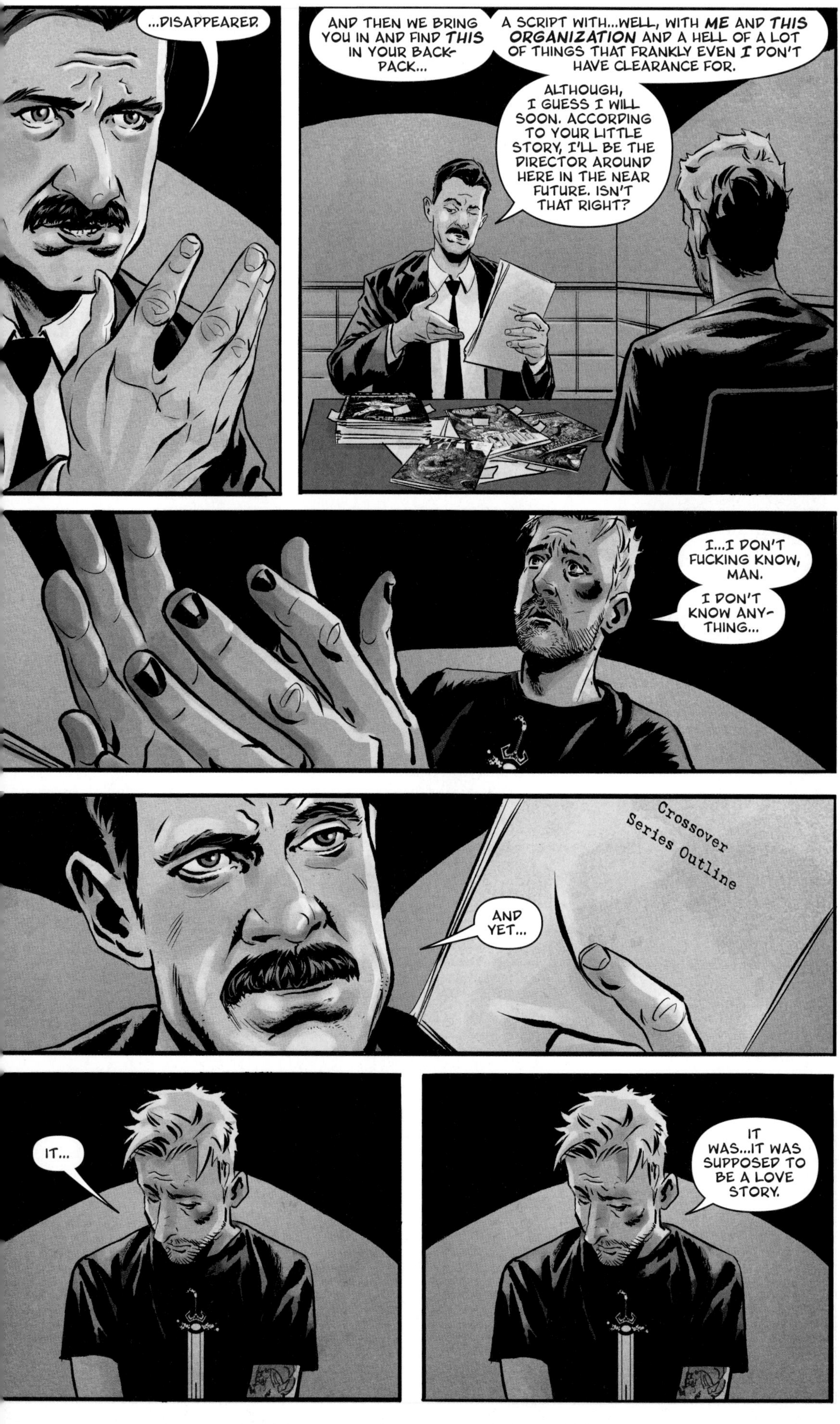
...DISAPPEARED.
AND THEN WE BRING YOU IN AND FIND THIS IN YOUR BACK-PACK...
A SCRIPT WITH...WELL, WITH ME AND THIS ORGANIZATION AND A HELL OF A LOT OF THINGS THAT FRANKLY EVEN I DON'T HAVE CLEARANCE FOR.
ALTHOUGH, I GUESS I WILL SOON. ACCORDING TO YOUR LITTLE STORY, I'LL BE THE DIRECTOR AROUND HERE IN THE NEAR FUTURE. ISN'T THAT RIGHT?
I...I DON'T FUCKING KNOW, MAN.
I DON'T KNOW ANY-THING...
Crossover
Series Outline
AND YET...
IT...
IT WAS...IT WAS SUPPOSED TO BE A LOVE STORY.

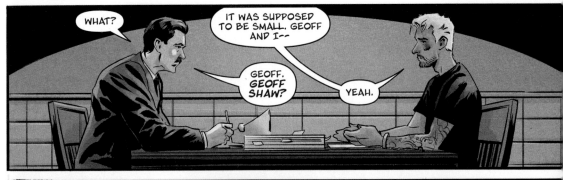

WHAT?

IT WAS SUPPOSED TO BE SMALL. GEOFF AND I--

GEOFF. GEOFF SHAW?

YEAH.

WE WANTED TO DO SOMETHING PERSONAL AND SMALL AFTER OUR MARVEL STUFF. SOMETHING LIKE GOD COUNTRY. BUT--

LIKE WHAT?

NOTHING.

LOOK...THE BOOK I WROTE. THAT OUTLINE...IT JUST... GOT AWAY FROM ME. IT GOT TOO BIG, SO I SHELVED IT AND I WROTE THANOS INSTEAD.

BUT GEOFF...HE NEVER LET IT GO. I DON'T KNOW. I DON'T KNOW IF THAT'S WHY HE--

WHERE IS GEOFF SHAW?

HE...HE LIVES IN DENVER. OR...HE LIVED IN DENVER. I DON'T KNOW.

WE WERE VISITING HIM. HE... I DON'T KNOW. HE WASN'T HIMSELF, SO, WE WENT TO GO CHECK ON HIM. ME...AND...

...AND MEGAN.

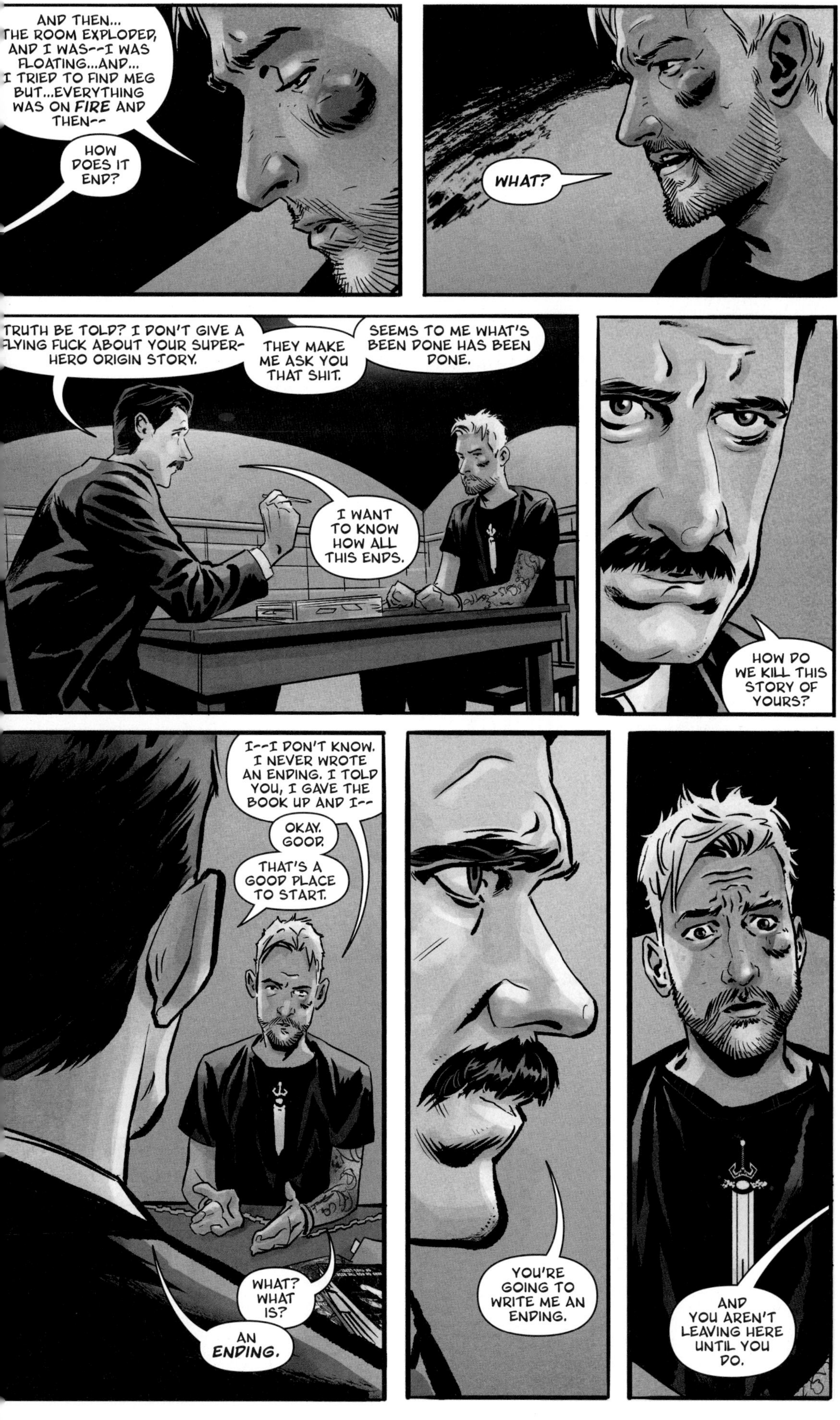
AND THEN... THE ROOM EXPLODED, AND I WAS--I WAS FLOATING...AND... I TRIED TO FIND MEG BUT...EVERYTHING WAS ON FIRE AND THEN--
HOW DOES IT END?
WHAT?
TRUTH BE TOLD? I DON'T GIVE A FLYING FUCK ABOUT YOUR SUPER-HERO ORIGIN STORY.
THEY MAKE ME ASK YOU THAT SHIT.
SEEMS TO ME WHAT'S BEEN DONE HAS BEEN DONE.
I WANT TO KNOW HOW ALL THIS ENDS.
HOW DO WE KILL THIS STORY OF YOURS?
I--I DON'T KNOW. I NEVER WROTE AN ENDING. I TOLD YOU, I GAVE THE BOOK UP AND I--
OKAY. GOOD.
THAT'S A GOOD PLACE TO START.
WHAT? WHAT IS?
AN ENDING.
YOU'RE GOING TO WRITE ME AN ENDING.
AND YOU AREN'T LEAVING HERE UNTIL YOU DO.

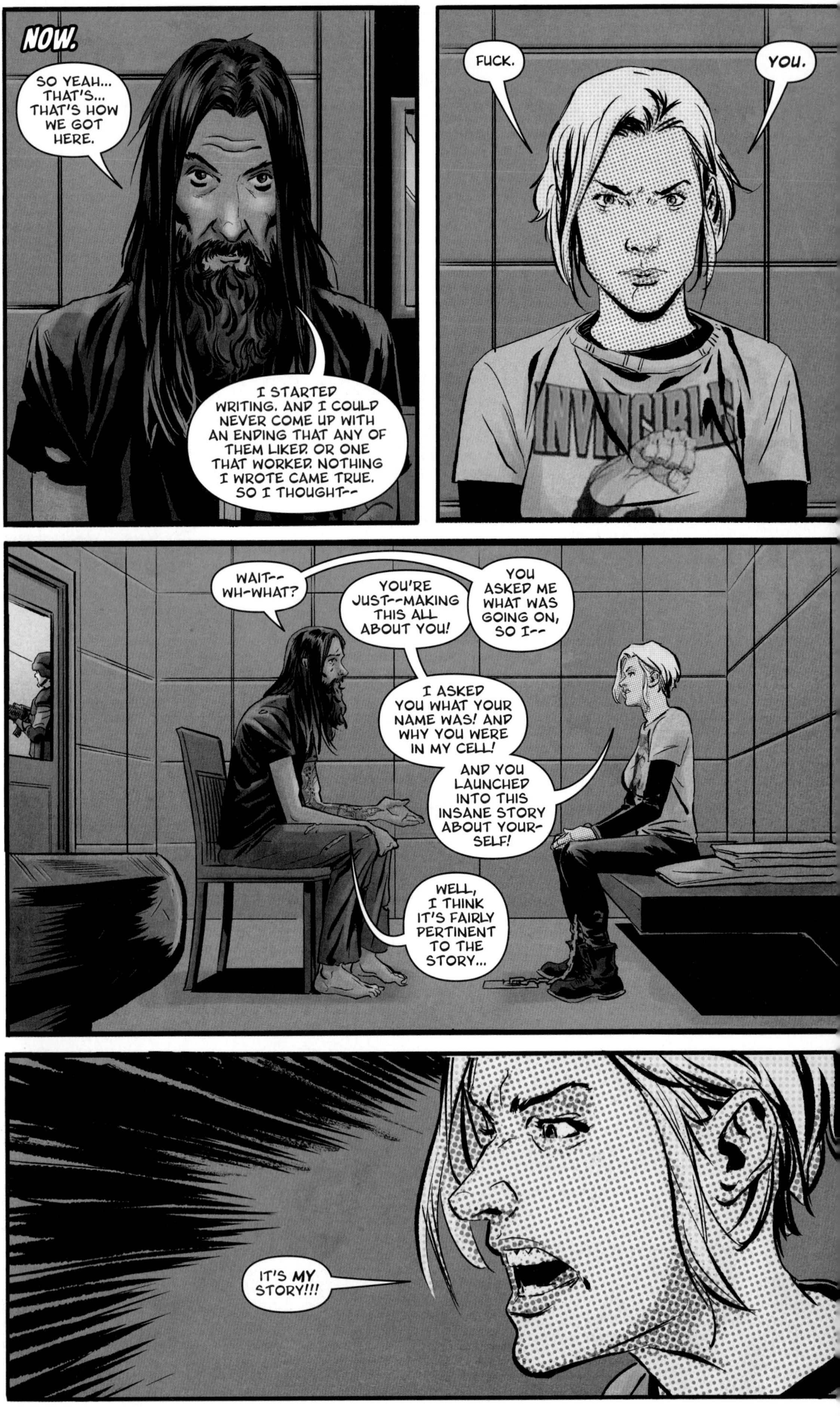
NOW.
SO YEAH... THAT'S... THAT'S HOW WE GOT HERE.
I STARTED WRITING. AND I COULD NEVER COME UP WITH AN ENDING THAT ANY OF THEM LIKED. OR ONE THAT WORKED. NOTHING I WROTE CAME TRUE. SO I THOUGHT--
FUCK.
YOU.
INVINCIBLE
WAIT-- WH-WHAT?
YOU'RE JUST--MAKING THIS ALL ABOUT YOU!
YOU ASKED ME WHAT WAS GOING ON, SO I--
I ASKED YOU WHAT YOUR NAME WAS! AND WHY YOU WERE IN MY CELL!
AND YOU LAUNCHED INTO THIS INSANE STORY ABOUT YOURSELF!
WELL, I THINK IT'S FAIRLY PERTINENT TO THE STORY...
IT'S MY STORY!!!

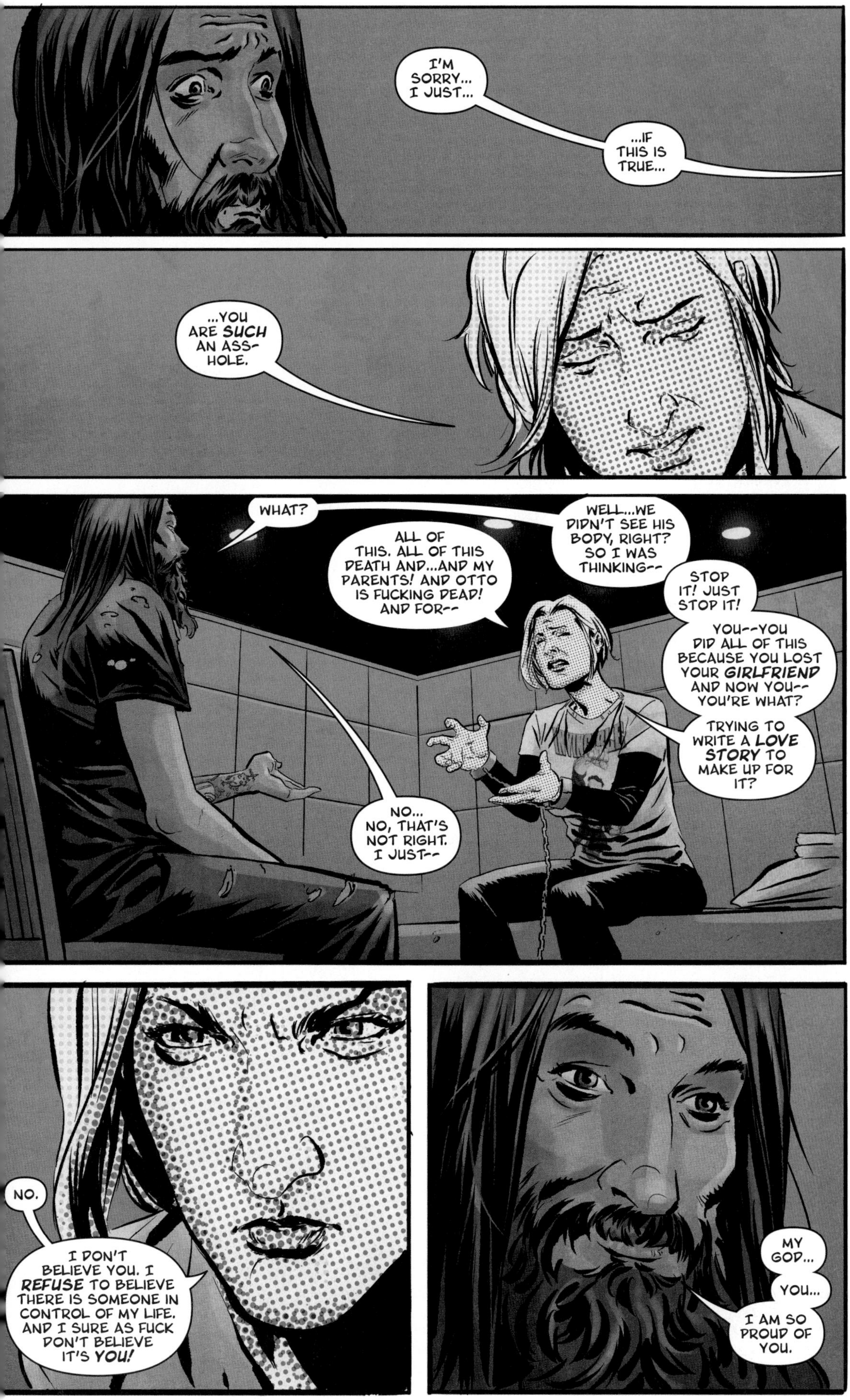
I'M SORRY... I JUST...
...IF THIS IS TRUE...
...YOU ARE SUCH AN ASS-HOLE.
WHAT?
WELL...WE DIDN'T SEE HIS BODY, RIGHT? SO I WAS THINKING--
ALL OF THIS. ALL OF THIS DEATH AND...AND MY PARENTS! AND OTTO IS FUCKING DEAD! AND FOR--
STOP IT! JUST STOP IT!
YOU--YOU DID ALL OF THIS BECAUSE YOU LOST YOUR GIRLFRIEND AND NOW YOU-- YOU'RE WHAT?
TRYING TO WRITE A LOVE STORY TO MAKE UP FOR IT?
NO... NO, THAT'S NOT RIGHT. I JUST--
NO.
I DON'T BELIEVE YOU. I REFUSE TO BELIEVE THERE IS SOMEONE IN CONTROL OF MY LIFE. AND I SURE AS FUCK DON'T BELIEVE IT'S YOU!
MY GOD...
YOU...
I AM SO PROUD OF YOU.

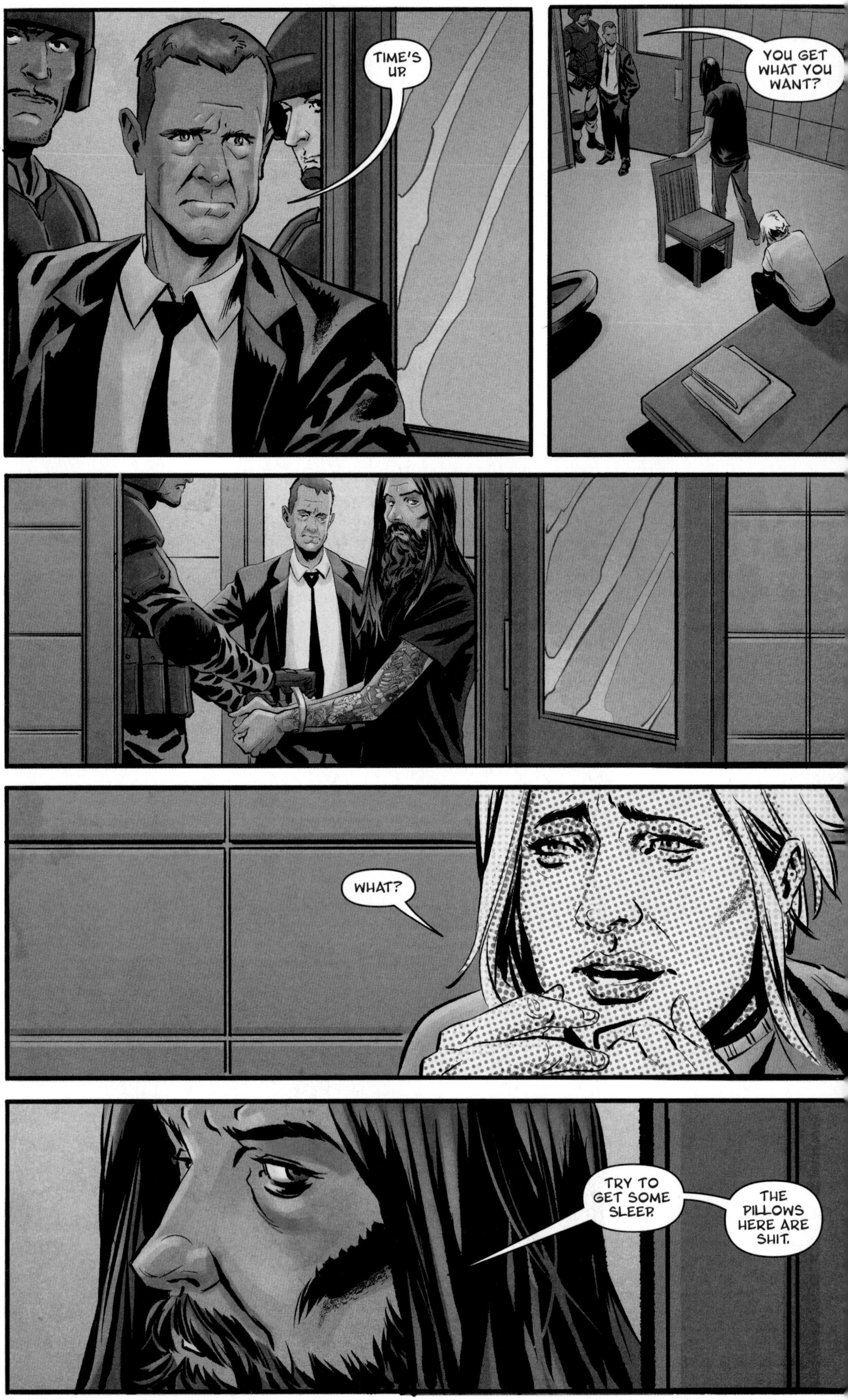
TIME'S UP.
YOU GET WHAT YOU WANT?
WHAT?
TRY TO GET SOME SLEEP.
THE PILLOWS HERE ARE SHIT.

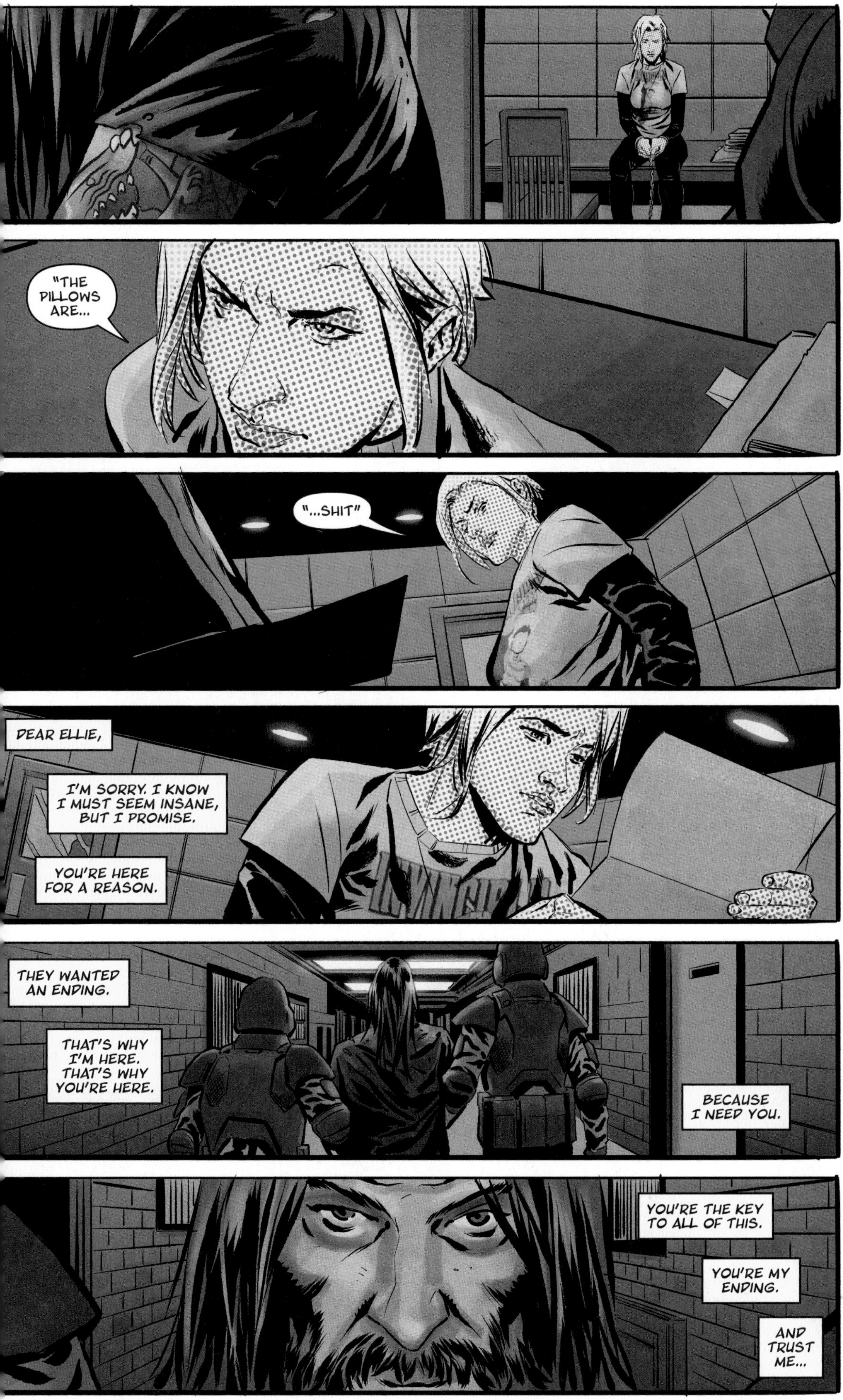

"THE PILLOWS ARE...
"...SHIT"
DEAR ELLIE,
I'M SORRY. I KNOW I MUST SEEM INSANE, BUT I PROMISE.
YOU'RE HERE FOR A REASON.
THEY WANTED AN ENDING.
THAT'S WHY I'M HERE. THAT'S WHY YOU'RE HERE.
BECAUSE I NEED YOU.
YOU'RE THE KEY TO ALL OF THIS.
YOU'RE MY ENDING.
AND TRUST ME...

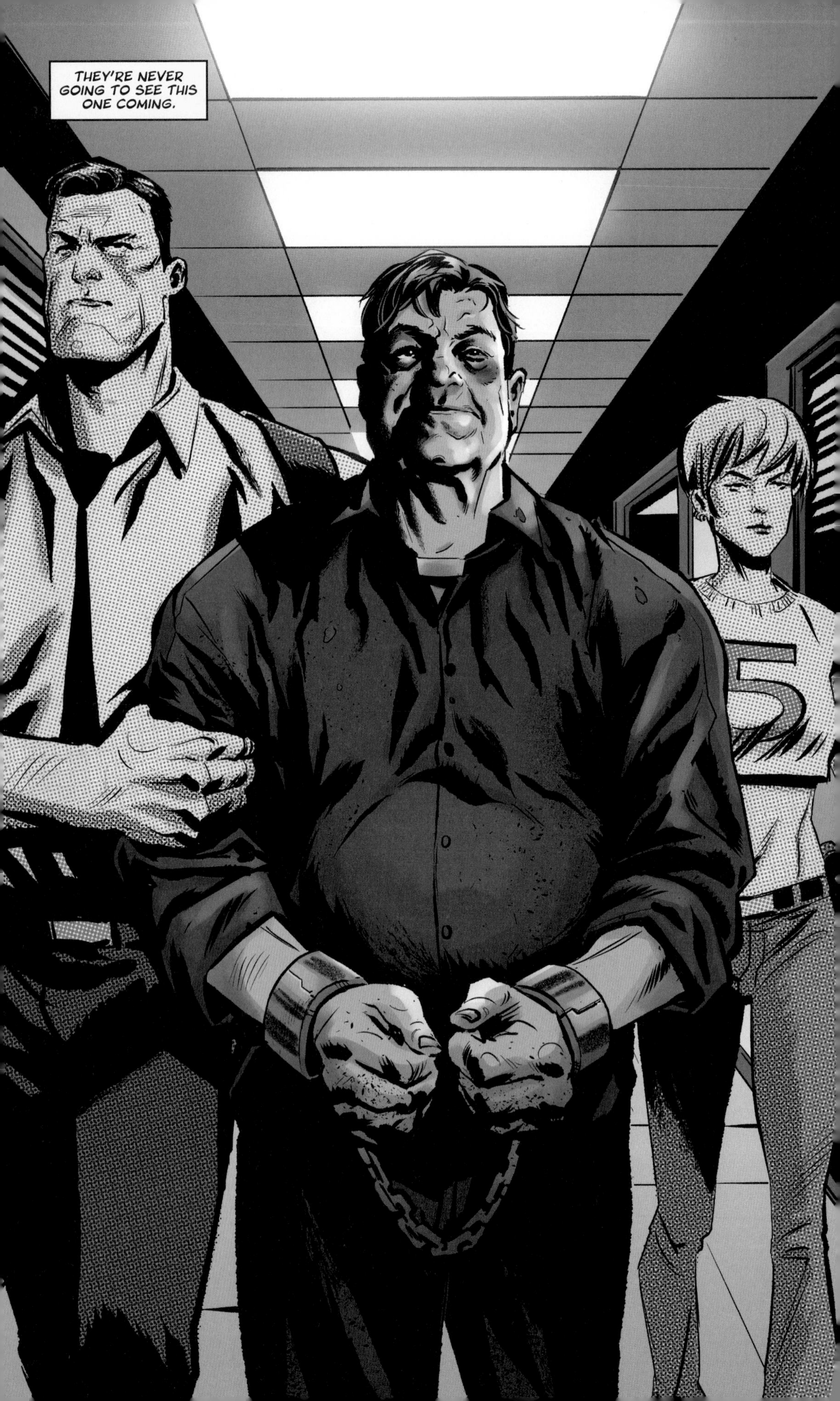
THEY'RE NEVER GOING TO SEE THIS ONE COMING.

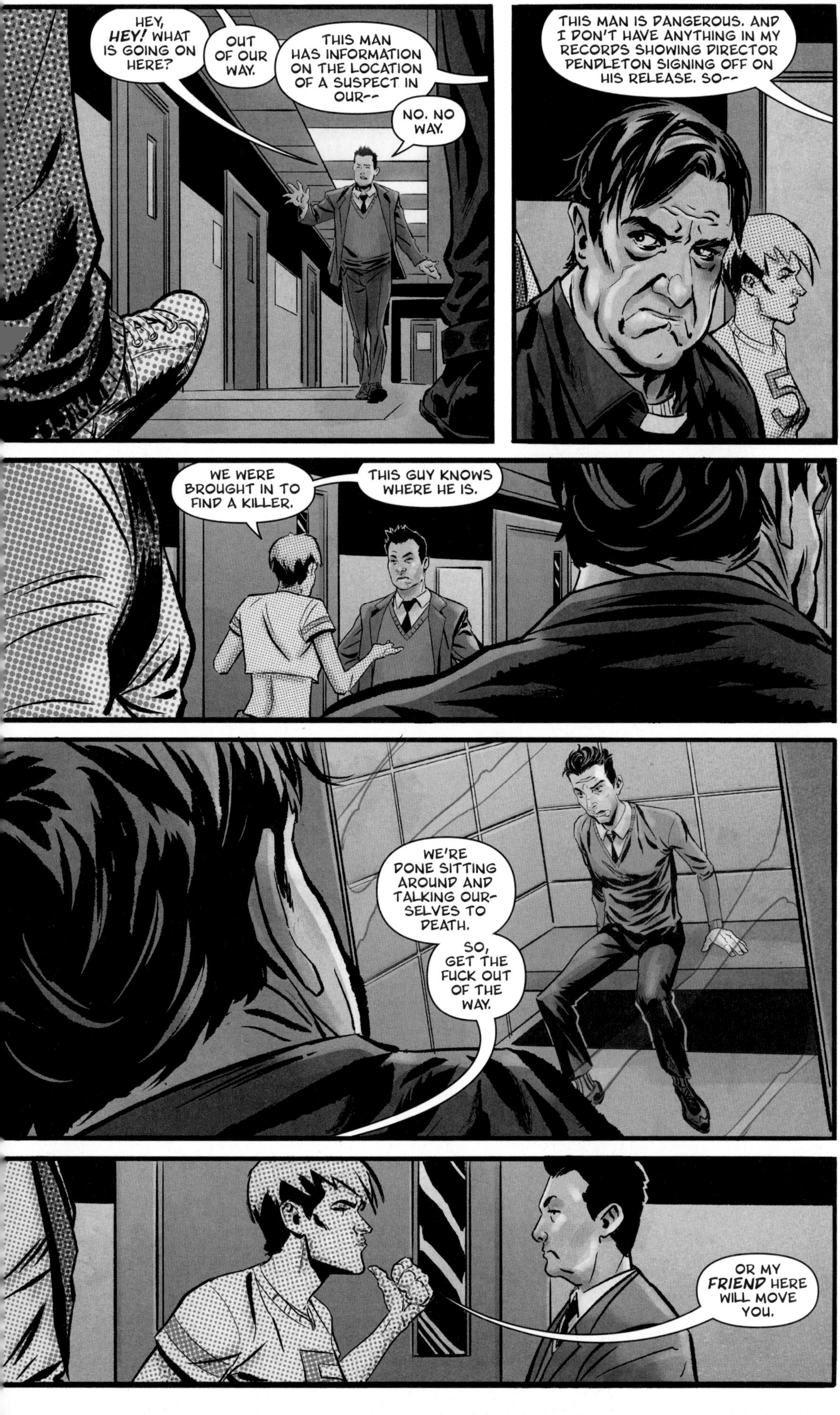
HEY, HEY! WHAT IS GOING ON HERE?
OUT OF OUR WAY.
THIS MAN HAS INFORMATION ON THE LOCATION OF A SUSPECT IN OUR--
NO. NO WAY.
THIS MAN IS DANGEROUS. AND I DON'T HAVE ANYTHING IN MY RECORDS SHOWING DIRECTOR PENDLETON SIGNING OFF ON HIS RELEASE. SO--
WE WERE BROUGHT IN TO FIND A KILLER.
THIS GUY KNOWS WHERE HE IS.
WE'RE DONE SITTING AROUND AND TALKING OURSELVES TO DEATH.
SO, GET THE FUCK OUT OF THE WAY.
OR MY FRIEND HERE WILL MOVE YOU.

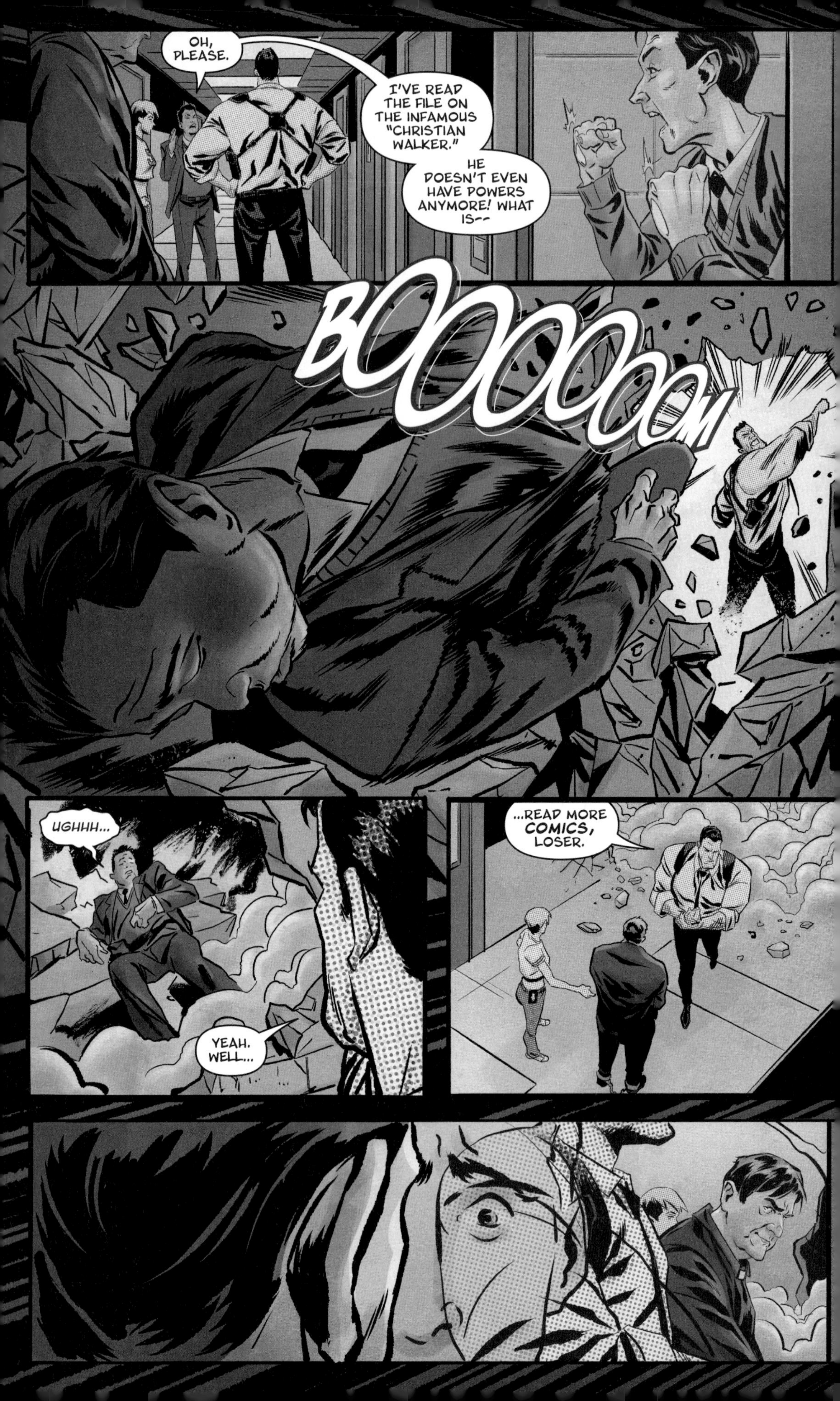
OH, PLEASE.
I'VE READ THE FILE ON THE INFAMOUS "CHRISTIAN WALKER."
HE DOESN'T EVEN HAVE POWERS ANYMORE! WHAT IS--
BOOOOOOOM
UGHHH...
YEAH. WELL...
...READ MORE COMICS, LOSER.

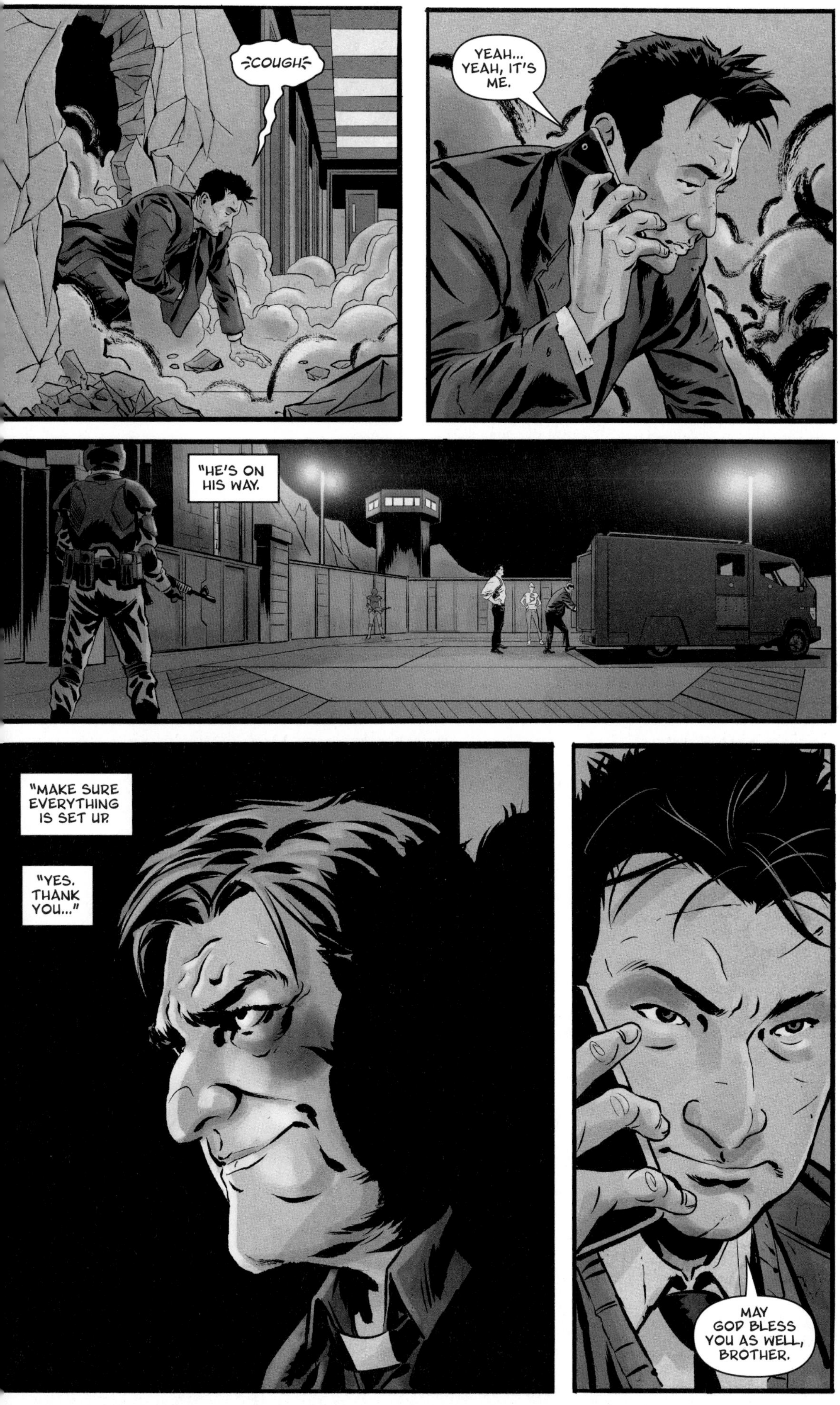
COUGH
YEAH... YEAH, IT'S ME.
"HE'S ON HIS WAY.
"MAKE SURE EVERYTHING IS SET UP.
"YES. THANK YOU..."
MAY GOD BLESS YOU AS WELL, BROTHER.

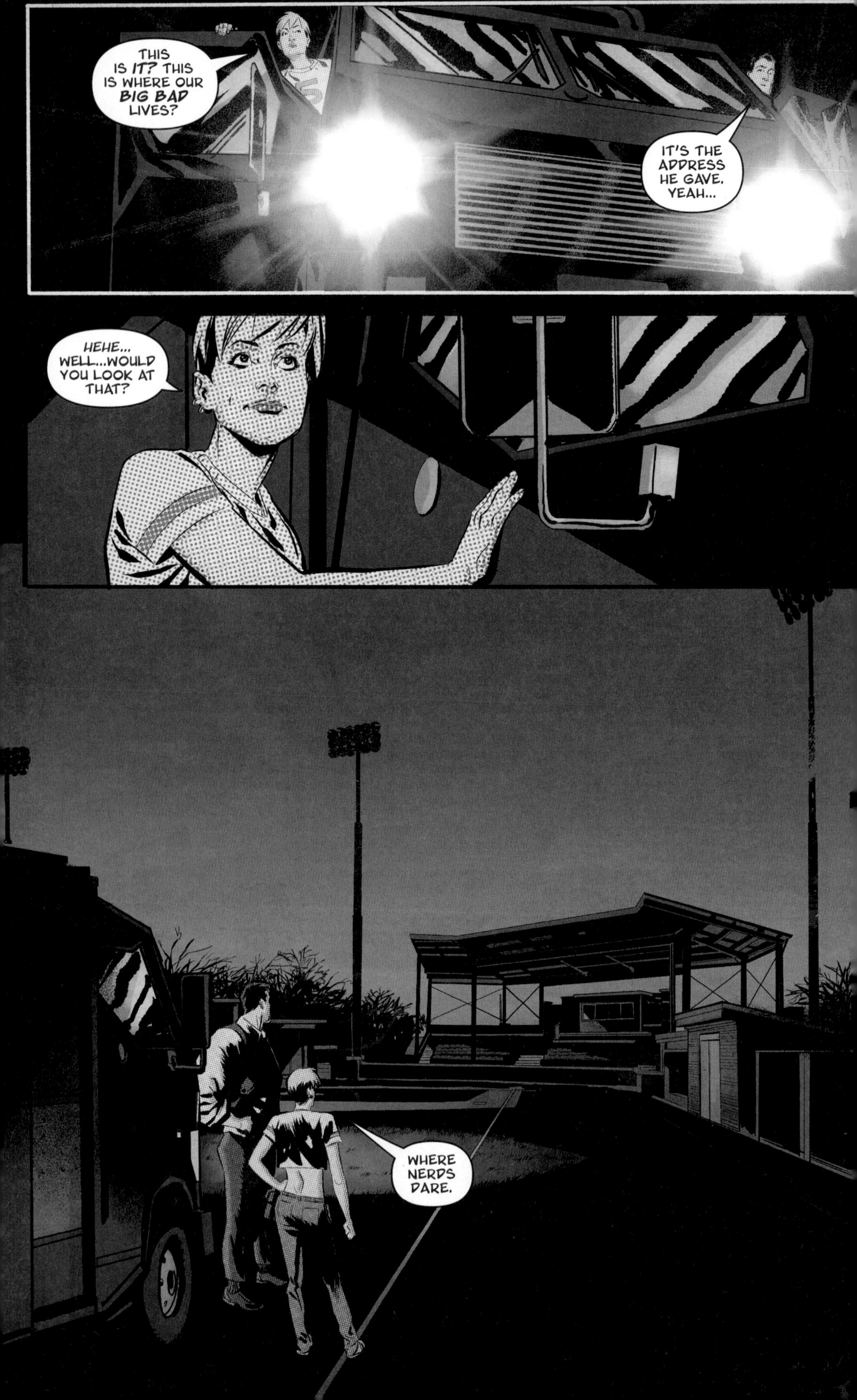

THIS IS IT? THIS IS WHERE OUR BIG BAD LIVES?
IT'S THE ADDRESS HE GAVE. YEAH...
HEHE... WELL...WOULD YOU LOOK AT THAT?
WHERE NERDS DARE.

OKAY PREACHER. YOUR TIME TO SHINE.

WHERE IS THIS ASSHOLE?

OH, HE'S HERE. I ASSURE YOU. I CAN *FEEL* HIM.

YOU'RE ABOUT TO FEEL YOUR BALLS IN YOUR FUCKING *THROAT* IF YOU DON'T STOP THE HIGH AND MIGHTY BULLSHIT, AND--

CHOOM CHOOOM CHOOM

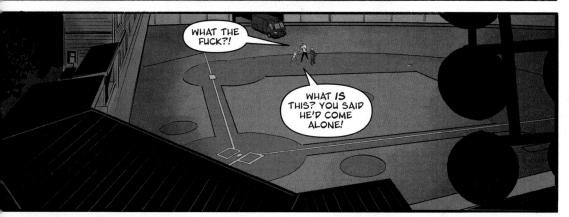

WHAT THE FUCK?!

WHAT *IS* THIS? YOU SAID HE'D COME ALONE!

OH, WE'RE NEVER ALONE, ARE WE?

THERE IS ALWAYS SOME-THING *BIGGER* WATCHING OVER US.

ISN'T THAT RIGHT, FRIEND?

WHO GIVES A SHIT?

NOW, YOU TWO, STAY WHERE THE *FUCK* YOU ARE...

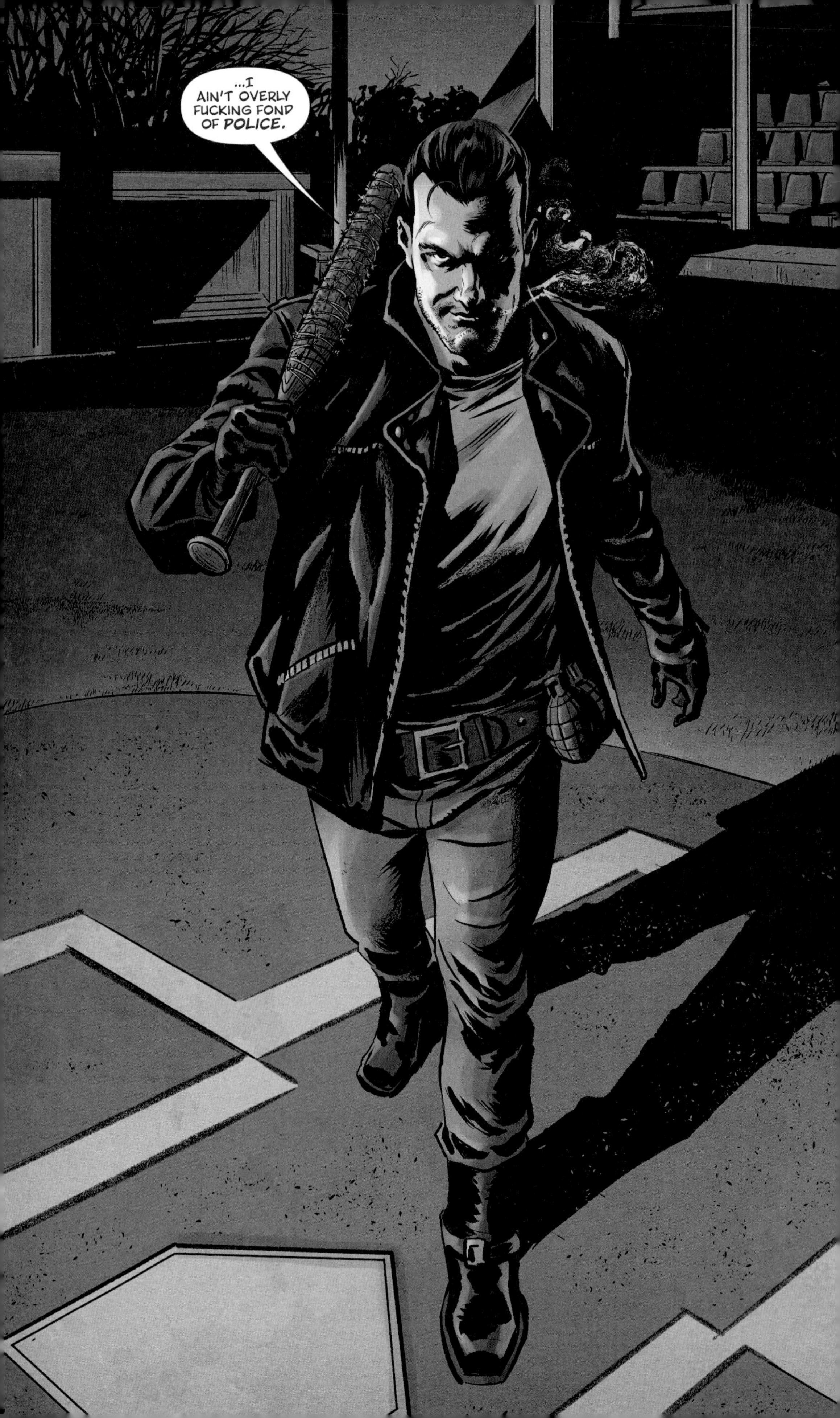
...I AIN'T OVERLY FUCKING FOND OF POLICE.

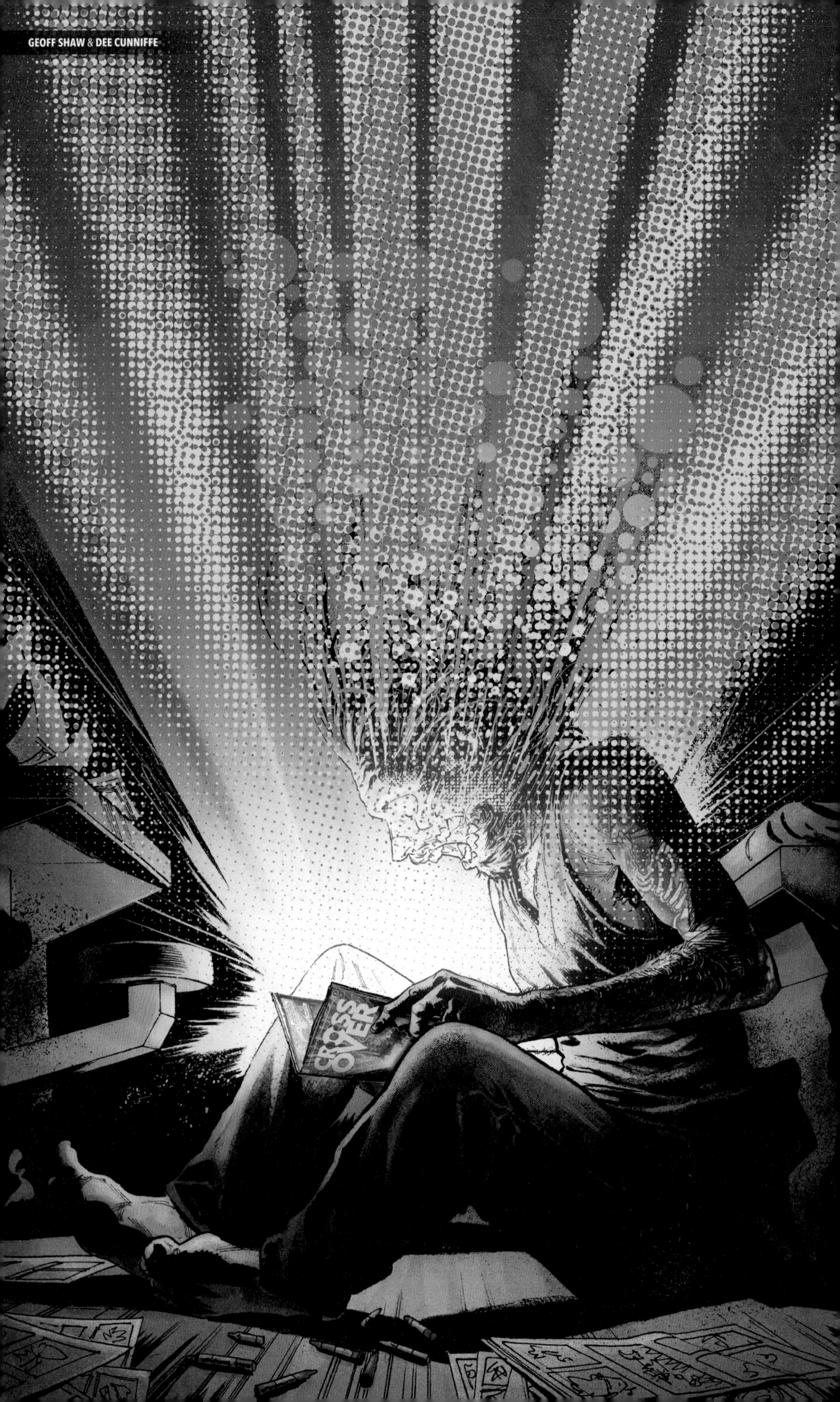
CROSS OVER

THE 10-CENT PLAGUE

CHAPTER FIVE

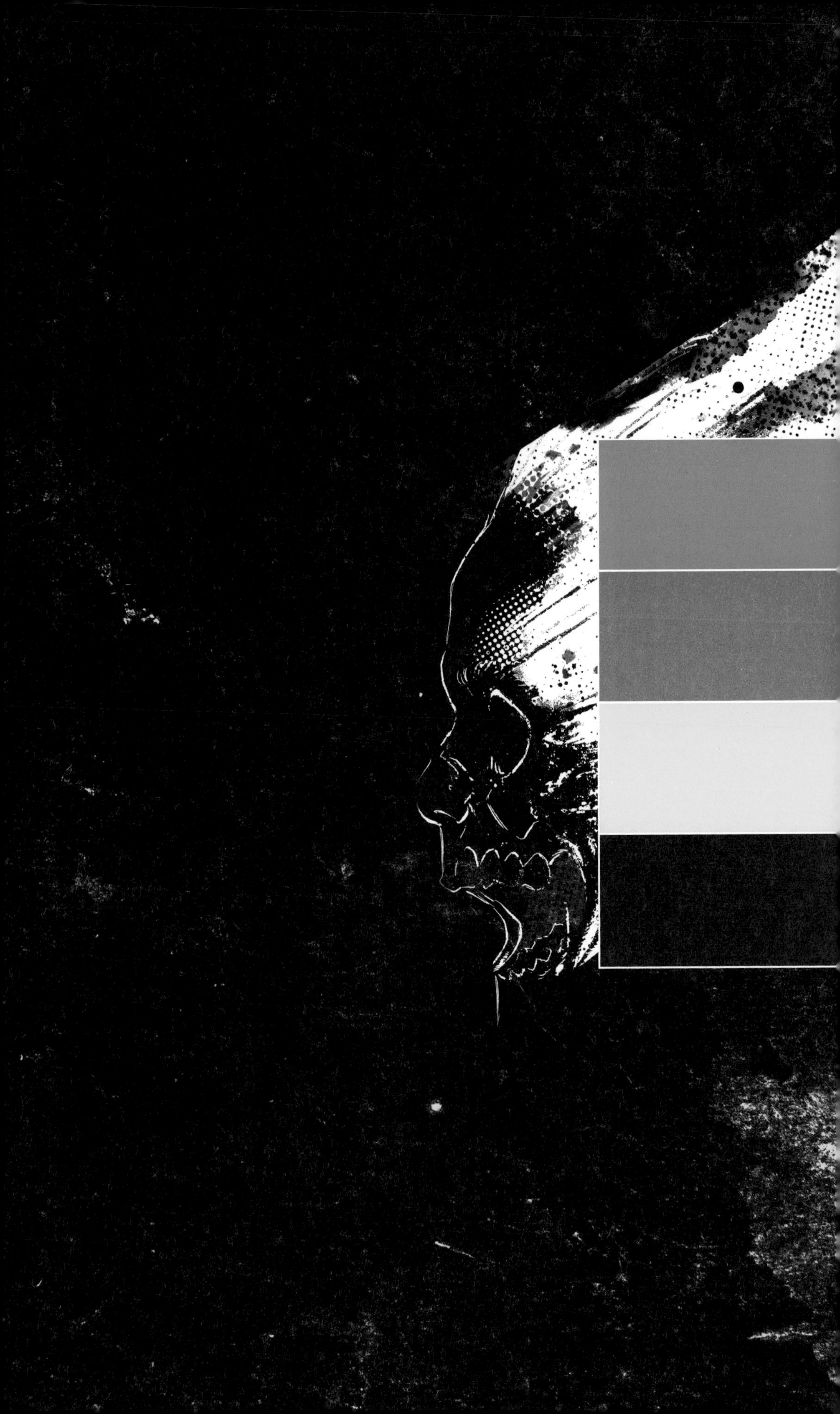

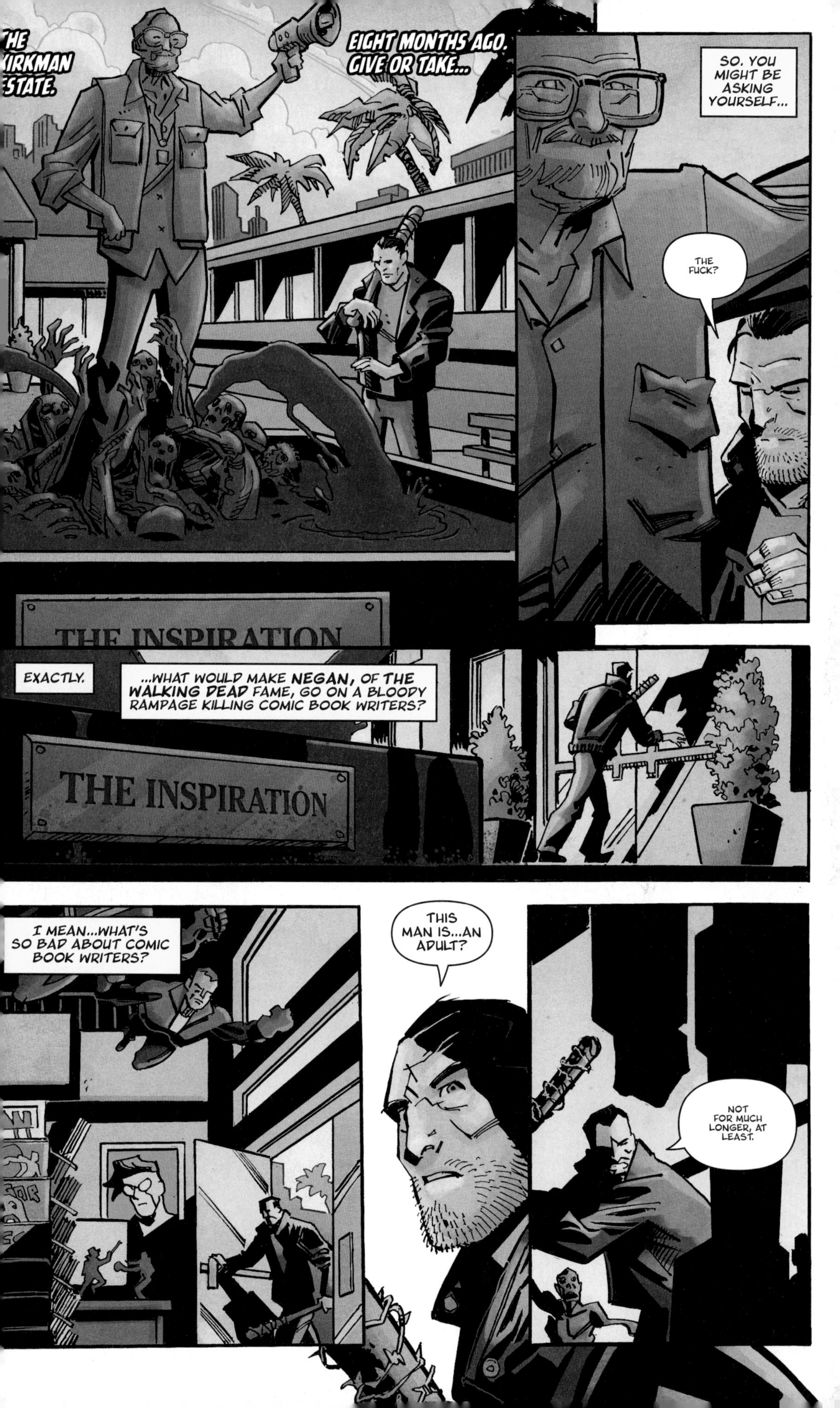

HE
IRKMAN
STATE.
EIGHT MONTHS AGO. GIVE OR TAKE...
SO. YOU MIGHT BE ASKING YOURSELF...
THE FUCK?
THE INSPIRATION
EXACTLY.
...WHAT WOULD MAKE NEGAN, OF THE WALKING DEAD FAME, GO ON A BLOODY RAMPAGE KILLING COMIC BOOK WRITERS?
THE INSPIRATION
I MEAN...WHAT'S SO BAD ABOUT COMIC BOOK WRITERS?
THIS MAN IS...AN ADULT?
NOT FOR MUCH LONGER, AT LEAST.

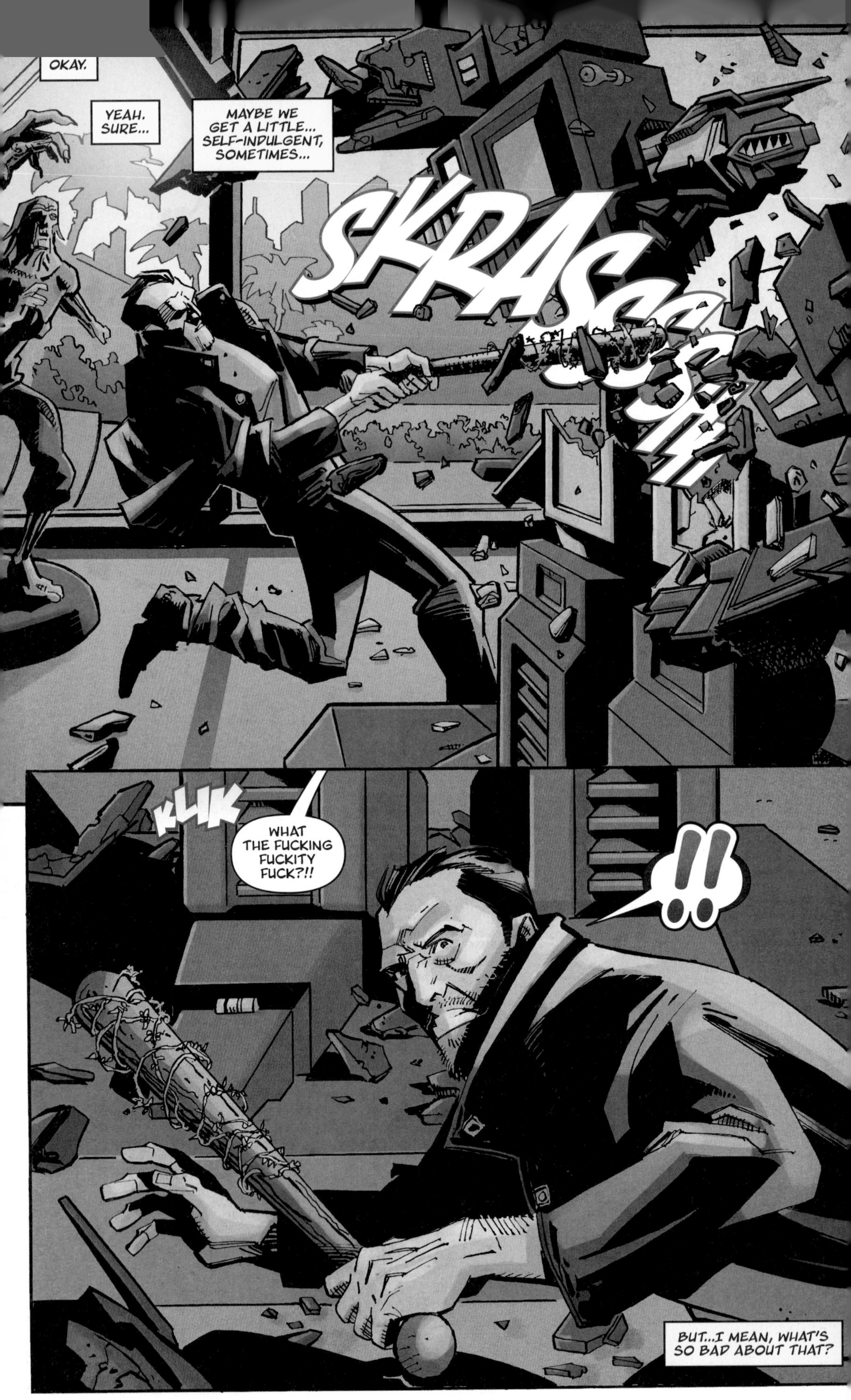
OKAY.
YEAH. SURE...
MAYBE WE GET A LITTLE... SELF-INDULGENT, SOMETIMES...
SKRASSSSH!
KLIK
WHAT THE FUCKING FUCKITY FUCK?!!
!!
BUT...I MEAN, WHAT'S SO BAD ABOUT THAT?

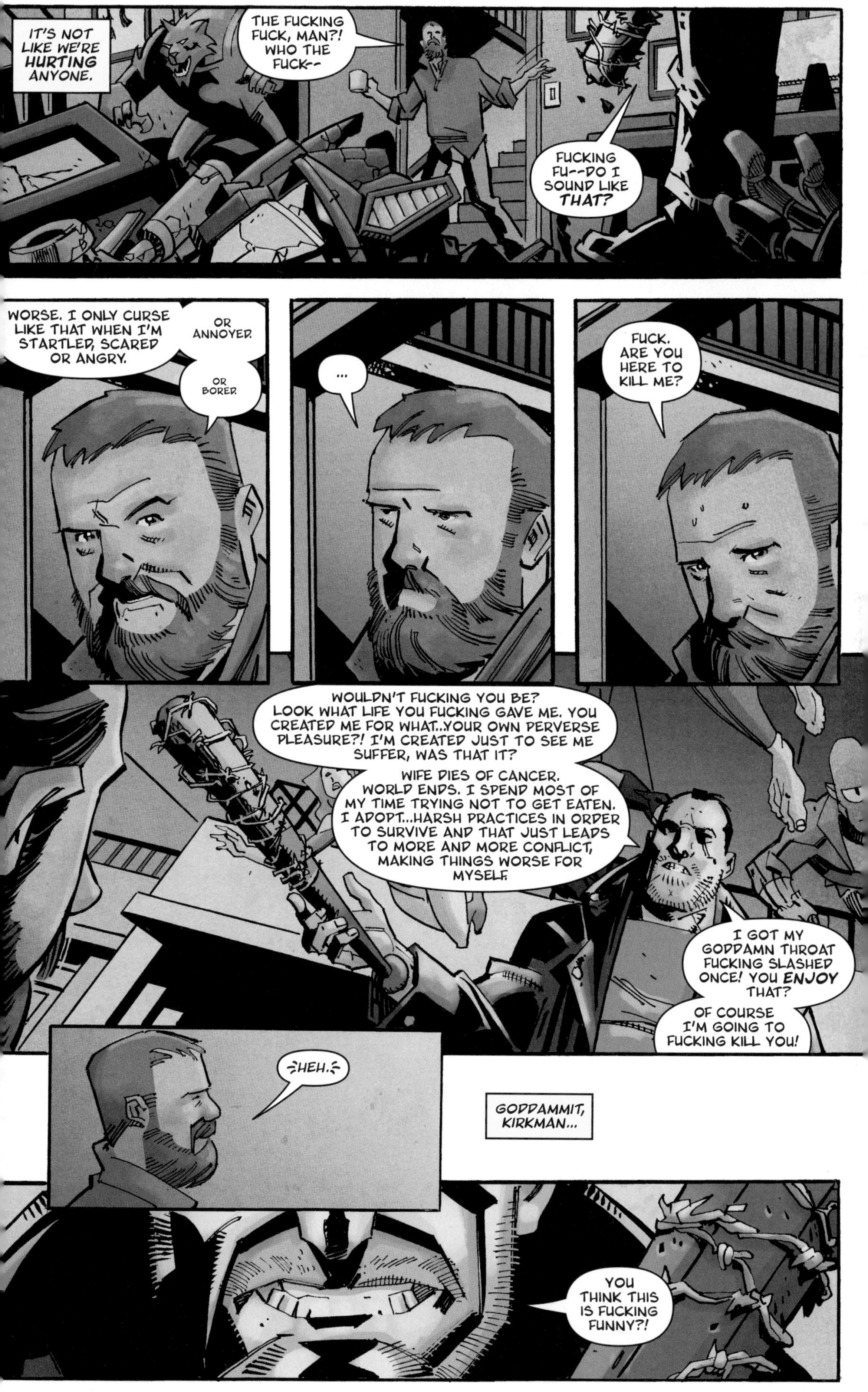
IT'S NOT LIKE WE'RE HURTING ANYONE.
THE FUCKING FUCK, MAN?! WHO THE FUCK--
FUCKING FU--DO I SOUND LIKE THAT?
WORSE. I ONLY CURSE LIKE THAT WHEN I'M STARTLED, SCARED OR ANGRY.
OR ANNOYED.
OR BORED.
...
FUCK. ARE YOU HERE TO KILL ME?
WOULDN'T FUCKING YOU BE? LOOK WHAT LIFE YOU FUCKING GAVE ME. YOU CREATED ME FOR WHAT...YOUR OWN PERVERSE PLEASURE?! I'M CREATED JUST TO SEE ME SUFFER, WAS THAT IT?
WIFE DIES OF CANCER. WORLD ENDS. I SPEND MOST OF MY TIME TRYING NOT TO GET EATEN. I ADOPT...HARSH PRACTICES IN ORDER TO SURVIVE AND THAT JUST LEADS TO MORE AND MORE CONFLICT, MAKING THINGS WORSE FOR MYSELF.
I GOT MY GODDAMN THROAT FUCKING SLASHED ONCE! YOU ENJOY THAT?
OF COURSE I'M GOING TO FUCKING KILL YOU!
HEH.
GODDAMMIT, KIRKMAN...
YOU THINK THIS IS FUCKING FUNNY?!

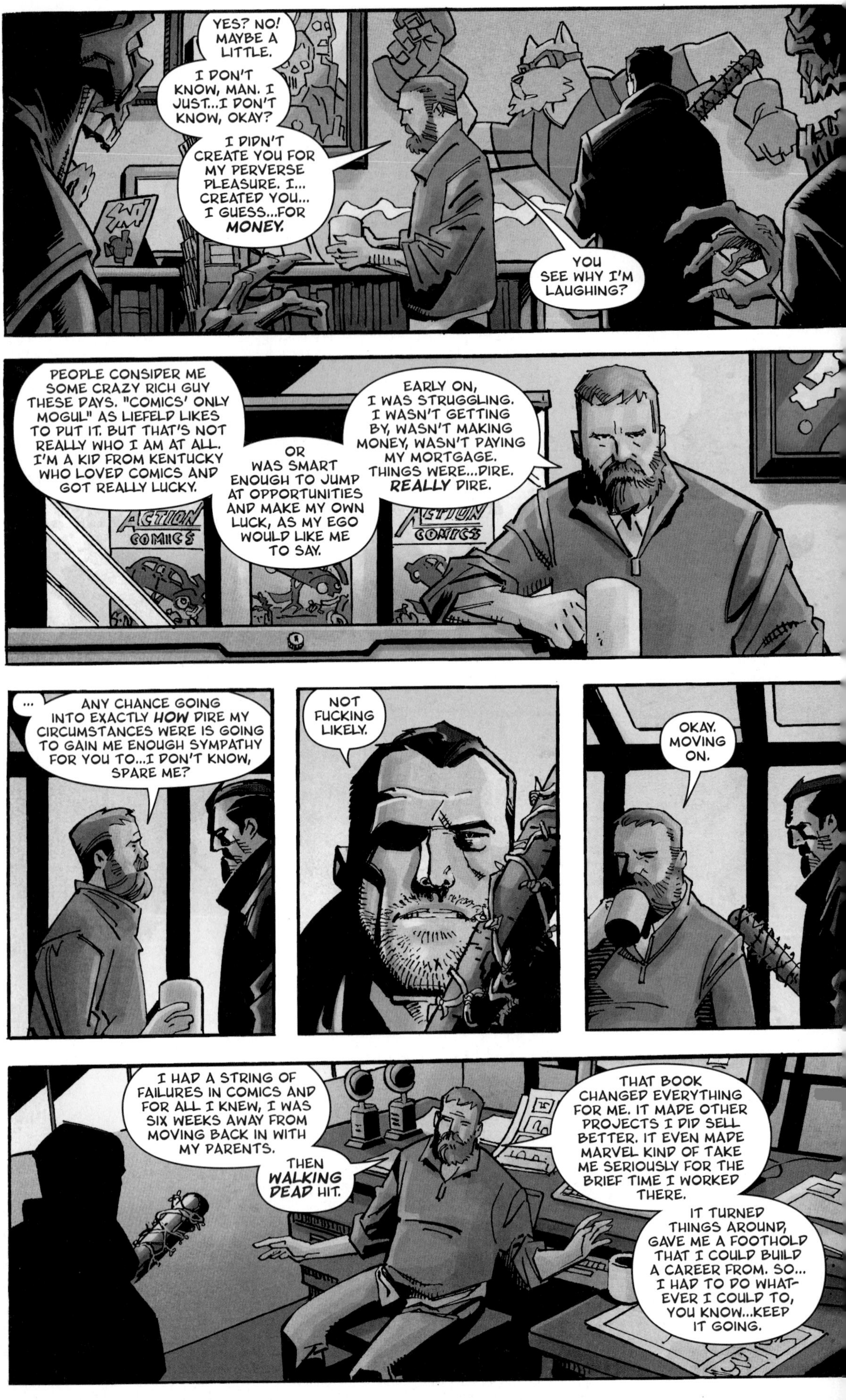
YES? NO! MAYBE A LITTLE.
I DON'T KNOW, MAN. I JUST...I DON'T KNOW, OKAY?
I DIDN'T CREATE YOU FOR MY PERVERSE PLEASURE. I... CREATED YOU... I GUESS...FOR **MONEY.**
YOU SEE WHY I'M LAUGHING?
PEOPLE CONSIDER ME SOME CRAZY RICH GUY THESE DAYS. "COMICS' ONLY MOGUL" AS LIEFELD LIKES TO PUT IT. BUT THAT'S NOT REALLY WHO I AM AT ALL. I'M A KID FROM KENTUCKY WHO LOVED COMICS AND GOT REALLY LUCKY.
OR WAS SMART ENOUGH TO JUMP AT OPPORTUNITIES AND MAKE MY OWN LUCK, AS MY EGO WOULD LIKE ME TO SAY.
EARLY ON, I WAS STRUGGLING. I WASN'T GETTING BY, WASN'T MAKING MONEY, WASN'T PAYING MY MORTGAGE. THINGS WERE...DIRE. **REALLY** DIRE.
...
ANY CHANCE GOING INTO EXACTLY **HOW** DIRE MY CIRCUMSTANCES WERE IS GOING TO GAIN ME ENOUGH SYMPATHY FOR YOU TO...I DON'T KNOW, SPARE ME?
NOT FUCKING LIKELY.
OKAY. MOVING ON.
I HAD A STRING OF FAILURES IN COMICS AND FOR ALL I KNEW, I WAS SIX WEEKS AWAY FROM MOVING BACK IN WITH MY PARENTS.
THEN **WALKING DEAD** HIT.
THAT BOOK CHANGED EVERYTHING FOR ME. IT MADE OTHER PROJECTS I DID SELL BETTER. IT EVEN MADE MARVEL KIND OF TAKE ME SERIOUSLY FOR THE BRIEF TIME I WORKED THERE.
IT TURNED THINGS AROUND, GAVE ME A FOOTHOLD THAT I COULD BUILD A CAREER FROM. SO... I HAD TO DO WHATEVER I COULD TO, YOU KNOW...KEEP IT GOING.

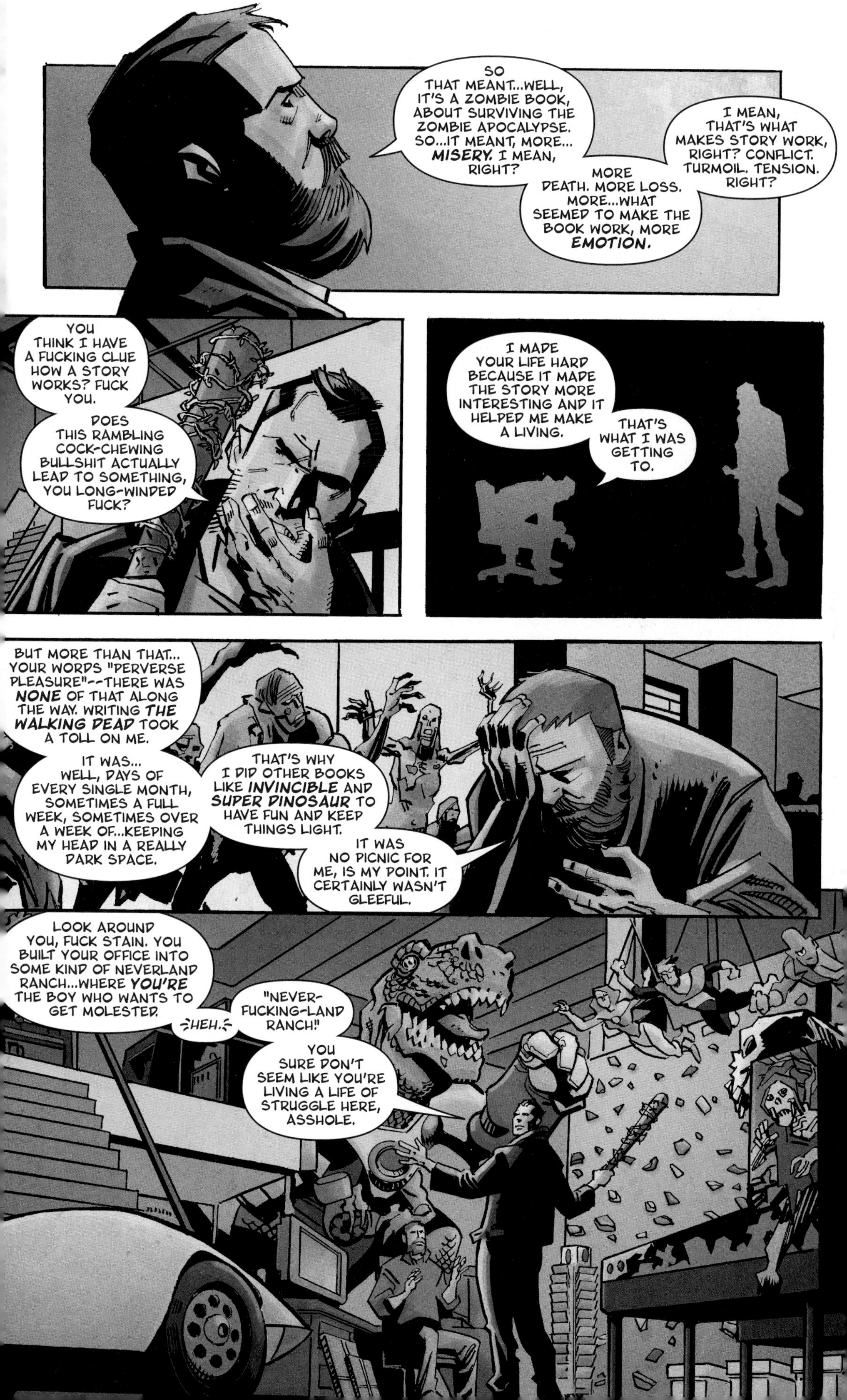
SO THAT MEANT...WELL, IT'S A ZOMBIE BOOK, ABOUT SURVIVING THE ZOMBIE APOCALYPSE. SO...IT MEANT, MORE... MISERY. I MEAN, RIGHT?
MORE DEATH. MORE LOSS. MORE...WHAT SEEMED TO MAKE THE BOOK WORK, MORE EMOTION.
I MEAN, THAT'S WHAT MAKES STORY WORK, RIGHT? CONFLICT. TURMOIL. TENSION. RIGHT?
YOU THINK I HAVE A FUCKING CLUE HOW A STORY WORKS? FUCK YOU.
DOES THIS RAMBLING COCK-CHEWING BULLSHIT ACTUALLY LEAD TO SOMETHING, YOU LONG-WINDED FUCK?
I MADE YOUR LIFE HARD BECAUSE IT MADE THE STORY MORE INTERESTING AND IT HELPED ME MAKE A LIVING.
THAT'S WHAT I WAS GETTING TO.
BUT MORE THAN THAT... YOUR WORDS "PERVERSE PLEASURE"--THERE WAS NONE OF THAT ALONG THE WAY. WRITING THE WALKING DEAD TOOK A TOLL ON ME.
IT WAS... WELL, DAYS OF EVERY SINGLE MONTH, SOMETIMES A FULL WEEK, SOMETIMES OVER A WEEK OF...KEEPING MY HEAD IN A REALLY DARK SPACE.
THAT'S WHY I DID OTHER BOOKS LIKE INVINCIBLE AND SUPER DINOSAUR TO HAVE FUN AND KEEP THINGS LIGHT.
IT WAS NO PICNIC FOR ME, IS MY POINT. IT CERTAINLY WASN'T GLEEFUL.
LOOK AROUND YOU, FUCK STAIN. YOU BUILT YOUR OFFICE INTO SOME KIND OF NEVERLAND RANCH...WHERE YOU'RE THE BOY WHO WANTS TO GET MOLESTED.
HEH.
"NEVER-FUCKING-LAND RANCH!"
YOU SURE DON'T SEEM LIKE YOU'RE LIVING A LIFE OF STRUGGLE HERE, ASSHOLE.

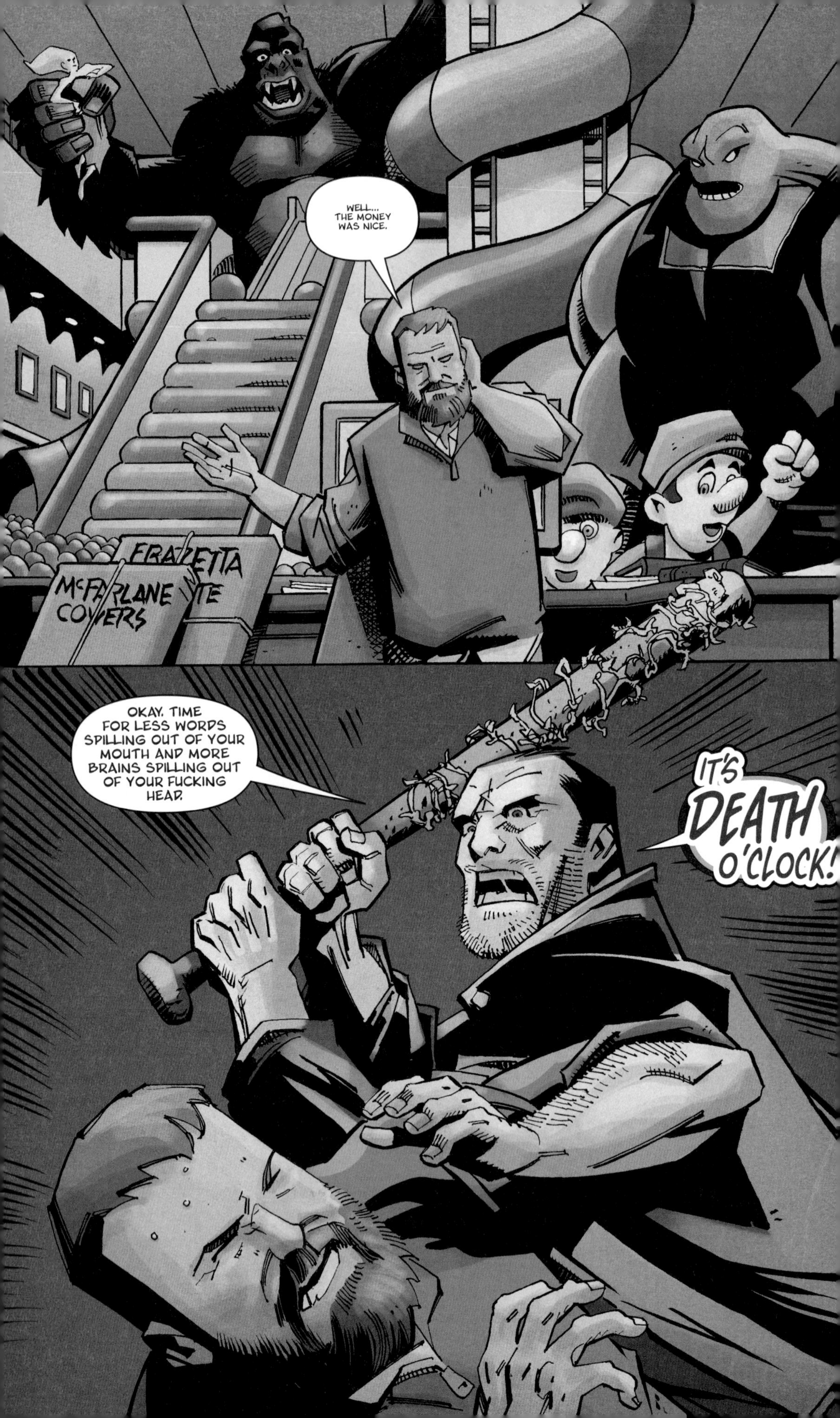
WELL... THE MONEY WAS NICE.
FRAZETTA
McFARLANE COVERS
OKAY. TIME FOR LESS WORDS SPILLING OUT OF YOUR MOUTH AND MORE BRAINS SPILLING OUT OF YOUR FUCKING HEAD.
IT'S DEATH O'CLOCK!

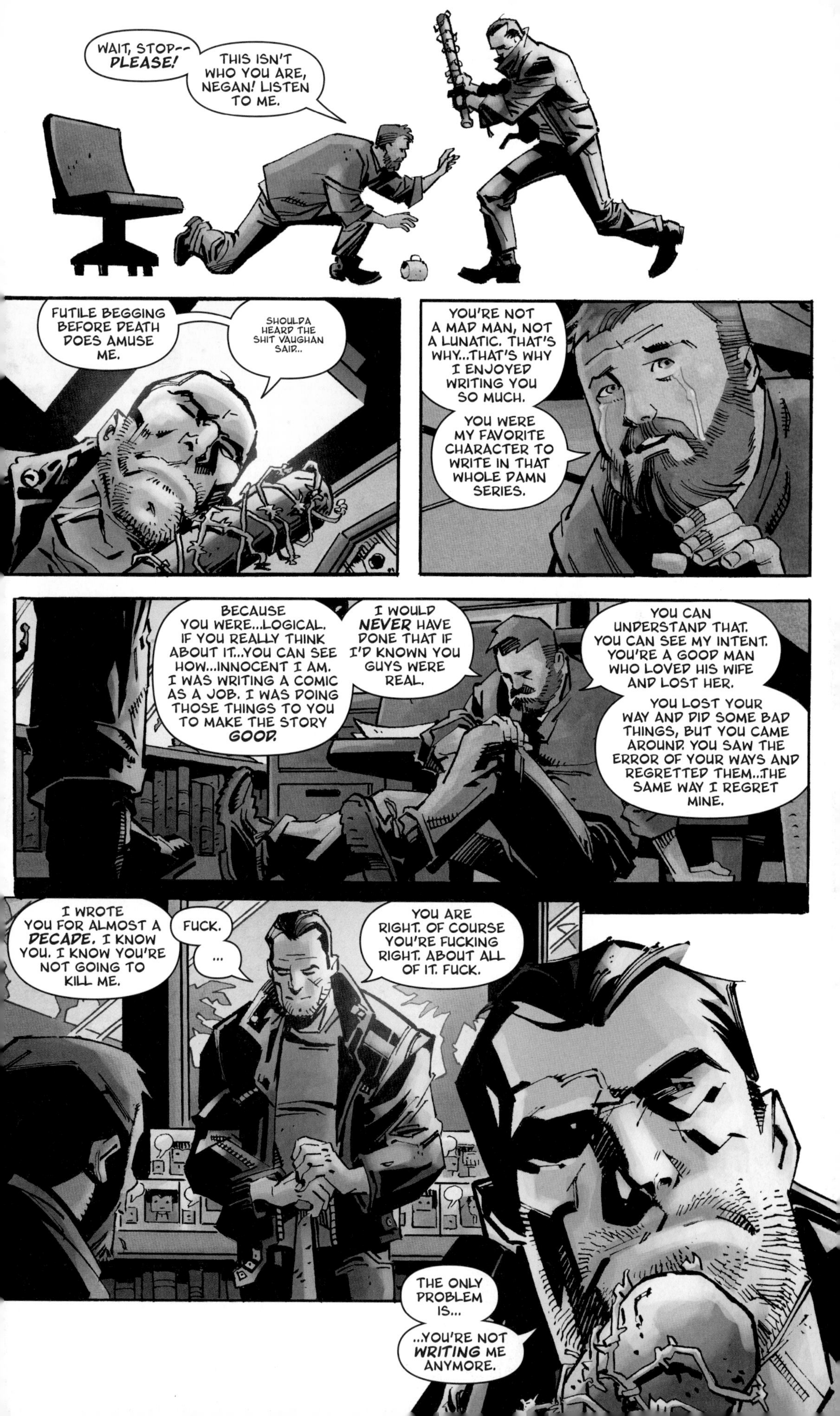
WAIT, STOP-- PLEASE!
THIS ISN'T WHO YOU ARE, NEGAN! LISTEN TO ME.
FUTILE BEGGING BEFORE DEATH DOES AMUSE ME.
SHOULDA HEARD THE SHIT VAUGHAN SAID...
YOU'RE NOT A MAD MAN, NOT A LUNATIC. THAT'S WHY...THAT'S WHY I ENJOYED WRITING YOU SO MUCH.
YOU WERE MY FAVORITE CHARACTER TO WRITE IN THAT WHOLE DAMN SERIES.
BECAUSE YOU WERE...LOGICAL. IF YOU REALLY THINK ABOUT IT...YOU CAN SEE HOW...INNOCENT I AM. I WAS WRITING A COMIC AS A JOB. I WAS DOING THOSE THINGS TO YOU TO MAKE THE STORY GOOD.
I WOULD NEVER HAVE DONE THAT IF I'D KNOWN YOU GUYS WERE REAL.
YOU CAN UNDERSTAND THAT. YOU CAN SEE MY INTENT. YOU'RE A GOOD MAN WHO LOVED HIS WIFE AND LOST HER.
YOU LOST YOUR WAY AND DID SOME BAD THINGS, BUT YOU CAME AROUND. YOU SAW THE ERROR OF YOUR WAYS AND REGRETTED THEM...THE SAME WAY I REGRET MINE.
I WROTE YOU FOR ALMOST A DECADE. I KNOW YOU. I KNOW YOU'RE NOT GOING TO KILL ME.
FUCK.
...
YOU ARE RIGHT. OF COURSE YOU'RE FUCKING RIGHT. ABOUT ALL OF IT. FUCK.
THE ONLY PROBLEM IS...
...YOU'RE NOT WRITING ME ANYMORE.

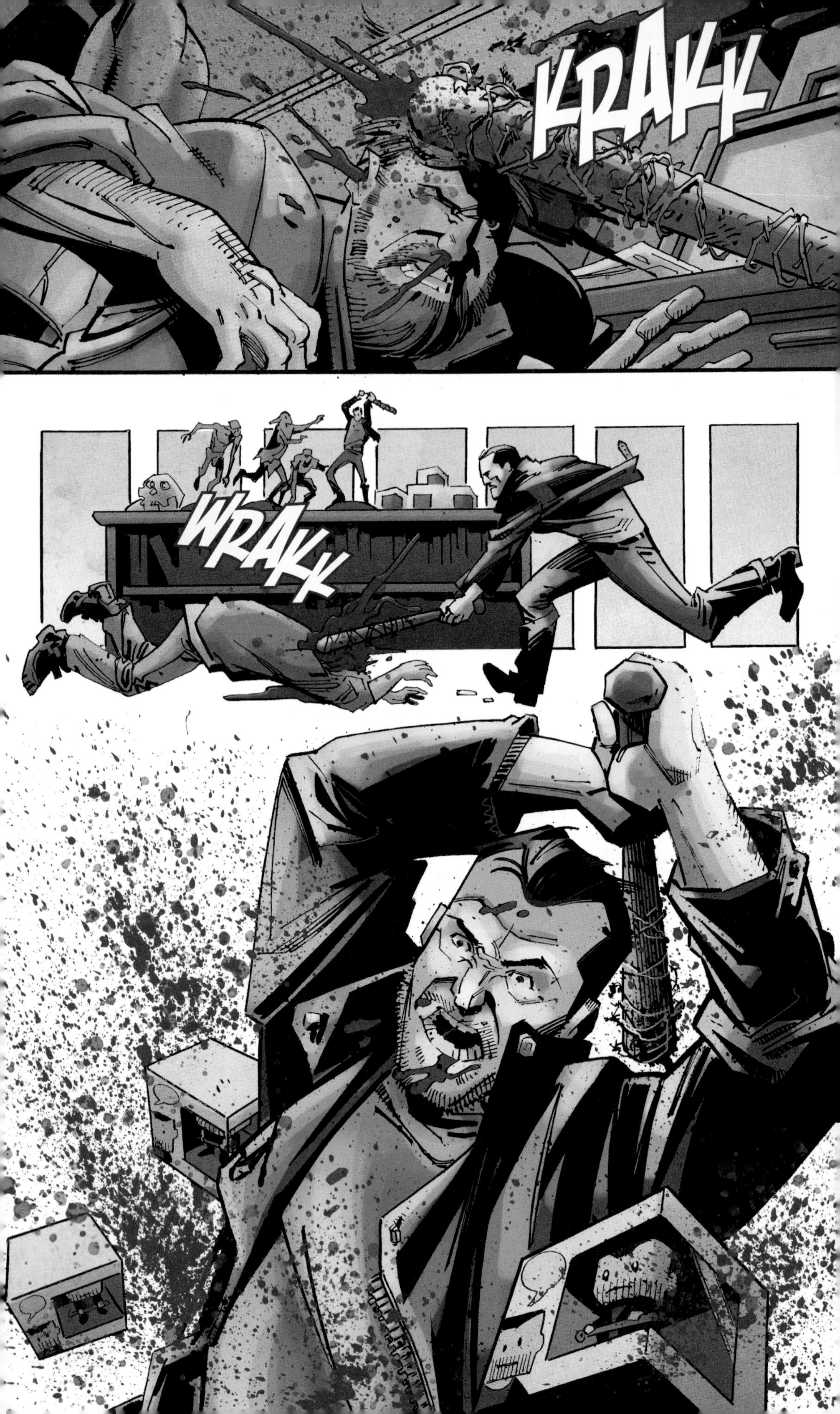
KRAKK
WRAKK

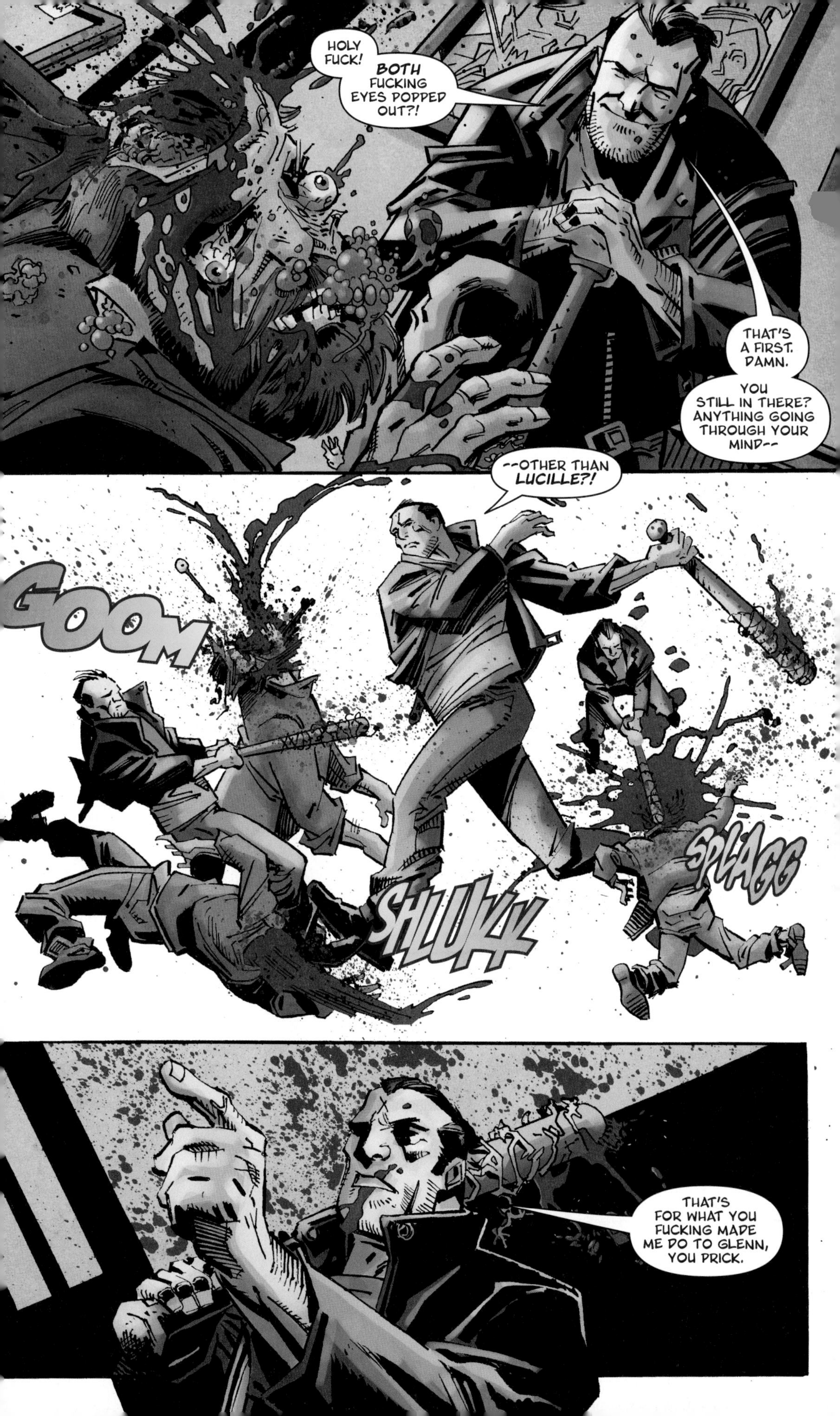
HOLY FUCK!
BOTH FUCKING EYES POPPED OUT?!
THAT'S A FIRST. DAMN.
YOU STILL IN THERE? ANYTHING GOING THROUGH YOUR MIND--
--OTHER THAN LUCILLE?!
GOOM
SHLUKK
SPLAGG
THAT'S FOR WHAT YOU FUCKING MADE ME DO TO GLENN, YOU PRICK.

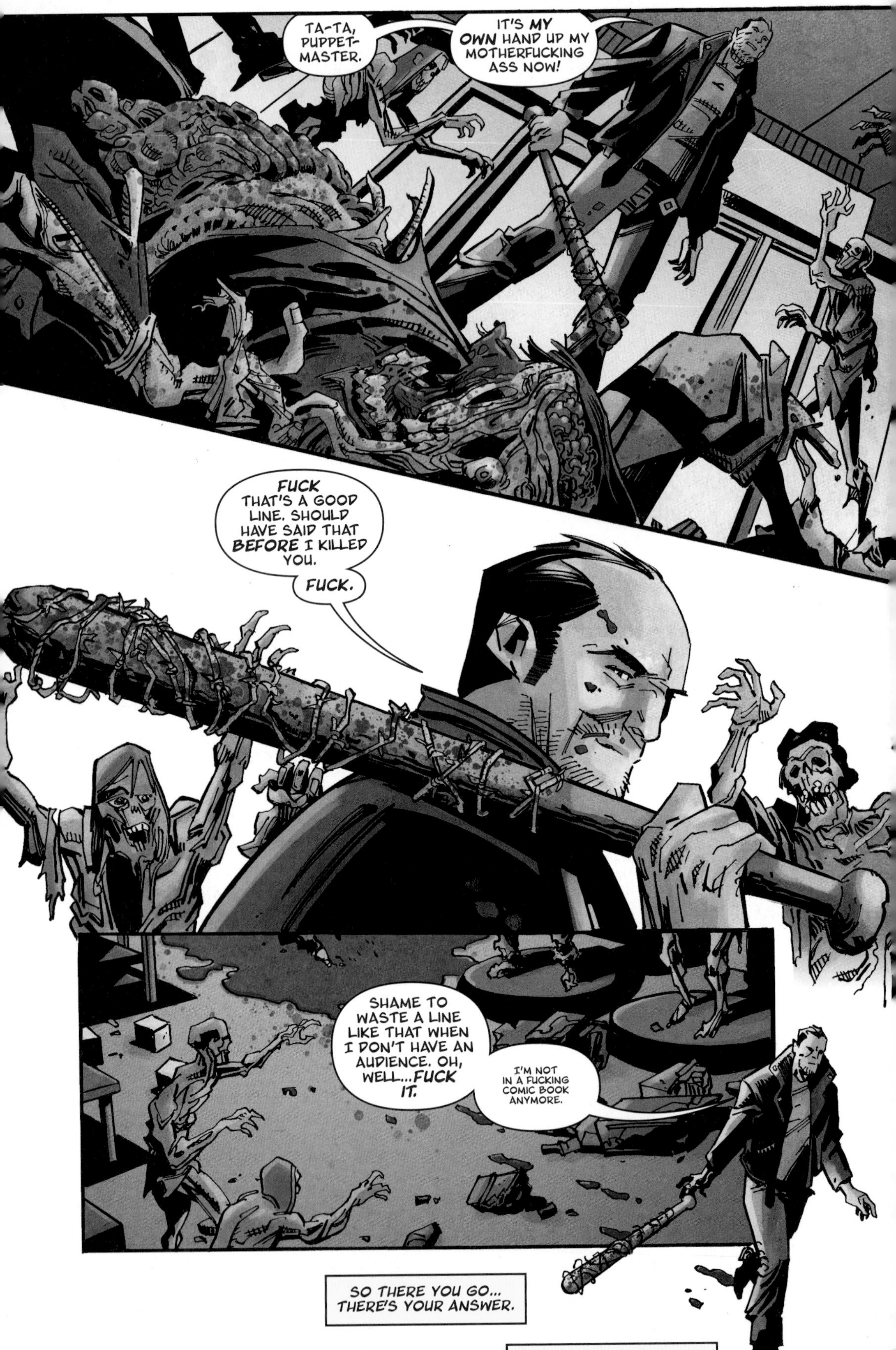
TA-TA, PUPPET-MASTER.
IT'S MY OWN HAND UP MY MOTHERFUCKING ASS NOW!
FUCK THAT'S A GOOD LINE. SHOULD HAVE SAID THAT BEFORE I KILLED YOU.
FUCK.
SHAME TO WASTE A LINE LIKE THAT WHEN I DON'T HAVE AN AUDIENCE. OH, WELL...FUCK IT.
I'M NOT IN A FUCKING COMIC BOOK ANYMORE.
SO THERE YOU GO... THERE'S YOUR ANSWER.
"WHY WOULD NEGAN START MURDERING COMIC BOOK WRITERS?"
WELL, AS IT TURNS OUT...

...APPARENTLY WE'RE THE BAD GUYS IN THIS STORY.

GODDAMMIT THAT'S SO COOL. WHY DIDN'T I THINK OF THAT?

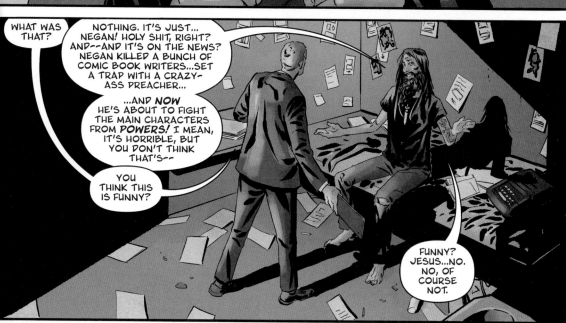

WHAT WAS THAT?

NOTHING. IT'S JUST... NEGAN! HOLY SHIT, RIGHT? AND--AND IT'S ON THE NEWS? NEGAN KILLED A BUNCH OF COMIC BOOK WRITERS...SET A TRAP WITH A CRAZY-ASS PREACHER...

...AND NOW HE'S ABOUT TO FIGHT THE MAIN CHARACTERS FROM POWERS! I MEAN, IT'S HORRIBLE, BUT YOU DON'T THINK THAT'S--

YOU THINK THIS IS FUNNY?

FUNNY? JESUS...NO. NO, OF COURSE NOT.

BUT IT IS... LIKE, RAD AS HELL...

GOD, I BET BLEEDING COOL WOULD EAT THIS SHIT UP...

THOSE GUYS. MAN, THEY'D WRITE A STORY ON ANY-THING.

...RIGHT?

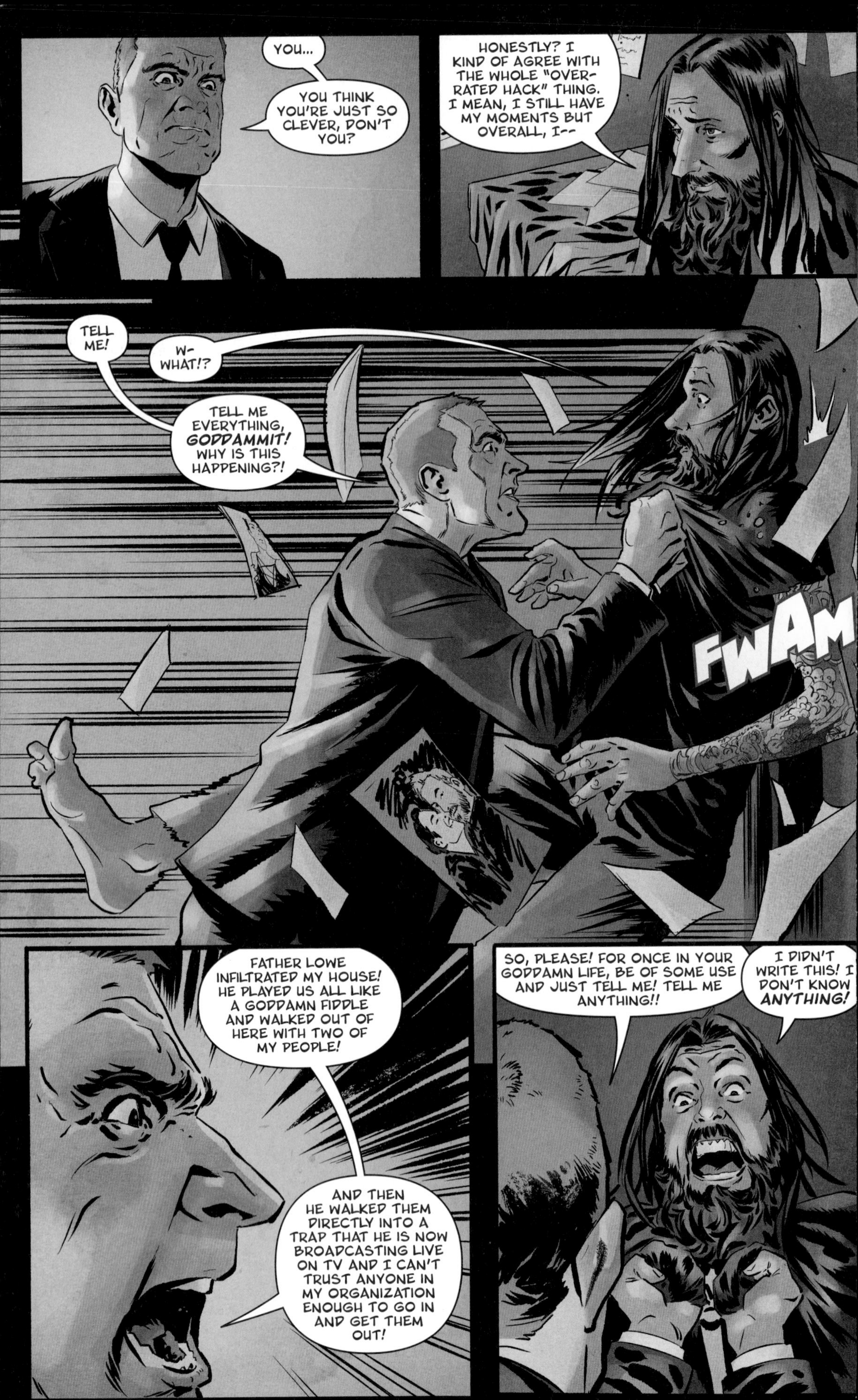
YOU...
YOU THINK YOU'RE JUST SO CLEVER, DON'T YOU?
HONESTLY? I KIND OF AGREE WITH THE WHOLE "OVER-RATED HACK" THING. I MEAN, I STILL HAVE MY MOMENTS BUT OVERALL, I--
TELL ME!
W-WHAT!?
TELL ME EVERYTHING, GODDAMMIT! WHY IS THIS HAPPENING?!
FWAM
FATHER LOWE INFILTRATED MY HOUSE! HE PLAYED US ALL LIKE A GODDAMN FIDDLE AND WALKED OUT OF HERE WITH TWO OF MY PEOPLE!
AND THEN HE WALKED THEM DIRECTLY INTO A TRAP THAT HE IS NOW BROADCASTING LIVE ON TV AND I CAN'T TRUST ANYONE IN MY ORGANIZATION ENOUGH TO GO IN AND GET THEM OUT!
SO, PLEASE! FOR ONCE IN YOUR GODDAMN LIFE, BE OF SOME USE AND JUST TELL ME! TELL ME ANYTHING!!
I DIDN'T WRITE THIS! I DON'T KNOW ANYTHING!

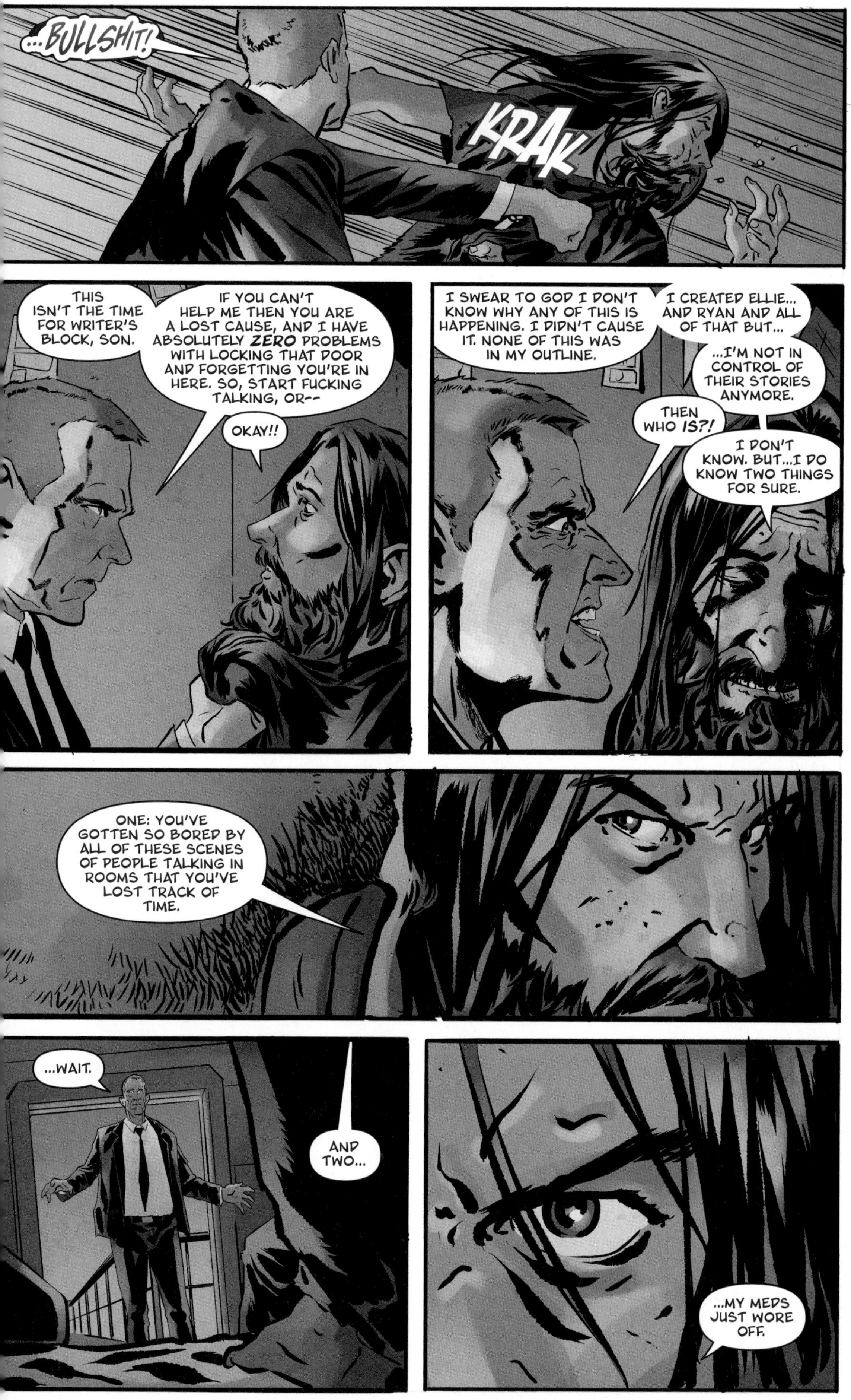
...BULLSHIT!
KRAK
THIS ISN'T THE TIME FOR WRITER'S BLOCK, SON.
IF YOU CAN'T HELP ME THEN YOU ARE A LOST CAUSE, AND I HAVE ABSOLUTELY ZERO PROBLEMS WITH LOCKING THAT DOOR AND FORGETTING YOU'RE IN HERE. SO, START FUCKING TALKING, OR--
OKAY!!
I SWEAR TO GOD I DON'T KNOW WHY ANY OF THIS IS HAPPENING. I DIDN'T CAUSE IT. NONE OF THIS WAS IN MY OUTLINE.
I CREATED ELLIE... AND RYAN AND ALL OF THAT BUT...
...I'M NOT IN CONTROL OF THEIR STORIES ANYMORE.
THEN WHO IS?!
I DON'T KNOW. BUT...I DO KNOW TWO THINGS FOR SURE.
ONE: YOU'VE GOTTEN SO BORED BY ALL OF THESE SCENES OF PEOPLE TALKING IN ROOMS THAT YOU'VE LOST TRACK OF TIME.
...WAIT.
AND TWO...
...MY MEDS JUST WORE OFF.

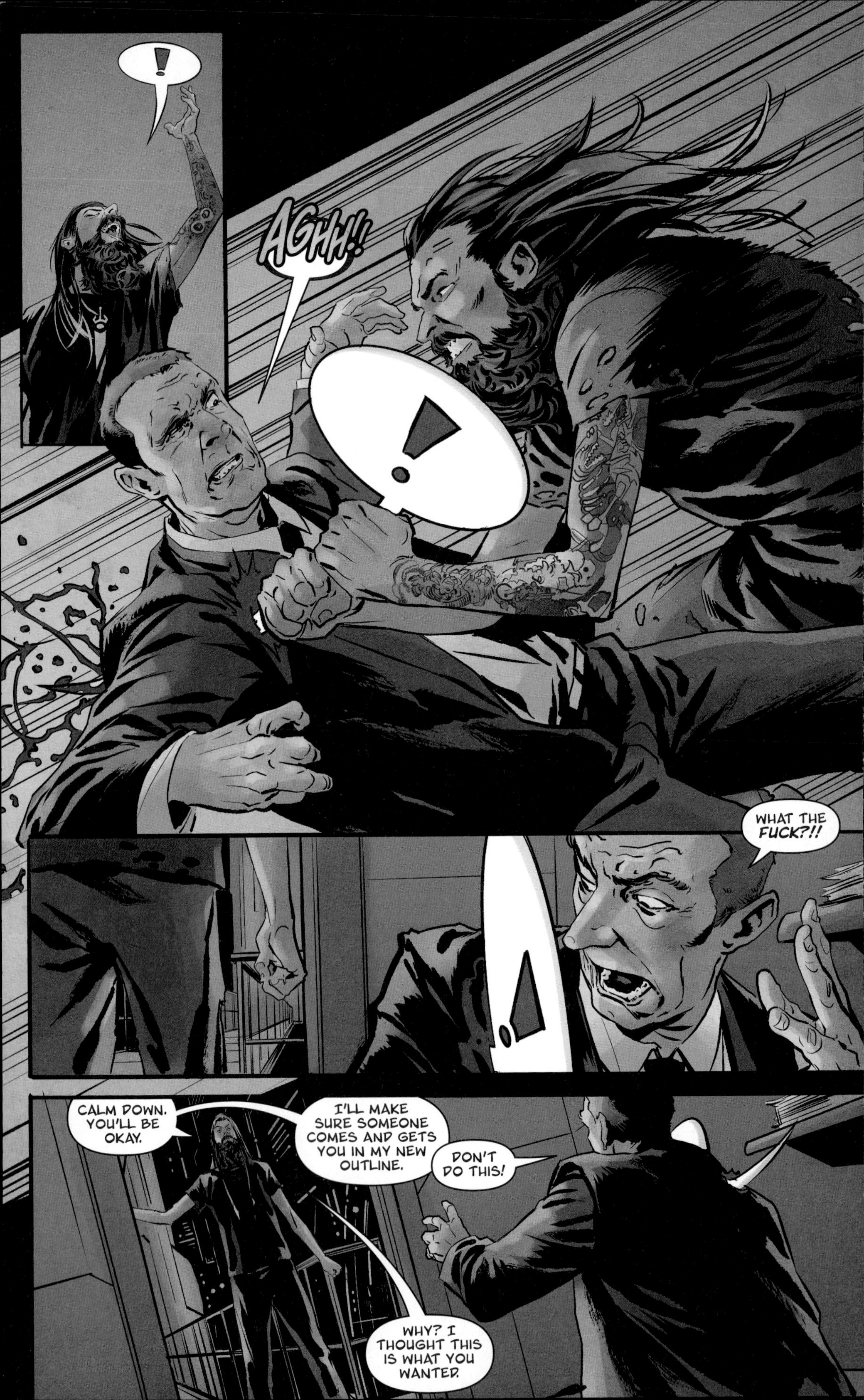
!
AGHH!!
!
WHAT THE FUCK?!!
!
CALM DOWN. YOU'LL BE OKAY.
I'LL MAKE SURE SOMEONE COMES AND GETS YOU IN MY NEW OUTLINE.
DON'T DO THIS!
WHY? I THOUGHT THIS IS WHAT YOU WANTED.

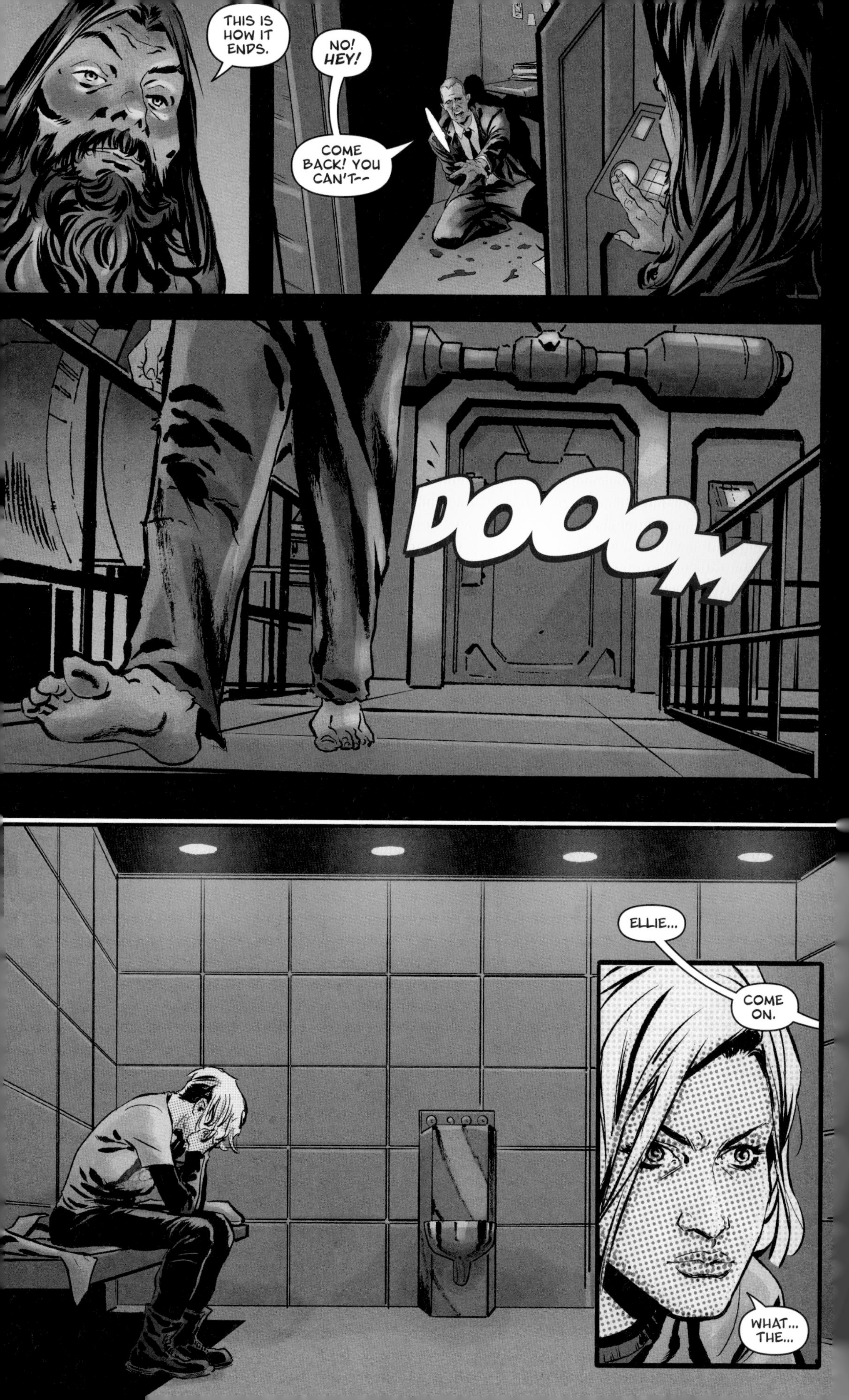
THIS IS HOW IT ENDS.
NO! HEY!
COME BACK! YOU CAN'T--
DOOOM
ELLIE...
COME ON.
WHAT... THE...

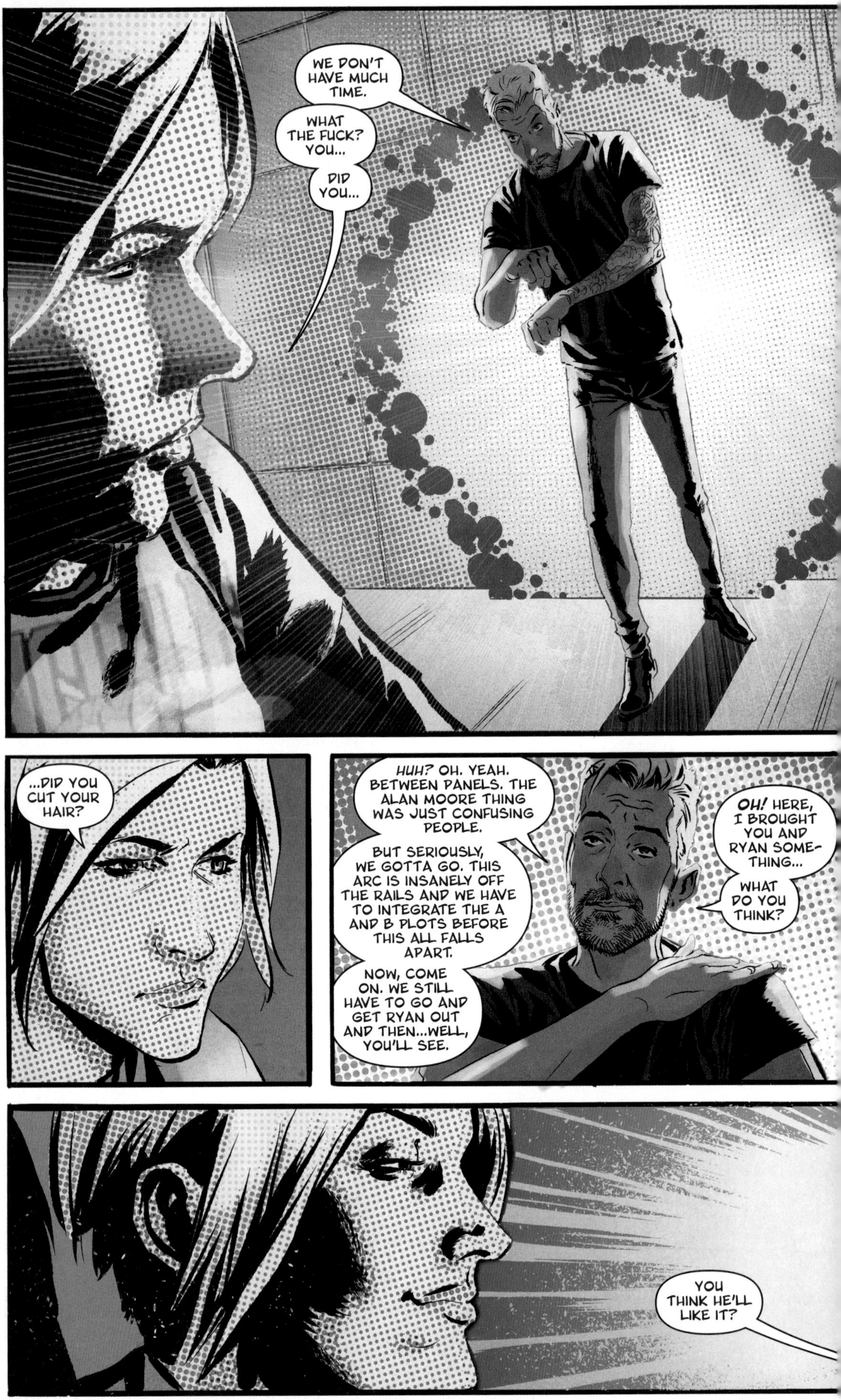
WE DON'T HAVE MUCH TIME.
WHAT THE FUCK? YOU...
DID YOU...
...DID YOU CUT YOUR HAIR?
HUH? OH. YEAH. BETWEEN PANELS. THE ALAN MOORE THING WAS JUST CONFUSING PEOPLE.
BUT SERIOUSLY, WE GOTTA GO. THIS ARC IS INSANELY OFF THE RAILS AND WE HAVE TO INTEGRATE THE A AND B PLOTS BEFORE THIS ALL FALLS APART.
NOW, COME ON. WE STILL HAVE TO GO AND GET RYAN OUT AND THEN...WELL, YOU'LL SEE.
OH! HERE, I BROUGHT YOU AND RYAN SOME-THING...
WHAT DO YOU THINK?
YOU THINK HE'LL LIKE IT?

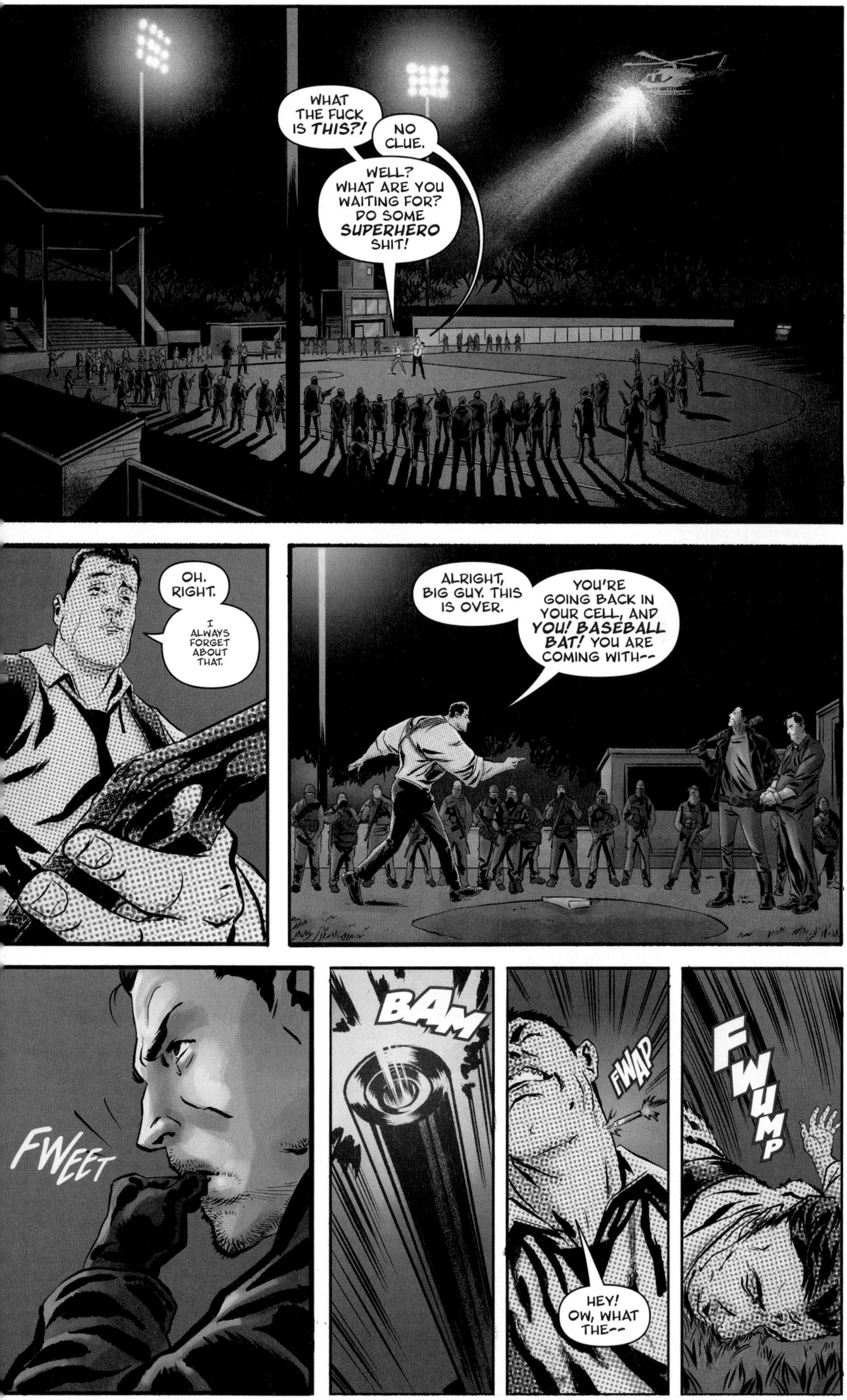

WHAT THE FUCK IS THIS?!
NO CLUE.
WELL? WHAT ARE YOU WAITING FOR? DO SOME SUPERHERO SHIT!
OH. RIGHT.
I ALWAYS FORGET ABOUT THAT.
ALRIGHT, BIG GUY. THIS IS OVER.
YOU'RE GOING BACK IN YOUR CELL, AND YOU! BASEBALL BAT! YOU ARE COMING WITH--
FWEET
BAM
FWAP
HEY! OW, WHAT THE--
FWUMP

WHAT...WHAT WAS THAT? WHAT DID YOU *DO* TO HIM?

DRAINER JUICE. NOW AVAILABLE IN HANDY-DANDY DART FORM! *HAHA*, WHAT THE FUCK WILL THEY THINK OF NEXT?!

WHAT DO YOU WANT? WHAT IS THIS?!

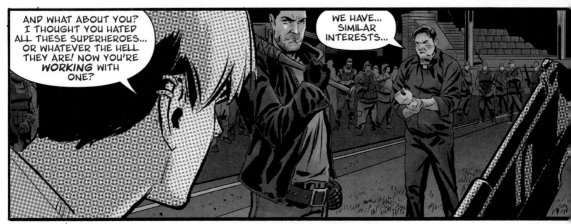

AND WHAT ABOUT YOU? I THOUGHT YOU HATED ALL THESE SUPERHEROES... OR WHATEVER THE HELL THEY ARE! NOW YOU'RE *WORKING* WITH ONE?

WE HAVE... SIMILAR INTERESTS...

WE BOTH WANT THIS SHIT OVER WITH.

I...WANT THIS WORLD FREE OF *YOUR KIND.* NO OFFENSE...

NONE TAKEN.

AND SEE, *ME?* I WANT THE SAME THING.

I WANT TO GO THE FUCK HOME.

...

WHAT? WHY? *THE WALKING DEAD* IS...I MEAN, IT SUCKS OVER THERE!

LOOK AT YOU! YOU'RE IN BLACK AND WHITE!

WHY WOULD YOU WANT TO GO BACK TO *THAT* HELL?

BECAUSE IT DOESN'T *HAVE* TO BE HELL.

SEE...I MET A MAN BACK INSIDE THAT DOME OUT IN COLORADO.

HE HAS POWER...*REAL* POWER...

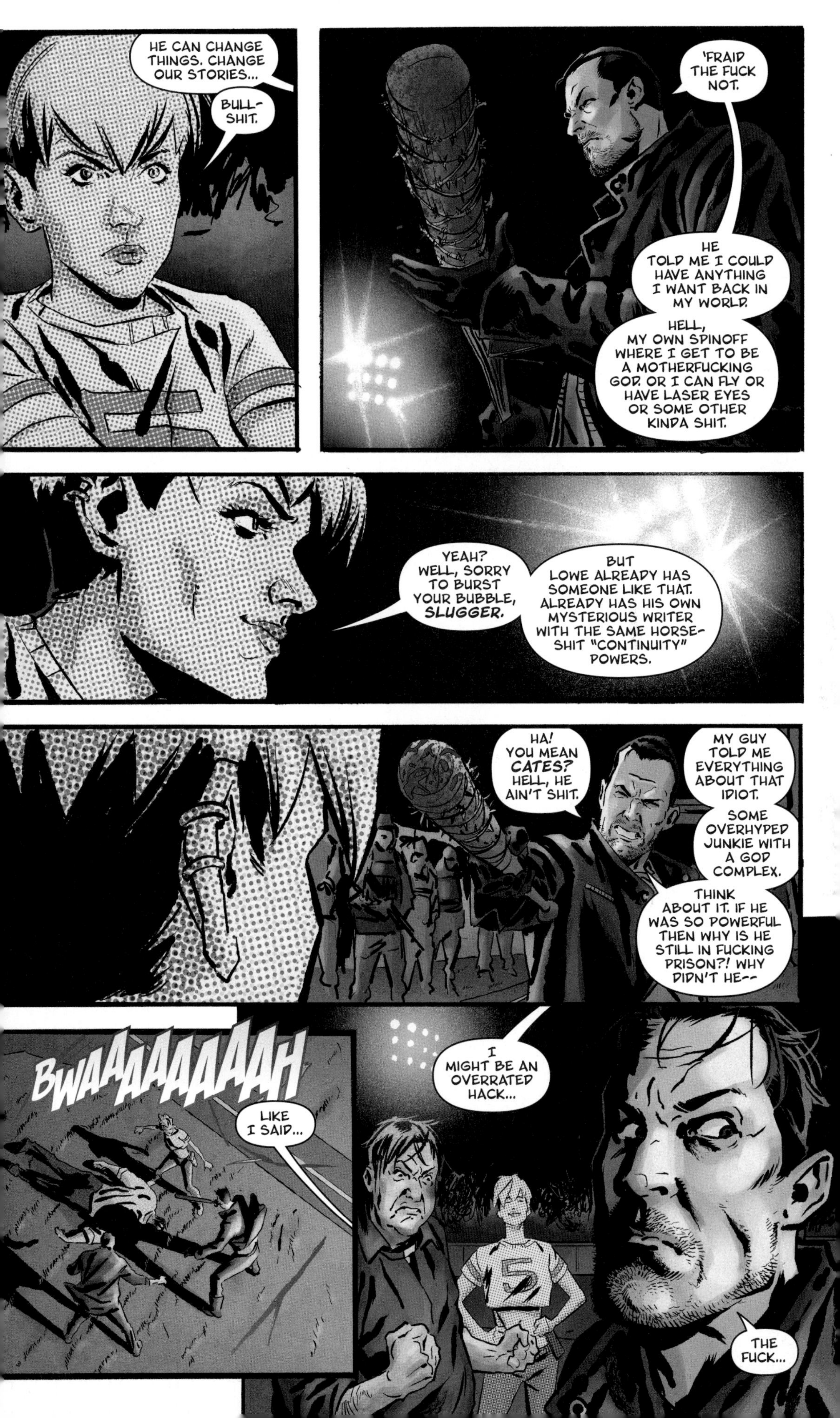

HE CAN CHANGE THINGS. CHANGE OUR STORIES...
BULL-SHIT.
'FRAID THE FUCK NOT.
HE TOLD ME I COULD HAVE ANYTHING I WANT BACK IN MY WORLD.
HELL, MY OWN SPINOFF WHERE I GET TO BE A MOTHERFUCKING GOD. OR I CAN FLY OR HAVE LASER EYES OR SOME OTHER KINDA SHIT.
YEAH? WELL, SORRY TO BURST YOUR BUBBLE, SLUGGER.
BUT LOWE ALREADY HAS SOMEONE LIKE THAT. ALREADY HAS HIS OWN MYSTERIOUS WRITER WITH THE SAME HORSE-SHIT "CONTINUITY" POWERS.
HA! YOU MEAN CATES? HELL, HE AIN'T SHIT.
MY GUY TOLD ME EVERYTHING ABOUT THAT IDIOT.
SOME OVERHYPED JUNKIE WITH A GOD COMPLEX.
THINK ABOUT IT. IF HE WAS SO POWERFUL THEN WHY IS HE STILL IN FUCKING PRISON?! WHY DIDN'T HE--
BWAAAAAAAAH
LIKE I SAID...
I MIGHT BE AN OVERRATED HACK...
THE FUCK...

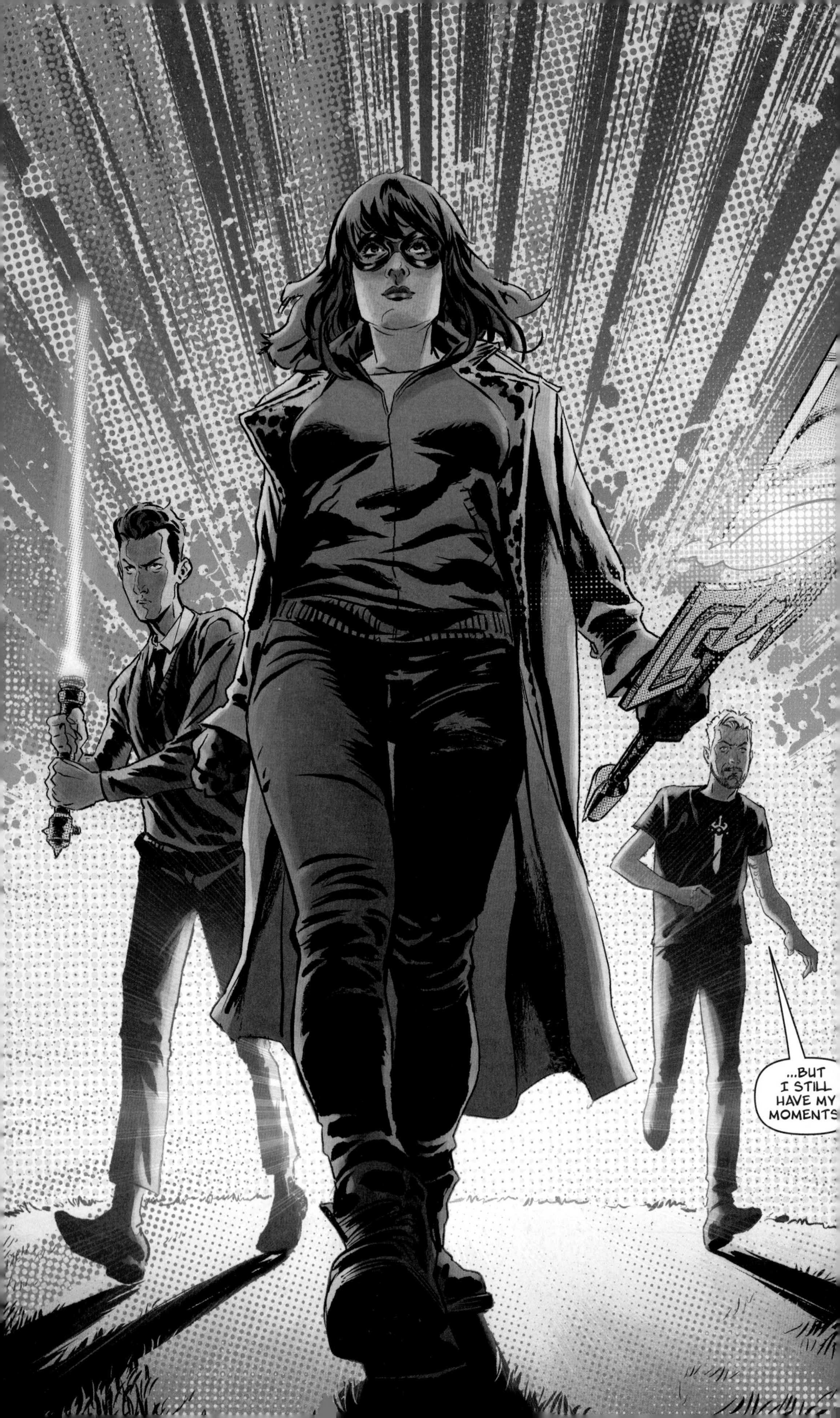
...BUT I STILL HAVE MY MOMENTS

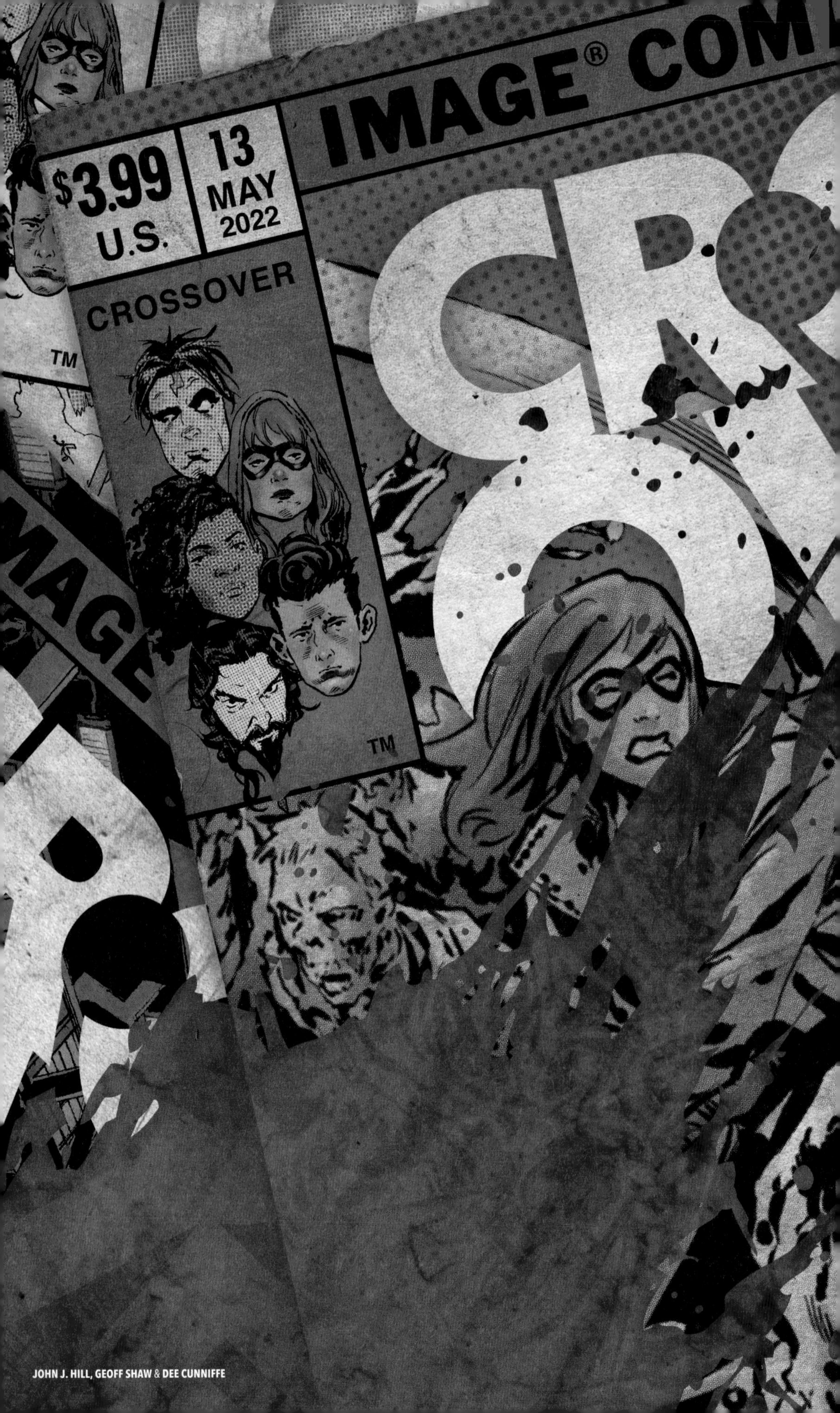
IMAGE® COM
$3.99
U.S.
13
MAY
2022
CROSSOVER
TM
TM
IMAGE
JOHN J. HILL, GEOFF SHAW & DEE CUNNIFFE

THE 10-CENT PLAGUE

PLAGUE

CHAPTER SIX

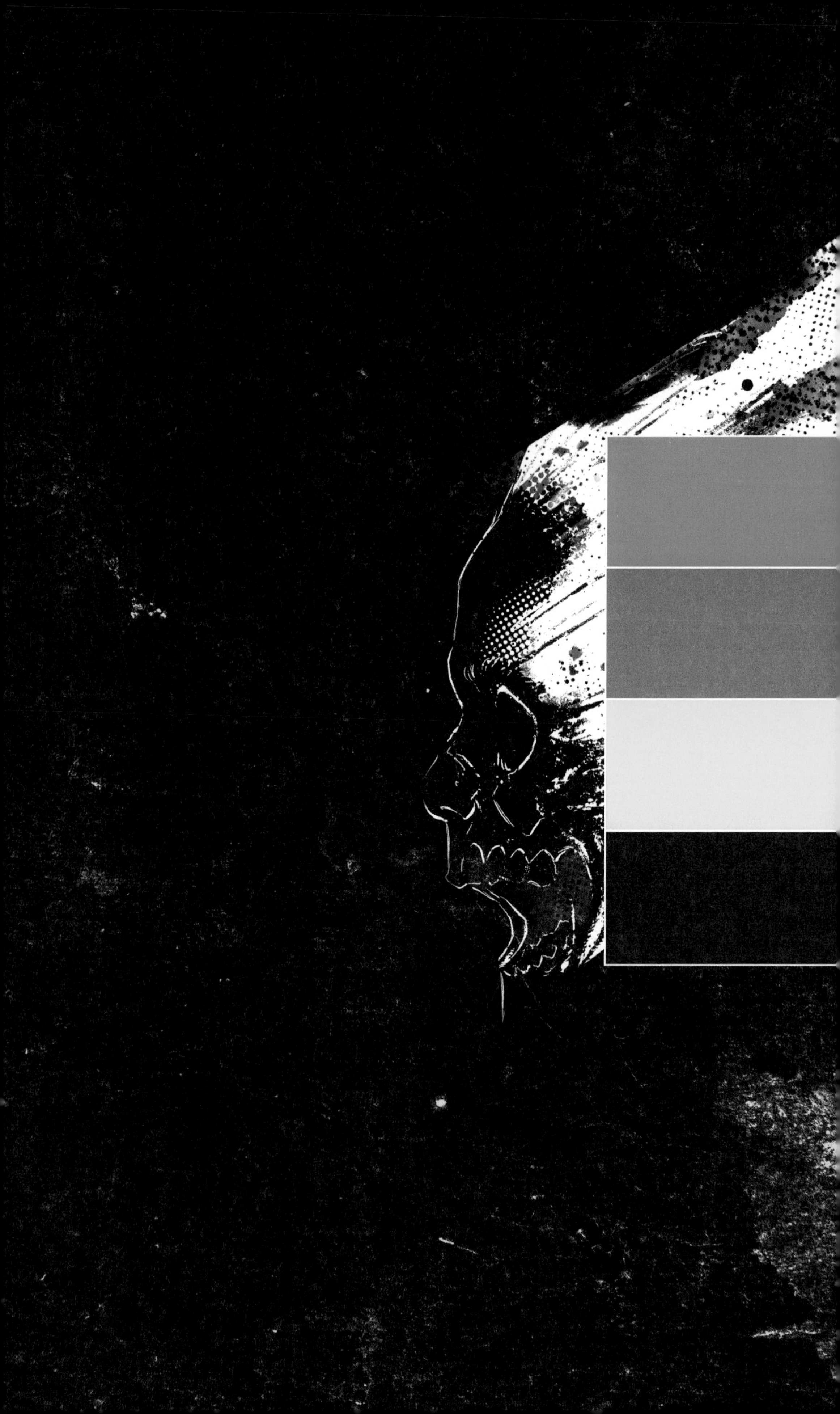

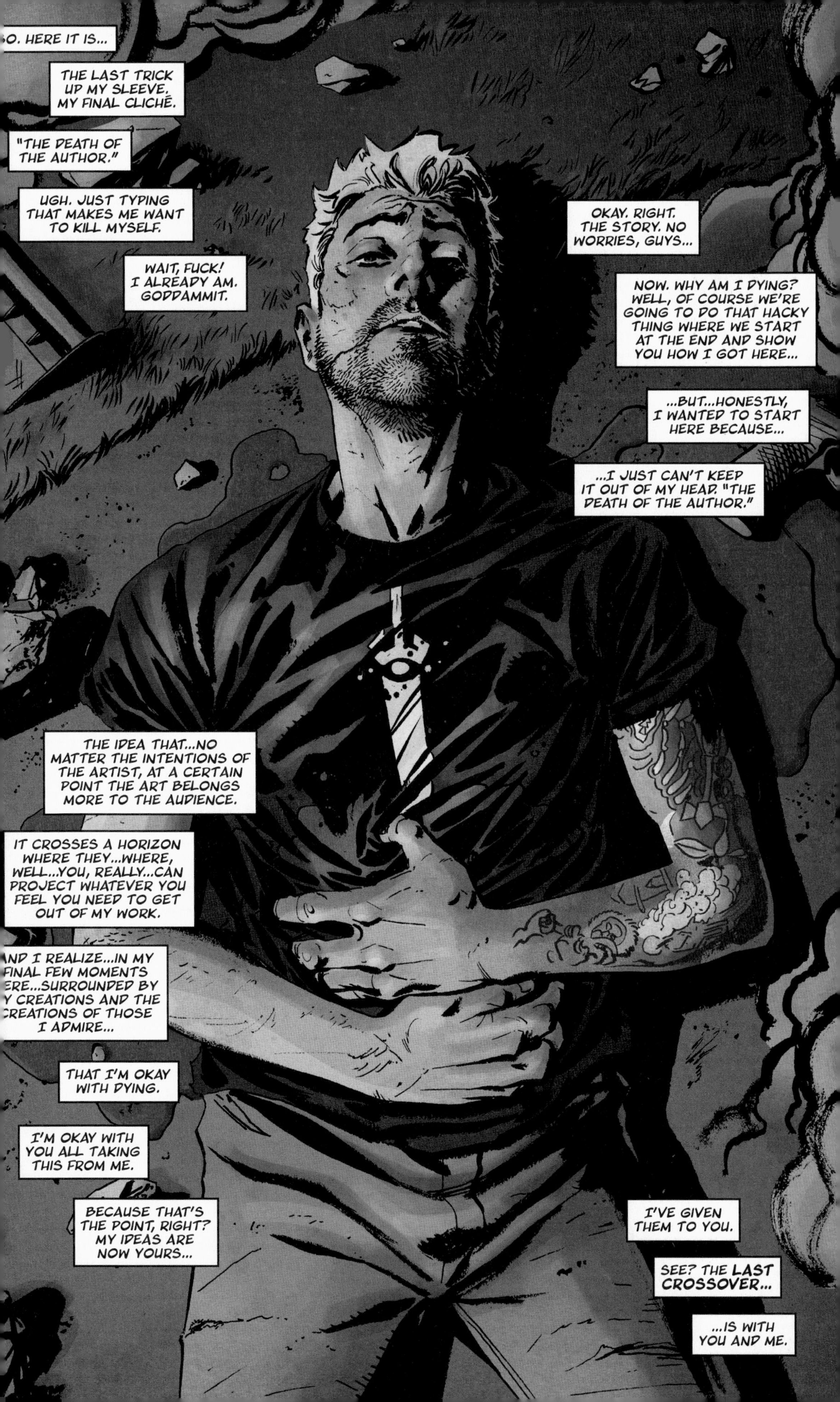

SO. HERE IT IS...
THE LAST TRICK UP MY SLEEVE. MY FINAL CLICHÉ.
"THE DEATH OF THE AUTHOR."
UGH. JUST TYPING THAT MAKES ME WANT TO KILL MYSELF.
WAIT, FUCK! I ALREADY AM. GODDAMMIT.
OKAY. RIGHT. THE STORY. NO WORRIES, GUYS...
NOW. WHY AM I DYING? WELL, OF COURSE WE'RE GOING TO DO THAT HACKY THING WHERE WE START AT THE END AND SHOW YOU HOW I GOT HERE...
...BUT...HONESTLY, I WANTED TO START HERE BECAUSE...
...I JUST CAN'T KEEP IT OUT OF MY HEAD. "THE DEATH OF THE AUTHOR."
THE IDEA THAT...NO MATTER THE INTENTIONS OF THE ARTIST, AT A CERTAIN POINT THE ART BELONGS MORE TO THE AUDIENCE.
IT CROSSES A HORIZON WHERE THEY...WHERE, WELL...YOU, REALLY...CAN PROJECT WHATEVER YOU FEEL YOU NEED TO GET OUT OF MY WORK.
AND I REALIZE...IN MY FINAL FEW MOMENTS HERE...SURROUNDED BY MY CREATIONS AND THE CREATIONS OF THOSE I ADMIRE...
THAT I'M OKAY WITH DYING.
I'M OKAY WITH YOU ALL TAKING THIS FROM ME.
BECAUSE THAT'S THE POINT, RIGHT? MY IDEAS ARE NOW YOURS...
I'VE GIVEN THEM TO YOU.
SEE? THE **LAST CROSSOVER**...
...IS WITH YOU AND ME.

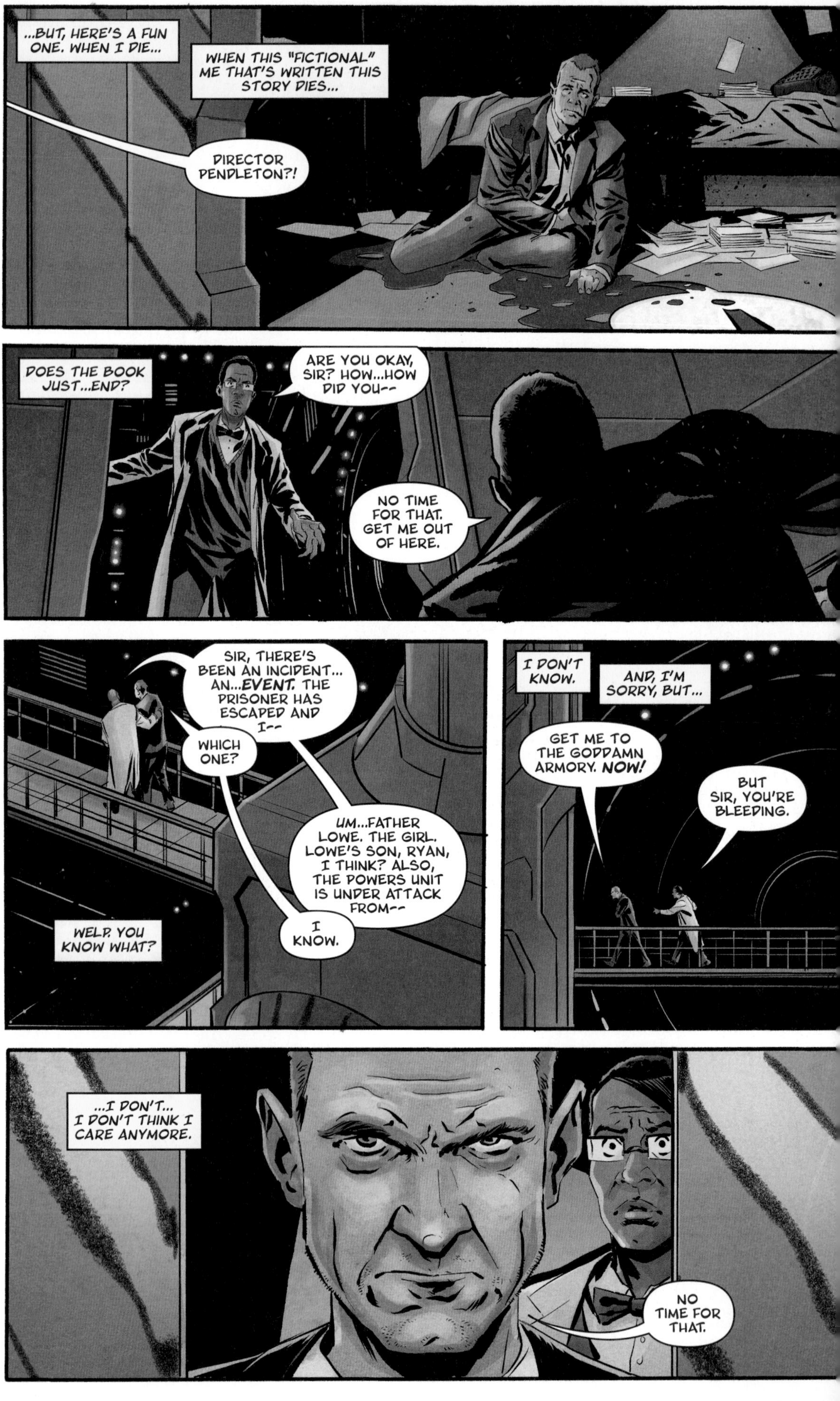

...BUT, HERE'S A FUN ONE. WHEN I DIE...
WHEN THIS "FICTIONAL" ME THAT'S WRITTEN THIS STORY DIES...
DIRECTOR PENDLETON?!
DOES THE BOOK JUST...END?
ARE YOU OKAY, SIR? HOW...HOW DID YOU--
NO TIME FOR THAT. GET ME OUT OF HERE.
SIR, THERE'S BEEN AN INCIDENT... AN...EVENT. THE PRISONER HAS ESCAPED AND I--
WHICH ONE?
UM...FATHER LOWE. THE GIRL. LOWE'S SON, RYAN, I THINK? ALSO, THE POWERS UNIT IS UNDER ATTACK FROM--
I KNOW.
WELP. YOU KNOW WHAT?
I DON'T KNOW.
AND, I'M SORRY, BUT...
GET ME TO THE GODDAMN ARMORY. NOW!
BUT SIR, YOU'RE BLEEDING.
...I DON'T... I DON'T THINK I CARE ANYMORE.
NO TIME FOR THAT.

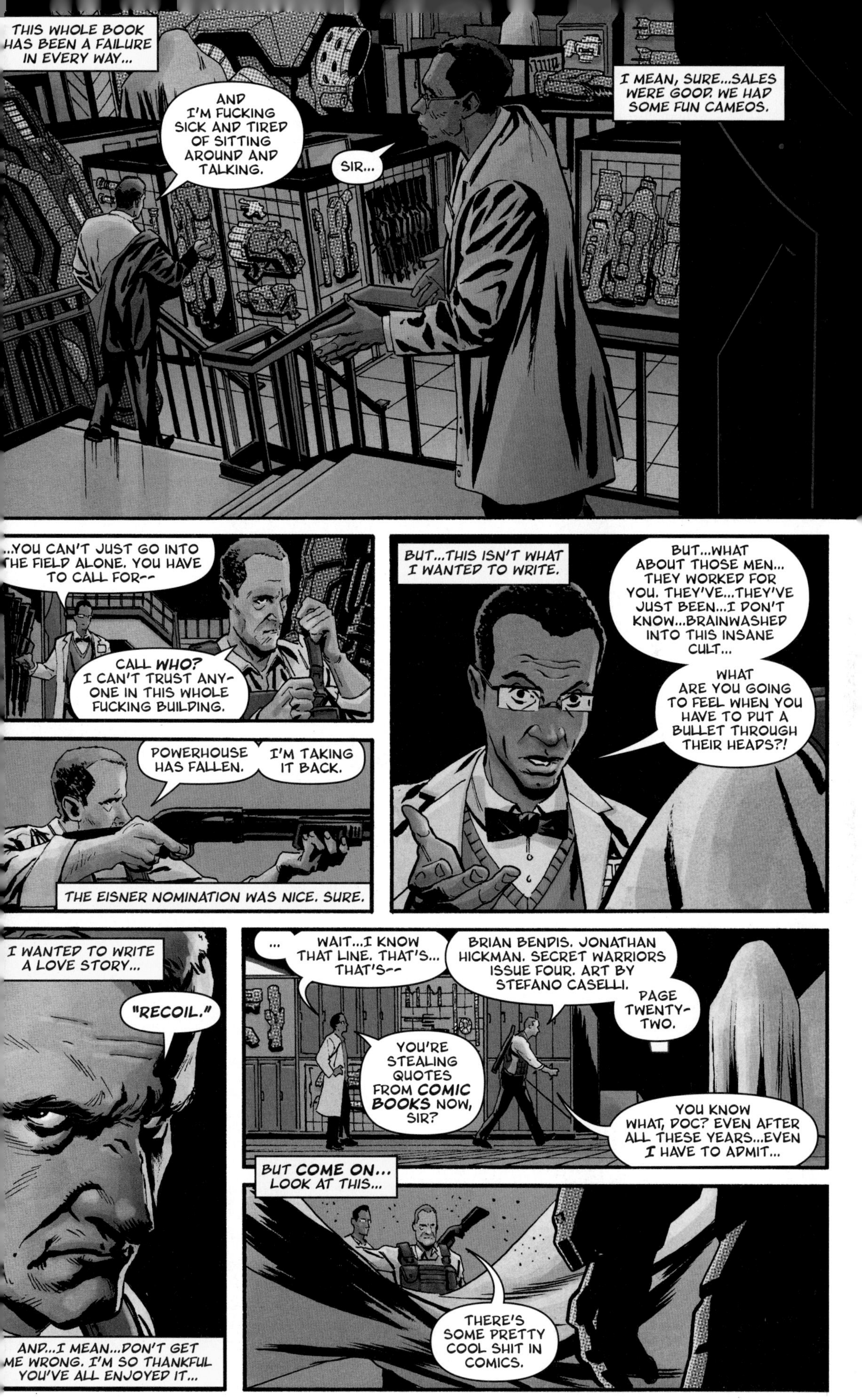
THIS WHOLE BOOK HAS BEEN A FAILURE IN EVERY WAY...
AND I'M FUCKING SICK AND TIRED OF SITTING AROUND AND TALKING.
SIR...
I MEAN, SURE...SALES WERE GOOD. WE HAD SOME FUN CAMEOS.
...YOU CAN'T JUST GO INTO THE FIELD ALONE. YOU HAVE TO CALL FOR--
CALL WHO? I CAN'T TRUST ANYONE IN THIS WHOLE FUCKING BUILDING.
POWERHOUSE HAS FALLEN.
I'M TAKING IT BACK.
THE EISNER NOMINATION WAS NICE. SURE.
BUT...THIS ISN'T WHAT I WANTED TO WRITE.
BUT...WHAT ABOUT THOSE MEN... THEY WORKED FOR YOU. THEY'VE...THEY'VE JUST BEEN...I DON'T KNOW...BRAINWASHED INTO THIS INSANE CULT...
WHAT ARE YOU GOING TO FEEL WHEN YOU HAVE TO PUT A BULLET THROUGH THEIR HEADS?!
I WANTED TO WRITE A LOVE STORY...
"RECOIL."
AND...I MEAN...DON'T GET ME WRONG. I'M SO THANKFUL YOU'VE ALL ENJOYED IT...
...
WAIT...I KNOW THAT LINE. THAT'S... THAT'S--
BRIAN BENDIS. JONATHAN HICKMAN. SECRET WARRIORS ISSUE FOUR. ART BY STEFANO CASELLI.
PAGE TWENTY-TWO.
YOU'RE STEALING QUOTES FROM COMIC BOOKS NOW, SIR?
YOU KNOW WHAT, DOC? EVEN AFTER ALL THESE YEARS...EVEN I HAVE TO ADMIT...
BUT COME ON... LOOK AT THIS...
THERE'S SOME PRETTY COOL SHIT IN COMICS.

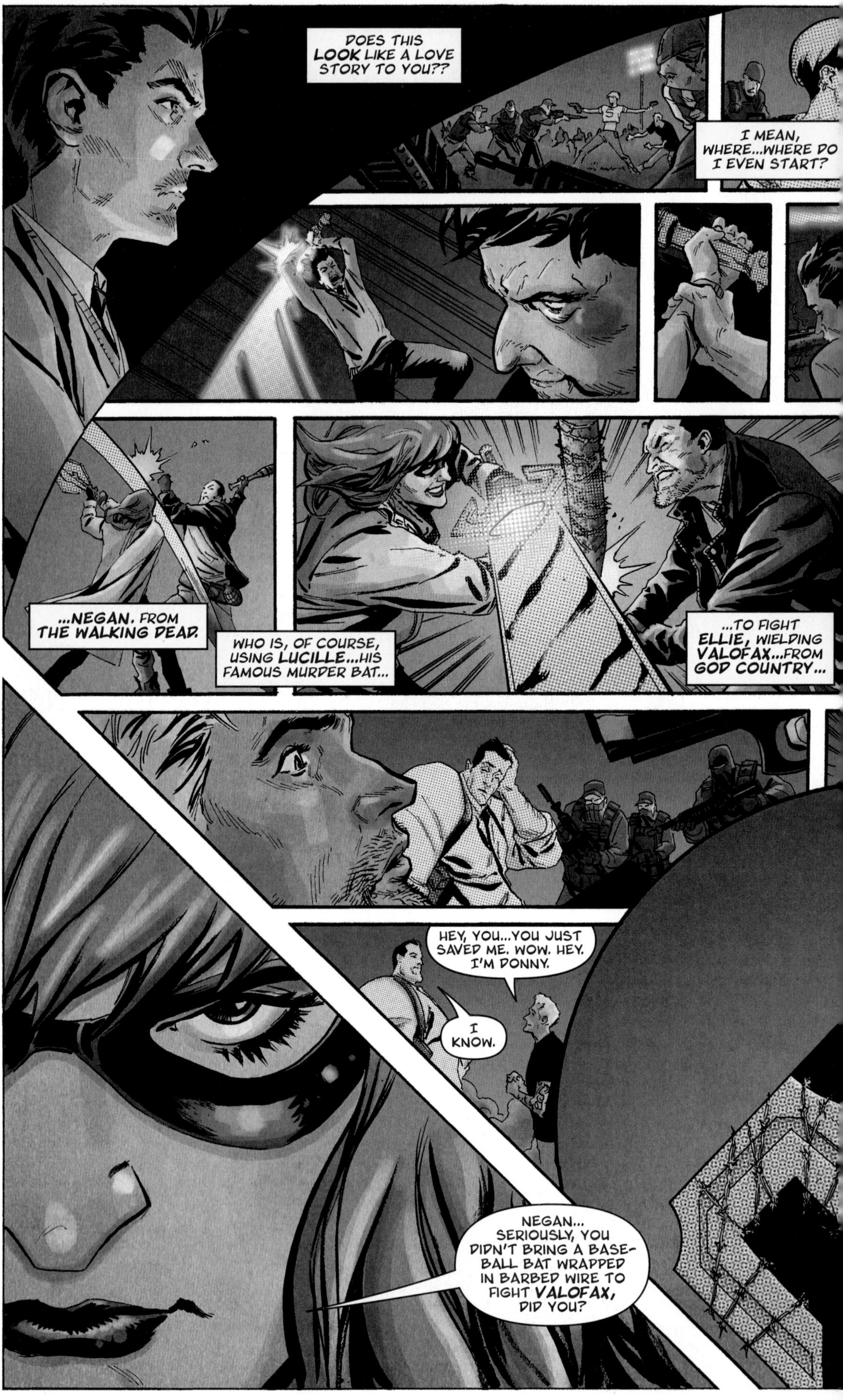
DOES THIS LOOK LIKE A LOVE STORY TO YOU??
I MEAN, WHERE...WHERE DO I EVEN START?
...NEGAN. FROM THE WALKING DEAD.
WHO IS, OF COURSE, USING LUCILLE...HIS FAMOUS MURDER BAT...
...TO FIGHT ELLIE, WIELDING VALOFAX...FROM GOD COUNTRY...
HEY, YOU...YOU JUST SAVED ME. WOW. HEY. I'M DONNY.
I KNOW.
NEGAN... SERIOUSLY, YOU DIDN'T BRING A BASE-BALL BAT WRAPPED IN BARBED WIRE TO FIGHT VALOFAX, DID YOU?

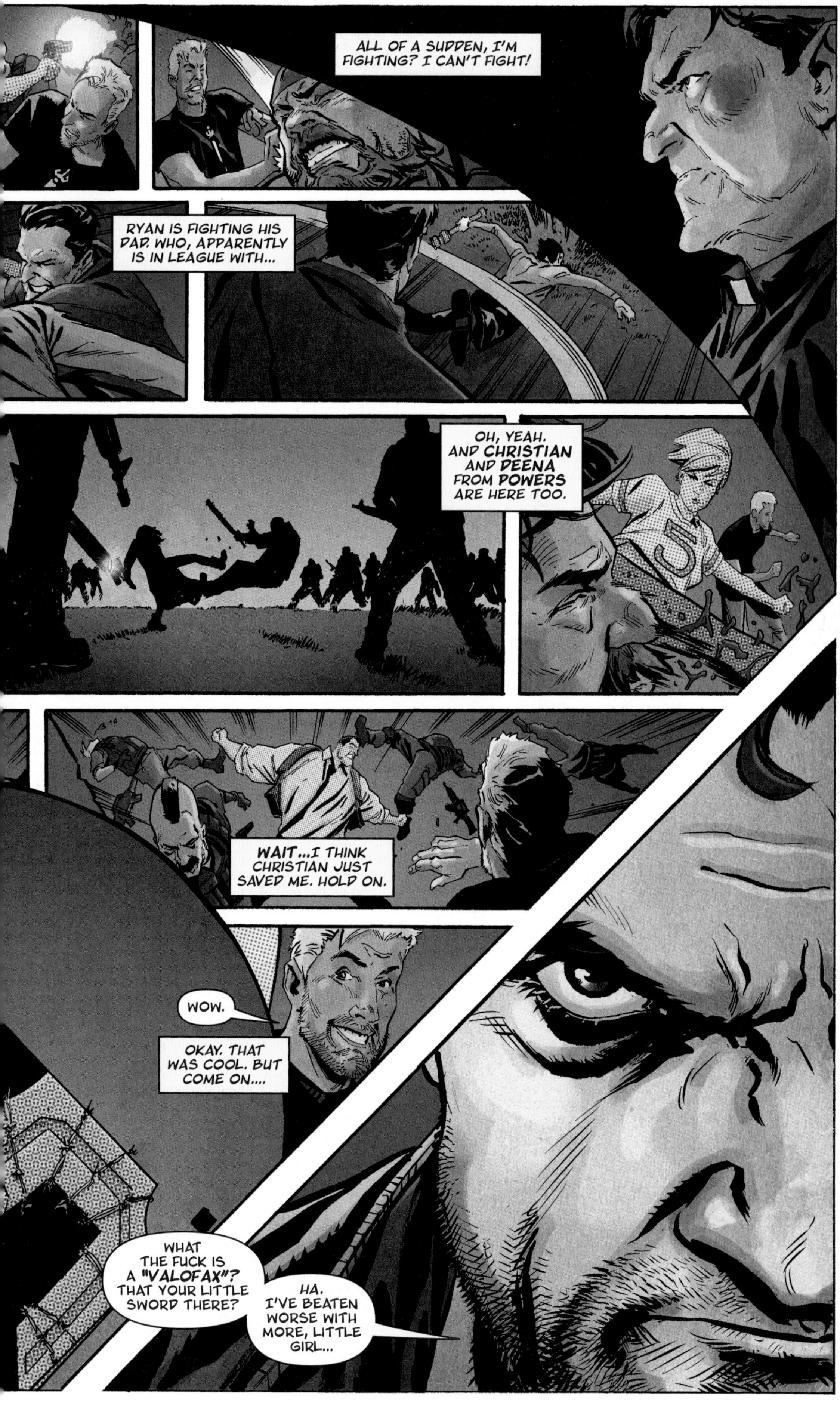
ALL OF A SUDDEN, I'M FIGHTING? I CAN'T FIGHT!
RYAN IS FIGHTING HIS DAD. WHO, APPARENTLY IS IN LEAGUE WITH...
OH, YEAH. AND CHRISTIAN AND DEENA FROM POWERS ARE HERE TOO.
WAIT...I THINK CHRISTIAN JUST SAVED ME. HOLD ON.
WOW.
OKAY. THAT WAS COOL. BUT COME ON....
WHAT THE FUCK IS A "VALOFAX"? THAT YOUR LITTLE SWORD THERE?
HA. I'VE BEATEN WORSE WITH MORE, LITTLE GIRL...

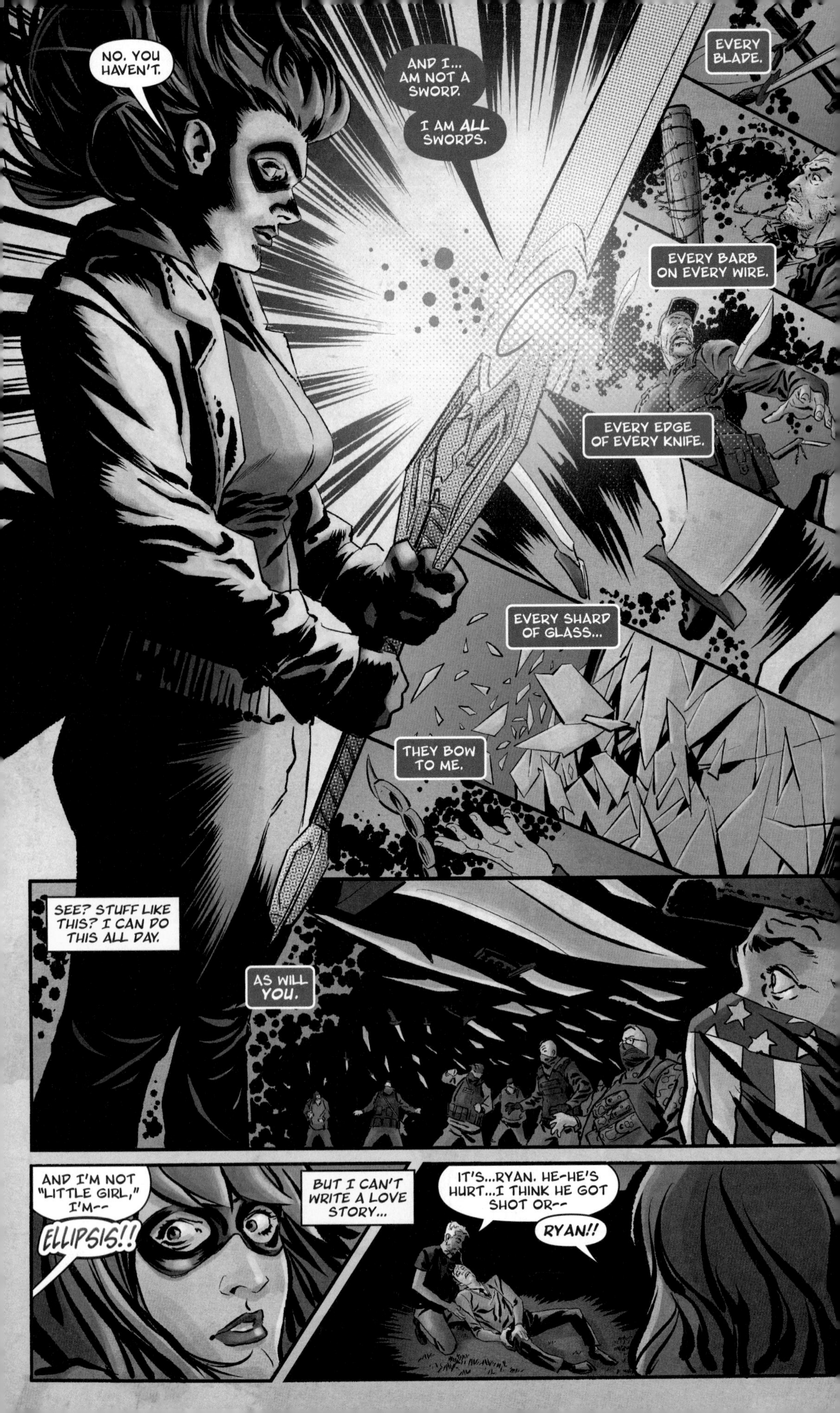
NO. YOU HAVEN'T.
AND I... AM NOT A SWORD.
I AM ALL SWORDS.
EVERY BLADE.
EVERY BARB ON EVERY WIRE.
EVERY EDGE OF EVERY KNIFE.
EVERY SHARD OF GLASS...
THEY BOW TO ME.
SEE? STUFF LIKE THIS? I CAN DO THIS ALL DAY.
AS WILL YOU.
AND I'M NOT "LITTLE GIRL," I'M--
ELLIPSIS!!
BUT I CAN'T WRITE A LOVE STORY...
IT'S...RYAN. HE-HE'S HURT...I THINK HE GOT SHOT OR--
RYAN!!

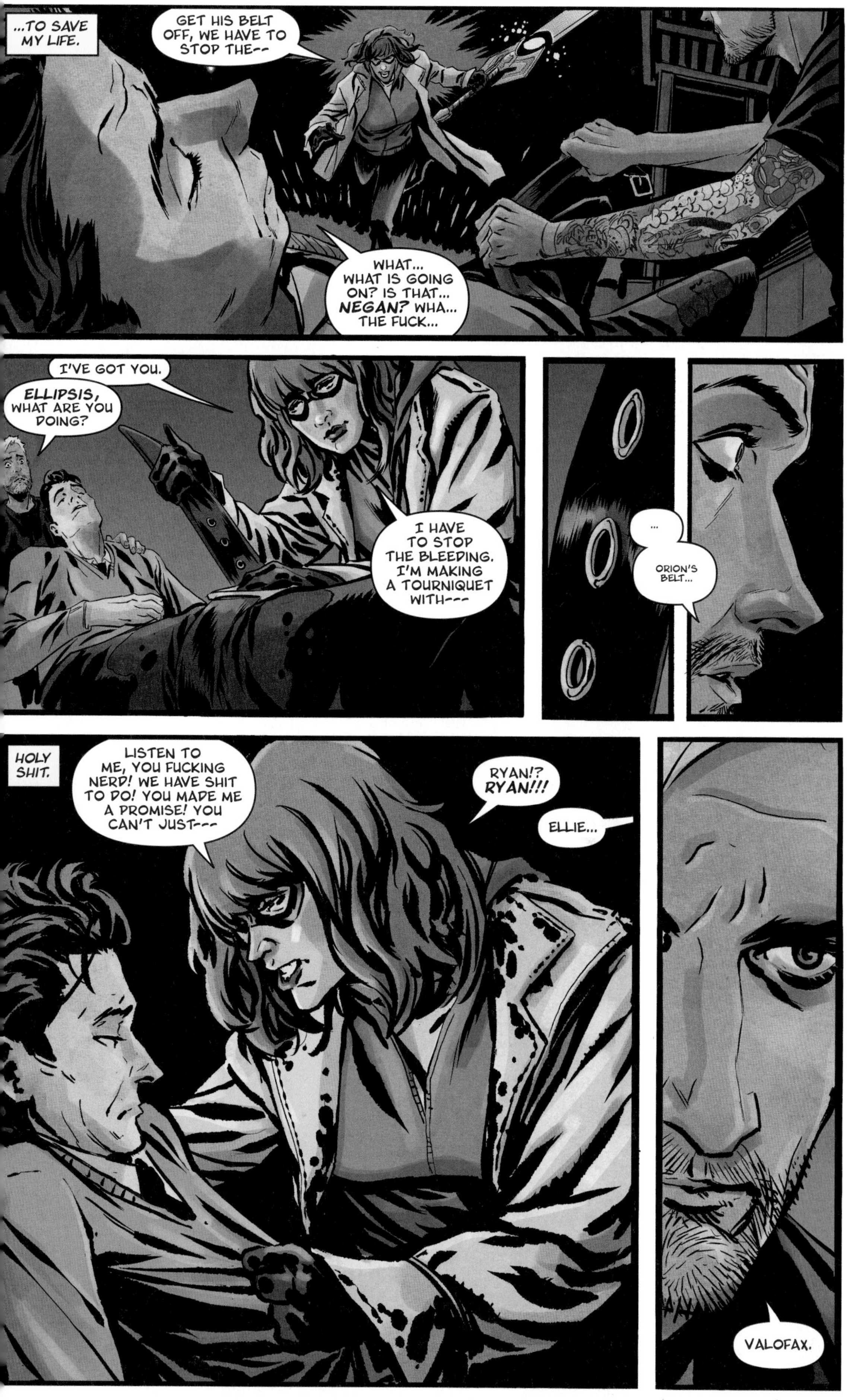
...TO SAVE MY LIFE.
GET HIS BELT OFF, WE HAVE TO STOP THE--
WHAT... WHAT IS GOING ON? IS THAT... NEGAN? WHA... THE FUCK...
I'VE GOT YOU.
ELLIPSIS, WHAT ARE YOU DOING?
I HAVE TO STOP THE BLEEDING. I'M MAKING A TOURNIQUET WITH---
...
ORION'S BELT...
HOLY SHIT.
LISTEN TO ME, YOU FUCKING NERD! WE HAVE SHIT TO DO! YOU MADE ME A PROMISE! YOU CAN'T JUST---
RYAN!? RYAN!!!
ELLIE...
VALOFAX.

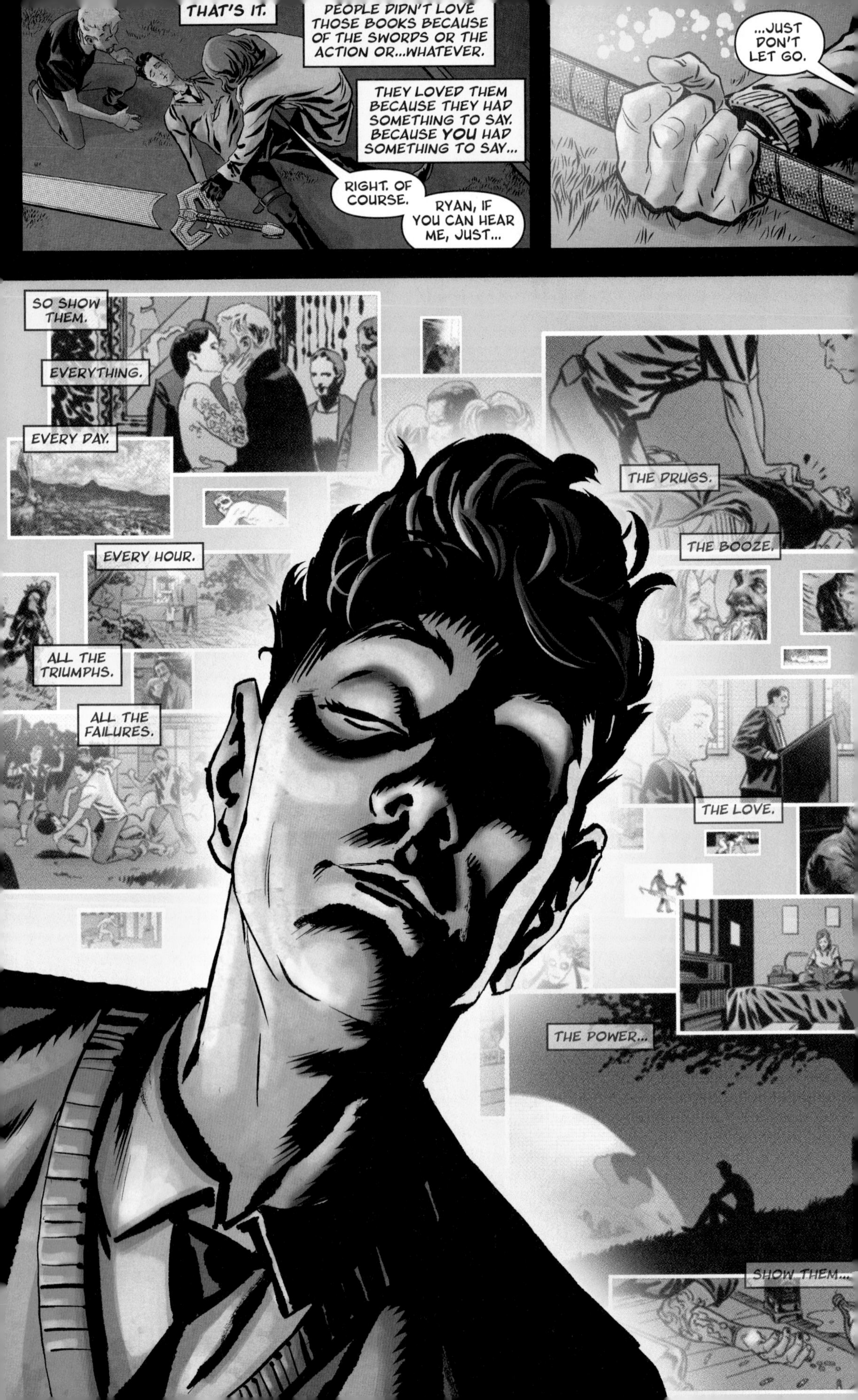
THAT'S IT.
PEOPLE DIDN'T LOVE THOSE BOOKS BECAUSE OF THE SWORDS OR THE ACTION OR...WHATEVER.
THEY LOVED THEM BECAUSE THEY HAD SOMETHING TO SAY. BECAUSE YOU HAD SOMETHING TO SAY...
RIGHT. OF COURSE.
RYAN, IF YOU CAN HEAR ME, JUST...
...JUST DON'T LET GO.
SO SHOW THEM.
EVERYTHING.
EVERY DAY.
EVERY HOUR.
ALL THE TRIUMPHS.
ALL THE FAILURES.
THE DRUGS.
THE BOOZE.
THE LOVE.
THE POWER...
SHOW THEM...

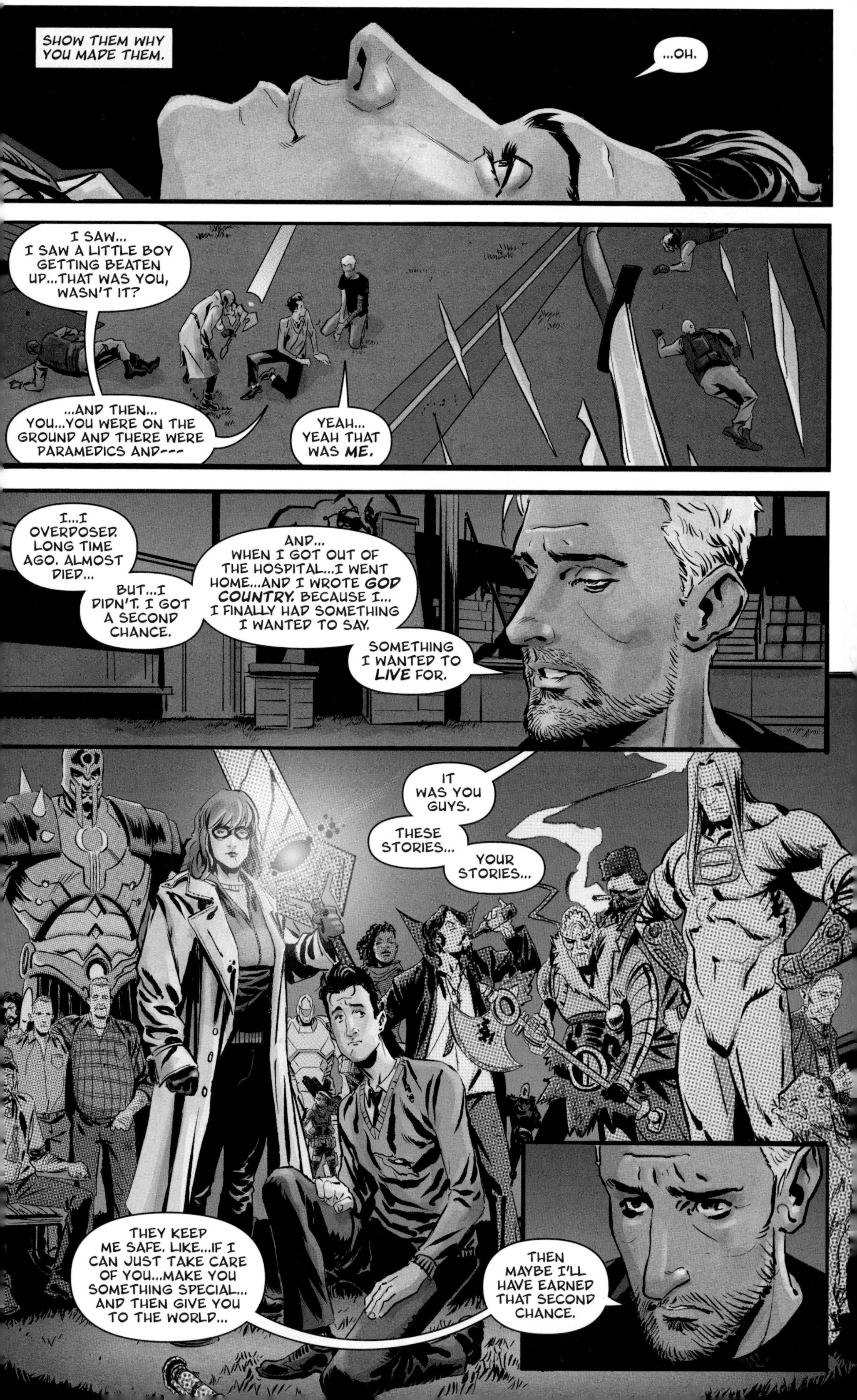
SHOW THEM WHY YOU MADE THEM.
...OH.
I SAW... I SAW A LITTLE BOY GETTING BEATEN UP...THAT WAS YOU, WASN'T IT?
...AND THEN... YOU...YOU WERE ON THE GROUND AND THERE WERE PARAMEDICS AND---
YEAH... YEAH THAT WAS **ME.**
I...I OVERDOSED. LONG TIME AGO. ALMOST DIED...
BUT...I DIDN'T. I GOT A SECOND CHANCE.
AND... WHEN I GOT OUT OF THE HOSPITAL...I WENT HOME...AND I WROTE ***GOD COUNTRY.*** BECAUSE I... I FINALLY HAD SOMETHING I WANTED TO SAY.
SOMETHING I WANTED TO ***LIVE*** FOR.
IT WAS YOU GUYS.
THESE STORIES...
YOUR STORIES...
THEY KEEP ME SAFE. LIKE...IF I CAN JUST TAKE CARE OF YOU...MAKE YOU SOMETHING SPECIAL... AND THEN GIVE YOU TO THE WORLD...
THEN MAYBE I'LL HAVE EARNED THAT SECOND CHANCE.

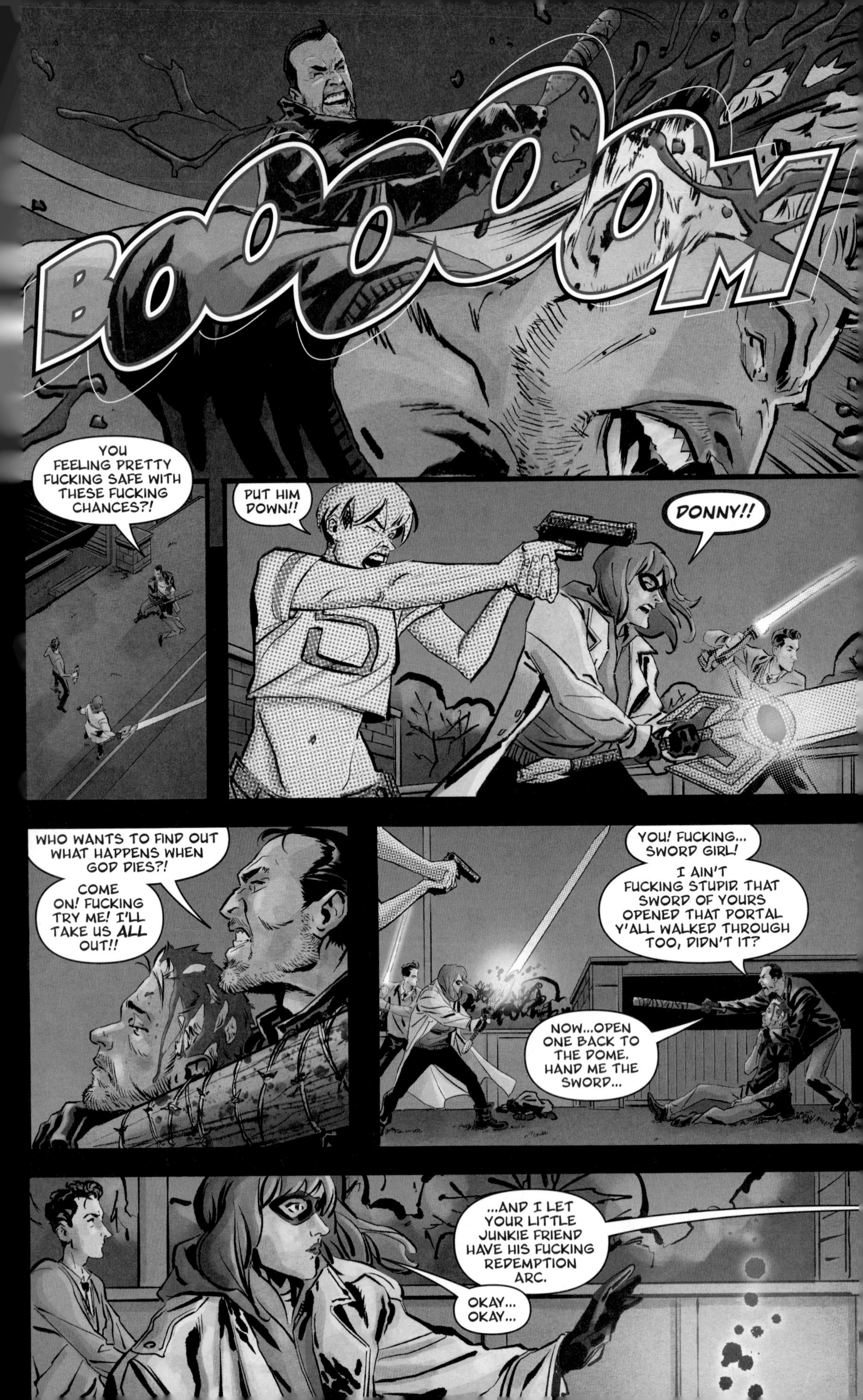
BOOOOOM
YOU FEELING PRETTY FUCKING SAFE WITH THESE FUCKING CHANCES?!
PUT HIM DOWN!!
DONNY!!
WHO WANTS TO FIND OUT WHAT HAPPENS WHEN GOD DIES?!
COME ON! FUCKING TRY ME! I'LL TAKE US ALL OUT!!
YOU! FUCKING... SWORD GIRL!
I AIN'T FUCKING STUPID. THAT SWORD OF YOURS OPENED THAT PORTAL Y'ALL WALKED THROUGH TOO, DIDN'T IT?
NOW...OPEN ONE BACK TO THE DOME. HAND ME THE SWORD...
...AND I LET YOUR LITTLE JUNKIE FRIEND HAVE HIS FUCKING REDEMPTION ARC.
OKAY... OKAY...

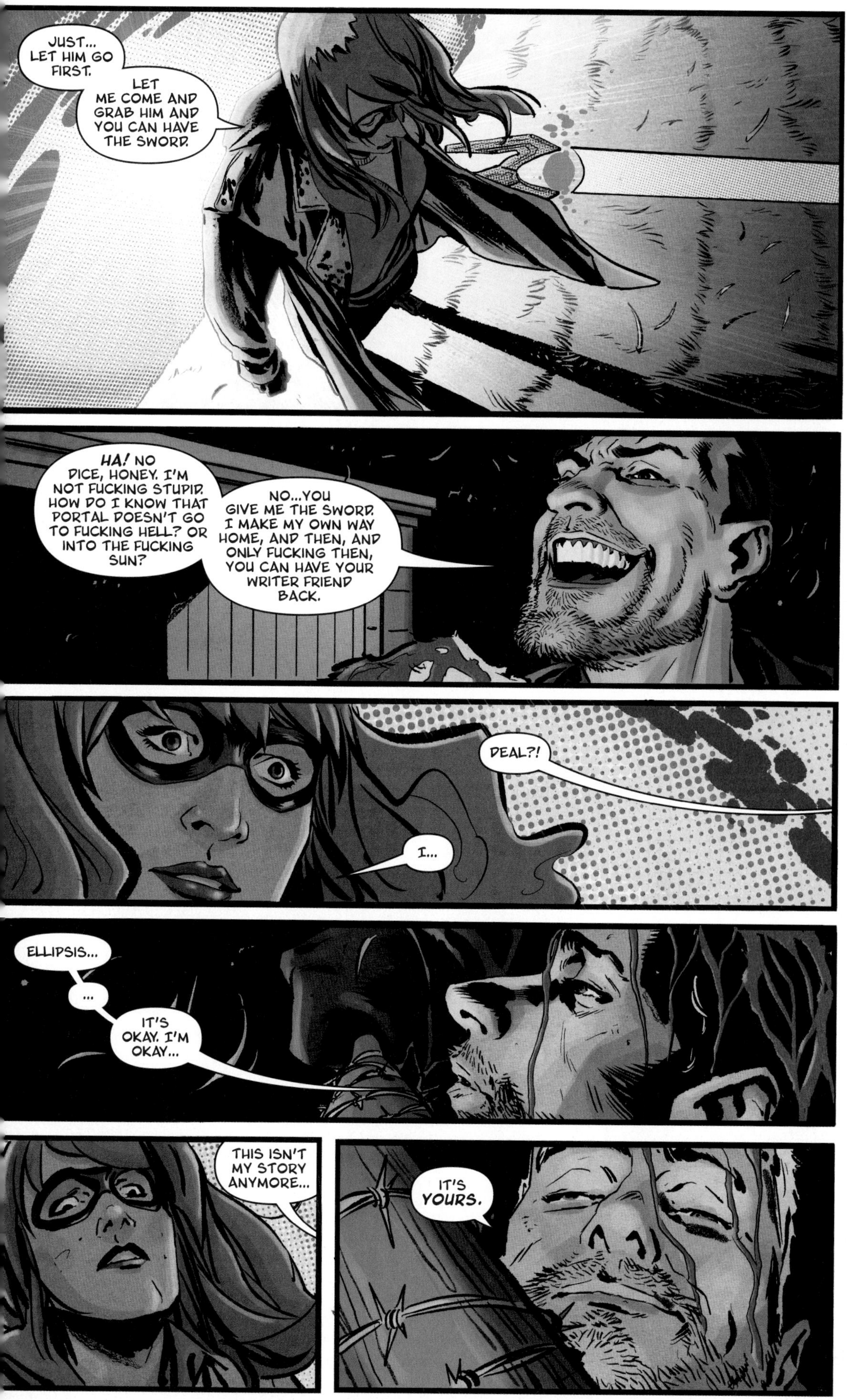
JUST... LET HIM GO FIRST.
LET ME COME AND GRAB HIM AND YOU CAN HAVE THE SWORD.
HA! NO DICE, HONEY. I'M NOT FUCKING STUPID. HOW DO I KNOW THAT PORTAL DOESN'T GO TO FUCKING HELL? OR INTO THE FUCKING SUN?
NO...YOU GIVE ME THE SWORD. I MAKE MY OWN WAY HOME, AND THEN, AND ONLY FUCKING THEN, YOU CAN HAVE YOUR WRITER FRIEND BACK.
DEAL?!
I...
ELLIPSIS...
...
IT'S OKAY. I'M OKAY...
THIS ISN'T MY STORY ANYMORE...
IT'S YOURS.

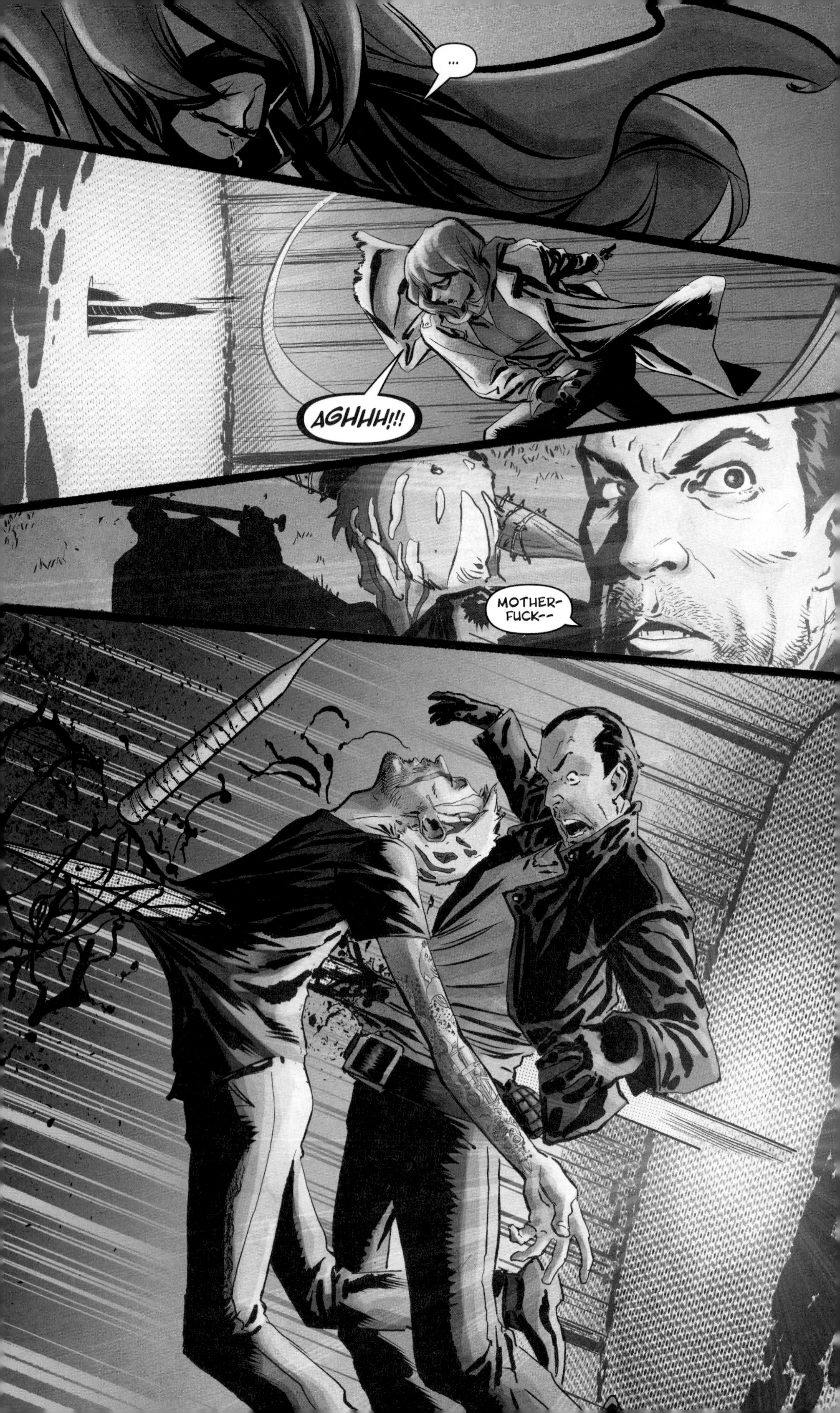
...
AGHHH!!!
MOTHER-FUCK--

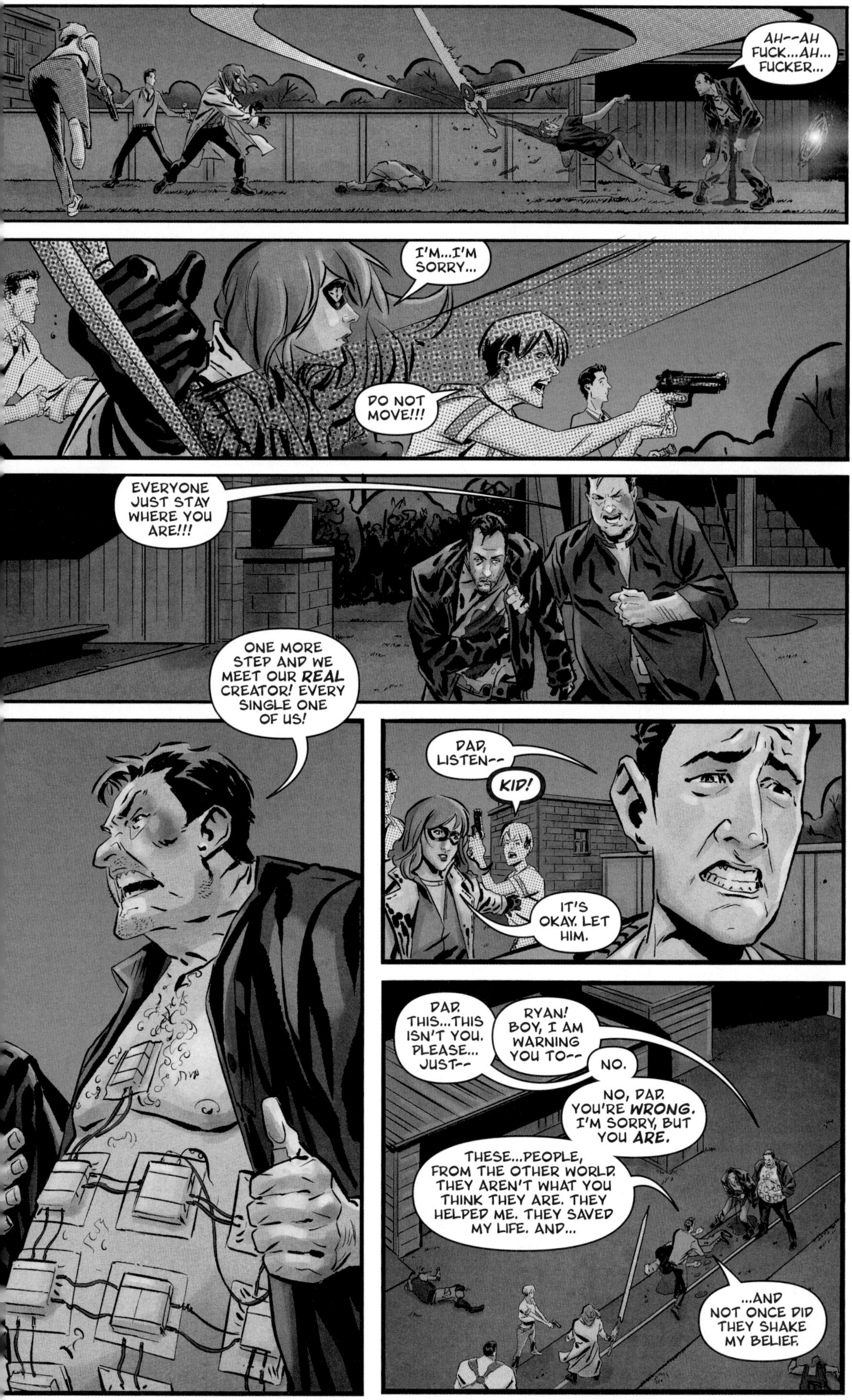

AH--AH FUCK...AH... FUCKER...
I'M...I'M SORRY...
DO NOT MOVE!!!
EVERYONE JUST STAY WHERE YOU ARE!!!
ONE MORE STEP AND WE MEET OUR REAL CREATOR! EVERY SINGLE ONE OF US!
DAD, LISTEN--
KID!
IT'S OKAY. LET HIM.
DAD. THIS...THIS ISN'T YOU. PLEASE... JUST--
RYAN! BOY, I AM WARNING YOU TO--
NO.
NO, DAD. YOU'RE WRONG. I'M SORRY, BUT YOU ARE.
THESE...PEOPLE, FROM THE OTHER WORLD. THEY AREN'T WHAT YOU THINK THEY ARE. THEY HELPED ME. THEY SAVED MY LIFE. AND...
...AND NOT ONCE DID THEY SHAKE MY BELIEF.

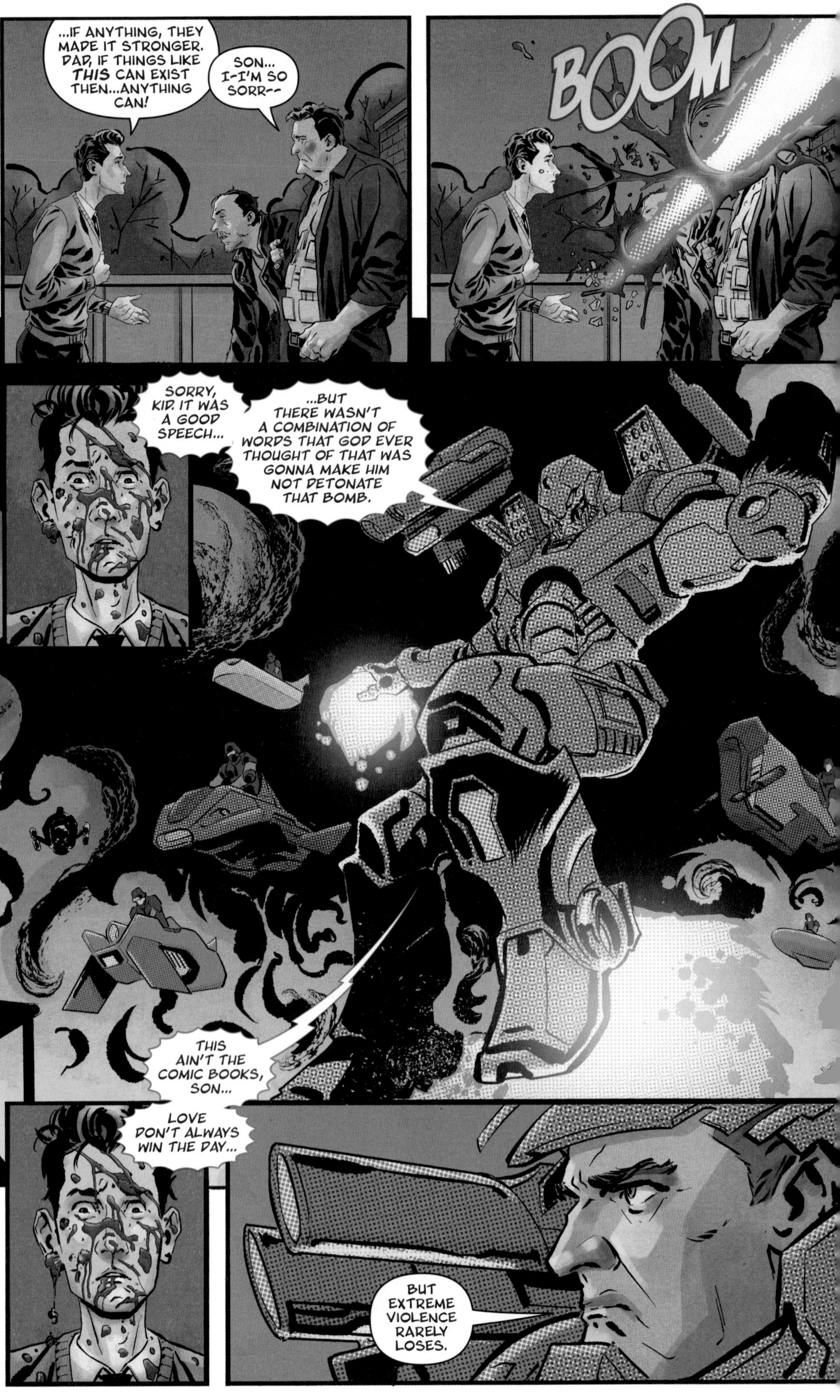

...IF ANYTHING, THEY MADE IT STRONGER. DAD, IF THINGS LIKE THIS CAN EXIST THEN...ANYTHING CAN!
SON... I-I'M SO SORR--
BOOM
SORRY, KID. IT WAS A GOOD SPEECH...
...BUT THERE WASN'T A COMBINATION OF WORDS THAT GOD EVER THOUGHT OF THAT WAS GONNA MAKE HIM NOT DETONATE THAT BOMB.
THIS AIN'T THE COMIC BOOKS, SON...
LOVE DON'T ALWAYS WIN THE DAY...
BUT EXTREME VIOLENCE RARELY LOSES.

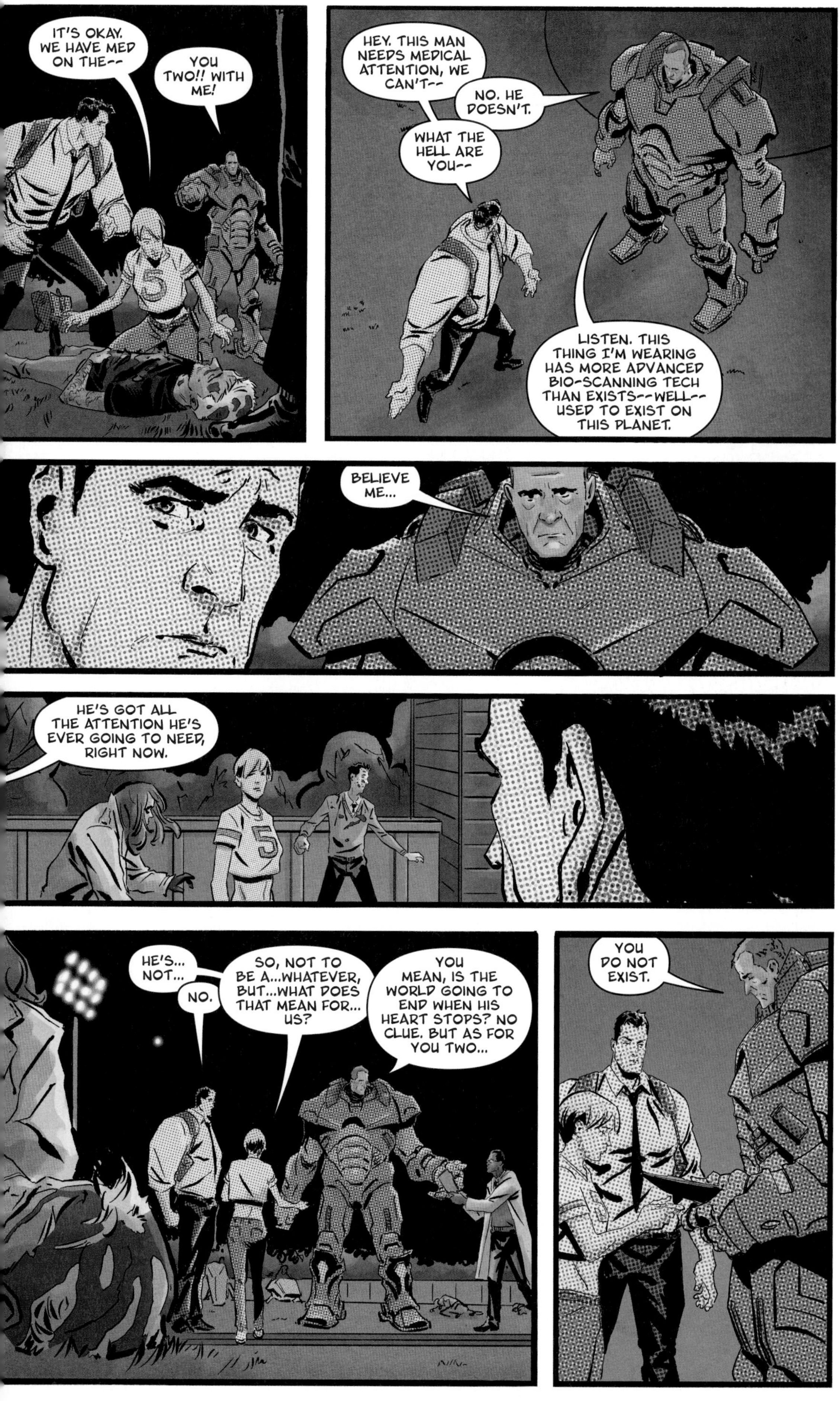
IT'S OKAY. WE HAVE MED ON THE--
YOU TWO!! WITH ME!
HEY. THIS MAN NEEDS MEDICAL ATTENTION, WE CAN'T--
NO. HE DOESN'T.
WHAT THE HELL ARE YOU--
LISTEN. THIS THING I'M WEARING HAS MORE ADVANCED BIO-SCANNING TECH THAN EXISTS--WELL--USED TO EXIST ON THIS PLANET.
BELIEVE ME...
HE'S GOT ALL THE ATTENTION HE'S EVER GOING TO NEED, RIGHT NOW.
HE'S... NOT...
NO.
SO, NOT TO BE A...WHATEVER, BUT...WHAT DOES THAT MEAN FOR... US?
YOU MEAN, IS THE WORLD GOING TO END WHEN HIS HEART STOPS? NO CLUE. BUT AS FOR YOU TWO...
YOU DO NOT EXIST.

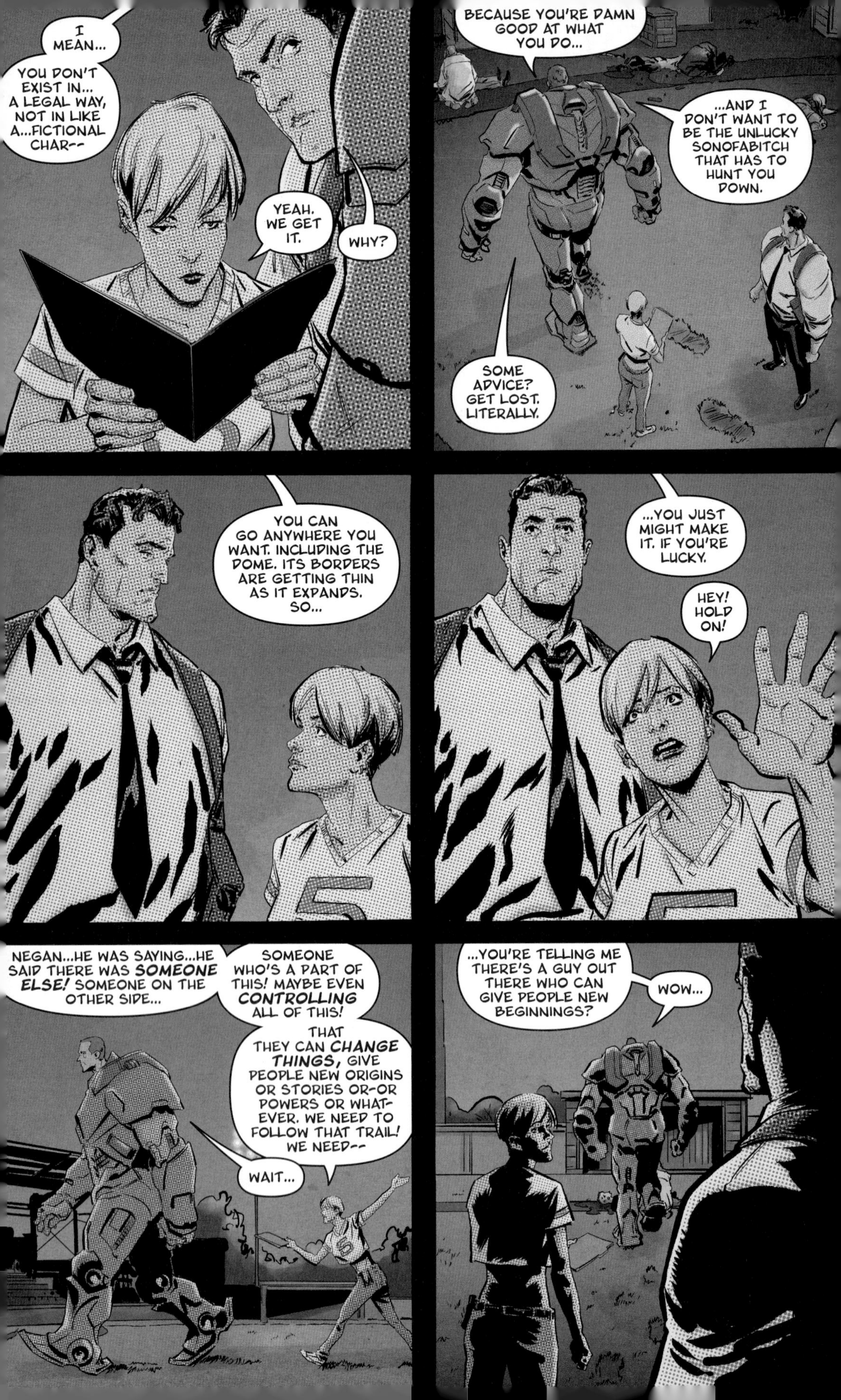
I MEAN...
YOU DON'T EXIST IN... A LEGAL WAY, NOT IN LIKE A...FICTIONAL CHAR--
YEAH. WE GET IT.
WHY?
BECAUSE YOU'RE DAMN GOOD AT WHAT YOU DO...
...AND I DON'T WANT TO BE THE UNLUCKY SONOFABITCH THAT HAS TO HUNT YOU DOWN.
SOME ADVICE? GET LOST. LITERALLY.
YOU CAN GO ANYWHERE YOU WANT. INCLUDING THE DOME. ITS BORDERS ARE GETTING THIN AS IT EXPANDS. SO...
...YOU JUST MIGHT MAKE IT. IF YOU'RE LUCKY.
HEY! HOLD ON!
NEGAN...HE WAS SAYING...HE SAID THERE WAS SOMEONE ELSE! SOMEONE ON THE OTHER SIDE...
SOMEONE WHO'S A PART OF THIS! MAYBE EVEN CONTROLLING ALL OF THIS!
THAT THEY CAN CHANGE THINGS, GIVE PEOPLE NEW ORIGINS OR STORIES OR-OR POWERS OR WHAT-EVER. WE NEED TO FOLLOW THAT TRAIL! WE NEED--
WAIT...
...YOU'RE TELLING ME THERE'S A GUY OUT THERE WHO CAN GIVE PEOPLE NEW BEGINNINGS?
WOW...

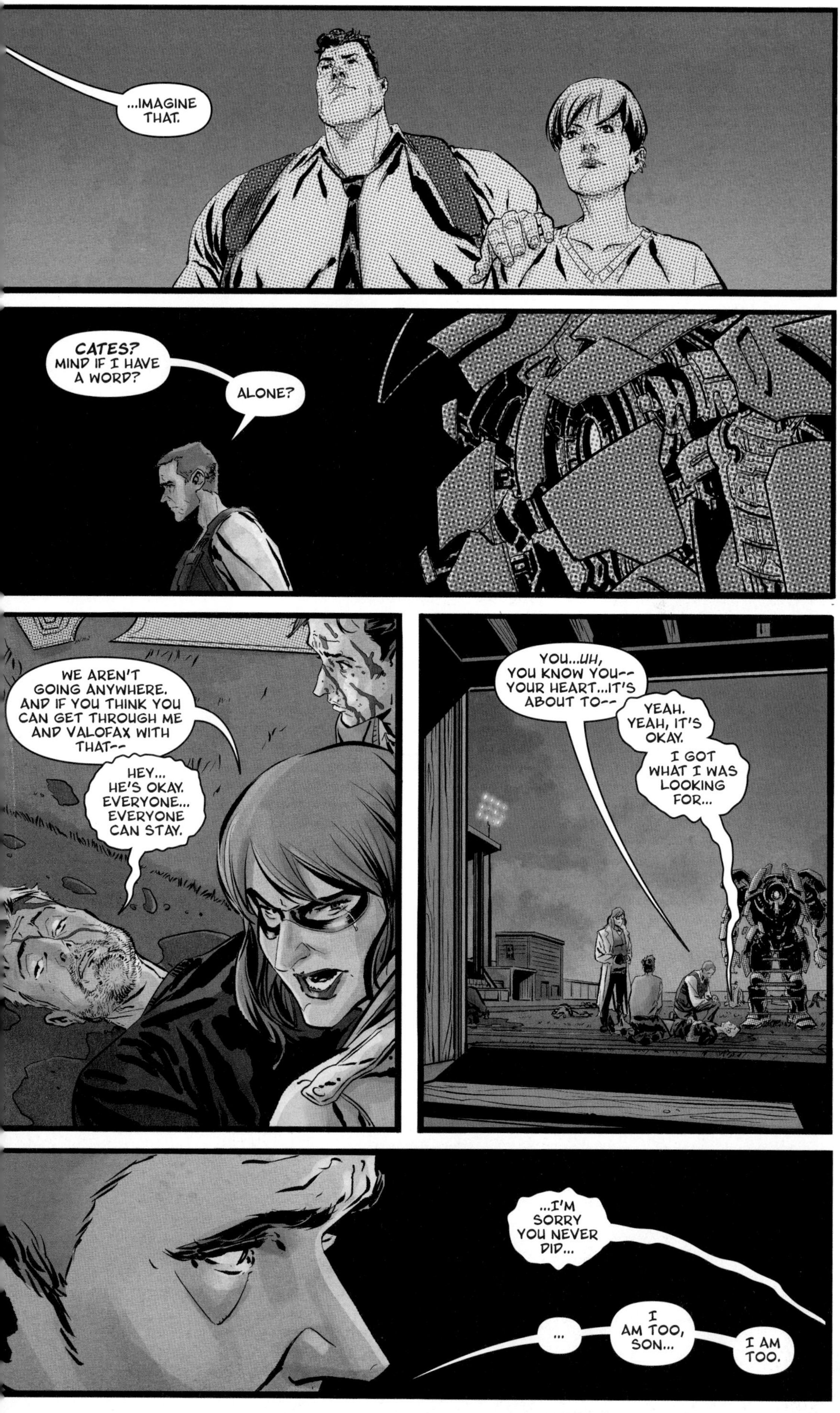
...IMAGINE THAT.
CATES? MIND IF I HAVE A WORD?
ALONE?
WE AREN'T GOING ANYWHERE. AND IF YOU THINK YOU CAN GET THROUGH ME AND VALOFAX WITH THAT--
HEY... HE'S OKAY. EVERYONE... EVERYONE CAN STAY.
YOU...UH, YOU KNOW YOU-- YOUR HEART...IT'S ABOUT TO--
YEAH. YEAH, IT'S OKAY.
I GOT WHAT I WAS LOOKING FOR...
...I'M SORRY YOU NEVER DID...
...
I AM TOO, SON...
I AM TOO.

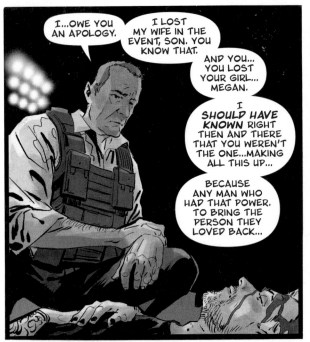

I...OWE YOU AN APOLOGY.

I LOST MY WIFE IN THE EVENT, SON. YOU KNOW THAT.

AND YOU... YOU LOST YOUR GIRL... MEGAN.

I SHOULD HAVE KNOWN RIGHT THEN AND THERE THAT YOU WEREN'T THE ONE...MAKING ALL THIS UP...

BECAUSE ANY MAN WHO HAD THAT POWER, TO BRING THE PERSON THEY LOVED BACK...

...I WOULD HAVE BROUGHT THE STARS DOWN OUT OF THE SKY.

JUST TO SEE HER. JUST ONE MORE TIME...

BUT... I CAN'T. I'VE BEEN TRYING TO TELL YOU...I'M NOT IN CONTROL OF ANY OF THIS.

BUT...YOU CAN DO THINGS? YOU BROKE US OUT OF JAIL AND GOT RYAN A LIGHTSA--

EXACTLY. I CAN DO SOME THINGS HERE... ALL WRITERS CAN.

THAT'S WHY HE WAS TARGETING THEM...

WHO? WHO ARE YOU TALKING ABOUT?

I-- GODDAMMIT, I CAN'T BELIEVE IT'S TAKEN ME SO LONG TO FIGURE THIS OUT.

GUYS. LOOK! I'M ABOUT TO DIE AND THE WORLD IS STILL HERE! DO YOU KNOW WHAT MEANS?!

I'M ACTUALLY NOT THE CENTER OF THE UNIVERSE...

...THE WORLD DOESN'T REVOLVE AROUND ME! HAHA!!

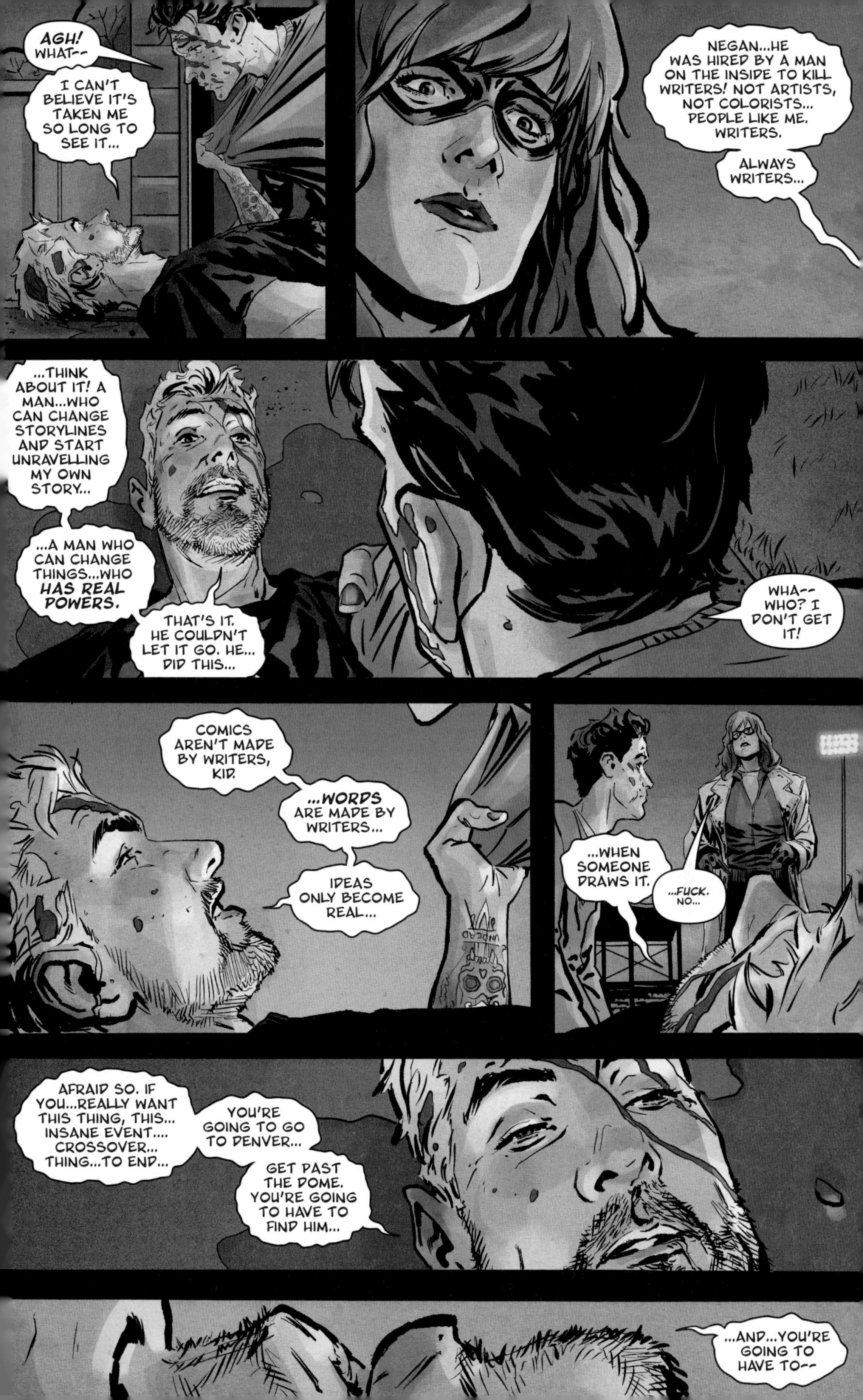

AGH! WHAT--
I CAN'T BELIEVE IT'S TAKEN ME SO LONG TO SEE IT...
NEGAN...HE WAS HIRED BY A MAN ON THE INSIDE TO KILL WRITERS! NOT ARTISTS, NOT COLORISTS... PEOPLE LIKE ME. WRITERS.
ALWAYS WRITERS...
...THINK ABOUT IT! A MAN...WHO CAN CHANGE STORYLINES AND START UNRAVELLING MY OWN STORY...
...A MAN WHO CAN CHANGE THINGS...WHO HAS REAL POWERS.
THAT'S IT. HE COULDN'T LET IT GO. HE... DID THIS...
WHA-- WHO? I DON'T GET IT!
COMICS AREN'T MADE BY WRITERS, KID.
...WORDS ARE MADE BY WRITERS...
IDEAS ONLY BECOME REAL...
...WHEN SOMEONE DRAWS IT.
...FUCK. NO...
AFRAID SO. IF YOU...REALLY WANT THIS THING, THIS... INSANE EVENT.... CROSSOVER... THING...TO END...
YOU'RE GOING TO GO TO DENVER...
GET PAST THE DOME. YOU'RE GOING TO HAVE TO FIND HIM...
...AND...YOU'RE GOING TO HAVE TO--

KILL GEOFF SHAW

THANK YOU FOR LETTING
US PLAY WITH YOUR TOYS...

MICHAEL ALLRED
MADMAN

IAN BEDERMAN
ATOMAHAWK

CHIP ZDARSKY
CHIP ZDARSKY

BRIAN MICHAEL BENDIS &
MICHAEL AVON OEMING
POWERS

ROBERT KIRKMAN &
TONY MOORE &
CHARLIE ADLARD
THE WALKING DEAD

ELIOT RAHAL
THE PAYBACKS

MARK REZNICEK
BUZZKILL

MARC SILVESTRI
THE DARKNESS

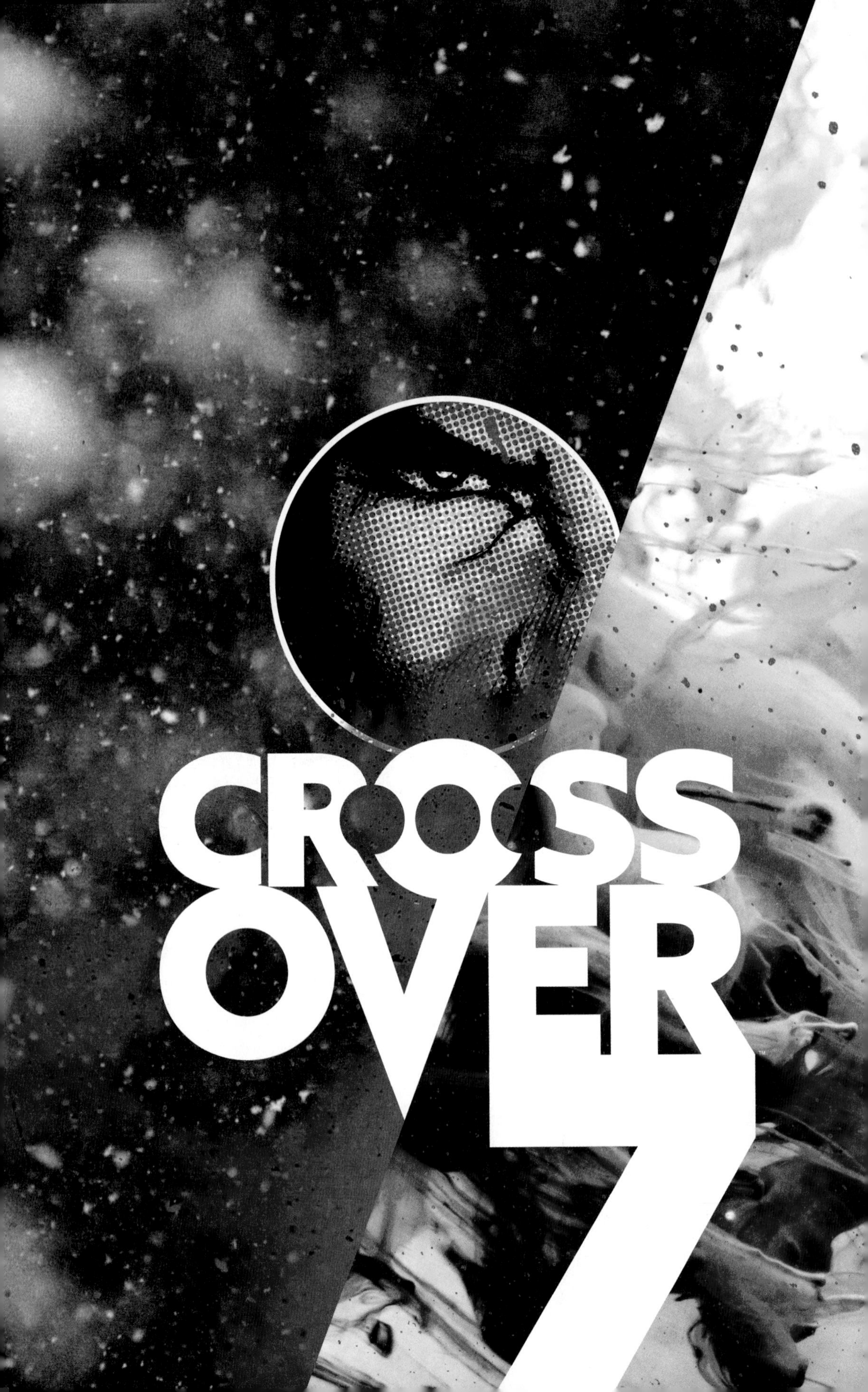
CROSS
OVER
7

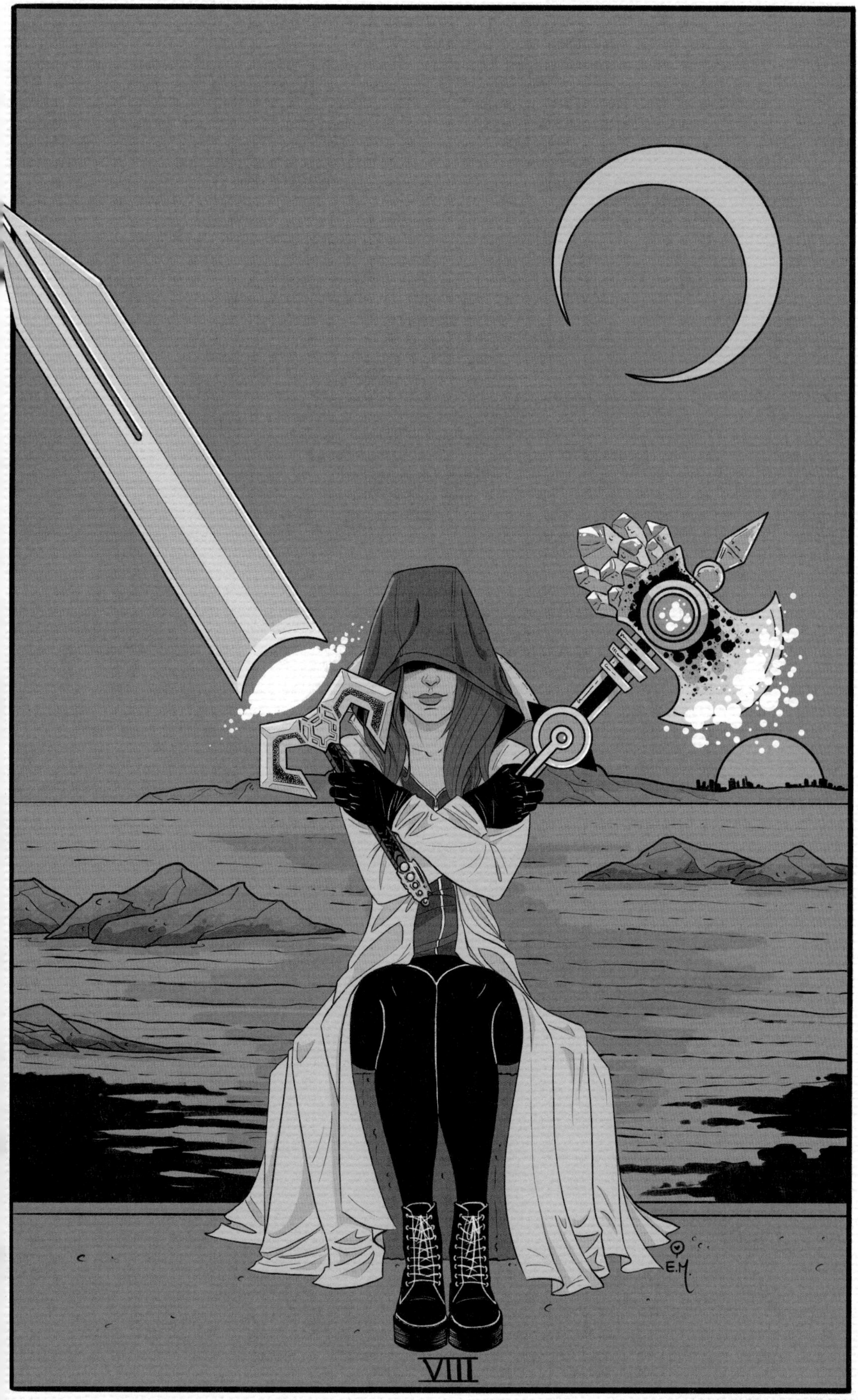
E.M.
VIII

EIGHT / VARIANT COVER / **MEGAN HUTCHISON-CATES**

NINE / VARIANT COVER
DAN PANOSIAN

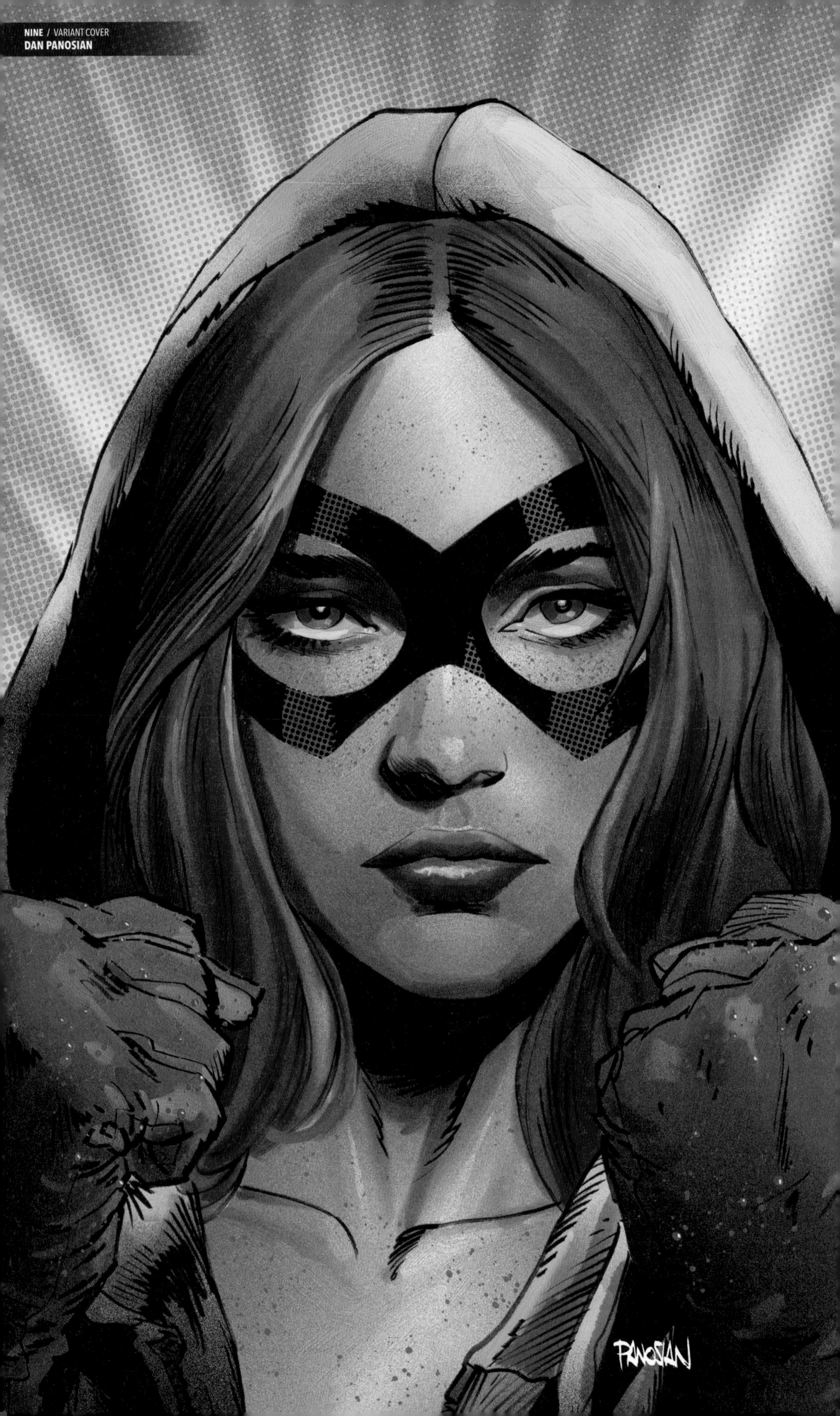
PANOSIAN

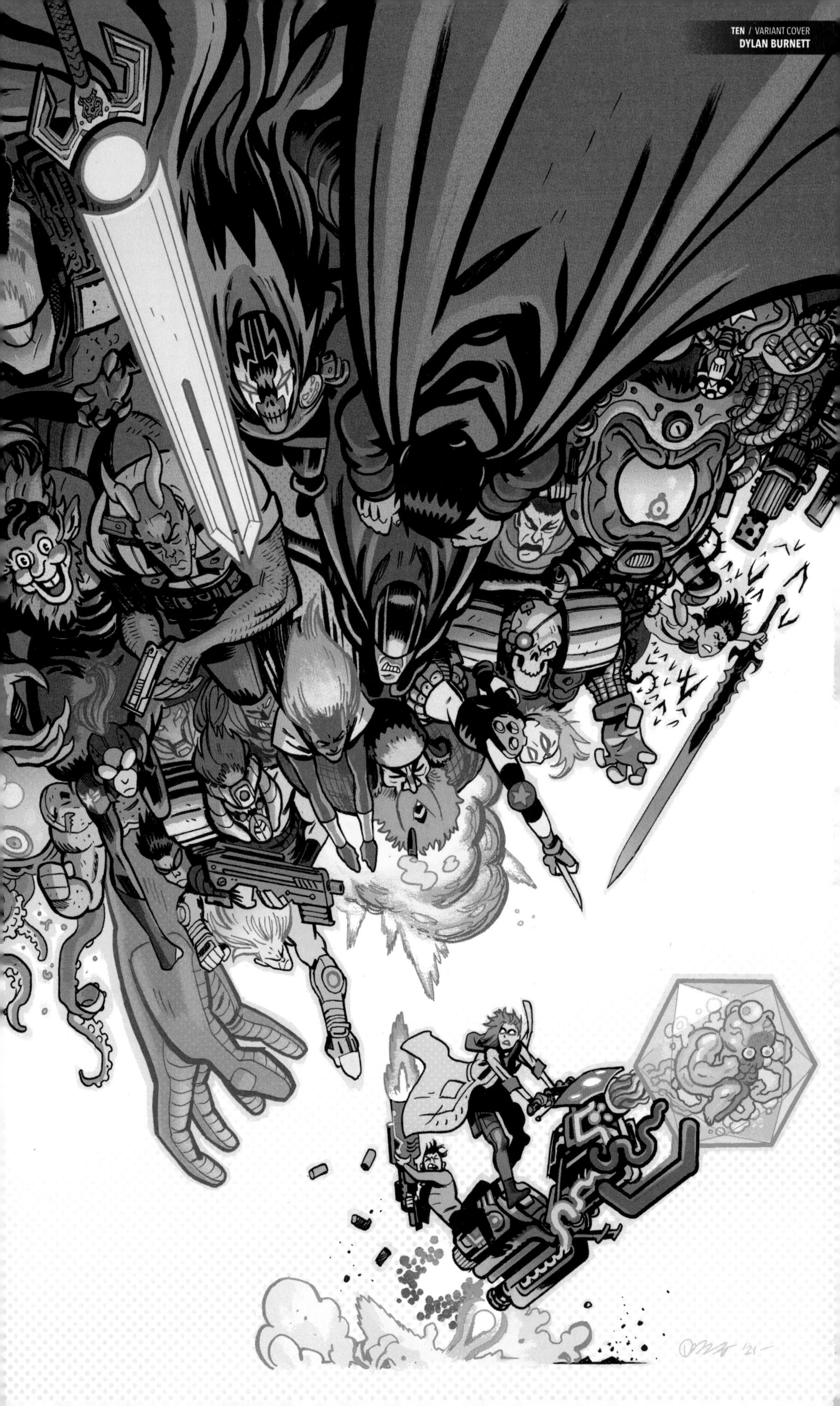

ELEVEN / VARIANT COVER
ADAM GORHAM & **DEE CUNNIFFE**

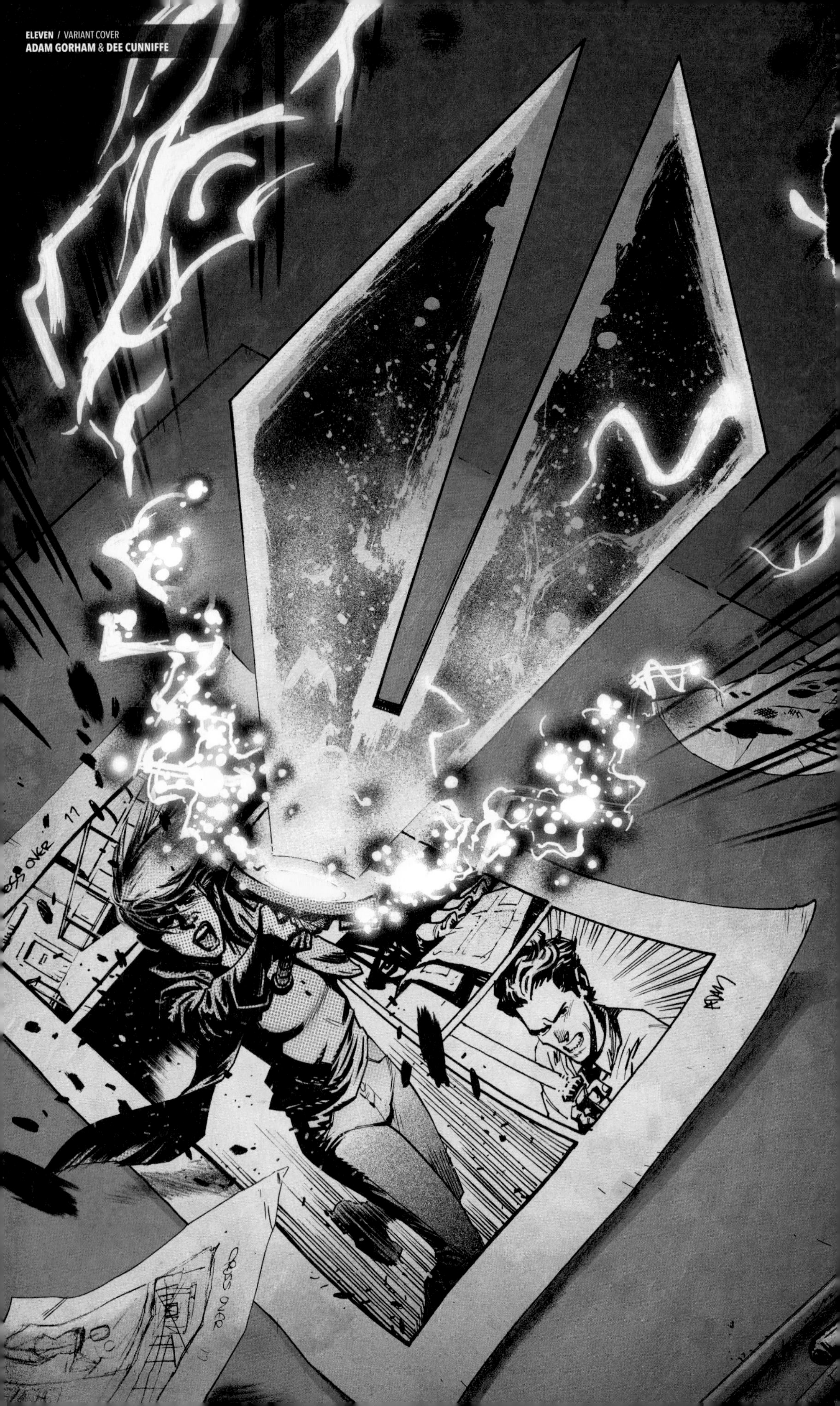
CROSS OVER
CROSS OVER

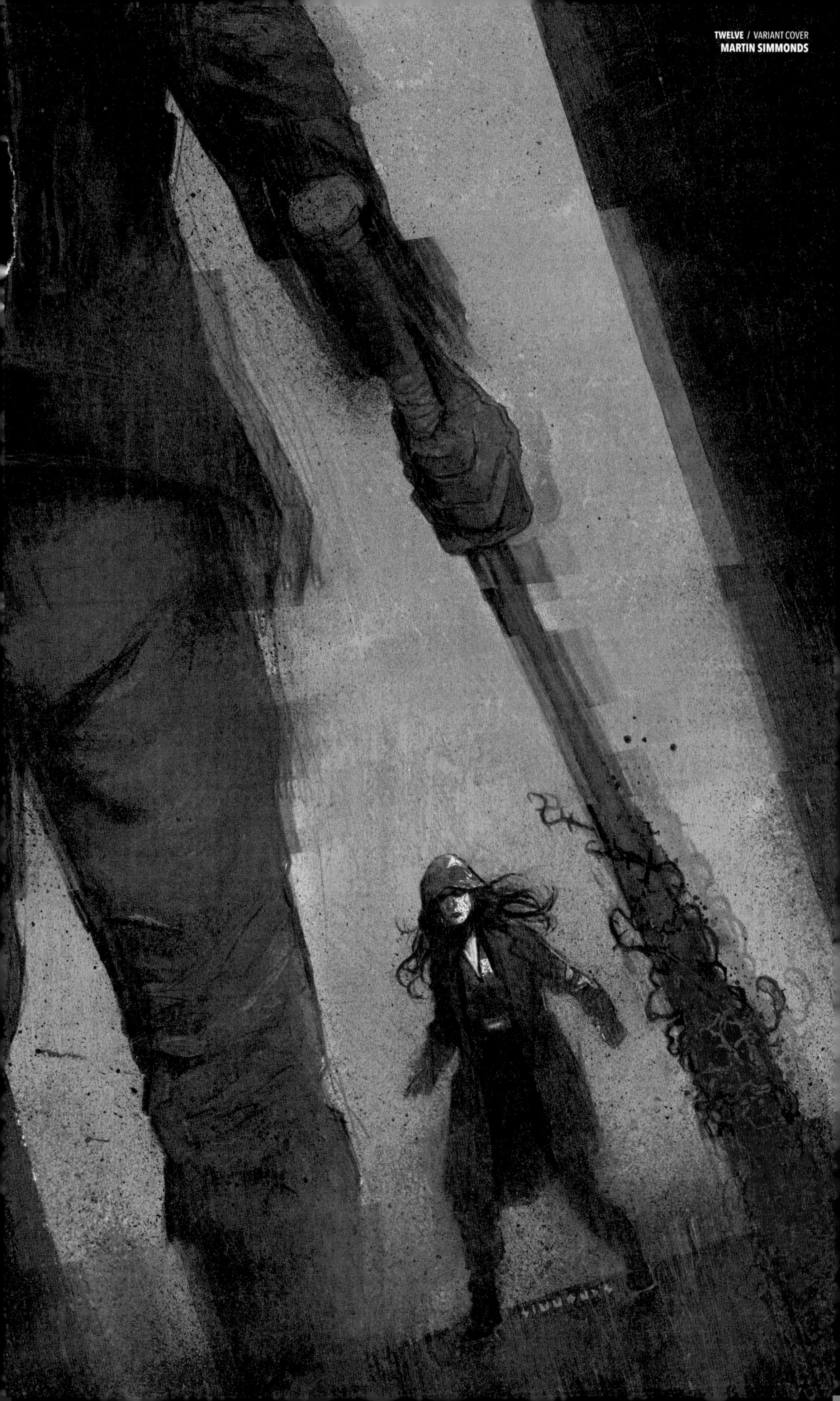

TWELVE / VARIANT COVER
MARTIN SIMMONDS

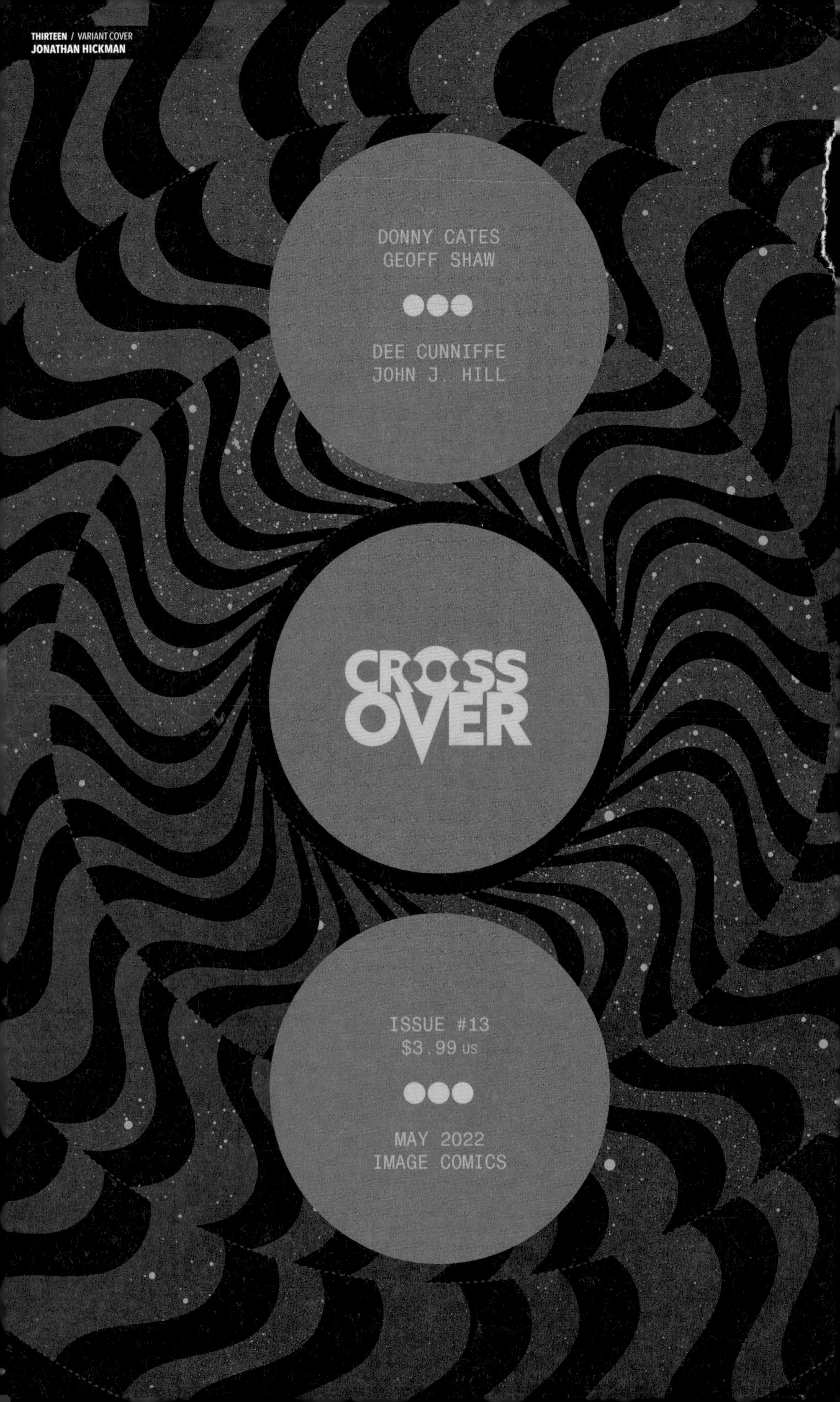
THIRTEEN / VARIANT COVER
JONATHAN HICKMAN
DONNY CATES
GEOFF SHAW
DEE CUNNIFFE
JOHN J. HILL
CROSSOVER
ISSUE #13
$3.99 US
MAY 2022
IMAGE COMICS